A whirlwind

DESTINAT...
SUMM...
Weddings!

Stunning, exotic and mysterious places –
dream destinations in which to fall in love.

From glorious beaches to towns buzzing with
activity and culture, every setting is glamorous,
colourful and, most importantly, sets the scene
for a beautiful romance!

Don't miss your special bonus treat – go to
www.millsandboon.co.uk for your
FREE online read!

DESTINATION: SUMMER

Weddings!

AND THE BRIDE WORE RED
by Lucy Gordon

A TRIP WITH THE TYCOON
by Nicola Marsh

HONEYMOON WITH THE BOSS
by Jessica Hart

M&B™ and M&B™ with the Rose Device
are trademarks of the publisher.
Harlequin Mills & Boon Limited, Eton House,
18-24 Paradise Road, Richmond, Surrey TW9 1SR

DESTINATION: SUMMER WEDDINGS!
© by Harlequin Books SA 2010

And the Bride Wore Red © Lucy Gordon 2009
A Trip with the Tycoon © Nicola Marsh 2009
Honeymoon with the Boss © Jessica Hart 2009

ISBN: 978 0 263 87895 0

25-0610

Harlequin Mills & Boon policy is to use papers that are
natural, renewable and recyclable products and made from
wood grown in sustainable forests. The logging and
manufacturing processes conform to the legal environmental
regulations of the country of origin.

Printed and bound in Spain
by Litografia Rosés S.A., Barcelona

And the Bride
Wore Red

LUCY GORDON

Lucy Gordon cut her writing teeth on magazine journalism, interviewing many of the world's most interesting men, including Warren Beatty, Charlton Heston and Sir Roger Moore. She also camped out with lions in Africa and had many other unusual experiences, which have often provided the background for her books. Several years ago, while staying in Venice, she met a Venetian who proposed within two days. They have been married ever since. Naturally this has affected her writing, where romantic Italian men tend to feature strongly. Two of her books have won the Romance Writers of America RITA® Award. You can visit her website at www.lucy-gordon.com.

Dear Reader,

A couple of years ago I visited China and was overwhelmed by its beauty, its magnificence and above all its mystery. In Beijing I saw the Forbidden City, where the Emperors lived and where their concubines had their apartments. Later I visited the Terracotta Warriors. I'd heard so much about them, but nothing could have prepared me for their breathtaking, lifelike reality.

After that came a cruise along the Yangtze River, marvelling at the high banks that rise on each side, giving the feeling of being enclosed in a separate world. It could be a perfect place for lovers, as my hero and heroine Lang and Olivia discovered. But at last the outside world intruded, facing them with decisions that threatened to tear them apart.

When they finally found their destiny it was because they were true to themselves and also because they had answered the magical call of China. It was a call that would always draw them back – just as it has drawn me back and will do again.

Warm wishes,

Lucy Gordon

This book is dedicated to my friend Xin Ying,
who lives in Beijing and whose assistance with
Chinese social customs was invaluable.

CHAPTER ONE

'OLIVIA, come quickly! There's been a terrible disaster!'

Olivia looked up from the school books she was marking to where Helma, the young teaching assistant, stood in the doorway. She was only mildly alarmed by the girl's agitated words. Helma had a wild sense of drama and 'a terrible disaster' might mean no more than the school cat making off with someone's lunch.

'It's Yen Dong!' Helma wailed.

Ten-year-old Dong was the brightest pupil in Olivia's class at the Chang-Ming School in Beijing. He was also the most mischievous, using his impish charm to evade retribution for his many escapades.

'What's he done now?' Olivia asked. 'Set a booby trap for the headmistress?'

'He's climbed a tree.'

'Again? Then he can just come down. It's almost time for afternoon lessons.'

'But he's ever so high and I don't think he can get down.'

Olivia hurried out into the garden that formed the school's playground and looked up. Sure enough, there was the little rascal, high on the tallest tree, looking cheerful even while hanging on for dear life.

'Can you climb down?' Olivia called.

He ventured a step, but his foot slid on the next branch and he backed off hastily.

'All right, not to worry,' Olivia said, trying to sound more confident than she felt. 'I need a ladder.'

One was fetched immediately, but to everyone's dismay it fell short of Dong by several feet.

'No problem,' Olivia sang out, setting her foot on the bottom rung.

Luckily she was wearing jeans, which made climbing easier, and reaching the top of the ladder wasn't too hard. But the next bit didn't look so easy. Taking a deep breath, she set her foot on a branch. It trembled but held, and she was emboldened to haul herself up. In another moment she had reached Dong, who gave her a beaming smile.

'It is very nice up here,' he said in careful, perfect English. 'I like climbing trees.'

Olivia looked at him askance. At any other time she would have been delighted with his command of her language. In the six months she'd spent teaching English at the Chang-Ming School, she'd found that Dong was the one who grasped everything first. She was proud of him, but right now she had other things to worry about.

'I like climbing trees too,' she said. 'But I also like getting down safely. So let's try to do that.'

She began to edge down, encouraging him to follow her so that he descended into the safety of her arms. One branch, then two, then three and finally, to her immense relief, the top rung of the ladder.

'Just a little further,' she said. 'Nearly there.'

But it was the ladder which failed them, sliding away from the tree suddenly and depositing them on the ground with a bump.

Olivia gasped as she felt the bark scrape painfully against her arm, but her real fear was for Dong.

'Are you hurt?' she asked worriedly.

He shook his head, refusing to be troubled by a few bruises, and bounced back onto his feet.

'I am well,' he pronounced.

Clearly this was true, but Olivia knew she had to be sure.

'I'm getting you to a doctor,' she said.

The headmistress had arrived on the scene in time to hear this. She was in her late forties with an air of common sense.

'That's a good idea,' she said. 'He seems fine, but let's take no chances. There's a hospital ten minutes away. I'll call a taxi.'

A few minutes later they were on their way to the hospital. Olivia kept an anxious eye on Dong, but he was grinning, completely happy with the result of his escapade.

In the hospital someone showed them the way to the clinic, and they joined a short queue. A nurse gave Olivia some forms, and she filled them in while they waited to be seen.

A notice on the wall informed her that today's clinic was being taken by Dr Lang Mitchell. Briefly she wondered about that name; 'Mitchell' suggested that he might come from the West, but 'Lang' held a hint of Chinese.

After a few minutes the buzzer announced that the doctor was free, and they went in. Olivia saw a tall young man in his early thirties, with dark hair and eyes, and good-looking features that were mostly Western, yet with an intriguing hint of something else.

'What have you two been doing to yourselves?' he demanded, smiling and eyeing the state they were in.

'Miss Daley climbed a tree,' Dong said irrepressibly, 'and I went up to help her when she got stuck.'

Olivia looked aghast, which made Dr Mitchell grin in perfect comprehension.

'Perhaps it was the other way around?' he suggested.

'It certainly was,' Olivia declared, recovering her dignity. 'On the way down the ladder slipped, and we landed in a heap.'

He studied the forms. 'You are Miss Olivia Daley, a teacher at the Chang-Ming School?'

'That's right. Yen Dong is one of my pupils. I don't think he's hurt, but I have to be sure when I hand him back to his mother.'

'Of course. Let's have a look.'

After a thorough examination of Dong, he said, 'I agree that it doesn't look serious, but we'll have an X-ray just to be on the safe side. The nurse will take him.'

'Perhaps I should go too.'

But Dong shook his head, informing her that he was grown up and didn't need to be protected all the time. When he'd left with the nurse, the doctor switched to English to say, 'Let's see about your injuries.'

'Thank you. But I really don't need much done.'

Smiling, he said gently, 'Why don't you let me decide that?'

'Sorry,' she groaned. 'I just can't help it. My aunt says if I'd shut up occasionally I might learn something.'

He smiled again but didn't answer directly. Then he frowned, saying, 'It might be worse than you think.'

Now she saw the true extent of the damage. The final slide against the bark of the tree had not merely scratched her flesh but torn the top of her sleeve so that it was barely hanging on.

'I'm afraid I'll need to remove your blouse,' Dr Mitchell said. 'The scratches seem to go further than your arm. Don't worry, a nurse will be present.'

He went to the door and called, 'Nurse.' A smiling young woman entered, removed Olivia's blouse gently and remained

while he studied her abrasions. He eased her arm this way and
that with movements that were as neat as they were skilful.
His hands were large and comforting, both gentle and powerful together.

Disconcertingly she found herself becoming self-conscious.
The blouse was high-necked and modest, even severe, as
befitted a teacher, but beneath it she wore only a bra of fairly
skimpy dimensions. She had breasts to be proud of, an unusual
combination of dainty and luscious. Every bra she possessed
had been designed to reveal them to one man, and although he
was no longer part of her life she had never discarded them.

It had briefly crossed her mind to substitute underwear that
was more sober and serious, but she'd rejected the thought as
a kind of sacrilege. Now she wished she'd heeded it. Her generous curves were designed to be celebrated by a lover, not
viewed clinically by a man who seemed not to notice that they
were beautiful.

But that was as it should be, she reminded herself. The
doctor was being splendidly professional, and deserved her
respect for the scrupulous way he avoided touching her except
when and where necessary. It was just disturbing that his restraint seemed to bring her physically alive in a way that only
one man's touch had before.

He was cleaning her arm, swabbing it gently with cotton
wool anointed with a healing spirit.

'This will sting a little,' he said. 'I'm sorry, are you all right?'

'Yes, I—'

'You jumped. I guess it stings more than I thought. Don't
worry, I'll soon be finished.'

To her own dismay she'd sounded breathless. She hoped
he didn't guess the reason, or notice the little pulse beating
in her throat.

'Your diagnosis was quite correct,' he said after a while. 'Just a light dressing, I think. Nurse?'

The nurse did the necessary work, then helped Olivia back on with her ruined blouse and departed. Dr Mitchell had retired behind his desk.

'How are you going to get home?' he asked, eyeing the tear.

'I look a bit disreputable, don't I?' she said with a laugh. 'But I've got this.' She took a light scarf from her bag and draped it over the spot. 'And I'll take a taxi. Just as soon as I know that Dong is all right.'

'Don't worry about him. I never saw such a healthy child.'

'I know,' she said with a shaky laugh. 'He's a rascal, I'm glad to say. No power on earth stops him getting up to mischief. He couldn't see the highest tree in the playground without wanting to climb it.'

'And that can be good,' Dr Mitchell said. 'Except that other people have to pick up the pieces, and often it is they who get hurt. I was much the same as a boy, and always in trouble for it. But I only recall my teachers reproving me, not risking their own safety to rescue me.'

'If he'd been seriously hurt, how could I have faced his mother?'

'But he isn't seriously hurt, because he had a soft landing on top of you.'

'Something like that,' she said ruefully. 'But nothing hurts me. I just bounce. And I should be getting him back to school soon, or he'll be late going home.'

'What about when you go home?' he asked. 'Is there anyone there to look after you?'

'No, I live alone, but I don't need anyone to look after me.'

He paused a moment before saying, 'Perhaps you shouldn't be too confident of that.'

'Why not?'

'It—can sometimes be dangerous.'

She wanted to ask him what he meant. The air was singing as though two conversations were happening together. Beneath the conventional words, he was speaking silently to a part of her that had never listened before, and it was vital to know more. She drew a breath, carefully framing a question...

'Here I am,' came a cheerful voice.

Suddenly she was back on earth, and there was Dong, trotting into the room, accompanied by the nurse with the X-ray.

'Excellent,' Dr Mitchell said in a voice that didn't sound quite natural to Olivia's ears. But nothing was natural any more.

As predicted, the X-ray showed no injury.

'Bring him back if he seems poorly,' Dr Mitchell told her, his tone normal again. 'But he won't.'

He showed her out and stood watching as she vanished down the corridor and around the corner. Closing the door, he reached automatically for the buzzer, but stopped. He needed a moment to think before he saw another patient.

He went to stand at the window. Here, two floors high, there was a close-up view of the trees hung with cherry blossom; the promise of spring had been gloriously kept, and still lingered.

Here in China cherry blossom was a symbol of feminine beauty; seemingly delicate, yet laden with hope and promise. Now he saw that wherever he looked it was the same, as fresh new life returned after the cold, bringing hope and joy for those who were eager to embrace it.

On the surface nothing very much had happened. Olivia Daley was strong, independent, concerned not for herself but those in her care, much like the kind of woman a medical man met every day. It might only have been his imagination that beneath her composure was someone else—someone tense, vulnerable, needing help yet defiantly refusing to ask for it.

He could hear her again, insisting, *Nothing hurts me. I just bounce.*

He wondered if she truly believed herself so armoured to life. For himself, he didn't believe a word of it.

A few minutes they'd been together, that was all. Yet he'd seen deep into her, and the sad emptiness he'd found there had almost overwhelmed him. He knew too that she'd been as disconcertingly alive to him as he had been to her.

He'd smothered the thought as unprofessional, but now it demanded his attention, and he yielded. She was different from other women. He had yet to discover exactly how different, and caution warned him not to try. Already he knew that he was going to ignore caution and follow the light that had mysteriously appeared on the road ahead.

It was a soft light, flickering and uncertain, promising everything and nothing. But he could no more deny it than he could deny his own self.

'Is everything all right?' asked the nurse from the doorway. 'You haven't buzzed.'

'I'm sorry,' he said with an effort. 'I just—got distracted.'

She smiled, following his gaze to the blossom-laden trees. 'The spring is beautiful, isn't it?'

'Yes,' he murmured. 'Beautiful.'

They arrived back at the school to find Mrs Yen, Dong's mother, waiting with a worried look that cleared as soon as she saw him waving eagerly.

'Perhaps you should take tomorrow off?' Mrs Wu, the headmistress, asked when they were finally alone.

'Thanks, but I won't need to.'

'Well, be sure. I don't want to lose one of my best teachers.'

They had been friends since the day Olivia had joined the school, charged with instructing the children in English. Now Mrs Wu fussed over her kindly until she went to collect her bicycle and rode it to her apartment, ten minutes away.

She had moved in six months ago, when she'd arrived to work in Beijing. Then she had been distraught, fleeing England, desperately glad to be embraced by a different culture which occupied her thoughts and gave her no time to brood. Now her surroundings and her new life were more familiar, but there were still new discoveries to be made, and she enjoyed every day.

She had a settled routine for when she arrived home. After a large cup of tea, she would switch on the computer and enter a programme that allowed her to make video contact with Aunt Norah, the elderly relative in England to whom she felt closest.

London was eight hours behind Beijing, which meant that back there it was the early hours of the morning, but she knew Norah would be ready, having set her alarm to be sure.

Yes, there she was, sitting up in bed, smiling and waving at the camera on top of her computer screen. Olivia waved back.

Norah was an old lady, a great-aunt rather than an aunt, but her eyes were as bright as they'd been her youth, and her vitality was undimmed. Olivia had always been close to her, turning to her wisdom and kindness as a refuge from the self-centred antics of the rest of her family.

'Sorry I'm late,' she said into the microphone. 'There was a bit of a kerfuffle at school today.'

She outlined the events of the afternoon, making light of them.

'And the doctor said you were all right?'

'He says I'm fine. I'll have an early night and be fit as a fiddle.'

'Are you going out with anyone?'

'You asked me that last night, and the night before. Honestly, Auntie, it's all you ever think of.'

'So I should hope. You're a pretty girl. You ought to be having a good time.'

'I'm having a wonderful time. And I do have dates. I just don't want to get serious. Now, tell me about yourself. Are you getting enough sleep?'

There was more in the query than just a desire to change the subject. Norah was in her seventies, and the only thing that had made Olivia hesitate about coming to China was the fear of possibly not seeing her again. But Norah had assured her that she was in the best of health and had urged her to go.

'Don't you dare turn down your chance because of me,' she'd insisted.

'I'm just trying to be sensible,' Olivia had protested mildly.

'*Sensible?* You've got the rest of your life for that sort of nonsense. Get out there, do things you've never done before, and forget that man who didn't deserve you anyway.'

Norah could never forgive the man who'd broken Olivia's heart.

'I'm sleeping fine,' Norah said now. 'I spent yesterday evening with your mother, listening to her complaining about her latest. That sent me right off to sleep.'

'I thought Guy was her ideal lover.'

'Not Guy, Freddy. She's finished with Guy, or he finished with her, one of the two. I can't keep up.'

Olivia sighed wryly. 'I'll call her and commiserate.'

'Not too much or you'll make her worse,' Norah said at once. 'She's a silly woman. I've always said so. Mind you, it's not all her fault. Her own mother has a lot to answer for. Fancy giving her a stupid name like Melisande! She was bound to see herself as a romantic heroine.'

'You mean,' Olivia said, 'that if Mum had been called something dull and sensible she wouldn't have eloped?'

'Probably not, although I think she'd have been self-centred whatever she was called. She's never thought of anyone but herself. She's certainly never thought of you, any more than your father has. Heaven alone knows what he's doing now, although I did hear a rumour that he's got some girl pregnant.'

'Again?'

'Yes, and he's going about preening as though he's the first man who's ever managed it. Forget him. The great fool isn't worth bothering with.'

Thus she dismissed her nephew—with some justice, as Olivia had to admit.

They chatted for a while longer before bidding each other an affectionate goodnight. Olivia delayed just long enough to make herself a basic meal, then fell thankfully into bed, ready to fall asleep at once.

Instead she lay awake, too restless for sleep. Mysteriously, Dr Mitchell had found his way into her thoughts, and she remembered him saying, *Other people have to pick up the pieces, and often it is they who get hurt.*

He'd given her a look full of wry kindness, as if guessing that she was often the person who had to come to the rescue—which was shrewd of him, she realised, because he'd been right.

As far back as she could remember she'd been the rock of stability in her family. Her parents' marriage had been a disaster. They'd married young in a fever of romance, had quickly been disillusioned by prosaic reality and had headed for divorce. Since then her mother had remarried and divorced again before settling for lovers. Her father had moved straight onto the lovers.

She herself had been passed from pillar to post, depending on whichever of them had felt she could be most useful. They had lavished noisy affection on her without ever managing to be convincing. Their birthday and Christmas gifts had been expensive, but she'd realised early on that they were aimed at scoring points off each other.

'Let's see what your father thinks of that,' her mother had said, proudly revealing a state-of-the-art, top-of-the-range, laptop. But she'd been too busy to come and see Olivia in the school play, which would have meant far more.

The person who'd always come to school functions was Norah, her father's aunt. When both her parents had been busy, Olivia had gone to Norah for long visits and found that here was someone she could talk to. Norah had encouraged her to say what she was thinking. She would argue, forcing the girl to define her ideas then enlarge on them, until Olivia had begun to realise that her own thoughts were actually worth discussing—something she'd never discovered with her parents, who could talk only about themselves.

There'd always been a bedroom for her in Norah's home, and when she'd turned sixteen she'd moved into it full-time.

'How did that pair of adolescents you call parents react to the idea?' Norah demanded.

'I'm not sure they quite realise that I've gone,' Olivia said. 'He thinks I'm with her, she thinks I'm with him. Oh, what do they matter?'

It was possible to cope with her parents' selfish indifference because Norah's love was there like a rock. Even so, it was painful to discover yet again how little they really cared about her.

Eventually her mother asked, 'Will you be all right with Norah? She's a bit—you know—' she'd lowered her voice as though describing some great crime '—*fuddy-duddy*.'

It crossed Olivia's mind that 'fuddy-duddy' might be a welcome quality in a parent, but she said nothing. She'd learned discretion at an early age. She assured her mother that she would be fine, and the subject was allowed to die.

Before leaving, Melisande had one final request.

'Would you mind not calling me Mum when there are people around? It sounds so middle-aged, and I'm only thirty-one.'

Olivia frowned. 'Thirty-three, surely? Because I was born when—'

'Oh, darling, must you be so literal? I only *look* thirty-one. In fact, I've been told I look twenty-five. Surely you understand about artistic licence?'

'Of course,' Olivia agreed with a touch of bitterness that passed her mother by. 'And if I start claiming you as my mother it spoils the effect.'

'Exactly!' Melisande beamed, entirely missing the irony in her daughter's voice. 'You can call me Melly if you like.'

'Gosh, thanks, Mum.'

Her mother gave her a sharp look but didn't make the mistake of replying.

That evening, she told Norah, who was disgusted.

'Fuddy-duddy! She means I don't live my life at the mercy of every wind that blows.'

'She just thinks you know nothing about love,' Olivia pointed out.

When Norah didn't answer, she persisted, 'But she's wrong, isn't she? There's someone you never talk about.'

That was how she'd first heard about Edward, who'd died so long ago that nobody else remembered him, or the volcano he'd caused in the life of the girl who'd loved him. Norah told her only a little that night, but more later on, as Olivia grew old enough to understand.

Norah had been eighteen when she'd met Edward, a young army-officer, nineteen when they'd celebrated his promotion by becoming engaged, and twenty when he'd died, far away in another country. She had never loved another man.

The bleak simplicity of the story shocked Olivia. Later she learned to set it beside her own parents' superficial romances, and was equally appalled by both.

Had that lesson hovered somewhere in her mind when she too had fallen disastrously in love?

Looking back, she could see that her life-long cynicism about emotion, far from protecting her, had left her vulnerable. She'd determinedly avoided the youthful experiences on which most girls cut their romantic teeth, proud of the way her heart had never been broken because she'd never become involved. But it meant that she'd had no yardstick by which to judge Andy, no caution to warn her of signs that other women would have seen. Her capitulation to him had been total, joyful, and his betrayal had left her defenceless.

She'd fled, seeking a new life here in China, vowing never to make the same mistake again. From now on men would no longer exist. Neither would love, or anything that reminded her of 'the whole romantic nonsense' as she inwardly called it. And so she would be safe.

On that comforting thought, she fell asleep.

But tonight her sleep was mysteriously disturbed. Phantoms chased through her dreams, making her hot and cold by turns, causing her blood to race and her heart to pound. She awoke abruptly to find herself sitting up in bed, not knowing when it had happened, not knowing anything, except that suddenly there was no safety in all the world.

CHAPTER TWO

THE next day Olivia felt down from the moment she awoke. The sight of herself in the bathroom mirror was off-putting. Where was the vibrant young woman in her twenties with a slender figure, rich, honey-coloured hair and large blue eyes that could say so much?

'I don't think she ever really existed,' she informed her reflection gloomily. 'You're the reality.'

She wondered if she might still be in shock from her nasty fall, but dismissed that as just making excuses.

'I'm a hag,' she muttered. 'I look older than I am. I'm too thin, and my hair is just plain drab. I'll be going grey next.'

The woman in the mirror stared back, offering not a glimmer of sympathy. Normally Olivia wore her wavy hair long and bouncy but today she pulled it back into an efficient-looking bun. It suited her mood.

The day continued to be glum for no apparent reason. Her students were attentive and well-behaved, lunch was appetizing and her friends on the staff made kindly enquiries as to her health. Mrs Wu even tried to send her home.

'It's a reaction to that fall,' she said. 'Go home and rest.'

'Dong doesn't seem to need rest,' Olivia pointed out. 'I actually had to stop him trying to climb that tree again.'

'It's up to you,' the headmistress said sympathetically. 'But feel free to leave when you feel like it.'

She stuck it out to the end of the day, tired and grumpy, wanting to go home yet not looking forward to the empty apartment. Finally she delivered some papers to the headmistress and slipped out of the building by a side door, instead of the main entrance that she would normally have used. Then she stopped, arrested by the sight that met her eyes.

Dr Mitchell was there.

Now she knew that this moment was always meant to happen.

He was sitting on a low wall near the main entrance. Olivia paused for a moment just as he rose and began to pace restlessly and look at the main door as though expecting somebody to come through it. Occasionally he consulted his watch.

She backed off until she was in shadow under the trees, but still able to see him clearly. She realised that her view of him the day before had been constricted by the surroundings of his office. He was taller than she remembered, not muscular, but lean with a kind of casual elegance that yet hinted at tension and control.

Yesterday he'd been in command on his own territory. Now he was uncertain.

She began to walk towards him, calling, 'Can I help you?'

His face brightened at once, convincing her that she was the one he'd been awaiting. Mysteriously the day's cares began to fall away from her.

'I thought I'd drop in to see how my patients are,' he said, moving towards her.

'Do you always do follow-up visits from the clinic?'

He shook his head. His eyes were mischievous.

'Just this time,' he said.

'Thank you. Dong has already gone home, but he's fine.'

'But what about you? You were hurt as well.'

'It was only a few scratches, and I was cared for by an excellent doctor.'

He inclined his head in acknowledgement of her compliment, and said, 'Still, perhaps I should assure myself that you're really well.'

'Of course.' She stood back to let him enter the building, but he shook his head.

'I have a better idea. There's a little restaurant not far from here where we can talk in peace.'

His smile held a query, asking if she would go along with his strategy, and she hurried to reassure him, smiling in return and saying, 'What a lovely idea!'

'My car's just over there.'

To her pleasure he drove to a place that had a look that she thought of as traditionally Chinese. Much of Beijing had been rebuilt in a modern style, but she yearned for the old buildings with their ornate roofs turning up at the corners. Here she found them glowing with light from the coloured lamps outside.

The first restaurant they came to was full. So was the second.

'Perhaps we should try—'

He was interrupted by a cheerful cry. Turning, they saw a young man hailing him from a short distance away, and urgently pointing down a side street. He vanished without waiting to see if they followed him.

'We're caught,' her companion said ruefully. 'We'll have to go to the Dancing Dragon.'

'Isn't it any good?'

'It's the best—but I'll tell you later. Let's go.'

There was no mistaking the restaurant. Painted dragons swirled on the walls outside, their eyes alight with mischief. Inside was small and bright, bustling with life and packed.

'They don't have any tables free,' she murmured.

'Don't worry. They always keep one for me.'

Sure enough the man from the street reappeared, pointing the way to a corner and leading them to a small, discreet table tucked away almost out of sight. It had clearly been designed for lovers, and Lang must have thought so too, because he gave a hurried, embarrassed mutter, which Olivia just managed to decipher as, 'Do you have to be so obvious?'

'Why not?' the waiter asked, genuinely baffled. 'It's the table you always have.'

Olivia's lips twitched as she seated herself in the corner, but she controlled her amusement. Dr Mitchell was turning out to be more interesting than she would have guessed.

The restaurant was charming, the lanterns giving out a soft, red light, the walls covered in dragons. She regarded them in delight. Dragons had been part of her love affair with China ever since she'd discovered their real nature.

Raised in England, the only dragon she'd heard of had been the one slain by St George, a devil breathing fire and death, ravaging villages, demanding the sacrifice of innocent maidens, until the heroic knight George had overcome him and become the country's patron saint as a result.

In China it was different. Here the dragon had always been the harbinger of good luck, wealth, wisdom, a fine harvest. Delightful dragons popped up in every part of life. They danced at weddings, promenaded in parades, breathing their friendly fire and spreading happiness. They were all around her now.

Perhaps that was why she suddenly felt better than she'd done all day. There surely couldn't be any other reason.

Looking at a dragon painted onto a mirror, she caught sight of her own reflection and realised that her hair was still drawn back severely, which no longer felt right. With a swift movement she pulled at the pins until her tresses were freed, flowing lusciously again, in keeping with her lighter mood.

The dragon winked at her.

While Dr Mitchell was occupied with the waiter, Olivia remembered a duty that she must perform without delay. Whenever she was unable to make computer contact with Norah she always called to warn her so that the old woman wouldn't be left waiting in hope. Quickly she used her mobile phone and in a moment she heard Norah's voice.

'Just to let you know that I'm not at home tonight,' she said.

'Jolly good,' Norah said at once, as Olivia had known she would say. 'You should go out more often, not waste time talking to me.'

'But you know I love talking to you.'

'Yes, I do, but tonight you have more important things to think of. At least, I hope you have. Goodnight, darling.'

'Goodnight, my love,' Olivia said tenderly.

She hung up to find her companion regarding her with a little frown.

'Have I created a problem?' he asked delicately. 'Is there someone who—' he paused delicately '—would object to your being with me?'

'Oh, no! I was talking to my elderly aunt in England. There's nobody who can tell me who to be with.'

'I'm glad,' he said simply.

And she was glad too, for suddenly the shadows of the day had lifted.

'Dr Mitchell—'

'My name is Lang.'

'And mine is Olivia.'

The waiter appeared with tea, filling Olivia's cup, smiling with pleased surprise as she gave the traditional thank-you gesture of tapping three fingers on the table.

'Most Westerners don't know to do that,' Lang explained.

'It's the kind of thing I love,' she said. 'I love the story too—about the emperor who went to a tea-house incognito with some friends and told them not to prostrate themselves before him because it would give away his identity. So they tapped their fingers instead. I don't want to stand out. It's more fun fitting in.'

When the first dishes were laid out before them, including the rice, he observed her skill using chopsticks.

'You really know how to do that,' he observed as they started to eat. 'You must have been in China for some time.'

He spoke in Mandarin Chinese and she replied in the same language, glad to demonstrate that she was as expert as he.

'About six months,' she said. 'Before that I lived in England most of the time.'

'Most?'

'I've always travelled a lot to improve my languages. They were all I was ever good at, so I had to make the most of them.'

'How many languages do you speak?'

'French, German, Italian, Spanish…'

'Hey, I'm impressed. But why Chinese?'

'Pure show-off,' she chuckled. 'Everyone warned me it was difficult, so I did it for the fun of proving that I could. That showed 'em!'

'I'll bet it did,' he said admiringly, reverting to English. 'And I don't suppose you found it difficult at all.'

'Actually, I did, but I kept that to myself. You're the only person I've ever admitted that secret to.'

'And I promise not to reveal it,' he said solemnly. 'On pain of your never speaking to me again.'

She didn't have to ask what he meant by that. They both knew that the connection between them had been established in those few minutes of devastating consciousness in his surgery, and today he'd come looking for her because he had to.

Olivia thought back to last night, to the disturbance that had haunted her dreams, waking her and refusing to let her sleep again. Instinct told her that it had been the same with him.

They might spend no more than a few fleeting hours in each other's company, or they might travel a little distance along the road together. Neither could know. But they had to find out.

'So you came out here to improve your Chinese?' he asked in a tone that suggested there must be more to it.

'Partly, but I needed to get away from England for a while.'

He nodded, understanding at once. 'Was he a real louse?'

'I thought so at the time, but I think now I had a lucky escape. He almost made me forget my prime directive. But when I discovered what a louse he really was, I realised that the prime directive had been right all the time.'

'Prime directive,' he mused, his eyes glinting with amusement. 'Now, let me see—what would that be? "Only learning matters." "Life can be reduced to graphs on a page." How am I doing?'

'You're part of the way there, but only part. Beware people, beware relationships—'

'Beware men!'

'Hey, you guessed.'

'It was obviously what you were building up to. Are we all condemned?'

'It's not that simple. I don't just condemn men, I blame women, as well.'

'Well, that seems to take care of the entire human race. Having disposed of the whole lot of them, let's go on eating.'

His wryly mocking tone made her laugh.

'My parents were both wild romantics,' she went on, 'and I can't tell you what a misfortune that is.'

'You don't need to. Romance isn't supposed to be for parents. Their job is to be severe and straight-laced so that their kids have a safety net for indulging in mad fantasies.'

'Right!' she said, relieved at his understanding. 'According to Aunt Norah it was love at first sight, then a whirlwind romance—moon rhyming with June. All that stuff.'

Lang regarded her curiously. Something edgy in the way she'd said *all that stuff* had alerted him.

'What happened?'

'She was seventeen, he was eighteen. Nobody took it seriously at first, just kids fooling around. But then they wanted to get married. The parents said no. He had to go to college. So she got pregnant—on purpose, Norah thinks. They ended up making a runaway marriage.'

'Wonderfully romantic,' Lang supplied. 'Until they came down to earth with a bump. He had to get a job, she found herself with a crying baby….'

'Apparently I cried more than most—for no reason, according to my mother.'

'But babies can sense things. You must have known instinctively that she was dissatisfied, wanting to go out and enjoy herself, and your father probably blamed her for his blighted career-prospects.'

She stared at him, awed by this insight.

'That's exactly how it was. At least, that's how Norah says it was. I don't remember, of course, except that I picked up the atmosphere without knowing why. There was lots of shouting and screaming.

'It got worse because they both started having affairs. At last they divorced, and I found I didn't really have a home. I stayed with her, or with him, but I always felt like a guest. If there was a new girlfriend or new boyfriend I'd be in the way and I'd stay with Norah. Then the romance would break up and my mother would cry on my shoulder.'

'So you became *her* mother,' Lang observed.

'Yes, I suppose I did. And, if that was what romance did to you, I decided I didn't want it.'

'But wasn't there anyone else in your family to show you a more encouraging view of love? What about Norah?'

'She's the opposite to them. Her fiancé died years ago. There's been nobody else for her since, and she's always told me that she's perfectly content. She says once you've found the right man you can't replace him with anyone else.'

'Even when she's lost him?'

'But according to Norah she hasn't lost him. He loved her to the end of his life, so she feels that they still belong to each other.'

'And you disapprove?' he asked, frowning a little.

'It sounds charming, but it's really only words. The reality is that it's turned Norah's life into a desert that's lasted fifty years.'

'Perhaps it hasn't. Do you really know what's inside her heart? Perhaps it's given her a kind of fulfilment that we can't understand.'

'Of course you could be right, but if that's fulfilment…' She finished with a sigh. 'I just want more from life than dreaming about a man who isn't there any more. Or,' she added wryly, 'in my mother's case, several men who aren't there any more.'

'But what about the louse? Didn't he change your mind?'

For the first time he saw her disconcerted.

'I kind of lost the plot there,' she admitted. 'But it sorted itself out. Never mind how. I'm wiser now.'

She spoke with a shrug and a cheerful smile, but she had

the feeling that he wasn't fooled. Some instinct was telling him the things she wouldn't, couldn't say.

She'd been dazzled by Andy from the first moment. Handsome, charming, intelligent, he'd singled her out, wooed her passionately and had overturned all the fixed ideas of her life. For once she'd understood Norah's aching fidelity to a dead man. She'd even partly understood the way her mother fell in love so often.

Then, just when she'd been ready to abandon the prejudices of a lifetime, he'd announced that he was engaged to marry someone else. He'd said they'd had a wonderful few months together but it was time to be realistic, wasn't it?

The lonely, anguished nights that had followed had served to convince her that she'd been right all the time. Love wasn't for her, or for anyone in their right mind. She couldn't speak of it, but there was no need. Lang's sympathetic silence told her that he understood.

'Tell me about you,' she hastened to say. 'You're English too, aren't you? What brought you out here?'

'I'm three-quarters English. The other quarter is Chinese.'

'Ah,' she said slowly.

'You guessed?'

'Not exactly. You sound English, but your features suggest otherwise. I don't know—there's something else…'

She gave up trying to explain. The 'something else' in his face seemed to come and go. One moment it almost defined him, the next it barely existed. It intrigued and tempted her with its hint of another, mysterious world.

'Something different—but it's not a matter of looks,' she finished, wishing she could find the right words.

He seemed satisfied and nodded.

'I know. That "something different" is inside, and it has always haunted me,' he said. 'I was born in London, and I grew up there, but I knew I didn't quite fit in with the others. My mother was English, my father was half-Chinese. He died soon after I was born. Later my mother married an Englishman with two children from a previous marriage.'

'Wicked stepfather?' Olivia enquired.

'No, nothing so dramatic. He was a decent guy. I got on well with him and his children, but I wasn't like them, and we all knew it.

'Luckily I had my grandmother, who'd left China to marry my grandfather. Her name was Lang Meihui before she married, and she was an astonishing woman. She knew nothing about England and couldn't speak the language. John Mitchell couldn't speak Chinese. But they managed to communicate and knew that they loved each other. He brought her home to London.'

'She must have found it really hard to cope,' Olivia mused.

'Yes, but I'll swear, nothing has ever defeated her in her life. She learned to speak English really well. She found a way to live in a country that probably felt like being on another planet, and she survived when her husband died ten years later, leaving her with a son to raise alone.

'He was called Lang too. She'd insisted on that. It was her way of keeping her Chinese family-name alive. When I was born she more or less bullied him into calling me Lang, as well. She told me later that she did it so that "we don't lose China."

'My father died when I was eight years old. When my mother remarried, Meihui moved into a little house in the next street so that she could be near me. She helped my mother with the children, the shopping, anything, but then she slipped away to her own home. And in time I began to follow her.'

He gave her a warm smile. 'So you see, I had a Norah too.'

'And you depended on her, just as I did on mine.'

'Yes, because she was the only one who could make me understand what was different about me. She taught me her language but, more than that, she showed me China.'

'She actually brought you here?'

'Only in my head, but if you could have seen the fireworks she set off in there.' He tapped his forehead. 'She used to take me out to visit London's Chinatown, especially on Chinese New Year. I thought I was in heaven—all that colour, the glittering lights and the music—'

'Oh, yes, I remember,' Olivia broke in eagerly.

'You saw it too?'

'Only once. My mother visited some friends who lived near there, and they took us out a couple of nights to see what was happening. It was like you said, brilliant and thrilling, but nobody could explain it to me. There was a lot of red, and they were supposed to be fighting somebody, but I couldn't tell who or what.'

'Some people say they're fighting the Nian,' Lang supplied. 'A mythical beast rather like a lion, who devours crops and children. So they put food out for him and let off firecrackers, because he's afraid of loud noises and also of the colour red. So you got lots of red and fireworks and lions dancing. What more could a child want?'

'Nothing,' Olivia said, remembering ecstatically. 'Oh, yes, it was gorgeous. So much better than the English New Year celebrations, which always seemed boringly sedate after that.'

'Me too. It was the one thing I refused ever to miss, and that drove my mother mad, because the date was always changing—late January, mid-February—always lasting fifteen days. Mum complained that she couldn't plan for anything, except that I'd be useless for fifteen days. I said, "Don't worry, Mum, I'm always useless".' He made a face. 'She didn't think that was at all funny.'

LUCY GORDON

33

'Your grandmother sounds wonderful,' Olivia said sincerely.

'She was. She told me how everyone is born in the year of an animal—a sheep, an ox, a rat, a dragon. I longed to find I was born in the year of the dragon.'

'And were you?'

He made a face. 'No, I was born in the year of the rabbit. *Don't laugh!*'

'I'm not laughing,' she said, hastily controlling her mirth. 'In this country, the rabbit is calm and gentle, hardworking—'

'Dull and plodding,' he supplied. 'Dreary, conventional—'

'Observant, intelligent—'

'Boring.'

She chuckled. 'You're not boring, I promise.'

It was true. He delighted her, not with any flashy display of personality, but because his thoughts seemed to reach out and take hers by the hand in a way that, she now realized, Andy had never done.

He gave her a rueful grin.

'Thank you for those kind words, even if you had to scrape the bottom of the barrel to find them.'

'According to everything I've read, there's nothing wrong with being born in the year of the rabbit.'

'And you've obviously read a lot, so I guess you know your own year.' He saw her sheepish look and exclaimed, 'Oh, no, please don't tell me—!'

'I'm sorry, I really am.'

'The year of the dragon?'

'It not my fault,' she pleaded.

'You know what that means, don't you?' He groaned. 'Dragons are free spirits, powerful, beautiful, fearless, they soar above convention, refusing to be bound by rules and regulations.'

'That's the theory, but I never felt it quite fitted me,' she said, laughing and trying to placate him. 'I don't see myself soaring.'

'But perhaps you don't know yourself too well,' he suggested. 'And you've yet to find the thing that will make you soar. Or the person,' he added.

The last words were spoken so quietly that she might have missed them, except that she was totally alive to him. She understood and was filled with sudden alarm. Things were happening that she'd sworn never to allow happen again.

She would leave right now and retreat into the old illusion of safety. All she had to do was rise, apologise and leave, trying to avoid his eyes that saw too much. It was simple, really.

But she didn't move, and she knew that she wasn't going to.

CHAPTER THREE

'THE trouble with soaring,' she murmured, 'is that you fall to earth.'

'Sometimes you do,' he said gently. 'But not always.'

'Not always,' she murmured. 'Perhaps.'

But it was too soon. Her nerve failed her and in her mind she crossed hastily to the cautious side of the road.

'What about your grandmother? What was her year?'

Tactfully he accepted her change of subject without demur.

'She was a dragon too,' he said. 'With her courage and sense of adventure she couldn't have been anything else—a real dragon lady. Everything she told me about this country seemed to bring me alive, until all I could think of was coming here one day.

'We planned how we'd make the trip together, but she became very ill. I'd qualified as a doctor by then, and I knew she wasn't going to recover, but she still talked as though it would happen soon.

'At last we had to face the truth. On her deathbed she said, "I so much wanted to be there with you." And I promised her that she would be.'

'And she has been, hasn't she?' Olivia asked, marvelling.

'Every step of the way,' he confirmed. 'Wherever I go, I

remember what she told me. Her family welcomed me with open arms.'

'Did you find them easily?'

'Yes, because she'd stayed in touch. When I landed at Beijing Airport three years ago there were thirty people to welcome me. They recognised me at once from the pictures she'd sent them, and they all cheered.

'It's an enormous family. Not all of them live in Beijing, and many of those who lived further out had come in especially to see Meihui's grandson.'

'They weren't put off by your being three-quarters English?'

He laughed. 'I don't think they even see that part of me. I'm one of the Lang family. That's all that counts.'

'It was clever of your grandmother to name you and your father Lang,' Olivia mused. 'In England it's your first name, but here the family name comes first.'

'Yes, my uncles are Lang Hai and Lang Jing, my great uncle is Lang Tao, my cousin is Lang Dai, so I fitted in straight away.'

A sudden look of mischief crossed her face. 'Tell me something—have your stepbrothers given you any nephews and nieces?'

He looked puzzled. 'Three, but I don't see...'

'And I'll bet they call you Uncle Lang.'

'Yes, but—'

'And what do the children of the Lang family call you? It can't be Uncle Lang, because that would be nonsense to them. So I guess they must call you Uncle Mitch.'

A glazed look came into his eyes and he edged away from her with a nervous air that made her laugh.

'Are you a witch to have such second sight?' he demanded. 'Should I be scared?'

'Are you?' she teased.

'A bit. More than a bit, actually. How did you know that?'

'Logical deduction, my dear Watson. Second sight doesn't come into it.'

He could see that she was right, but it still left him with an enchanted feeling, as though she could divine what was hidden from others. A true 'dragon lady', he thought with delight, with magic arts to entice and dazzle a man.

'You're right about my grandmother,' he said. 'In her heart, she never really left China.'

'How did her relatives feel about her marrying an Englishman and leaving the country?'

'They were very supportive, because it's in the family tradition.'

'You all believe in marrying for love?'

'Much more than that. Marrying in the face of great difficulties, putting love first despite all obstacles. It goes back over two-thousand years.'

'Two thou...?' She laughed in astonishment. 'Are you nobility or something?'

'No, just ordinary people. Over the centuries my family has tilled the land, sold farm produce, perhaps made just enough money to start a little shop. We've been carpenters, wheelwrights, blacksmiths—but never noble, I promise you.'

The arrival of the waiter made him fall silent while plates were cleared away and the next course was served. It was fried pork-belly stewed in soy and wine, and Olivia's mouth watered at the prospect.

'We're also excellent cooks,' Lang observed, speaking very significantly.

'You mean...?'

'This was cooked by my cousin Lang Chao, and the guy who served it is his brother, Lang Wei. Later Wei's girlfriend, Suyin, will sing for us.'

'Your family own this restaurant?'

'That's why they virtually hijacked us. I wasn't planning to bring you here because I knew we'd be stared at—if you glance into the corner you'll see Wei sneaking a peek and thinking we can't see him—but they happened to spot me in the street, and after that we were lost.'

'We seem to be providing the entertainment,' she said, amused. 'Wei's enjoying a good laugh over there.'

'I'm going to strangle him when I get home,' Lang growled. 'This is why I didn't want them to see you because I knew they'd think— Well…'

'That you'd brought one of your numerous girlfriends here?' Olivia said.

She was teasing but the question was important.

'I occasionally bring a lady here to dine,' he conceded. 'Purely in a spirit of flirtation. Anything more serious, I wouldn't bring her here. Or at least,' he added, grinding his teeth and glaring at the unrepentant Wei, 'I'd *try* not to.'

'No problem.' Olivia chuckled. 'You tell him that he's completely wrong in what he's thinking, that we're just a pair of fellow professionals having a quiet meal for companionship. There's no more to it than that.'

'No more to it than that,' he echoed in a comically robotic voice.

'*Then* you can strangle him.'

'That sounds like a good idea. But what do I tell him when I take you out again?'

'Tell him to mind his own business?' she suggested vaguely.

'I can see you've never lived with a family like mine.'

'Wait a minute, you said when you "get home"? You don't live in the same house, do you?'

'Sometimes. I have a room there, but also a little place of

my own near the hospital where I go if I've done a long stint
at work and need to collapse. But if I want warmth, noise and
cousins driving me crazy I go to the family home, so they tend
to know what I do. But next time we'll avoid this place and
have some privacy.'

'Look—'

'It's all right.' He held up a hand quickly. 'I don't mean to
rush you. I know you haven't decided yet. But, when you do,
let me know where you want to go.'

Her eyebrows rose at this quiet assurance but his smile
disarmed her, making her complicit.

'I didn't finish telling you about our tradition,' he said.

'Yes, I'm curious. How did a family that had to work so
hard come to put such a high value on romantic love? Surely
it made more sense for a man to marry the girl whose father
owned a strip of land next to his own?'

'Of course, and many marriages were made for such practical reasons. But the descendants of Jaio and Renshu always
hoped for more.'

'Who were they?'

'They lived in the reign of the Emperor Qin, of whom I'm
sure you've heard.'

She nodded. In reading about China, she'd learned about
the time when it had been divided into many states. Qin Shi
Huang, king of the state of Qin, had conquered the other
states, unifying them into one gigantic country. Since Qin was
pronounced 'chin' the country had come to be called China.
Qin had proclaimed himself emperor, and on his death he'd
been buried in a splendid mausoleum accompanied by any of
his concubines who hadn't born him a child.

'One of those concubines was Jaio,' Lang told her now.
'She didn't want to die, and she was in love with Renshu, a
young soldier who also loved her. Somehow he managed to

rescue her, and they fled together. Of course, they had to spend the rest of their lives on the run, and they only had about five years before they were caught and killed. But by then they'd had a son, who was rescued and spirited away by Jaio's brother.

'Nobody heard anything for years, but when the son was an old man he revealed the writings that Jaio and Renshu had left, in which they said that their love had been worth all the hardship. Of course, they had to be kept secret, but the family protected them and still has them to this day.

'Because of this the Langs have always cherished a belief in love that has seen them through many hard times. Often their neighbours have thought them mad for trusting in love when there were so many more *important* things in life, but they have clung to their ideals. It was that trust that made Meihui leave China and follow John Mitchell to England. And she never regretted it. She missed her homeland, but she always said that being with the man she loved mattered more than anything in life.'

Hearing these words, Olivia had a strange sense of familiarity. Then she realised that this was exactly what Norah would have said.

She sipped her wine, considering what she had just been told. On the surface it was a conventional legend— charming, a tad sentimental. What made it striking was that this serious man should speak as though it had a deep meaning for him.

'It's a lovely story,' she said wistfully. 'But did it really happen that way?'

'Why not?' he asked, giving her a quizzical smile.

She suppressed the instinct to say, *Because it's too absurdly romantic to be real*, and said, 'I only meant that two-thousand years is a terribly long time. So many things get lost in the mists, and you could never really know if they were true or not.'

'It's true if we want it to be,' he said simply. 'And we do.'

For a moment she almost queried who 'we' were, and then was glad she hadn't, because he added, 'All of us, the whole family—my aunts, great-aunts, my uncles, cousins—we all want it to be true. And so it is—for us.'

'That's a delightful idea,' she mused. 'But perhaps not very practical.'

'Ah, yes, I'd forgotten that you must always be practical and full of common sense,' he teased.

'There's a lot to be said for it,' she protested defensively. 'If you're a schoolteacher.'

'Doesn't a doctor need common sense, as well?'

'Often, but not always. Sometimes common sense is a much over-rated virtue.'

'And sometimes it can come to your rescue,' she said wryly.

She didn't realise that she'd spoken aloud until she saw him looking at her with a question in his eyes.

'Has it rescued you very often?' he asked gently.

'Now and then. It's nice to know I can always rely on it.'

'That's just what you can't do!' he said with sudden urgency. 'You must never rely completely on your head, because sooner or later it will always let you down.'

'And you think the heart doesn't?' she retorted with a touch of indignation. 'We're not all as lucky as Meihui.'

'Or Norah.'

'I'd hardly call her lucky.'

'I would,' he said at once. 'The man she loved died, but he didn't betray her. That makes her luckier than many women, and men too, who live for years with the shadows of failed love, bad memories, regrets. Or the others, who never dared risk love at all and have only thoughts of what might have been if only they'd had a little more courage.'

'That sounds very fine,' she said. 'But the fact is that most people are unlucky in love. Is there really much to choose between taking the risk and regretting it, and deciding not to take it at all?'

'And regretting that?'

'And living free,' she said defiantly. 'Free of regrets, free of pain—'

'Free of joy, free of the sense that life is worth living or ever has been?' he interrupted her firmly. 'Being free of pain can come at a heavy price.'

How had they strayed into this argument? she wondered. And why? The conversation was becoming dangerous, and she acted instinctively to get back into control.

'I see Wei coming towards us,' she said brightly.

If he noticed her abrupt change of subject he didn't say so. Instead he turned sardonic eyes on his cousin, who bustled forward eagerly, his gaze darting between the two of them.

'We'd like some fruit, please,' Lang said firmly. 'And then, *vanish*!'

Wei gave him a hurt look and departed with dignity. Lang ground his teeth.

'Sometimes I think I should have stayed well clear of my family,' he said.

Fruit was served, then tea, and then it was time for the entertainment. Two girls identically dressed in white-embroidered satin glided in. One, holding a small lute, seated herself, ready to play. The other stood beside her.

The lights dimmed except for the one on the performers. The first notes came from the lute and the singer began to make a soft crooning noise, full of a poignancy that was like joy and sadness combined. As Olivia listened an aching feeling came over her, as though the music had sprung all the locks by which she protected herself, leaving her open and defenceless as she had sworn never to be again.

The girl was singing in a soft voice:

'The trees were white with blossom.
We walked together beneath the falling petals.
But that is past and you are gone.
The trees do not blossom this year.
Aaaii-eeeii!'

That was how it had been; the trees hadn't blossomed this year and she knew they never would again. Andy had been an abject lesson in the need to stay detached. In future no man would hurt her like that because she wouldn't let it happen.

'The bridge still leads across the river,
Where we walked together.
But when I look down into the water,
Your face is not beside me.
Never again…'

Never again, she thought, not here or anywhere. She closed her eyes for a moment. But suddenly she opened them again, alerted by a touch on her cheek.

'Don't cry,' Lang said.

'I'm not crying,' she insisted.

For answer he showed her his fingertips, wet with her tears.

'Don't weep for him,' he said softly.

It would have been useless to utter another denial when he hadn't believed the first.

'I get sentimental sometimes.' She tried to laugh it away. 'But I'm really over him.'

In the dim light she could see Lang shake his head, smiling ruefully.

'Perhaps you belong together after all,' he said. Suddenly he reached into his pocket, took out his mobile phone and pushed it towards her, then he leaned close to murmur into her ear without disturbing the singer.

'Call him. Say that your quarrel was a mistake, and you love him still. Go on. Do it now.'

The dramatic gesture astonished and intrigued her. With a gasp of edgy laughter, she pushed the phone back to him.

'Why are you laughing?' he demanded.

'I was just picturing his face if he answered the phone and found himself talking to me. There was no quarrel. He left me for someone else. She had a lot of money, so he obviously did the right thing. I believe they're very happy. She bought him a posh car for a wedding present.'

'And that makes it the right thing?' he enquired.

'Of course.'

'So if a millionaire proposed you'd accept at once?'

'No way! He'd have to be a billionaire at least.'

'I see.' The words were grave but his lips were slightly quirked, as if he were asking who she thought she was fooling.

But he said nothing more. The music had ended. The singer bowed to the heartfelt applause and embarked on another song, slightly more cheerful. Lang turned his head towards the little stage, but reached back across the table to take hold of Olivia's hand, and kept it.

She found that her nostalgic sadness had vanished, overtaken by a subtle pleasure that seemed to infuse the whole evening. Everything was a part of it, including the man sitting opposite her, looking away, giving Olivia the chance to study him unobserved.

She could appreciate him like this. His regular features were enough to make him good-looking, but they also had a mobility that was constantly intriguing. His eyes could be bland and conventional, or wickedly knowing in a way that gave him a disconcerting charm. She wondered if there was anyone he regretted from his own past. A warm-natured man in his thirties, with a deep belief in the value of romantic love, had surely not reached this point without some sadness along the road.

She began to muse on the subject, wondering if there was a way to question him without revealing too much interest. There wasn't, of course, and an alarm bell sounded in her head. This was just the kind of atmosphere she'd learned to fear—seductive, romantic, lulling her senses and her mind in dangerous harmony.

It was time for common sense to take over. In a few minutes she would suggest that the evening should end soon, phrasing it carefully. She began to plan the words, even deciding what she would say when he protested.

Lang was beckoning to Wei, paying the bill, and ordering him to stop giggling and make himself scarce. Wei departed jauntily. Olivia took a deep breath to make her speech.

'We'd better go,' Lang said.

'Pardon?'

'We both have to work tomorrow, so I'll get you home quickly. I'm sorry to have kept you out so late.'

'Don't mention it,' she said faintly.

On the journey she wondered what was going to happen now. Lang had recognised that she wasn't ready for a decision, while subtly implying that he was attracted to her. He was charming and funny, with a quiet, gentle strength that appealed to her, perhaps because she could sense something quirky and irreverent beneath it.

A light-hearted flirtation could be agreeable, but if he wanted more, if he planned to end the evening in her arms—or even in her apartment—what then? A gentle let-down? How did you half-reject someone you more than half-liked? Again she began to think about what she would say to him.

When they arrived, he came with her to the apartment block.

'How far up are you?' he asked.

'Second floor.'

He rode up with her and came to her door.

'Lang?' she began uneasily.

'Yes?'

She lost her nerve. 'Would you care to come in for a drink?'

'I certainly want to come in, but not for a drink. Let's get inside and I'll explain, although I'm sure you know what the problem is.'

Once inside he took off his jacket and helped her off with hers.

'You'll need to remove your blouse as well,' he said, beginning to work on her buttons.

'Lang…'

He took no notice, opening the buttons one by one until he could remove the blouse, revealing her as he had the day before. She was astonished at his effrontery. Did he think he could simply undress her, seduce her, do as he liked with her?

'Now let me look at that arm,' he said.

'My arm?' she echoed, thunderstruck.

'That's why I came to find you tonight, isn't it?'

'Oh, yes—I remember.'

She had a horrible feeling that she sounded idiotic, but that was how she felt. He hadn't come here to seduce her, but to tend her. Her wild thoughts had been nonsense. She felt her-self blushing from head to toe.

Then she thought she caught a gleam of mischief in his eyes, although it was gone before she could be certain.

With her blouse removed, he held her arm up, moving his head this way and that without appearing to notice anything but her injury. He had no eyes for the peachy, youthful glow of her skin, the way her waist narrowed and the lamp threw shadows between her breasts. It was almost insulting.

'This is the last time it will need covering,' he said. 'It's healing nicely.'

He'd brought a small bag in with him, and from it he took replacement dressings. He covered the grazes lightly, and fixed everything in place.

'Now get a good night's sleep,' he instructed.

Then he was heading out of the apartment, without having touched her, except as a doctor.

'Wait,' she said desperately. 'What did you mean about "the problem"?'

He paused in the doorway.

'The problem,' he said, 'is that you're still my patient. Later…'

'Later?'

His gaze moved over her slowly, lingering just a little on the beauty he had so dutifully ignored.

'Later you won't be. Goodnight.'

The school term was nearly over. Olivia was busy writing re-ports, talking to parents and consulting with the headmistress, who looked in on her on the penultimate day.

'I'm just making plans for next year,' she said cheerfully. 'I'm so glad you're staying.'

'Staying?' Olivia echoed vaguely.

'You originally came for six months, but when I asked if you were going to stay on you said you would. Don't you remember?'

'Oh, yes—yes.'

'You really sound in need of a holiday,' Mrs Wu said kindly.

'It's just that I've been wondering if I should go home.'

'But you can do that and still come back next term. From all you've told me about Norah, she wants you to stay here and spread your wings. I hope you come back. You're doing such a good job. But you've got my number if you have a last-minute change of mind.'

Olivia went home, thoughtful. Everything that had seemed simple only a short while ago had suddenly become complicated.

It was true that Norah showed no sign of wanting her early return. Only last night she'd been at her most lively, talking furiously about Melisande's latest lover.

'You mean, Freddy?' Olivia had queried.

'No. Freddy's finished since she caught him sleeping with a pole dancer. It's your father.'

'Mum and Dad? What are they playing at?'

'I gather he went to see her, seeking solace from a broken heart.'

'I thought you said he'd made some girl pregnant.'

'He thought he had, but apparently it's not his, so he went to cry on your mother's shoulder because, and I quote, "she's the only one who understands".'

'Give me patience!'

'That's what I said. Anyway, it seems that they looked at each other across the barrier of years, heart spoke to heart as though time and distance had never been…'

'*What?*'

'I told her to get out before she made me ill. It's just her putting herself centre-stage again, as always.'

Olivia had had to agree. She'd seen, and suffered from, enough of her parents' selfish grandstanding to dismiss this great romance as just another show in the spotlight.

You could say much the same of all great romances, she thought. Her father would let her mother down again, because that was what men did. It was what Andy had done. And who cared if Lang called her or not?

Several days had passed since their last meeting. After talking so significantly he had fallen silent, and with every passing hour Olivia had condemned herself more angrily as a fool.

It wasn't as if she hadn't been warned, she told herself crossly. When Andy had appeared in her life, she'd abandoned the caution so carefully built up over a lifetime because she'd convinced herself that *this* man was different.

But no man was different, as she'd learned in anguish and bitterness. She'd vowed 'never again', but then she'd been tricked into ignoring those resolutions because Lang had charmed her.

No, it was more than charm, she admitted. It was the sense of quiet understanding, the feeling that his mind and heart were open to hers, and that she would find in him generosity and understanding.

Heart spoke to heart as though time and distance had never been.

Her mother's melodramatic words shrieked a warning in her head. She and Lang had met only a couple of times, and came from different worlds, yet time and distance did not exist, hadn't existed between them from the first moment.

Which meant that she would fight him all the harder. If she made the foolish mistake of falling in love with Lang, the misery would be far greater than before.

It was useful that he'd shown his true colours in time to prevent a disaster. She repeated that to herself several times.

But no way would she stay here, pining. If she didn't return to England, she'd go somewhere else. She got a brochure advertising cruises along the great Yangtze River and booked herself a cabin. She would board the boat at Chongqing, leave it at Yichang and travel on to Shanghai. After that, who could tell where she would travel? And what did it matter? What did anything matter as long as she had no time to think?

CHAPTER FOUR

ON THE last day of term Olivia counted the minutes until it was time to go. Just a little longer and she need never think of Lang again. *Concentrate on the Yangtze. Think of Shanghai.*

The last pupil had gone home. She was gathering up her things when a buzz made her look at her mobile phone, where there was a text: *I'm outside.*

For a brief moment her heart leapt, then indignation took over. Cheek! Like he only had to announce his presence and she must jump.

She texted back: *I'm busy.*

The reply came at once: *I'll wait.*

Mrs Wu looked in to say goodbye and they left the building together.

'Have a good holiday,' she said. 'And please dispose of that young man hanging around the gate. Loiterers are bad for the school's reputation.'

'He's nothing to do with me.'

'Of course he isn't. That's why his eyes are fixed on you. Goodbye for now.'

Lang was leaning against the wall as though there was all the time in the world, which did nothing to improve her mood.

She advanced on him in a confrontational mood, and thrust out her arm, from which she'd removed the dressing.

'Just a few scratches and healing nicely, thank you,' she said in a formal voice.

'You don't know how glad I am to hear that.'

'And the headmistress says I'm to get rid of you. You're giving the place a bad name.'

'In that case, let's go.'

'I don't think—'

'Let's not waste any more time.' He already had hold of her arm and was ushering her into his car, which he started up quickly, as though afraid to give her time to think.

Had he known it, she was beyond coherent thought, beyond anything but wild emotion. He hadn't abandoned her, hadn't turned away, leaving her desolate. He had come for her because he could no more escape the bonds tightening around them than she could.

She knew she should try to control the heady, idiotic feeling that pervaded her. It was too much like joy: terrifying, threatening, destructive, glorious joy.

At last she managed to speak and ask where they were going. At least, that was what she thought she'd asked. She was too confused to be sure.

'I'm taking you somewhere that will help you get over being grumpy,' he replied.

'I'm not grumpy.'

'Yes you are. When you saw me outside the school, you glared hard enough to terrify the devil.'

'Well, it was very inconsiderate of you to arrive in the last five minutes.'

'You couldn't possibly have been hoping to see me earlier?'

'Certainly not. You just disrupted my schedule. I like things done in the proper order.'

'Just as I said, grumpy. Meihui used to have a way of deal-ing with my bad moods—several ways, actually—but this was our favourite one.'

More than that he would not say, but he drove for half an hour in silence, glad of the chance to say nothing and collect his thoughts. Unusually for him, they were chaotic.

After their last meeting he'd resolved not to approach Olivia again, at least, not soon. He was an ambitious man, and his career was beginning to look promising. He needed no dis-tractions, and the sensible course would be to let the summer vacation pass before they met again. The passage of a little time would put him in control of himself again.

It had all been very simple. Until today.

The summer break from his job had already started, which was unlucky, because if he'd been at work he couldn't have yielded to temptation. As it was, the realisation that she would be leaving any minute had galvanised him. Suddenly his reso-lutions were rubbish, his strength of will non-existent. He'd barely made it to the school in time.

Now he was calling himself names, of which 'weakling' was the kindest. But the abusive voice was bawling only from the back of his head; the front was full of relief that he'd made it in time.

There was another voice too, not yelling, but muttering. This was his conscience, warning him that there was something he must confess to her without delay. He wasn't sure what her reaction would be. That troubled him more than anything.

'Here we are,' he said, drawing up outside a huge gate.

'You've brought me to a zoo?' she said, astounded.

'Meihui said nobody could stay cross in a zoo. So let's go in.'

He was right, after only a few minutes of wandering around the animals, her spirits lightened. Who cared about anything else when there were lions to be viewed, bears to watch, exotic birds?

Lang was like no other man. When was the last time any-one had taken her to a place like this? she wondered as they gazed at the giant pandas.

'I've never seen anything so beautiful,' she murmured.

'They're magnificent, aren't they?' he agreed warmly.

'But how do you tell one from the other? Pandas all look exactly alike.'

'The one over there on her own in the tree is the female. Earlier this year she was in heat for a couple of days, and had all the males swooning after her. Now she's safely pregnant, and they can go and jump in the lake for all she cares.'

'I wonder which male she favoured.'

'The highest ranking one. He proved his status by knocking seven bells out of the competition.'

'Very sensible,' Olivia said. 'None of that sentimental non-sense. If ever I'm reborn, I shall come back as a panda.'

He laughed but said, 'Why do you have to be so severe?'

'I'm not severe.'

'You are from where I'm standing.'

'Oh, I see, a *male* version of severe—meaning a woman who doesn't collapse in a sentimental heap at the mention of *lurve*.' She gave the word a satirical inflection that made him wince. '*That* kind of severe.'

'You put it very crudely,' he complained.

'The truth is usually crude, and definitely unromantic. Like life. We just have to face up to it.'

She was saying the first thing that came into her head and enjoying the sight of his face. For once the confident Dr Mitchell was struggling for words, and that was fun.

'Why are you so determined not to believe in love?' he asked. 'I know you had a bad experience, but so have most people, and they don't abandon hope. I didn't give up when Becky Renton told me it was all over.'

'Oh, yes? And I'll bet the two of you were about twelve when that happened.'

He grinned. 'A little older than that, but you've got the right idea.'

She wondered if this handsome, assured man had ever been dumped in his life. Not by anyone he really cared about, she would have bet on it.

'Joking apart,' he resumed, 'people really do do things for love. I know you don't believe it, but it's true.'

'If you're talking about your romantic ancestors, allow me to point out that there's no reason to believe that Jaio was ever in love. They were going to lock her in the tomb and Renshu offered escape. She might simply have thought that going with him was better than dying.'

'But what about him? He must have loved her a lot because he sacrificed everything to be with her.' Lang added provocatively, 'Perhaps it really means that a man can love more deeply than a woman. It could even be doubted that women know how to love at all. They believe in logic rather than sentiment—like pandas.'

Olivia eyed him askance. 'Did you say that just to be annoying?'

'No, I think it's an interesting theory.' Catching her expression, he couldn't resist adding, 'But I must admit I also enjoy annoying you.'

'You'll go too far.'

'I hope so. Better too far than not far enough.'

His grin was her undoing, leaving her no choice but to smile back.

'Let's find the snack bar,' he said, slipping an arm around her shoulders.

As they sat down over coffee, Lang suddenly said, 'I hope you can forgive my clumsiness.'

'About what?'

'That remark about choosing a mate through logic rather than sentiment. It's exactly what your louse boyfriend did, isn't it? I'm sorry. I didn't mean to hurt you.'

'You didn't,' she said, realising that it was true. She hadn't even thought about Andy. Nor, now she thought of it, had she ever enjoyed such a day as this, strolling calmly through pleasant gardens, teasing and testing each other.

There had been no jokes with Andy, only passion and violent emotion, which at the time she'd thought was enough. But with Lang she was discovering how emotion could be tempered with humour. He was a patient man who knew when to back off. It made him a restful companion, as well as an exciting one, and that too was a new pleasure.

'I've dismissed Andy from my mind,' she told him, adding with a flourish, 'It was the common sense thing to do.'

'That easy, huh?'

'Of course. Logic over sentiment any day. I reckon the female panda knows exactly what she's doing.'

'Then I'm glad I'm not a panda,' he said, matching her flourish with one of his own.

Before they left the zoo he took her to the gift shop and bought her a small soft toy in the shape of a panda.

'She's a female,' he declared.

'How can you tell?'

'Because that's what I want her to be,' he said, as though explaining the obvious. 'Her name is Ming Zhi. It means wise.' His eyes gleamed with mischief. 'It was the nearest I could get to logic and common sense.'

'Then she and I will get on very well,' Olivia declared, taking the delightful creature and rubbing her face against its soft black-and-white fur. 'If I forget what's important, she's bound to remind me.'

'To the victory of logic,' he proclaimed.

'Every time.'

'Let's go and have some supper.'

They found a small, old-fashioned restaurant.

'Why were you in such a bad mood when we met earlier?' he asked when they were settled. 'Is it me you're annoyed with?'

'No, my parents. According to Norah, they've rediscovered each other, acting like love's young dream.'

'Which could be charming.'

'If it was anyone else, it could, but this pair of raging play-actors are heading for disaster.'

'Don't be so sure,' Lang said. 'Maybe they just married too young and were always meant to find each other again.'

She gave him a look.

'Maybe not,' he said hastily.

'In the end it'll collapse in lies, as it did the first time.' Olivia sighed. 'And there's nothing so fatal as deception.'

'Sometimes a deception can be fairly innocent,' Lang observed casually.

'But it's always destructive,' she insisted. 'Once you know he hasn't been straight with you, it's over, because—I don't know. I'm going to eat.'

Concentrating on her chopsticks, she didn't see the uncomfortable look that came over Lang's face.

'This food is nice,' she said after a while. 'But not as nice as at the Dancing Dragon.'

To her surprise he didn't respond to the compliment. He seemed sunk in thought, and strangely uneasy.

'Is everything all right?' she asked.

'No,' he said with an effort. 'There's something I have to tell you.'

There was a heaviness in his voice that filled Olivia with foreboding.

'I must admit that I've been putting this moment off,' Lang continued awkwardly. 'I was afraid it would make you think badly of me. I know I've done wrong, but I didn't want to risk not seeing you again.'

Now she knew what he was trying to say: he had a wife.

Impossible. In that case he would never have taken her to the Dancing Dragon where they would be seen by his family. But perhaps the family's attitude had simply been curiosity that their foreign relative was playing around. She tried to recall exactly what they had said, and couldn't.

'Will you promise to let me finish explaining before you condemn me?' he asked.

By ill luck, Andy had said much the same thing: 'If only you'd let me explain properly, it really wasn't my fault...'

A chill settled over her heart.

'Go on then,' she said. 'Tell me the worst.'

Lang took a deep breath and seemed to struggle for words.

'The fact is—' he began, stopped then started again. 'When we met—' He was floundering.

'Look,' she said edgily, 'why don't we just skip it and go home?'

'Don't you want to know what I have to say?'

'I probably already know what you're going to say,' she observed with a faint, mirthless laugh.

'You guessed? I don't see how you could have done.'

'Let's say I have a nose for some things. Call it my cynical nature.'

'I don't think you're as cynical as you try to pretend.'

Her temper flared. 'And I don't think you know anything about me.'

He stared. 'All right, don't jump on me. I'm harmless, I

swear it. I'll believe that you're anything you say—hard, cynical, unfeeling…'

'Ruthless, unforgiving, cold-hearted,' she supplied. 'I'm glad you understand.'

'I wish you hadn't said unforgiving,' he observed gloomily.

'Well, I did say it. I never give second chances. Now, if we've got that settled, what were you going to confess? Something unforgivable, obviously.'

'Well, you might think so.'

Her dismay increased. 'All right. I'm listening.'

'It's like this. When we met in that clinic—I wouldn't normally be there. I work in another part of the hospital, and I'd just started a vacation. But a friend who does work in the clinic got a stomach upset and had to take time off. They were short staffed, so I filled in.'

'But what's so terrible about that?' she asked, trying to think straight through the confusion of reactions storming through her.

'The thing is, he was back next morning. I did try to persuade him that he needed another day off, but he got an attack of heroics and insisted on returning.' Lang sighed and added distractedly, 'A man can't trust his friends for anything, not even to be ill when he needs them to be.'

'What on earth are you—?'

'So when I came to see you next day I wasn't working in the clinic any more, and strictly speaking you were no longer my patient.'

Olivia stared at him in mounting disbelief. 'Are you saying…?'

'That I lied to you,' he said mournfully. 'I approached you under false pretences, claiming that you were my patient when you no longer were. I deceived you.'

Olivia met his eyes and drew a quick breath at what she

saw there, a look of suspiciously bland innocence that masked something far from innocent. This man wasn't worried about being in trouble. He was inviting her into a conspiracy.

'You're overdoing it,' she said wryly.

'No, honestly! On the pretext of medical privilege, I gained access to your body.'

'To my—? Oh, yes, you saw my bare arm, didn't you?' she said sardonically. 'How could I have forgotten that? Shocking!'

'It was a little more than your arm,' he reminded her. 'If you want to report me to the medical authorities, well, I'll just have to accept it, won't I?'

'And if I kicked your shins you'd just have to accept that, wouldn't you?' she said sweetly.

'It would be my just deserts.'

'Don't get me started on your just deserts or we'll be here all night.'

'Would we? Tell me more.'

'Let's just say that you're a devious, treacherous— I can't think of anything bad enough.'

'I'll wait while you think of something. After all, it was shocking behaviour on my part.'

'I didn't mean that. I meant just now, making me think—'

'What?'

She pulled herself together. 'Making me think it was something really serious, instead of just fooling.'

She could barely speak for the confusion of relief and fear that warred in her: relief that he was a free man, fear that it mattered so much. She tried to bring herself under control lest he guess the truth.

Or did he already know? He was watching her intently but cautiously, as though trying to discover something that was important to him.

'I wanted to see you again,' he said simply. 'And that was the best excuse I could find.'

The storm died down. The relief was still there, but now tinged with laughter. The world was bright.

'Well, I guess I'm glad you thought of something,' she admitted.

He took her hand. 'So am I.'

'I'm still annoyed with you, but I forgive you—on a purely temporary basis.'

'That's all I ask.'

'So what is your job in the hospital?'

Lang shrugged. 'I fill in a lot, do the stuff nobody else wants.' He squeezed her hand gently. 'Sometimes I get a good day.'

He didn't pursue the subject and she was glad. The attraction between them was growing slowly, delicately, and she liked it that way. Any sudden movements might be fatal.

He was looking down at her hand, rubbing his fingers against it softly, and she had the feeling that he was uneasy again.

'What is it?' she asked. 'What terrible crime do you have to admit now?'

'We-ell…'

'Be brave. It can't be worse than you've already confessed.'

'The fact is there have been some repercussions to the other night. Wei, the great blabbermouth, went home and sounded off to my family, telling them all about you.'

'But he doesn't know anything about me—unless, of course, you've told him, which would be another abuse of medical privilege.' She considered him, her head on one side. 'You really are proving to be a disreputable character. Interesting, but disreputable.'

'This time I plead not guilty. Anything I know about you—which is frustratingly little—I keep firmly to myself. Wei's method is to invent what he doesn't know. The family's curiosity is aroused, and now there'll be no peace until I take you home for dinner.'

'Let me get this straight. You want to take me home just to save yourself from nagging?'

'That's about the size of it.'

'It's got nothing to do with wanting my company?'

'Certainly not,' he said in a shocked voice.

'It wouldn't mean that you were glad to be seen with me, liked me for myself, and maybe, I don't know…?'

'Maybe thought you were the prettiest girl I'd ever seen and the nicest I'd ever been out with?' he supplied helpfully.

'No, nothing like that. Don't worry.'

'You relieve my mind,' she said gravely.

He raised her hand and brushed his cheek against the back of her fingers.

'I think we should stay level-headed,' he said. 'I wouldn't want to offend you by indulging in the kind of sentimental behaviour I know you despise.'

'That's thoughtful of you. On the other hand, your family are going to expect us to seem at ease with each other. We mustn't disappoint them by being too distant.'

He nodded as though giving this judicious consideration.

'True. We need to get it just right.'

Before she knew what he meant to do, he leaned across the table and laid his lips softly against hers.

It was the briefest of contacts. No sooner was his mouth there than it was gone again. It might never have happened, yet it went through her like lightning, making nonsense of logic and control, leaving her changed and the world a different place.

She tried to smile with careless unconcern, but her heart was thumping, and there was no way she could seem indifferent. To hide her confusion she looked down, but when she raised her head again everything was more confusing, because now she could see that Lang was startled too.

'That should be about right,' she managed to say.

She was lying. It wasn't about right, it wasn't nearly enough. One whispering touch and something inside her had sprung to life, making her tingle with frustration. She wanted more, and so did he. His expression had told her that. Yet here they were, two well-behaved dolls, bound and gagged by the constraints that they had set themselves. Only a moment ago it had seemed amusing.

'So what can I tell the family?' he asked, and she wondered if she only imagined that his voice was shaking.

'I'd be delighted to accept their kind invitation when I return from my travels.'

'You're going away? When? Where?'

'I'm taking a cruise down the Yangtze.'

'But not tomorrow?'

'No, in three days but—'

'Fine, that gives us plenty of time.' He whipped out his mobile phone and dialled hurriedly. 'Better do this before you can change your mind. You're a very confusing person. I never know where I am with you.'

After the days she'd spent longing to hear from him— which she now admitted to herself she had—this left her speechless with indignation. While she was still trying to think of something bad enough to call him, he began talking into the phone.

'Hallo, Aunt Biyu? Olivia says she'd be delighted. Yes, yes.' He looked back at Olivia. 'Do you like dumplings?'

'I love them,' she said promptly.

'She loves them, Aunt Biyu— What's that? All right, I'll ask her. Do you prefer meat or vegetables?'

'I'm happy with either.'

'She's happy with either. Oh, yes, that sounds nice.' To Olivia he said, 'Shrimp and bamboo, OK?'

'Yes, splendid,' she said, slightly confused.

Lang turned back to the phone. 'Olivia is thrilled with shrimp and bamboo. Tomorrow evening?' He raised an eyebrow and Olivia nodded. 'Tomorrow's fine. Goodnight.'

He hung up. 'Aunt Biyu is married to Uncle Hai. She's preparing you the best shrimp and bamboo you ever tasted, and the whole family is helping. You're a very important guest.'

She knew enough about Chinese culture to recognise that this was true. In the old days of poverty, dumplings had been the staple food, and had subsequently acquired a place of honour. To lay out a banquet of dumplings for a guest was to pay a compliment.

She began to wonder exactly what Lang had told them. As he drove her home later, he was smiling.

At her apartment block he saw her to the main front door, but didn't try to come any further.

'I'll collect you at six o'clock tomorrow evening,' he said.

'Yes. Goodnight.'

'Goodnight.'

He hesitated for a moment, then leaned forward suddenly and gave her the briefest possible kiss before hurrying away.

Olivia was thoughtful as she entered her apartment. Nothing in the world seemed clear or simple, and it was because of Lang, a man she'd met only three times.

Reaching into her bag, she felt something soft and silky, and realised that she'd forgotten all about Ming Zhi. The little panda regarded her severely, reminding her that she was a sensible woman who had renounced love in favour of logic.

'Oh, shut up!' Olivia said, tossing her onto the bed. 'I don't care if he did give you to me. You're a pain in the whatsit. And so is he.'

That night she slept with Ming Zhi in the crook of her arm.

NEXT morning she went online to Norah and was rewarded by the sight of the old woman waving and smiling at the camera.

'So, what are you going to do with your holidays?' she asked. 'Did you book that cruise?'

'Yes, I'll be off in a few days.'

'And?' Norah probed, for Olivia's tone clearly hinted at something else.

'I've met this madman…'

She tried to describe Lang. It wasn't easy, for he seemed to elude her even as she spoke. Calling him a madman was the truth, but far from the whole truth, and she was still discovering the rest.

'He can make me laugh,' she said.

'That's always a good beginning.'

'And he gave me this.' She held up Ming Zhi. 'When we went to the zoo.'

'Now, that looks like getting serious. When are you seeing him again?'

'This evening. He's taking me to have dinner with his family.'

'Already? My dear, he's moving very fast.'

'No, it's not like that. One of his relatives saw us together and the family got curious. He's only taking me home to shut them up.'

'Is he a wimp, that he can't stand up to them?'

'No, he's not a wimp,' Olivia said, smiling and remembering how Lang gave the impression of being quietly in command, except when he was being jokingly deferential to make her laugh. 'He pretends to be sometimes, but that's just his way of catching me off-guard.'

'And does he often succeed?'

'Yes,' Olivia admitted wryly. 'He does.'

'Then he must be a very clever man indeed. I look forward to meeting him.'

'Norah, please! You're going much too fast. Lang and I have only met a few times. I'm not looking for anything serious. We'll enjoy a brief relationship and then I'll come home. In fact—'

'Don't you dare start that again. You stay where you are, and *live* your life. Don't throw it away.'

'All right, I promise,' Olivia said. She was slightly startled by Norah's intensity; a kind of anguish almost seemed to possess her.

'You spend as much time with Lang as you can. He sounds nice. Is he good-looking?'

'Yes, he's good-looking?'

'*Really* good-looking?'

'Well…'

'On a scale of one to ten?'

'Seven. Oh, all right—eight.'

'Jolly good,' Norah said robustly. 'Now, go and buy a really nice, new dress. Splash out, do you hear?'

'Yes, Aunt,' Olivia said meekly, and they laughed together.

After a hasty breakfast she headed out to the shops, meaning to choose something from the Western fashions that were now available in Beijing. But before long her eye fell on a *cheongsam*, the traditional Chinese dress that was so flattering to a woman with a good figure. The neckline came modestly up to the throat, and there was a high-standing collar, but it was also figure-hugging, outlining her tiny waist, flared hips and delicately rounded breasts in a way that left no doubt that her shape was perfect.

It was heavily embroidered and made of the highest-quality silk, at a price that made her hesitate for half a second. But when she tried it on and saw what it did for her she knew she was lost. When she combined it with the finest heels she dared to wear, the effect was stunning.

She wondered if Lang would think so. Would he compliment her on her appearance?

He did not. Calling for her punctually at six, he handed her into the car without a word. But she'd seen the way his eyes had lingered on the swell of her breasts, so perfectly emphasised by the clinging material, and she knew he had remembered their first meeting. His expression told her all she wanted to know.

She settled down to enjoy herself. They were headed for the *hutongs*; she'd always been fascinated by these streets that had surrounded the Forbidden City for hundreds of years. A plentiful water supply had dictated the location, and the *hutongs* had always flourished, colourful places full of life and industry. Shops sprung up, especially butchers, bakers, fishmongers and anything selling domestic necessities. Change came and went. Other parts of the city had become wealthier, more fashionable, but the *hutongs*' vibrant character had ensured their survival.

Olivia had sometimes shopped there. Now for the first

time she would see the personal life that lay behind the little stores. A *hutong* was a street formed by lines of quadrangles, called *siheyuans*, each *siheyuan* consisting of four houses placed at right angles to each other. Here large families could live with the privacy of their own home, yet with their relatives always within calling distance.

As they drove there, Lang described his family's *siheyuan*.

'The north house belongs to Grandfather Tao. He's the centre of the family. Meihui was his kid sister and he remembers her as if it were yesterday. He says I remind him of her, but that's just affection, because I don't really look like her at all. Uncle Jing and his wife also live there, with their four children.

'One of the side houses is occupied by Uncle Hai, his wife and their two younger children. The one opposite is the home of their two elder sons and their wives. And the south house has been taken over by Wei. He's Jing's son, and he's living in the south house in preparation for his marriage.'

'He's the one I saw the other night? Married? He looks far too young.'

'He's twenty, but he's madly in love with Suyin, the girl who sang in the restaurant, and she seems to feel she can put up with him. Apart from him there are several other children, ranging from five to twelve. They're wonderful kids. Villains, mind you.'

'As the best youngsters always are.'

'Right,' he said, gratified.

'But how many people am I meeting?' she asked, beginning to be nervous.

'About eighteen.'

'Wow! I'm getting scared.'

'Not you. You're a dragon lady, remember? Brave, adventurous, ready for anything.'

'Thank you. But that big a family still makes me a bit nervous.'

'Eighteen isn't so many. There are at least another dozen in other parts of the country, and probably plenty more I have yet to meet.'

'Is that where you're going? You said something about travelling soon.'

'Something like that. Let's talk later. I must warn you that you're about to walk into the middle of a feud. Uncle Jing is furious with Uncle Hai because Hai's wife Biyu is cooking you dumplings. Jing thinks the privilege of cooking for you should have been his. He's a fishmonger, and also a wedding planner.'

'I've heard of that before,' Olivia said, much struck. 'It's because the words for fish and prosperity are so alike that fish gets served at weddings as a way of wishing the couple good luck. So fishmongers often plan weddings as well.'

'That's right. Hai does very well as an arranger of weddings, where of course he sells tons of his own fish. The trouble is he thinks he's entitled to arrange everything for everyone, and he's very put out about the dumplings.'

His solemn tone made Olivia burst out laughing.

'I promise to be tactful,' she said.

'Have I told you you're looking beautiful tonight?'

'Not a word.'

'Well, I'm being careful. If I said that deep blue does wonderful things for your eyes you'd find me very boring.'

'I might,' she said in a pensive voice. 'Or I might decide to forgive you.'

'Thank you, ma'am, but I feel sure you'd censure me for insulting you with that old-fashioned romantic talk. Heavens, this is the twenty-first century! Women don't fall for that kind of clap-trap any more.'

'Well, I wouldn't actually say any of that out loud,' she said, laughing.

'But you might think it silently, and that would be much worse. I'm wary of your unspoken thoughts.'

'But if they're unspoken you can't possibly know what they are,' she pointed out.

'You're wrong. I'm starting to understand the way you think.'

'That's an alarming prospect!' she observed.

'For which of us, I wonder?'

'For me,' she said without hesitation.

'Are you more alarmed at the thought of my getting it right, or getting it wrong?'

She considered this seriously. 'Right, I think. I don't mind you getting it wrong. I can always tread on your toes.'

'Good thinking.'

'But what woman wants to be understood too well by a man?' she mused.

'Most women complain that men don't understand them.'

'Then they're being foolish,' she said with a little smile. 'They should bless their luck.'

They both laughed and the moment passed, but she was left with the sense that beneath the banter they had really been talking about something else entirely. It was a feeling that often assailed her in Lang's company.

They continued the journey in companionable silence, until at last he said, 'Before we get there I'd better warn you of just how enthusiastically Wei has prepared them for you. I've explained that we barely know each other, and he mustn't run ahead, but he— Well…'

'Didn't take any notice?' Olivia finished sympathetically.

'And how!'

'All right, I'm prepared.'

'Grandfather Tao and Grandmother Shu have learned a few words in English, in your honour. The rest of the family speaks English, but those two are so old that they've lived a different kind of life. They've been practising all day to offer you this courtesy.'

'How kind.' She was touched. 'I know I'm going to love your family.'

At last she found herself in streets that she recognised.

'Weren't we here the other night?'

'Yes, that restaurant is just around the corner. Just a couple more streets, and here we are. Home.'

The car drew up before the north house of the *siheyuan*, and Olivia drew an astonished breath as she saw what looked like the entire family gathered to meet her. They spilled out of the doorway into the street.

In the centre stood an old man and woman: Grandfather Tao and Grandmother Shu. On either side of them were two middle-aged men—the uncles, their wives and children. Everyone was watching the car's arrival with delight, and two of the younger children dashed forward to open the door and provide Olivia with a guard of honour.

'My goodness!' she exclaimed.

Lang took her hand. 'Don't worry,' he whispered. 'I'm here, Dragon Lady.'

He slipped his arm protectively around her as they neared the family and it divided into two groups, with the oldest, Grandfather Tao and Grandmother Shu, at the centre. He took her to them first.

'Our family is honoured to meet you,' Tao said, speaking in careful, perfect English, and his wife inclined her head, smiling in agreement.

'It is I who am honoured,' Olivia said.

Tao repeated his compliment. The words and manner were

formal but his and Shu's expressions were warm, and their eyes followed her when she moved on.

Strictly speaking they were the host and hostess, but because of their age and frailty they performed only the most formal duties, delegating anything more energetic to the younger ones.

Although brothers, Hai and Jing were totally unalike. Jing was a great, good-natured bull of a man, tall, broad and muscular. Beside him Hai was like a mountain goat next to a gorilla, small, thin and sprightly, with a wispy beard and bright eyes.

As the elder, Hai was introduced first, then his brother, then their wives—starting with Biyu, wife of Hai, and Luli, wife of Jing. They too greeted her in English, which she appreciated, but Lang immediately said in Chinese, 'No, she speaks our language. I told you.'

They repeated their greetings in Mandarin and she responded accordingly, which made them smile with pleasure.

'Mrs Lang—' Olivia started to say, but there was a burst of laughter from several Mrs Langs.

'You can't say that,' Hai's wife declared merrily. 'There are so many of us. Please, call me Biyu.' She introduced the others as Ting, Huan, Dongmei, and Nuo.

There seemed to be at least a dozen grown-up youngsters, young men who studied Lang's lady with politely concealed admiration, and young girls who considered her with more open interest. The fact that Olivia had the figure to wear a *cheongsam* was particularly appreciated among her contemporaries.

It was a warm evening, and the first part was to be spent in the courtyard flanked by the four houses. Here tables had been laid out with a variety of small edibles, a foretaste of the banquet to come. Before anything was served, Biyu led her into the south house where Lang lived with Wei, and opened the door to a bedroom with its own bathroom.

'Should you wish to retire for a few moments alone,' she said, 'you will find this place useful.' She saw Olivia glance around at the room's functional, masculine appearance, and said, 'When Lang stays with us, this is his room, but this evening it is yours.'

'Thank you. I'll just refresh my face.'

'I'll be outside.'

Left alone, Olivia was able to indulge her frank curiosity, although she learned little. There were several books, some medical, some about China, but nothing very personal. Lang had revealed as little as possible about himself.

She went out to find that he had joined Biyu, and together they escorted her to where everyone was waiting. Now it was the turn of the children to crowd round. Just as she'd predicted, they called Lang 'Uncle Mitch', and even his adult relatives referred to him as Mitchell.

Glancing up, she caught his eye and he nodded, reminding her of the moment on the first evening when she'd anticipated this.

'The dragon lady always understands before anyone else,' he said lightly.

The children demanded to know what he meant by 'dragon lady'. He explained that she'd been born in the year of the dragon, and they regarded her with awe. Her stock had definitely gone up.

The children were frankly curious, competing to serve her and to ask questions about England. She answered them as fully as she could, they countered with more questions and the result was one of the most satisfying half-hours that she had ever spent. By the time they went inside to eat, the atmosphere was relaxed.

Olivia soon understood what Lang had meant about a feud. From the start the food was laid out like a banquet being displayed to her, dumplings in the place of honour, and a multitude of fish dishes which Hai kept trying to nudge to the fore, only to be beaten back by fierce looks from Biyu. To please them both, Olivia ate everything on offer and was rewarded with warm looks of pleasure.

Then she had a stroke of luck. Enquiring politely about Tao's life, she learned that he had once been a farmer. It happened that one of her mother's passing fancies had owned a small pig-farm where they had spent the summer. The relationship hadn't lasted, her mother having been unable to endure the quiet country life, but the fourteen-year-old Olivia had loved it. Now she summoned memories of that happy time, and she and Tao were soon in animated discussion. Pigs had provided Tao with a good living, and Olivia had enjoyed feeding time.

'There was a huge sow,' she recalled. 'She had a litter of fifteen, but only fourteen teats, and terrible fights would break out between the piglets over the last teat. I used to take a feeding bottle to make sure I could give something to the one who missed out. He'd just drink his fill and then go back to the fight.'

Tao roared with laughter and countered with the tale of a vast pig he'd once owned, who'd fathered larger litters than any other pig, and whose services had been much in demand among his neighbours. Everyone else round the table watched them with delight, and Olivia knew she'd scored a success by impressing the head of the family.

When the meal was over, Biyu showed her around the other houses. She was eager to know about her first meeting with Lang, and laughed at the story of the mischievous child.

'We are so proud of Mitchell,' Biyu said. 'He works very hard, and he's a big man at the hospital.'

'What does he actually do there?' Olivia asked. 'He was taking a clinic when we met, but apparently he was just filling in because they were short-staffed. I understand that his real job is something quite different.'

'That's true. He's a consultant.'

'A consultant?' Olivia echoed, amazed. 'He's young for that.'

'Oh, yes, he's only a *junior* consultant,' Biyu amended hastily. 'He keeps insisting on that. He gets cross if I make him sound too important—but I say he's going to be very, very important, because they know he's the best they have. There's a big job coming soon.'

She gave a knowing wink.

'You think he'll get it?'

'He will if there's any justice,' Biyu said firmly. 'But he's superstitious. He thinks if he gets too confident then some great power above will punish him by taking the job away from him.'

'Superstitious,' Olivia mused. 'You wouldn't think it.'

'Oh, he acts as if nothing could worry him,' Biyu confided. 'But don't you be fooled.'

It struck Olivia that this was shrewd advice. Lang's air of cool confidence had cracks, some of which he'd allowed her to see. The rest he seemed to be keeping to himself while their mutual trust grew.

'You're very proud of him, aren't you?' she said.

'Oh, yes. It was a great day for us when he came to China. We already knew a lot about him because Meihui had kept in touch, sending us news, and to see him was wonderful. The best thing of all was that he wanted to come, and then he wanted to stay. Some men from his country would have ignored their Chinese heritage, but he chose to find it and live with it, because it's important to him.'

'He's going away soon, isn't he, to do some exploring?'

'Actually, I thought he'd be gone by now. He spoke as though— Well, anyway, I'm glad he decided to wait a little longer, or we might not have met you.'

She tensed suddenly as Lang's voice reached them from outside.

'We're here,' she called back, showing Olivia out into the courtyard where he was waiting.

'Grandfather wants to bring out the family photographs,' he said. 'He's got hundreds of them, all ready to show Olivia.'

'And I'm longing to see them,' she said.

The largest room in the north house had been laid out in preparation, with a table in the centre covered in photographs. To Olivia's amazement the pictures stretched back sixty years to when Meihui had been a beautiful young girl. She must have been about sixteen in the first one, sitting in the curve of Tao's arm. His face as he looked down on his little sister bore an expression of great pride, and Olivia thought she could still see it there now as he regarded her picture. He was almost in tears over the little sister who had meant the world to him, and who he'd last seen when she was eighteen, departing for ever with the man she loved.

'And that's him?' Olivia asked as an Englishman appeared in the pictures.

'That's John Mitchell, my grandfather,' Lang agreed.

He seemed about twenty-three, not particularly handsome but with a broad, hearty face and a smile that beamed with good nature. Meihui's eyes, as she gazed at him, were alight with joy.

Then there were photographs that she had sent from England: herself and John Mitchell, proudly holding their new-born son, Lang's father. Then the child growing up, standing between his parents, until his father vanished because death had taken him far too soon. After that it was just Meihui and her son, until he married, and soon his own son appeared, a toddler in his father's arms.

'Let's leave them,' Lang groaned.

'But you were a delightful child!' Olivia protested.

He gave a grimace of pure masculine embarrassment, and she hastily controlled her mirth.

It was true that he seemed to have been a pleasant youngster, but even then his face held a sense of resolution beyond his years, already heralding the man he would become.

There were some pictures with his parents, then with his mother after his father's death, but mostly they showed the young Lang with Meihui. Then he appeared with his new family after his mother's remarriage. Looking at them, Olivia understood what he'd meant about not having been at ease. His stepfather looked as though he had much good nature, but no subtlety, and his offspring were the same. Standing in their midst, the young Lang smiled with the courteous determination of a misfit.

He grew older, graduated from school and passed his medical exams. One picture especially caught Olivia's attention— it showed him sitting down while Meihui stood behind him, her hands on his shoulders, her face beaming with pride. At that moment she had been the happiest woman in the world. Instead of looking at the camera, Lang was glancing up, connecting with her.

'No wonder your family recognised you at the airport,' she murmured, drawing him slightly aside. 'Thanks to Meihui, they'd been with you every step of the way while you were growing up.'

'Yes, they said much the same. It made me feel very much at home.'

He spoke just loud enough for Biyu to hear, making her

glance up and smile. He smiled back, yet strangely Olivia sensed a hint of tension in him, the last thing she'd expected. Now she thought about it, she felt there was a watchfulness about him tonight that wasn't usually there.

She wondered if she was the cause of his concern, lest she make a bad impression, but his manner towards her was full of pride. What was troubling him, then? she wondered.

As they left the room, Biyu announced, 'Now I'm going to show you our special place, devoted to Jaio and Renshu. I know Lang has told you about them.'

'Yes, it must be wonderful having such a great family tradition, going back so far.'

'It is. We have mementoes of them which normally we keep locked away for safety, but in your honour we have brought them out.' She gave a teasing smile. 'Lang tells us that you may need a little convincing.'

'Oh, did he? Just wait until I see him.'

'You mean, it isn't true?' Biyu asked.

'Of course— Well, I think it's a lovely story.'

'But perhaps a little unreal?' Biyu sighed. 'The world is so prosaic these days. People no longer believe in a love so great that it conquers everything. But few families have been as fortunate as we. We keep our mementoes because they are our treasures, not in the worldly way, but treasures of the heart. Come, let me show you our temple.'

Crossing the courtyard, she entered the south house that would soon belong to Wei and his bride.

'This is where we keep our temple,' she said, opening the door to a room at the back. 'Wei and his wife-to-be have promised to respect it.'

It was a small room. In the centre was a table on which some papers were laid out, and a piece of jade.

'These are our mementoes of them,' Wei said.

'Those papers,' Olivia said. 'They are actually the ones that—?'

'The very ones that were discovered after their deaths.'

'Two-thousand years ago,' Olivia murmured.

She tried to keep a touch of scepticism out of her voice. She liked Biyu, and didn't wish to seem impolite, but surely nothing could be certain at such a distance of time?

'Yes, two-thousand years,' Biyu said. 'We've had collectors offering us a lot of money for them, saying that they are valuable historical relics. They cannot understand why we will not sell. They say the money would make us rich.'

'But these are beyond price,' Olivia said.

Biyu nodded, pleased at her understanding.

'Their value is not in money,' she agreed.

'What do the papers say?' Olivia asked. 'Normally I can read Chinese but these are so faded.'

'They say "We have shared the love that was our destiny. Whether long or short, our life together has been triumphant. They say that love is the shield that protects us from harm, and we know it to be true. Nothing matters but that".'

'Nothing matters but that,' Olivia murmured.

How would it feel to know a love so all-embracing that it extinguished everything else in the world? She tried to remember her feelings for Andy, and realised that she couldn't recall his face. Now there was another face on the edge of her consciousness waiting to be allowed in, but only when she was ready.

A man with the gift of endless patience could be comforting, fascinating, perhaps even alarming. She hadn't yet decided.

'I will never forget the day we showed these to Lang,' her hostess said. 'He had heard of them from Meihui, but the reality was very powerful to him. He held them in his hands and kept saying, "It is really true".'

'I love the way you all feel so close to Lang,' Olivia said. 'You don't treat him differently at all.'

'But should we? Oh, you mean because he's a little bit English?'

'Three-quarters English,' Olivia said, laughing.

Biyu shrugged as if to say 'what is three quarters?'.

'That is just on the surface,' she said. 'In here—' she tapped her heart '—he is one of us.'

Lang came in at that moment and Olivia wondered if he'd heard these last words. If he had they must surely have pleased him, but it was hard to tell.

'There's a little more,' he said, indicating a side table where there were two wooden boxes and two large photographs which Olivia recognised as Meihui and John Mitchell.

'The boxes are their ashes,' Biyu confided, looking at Lang. 'He brought them.'

'Meihui kept John's ashes,' Lang said. 'And when she died I promised her that I would bring them both here.'

'We had a special ceremony in which we welcomed them both home and said that we would always keep them together,' Biyu said. 'And we laid them in this temple, so that Renshu and Jaio could always watch over them.'

She spoke with such simple fervour that Olivia's heart was touched. It didn't matter, she realised, whether every detail of the legend was exactly true. The family had taken it as their faith, and perhaps a trust in the enduring power of love was the best faith anyone could choose.

Silently, Biyu drew her attention to a hanging on the wall. It was a large sheet of parchment, and on it were written the words Jaio had spoken: *love is the shield that protects us from harm*.

In the end their love hadn't protected them from those who'd sought them out, but now Olivia knew that this wasn't the harm Jaio had meant. To live a lonely, useless life, separated from the one who could give it meaning—that was a suffering neither she nor Renshu had ever known. And, if there had been a price, they did not complain.

She began to understand a little more of the family's pride in Lang, the man who through his grandmother embodied the legend in the present day.

He was looking away at that moment so that she was able to observe him unseen. And it seemed to her that the mysterious 'something' in his face was now more evident than ever.

CHAPTER SIX

As it grew dark the lanterns came on in the courtyard and everyone gathered to hear Suyin sing. After a while Olivia slipped away and went to Lang's room in the south house, glad of a moment alone to mull over what she'd learned tonight. She was beginning to understand Lang a little better—he was a man who hung back behind a quiet, even conventional mask, but who behind that mask was a dozen other men. Some of those men were fascinating, and some she should perhaps be wary of.

After giving her hair a quick brush, she left the room and found him waiting in the hall outside. She faced him with an air of indignation that was not entirely assumed.

'I've got a bone to pick with you,' she said.

'Are you mad at me? I've offended you?'

'Don't you give me that deferential stuff. I see right through it. You can't open your mouth without fooling me about something.'

'What have I done now?'

'I asked you about your job and you gave me the impression that you were little more than the hospital porter. Now I find out you're an important man.'

'I deny it,' he said at once.

'A consultant.'

'*Junior* consultant. It's just a title that's supposed to make me feel pleased with myself. The real big man is the senior consultant.'

'Oh, really? And when is the big man going to retire and let you step into his shoes?'

'That's a long story. We should be getting back before they come looking for us.'

He was still smiling, but she had a feeling that she'd touched a nerve. The hospital was one of the biggest and most important in Beijing. If he was seriously hoping for a major promotion after only three years, then he was more ambitious than he wanted anyone to know.

'They've already come to seek us out. There they are,' Lang said, indicating outside where Biyu could be seen watching, accompanied by Wei, Suyin and an assortment of children. 'From where they're standing, you can see in through the window, and they're waiting to see if we fulfil expectations.'

This was so plainly true that she chuckled. Some people would have found the blatant curiosity intrusive and dismaying, but Olivia—child of a fractured family where there had been much hysterical emoting but little genuine kindness—felt only the warmth of a large family welcoming her, similar to what Lang himself had felt, she guessed.

'Then you'd better put your arm around my shoulders,' she said.

'Like that?' His hand rested lightly on her shoulder.

'I think you might manage to be a little more convincing,' she reproved him. 'We're supposed to be giving them what they want, and I doubt if they can even see anything from there.'

'You're right,' he agreed. 'It has to look real.'

Tightening his arm, he drew her closer to him. Slowly he lowered his head until his lips were just brushing hers.

'Is this real enough?' he murmured.

'I think—I think we might try a little harder.'

That was all the encouragement he needed. Next moment his mouth was over hers forcefully. There was no hesitancy now, but a full-scale declaration of intent; his lips moved urgently, asking a question but too impatient to await the answer.

Olivia responded with an overwhelming sense of relief. She had wanted this, and it was only now that she knew how badly. Since their first meeting she'd been fighting him on one level, responding on another. Now she was no longer torn two ways and could yield to the delight that flowed through her with dizzying speed.

She'd demanded that he be more convincing, and he was following her wishes to the letter. But then he lifted his head for a moment and she saw the truth in his eyes. The one brief touch of lips that they'd shared the day before had given barely a hint of what awaited them, and now he was as stunned as she by the reality.

'Olivia…'

'Don't talk,' she said huskily, pulling his head down.

Then there was only a silence more eloquent than words. She'd studied his mouth, not even realising she was doing so, wondering how its shape would feel against her own. Her imaginings had fallen far short of this overwhelming awareness of leashed power combined with subtlety.

He released her mouth and dropped his head so that his breath warmed her neck softly. He was trembling.

She wanted to say something, but there was nothing to say. No words would describe the feelings that pervaded her, feelings that she wanted to go on for ever. Tenderly she stroked his head, turning slightly so that they could renew the kiss. She wanted that so badly.

But one of the children outside gave an excited squeal and was hastily shushed. The noise seemed to come from a distance, yet it shattered the spell ruthlessly. Stranded back on earth again, they regarded each other in bewilderment.

'I think,' Lang said unsteadily, 'I think we'd better—'

'Yes, I guess we should,' she replied, not having the least idea what she was talking about.

They walked out, bracing themselves for an ironic cheer, but the others had melted tactfully away. They'd seen all they needed to.

When it was time to leave, everyone embraced her warmly. Tao and Shu presented her with a glass pig, insisting that she must come again soon, and everyone stood outside to wave them off.

Lang drove in silence. Olivia wondered if he would speak about what had happened, but she was neither surprised nor disappointed when he didn't. It wasn't to be spoken of.

'Let's stop for a while before we go home,' he said at last. 'There's a little place just down here.'

It turned out to be a teahouse constructed on old-fashioned lines, several connected buildings with roofs that curved dramatically up at the corners. Red lanterns hung inside, and stretched out to a small garden. They went to an outside table where their tea was served in elegant porcelain cups.

Lang wished he knew what to say. He'd come here hoping for time to think after having been disconcerted all evening. He'd wanted Olivia to make a good impression on his family, but she'd done more than that. She'd been a knockout. He smiled, remembering how brilliantly she'd swapped pig memories with Grandfather Tao, and how his female relatives had been won over by her fashion sense.

He'd been astonished, but he should not have been. In the

brief time he'd known her she'd taken him by surprise more often than he could count. It was alarming—it turned the world on its head in a way that constantly caught him off-guard—but it was also part of her charm.

As an attractive man he was used to having women put themselves out to get his attention. He wasn't conceited about it, he just didn't know any different. Now he was relishing an experience that nothing had prepared him for.

To find himself powerfully attracted to a woman who was fighting her own attraction to him, to have to persuade her and tease her into a sense of security so that he could convince her of the value of romantic love, intrigued him and made him wonder just where this road was leading.

Wherever it led, he knew that he was happy to go there, and that the time of decision had come. He must act now or lose what might be the most precious gift of his life.

The courtyard of the teahouse was enclosed on three sides. On the fourth there was a small pond where ducks quacked for titbits, and a bridge where they could linger after drinking their tea.

'Oh, this is so nice.' Olivia sighed, enjoying deep breaths of the sweet air and tossing a crumb into the water. She'd taken a small cake from the table for this purpose, but had eaten none of it herself.

'Are you sure you don't want anything else?' Lang asked.

She laughed. 'No, the tea was delicious and I've had enough food to last me for a month. It was wonderful food. I'm not complaining.'

'I am,' he said frankly. 'It felt like being fattened for the slaughter. They were in competition to see which one of us they could make collapse first.'

'But they're so nice,' Olivia said. 'It was all so warm and friendly, just like a family should be.'

'I'm glad you felt that. I love them dearly, but I was afraid you might find them a little overpowering.'

'I did.' She laughed. 'But I don't mind being overpowered with kindness. Not one bit.'

She tossed another crumb into the water and watched the quacking squabble. At last she said, 'Biyu mentioned something strange—apparently they'd expected you to be gone before now.'

He hesitated a brief moment before admitting, 'I stayed because of you. I didn't mean to. I've been packed and ready to go for several days, but I couldn't make myself leave, or even make up my mind to come and talk to you.'

She nodded. The discovery that his confusion matched her own seemed to draw them closer.

'When do you leave for the Yangzte cruise?' he asked.

'I join the boat at Chongqing in a couple of days.'

'I've been planning to go to Xi'an,' he said thoughtfully.

'To see the mausoleum that Jaio escaped?'

'In a way. It hasn't been excavated yet, so I can't go inside, but I can see the terracotta warriors nearby. They were based on the Emperor's army.'

'So one of them might be Renshu,' she supplied. 'It sounds a great trip, but if you've been in China for three years I can't understand why you haven't been there before.'

'I have. It was one of the first places I went. But since I've lived here for a while I see things with different eyes. Then I was still a stranger. Now I feel part of this country, and I want to retrace my steps and try to understand things better.' Suddenly he grasped her hand and said, 'Olivia?'

'Yes?'

He took a deep breath and spoke with the eagerness of a man who'd finally seen the way clear.

'Come with me. Don't say no. Ah, say you'll come.'

It was only when she heard Lang beg her that Olivia fully understood how desolate she would have been if he'd left without a backward glance at her.

Don't get flustered, said the voice within. You're a woman of the twenty-first century. Stay cool.

'You mean, to see the warriors?' she asked with a fair display of casualness.

'I want to find out if I can make you see them as I do. Or maybe you'll show me something I've missed.' He added reflectively, 'You have a way of doing that.'

'It's quite unconscious.'

'I know. That's why it's so alarming. It springs out at me suddenly, and I have no chance to guard against it.'

'Do you want to guard against it?'

'Sometimes.'

She waited, sensing that he had more to say, and at last he went on. 'Sometimes you take fright and want to flee back to your old, safe life where things follow a pattern and nothing is too unpredictable. But then you realise that that's a kind of death; the safety is an illusion, and there's nothing to do but take the next step—whatever it brings. And sometimes—' he made a rueful face '—you can't decide between the two.'

'I know,' she murmured, awed by his insight.

'I'm a coward,' he said. Looking up, he added, 'But maybe I'm not the only one.'

She nodded.

'Now and then,' she said slowly, 'what passes for common sense is only cowardice in disguise.'

'Does that mean you'll come with me or not?' he asked urgently. 'We could leave for Xi'an tomorrow, and go on to Chongqing afterwards, if you wouldn't mind my joining you on the cruise. And after that, well, we go wherever we fancy and do whatever we fancy.'

'Whatever we fancy,' Olivia murmured longingly. 'I wonder...'

He drew her down the far side of the bridge and under the trees. There in the shadows he could take her into his arms and remind her silently of the things that united them. She came willingly, letting her own lips speak of feelings for which there were as yet no words.

She ought to refuse; she knew that. Step by seemingly innocent step he was enticing her along a path she'd sworn never to tread again, a path on which the delight in one man's presence would silence all warnings until her life spun into turmoil. How virtuous it would be to be strong. How sensible. How justified! How impossible!

With every caress his mouth begged her to trust him with her heart and follow him to an unknown destination. Except that it wasn't really unknown. It was the place where he wanted to be with her, and no questions were needed.

He kissed her again and again, breathing hard as his urgency and need threatened to overcome his control.

'We'll have the whole summer together,' he managed to say. 'That is, if the idea pleases you.'

'It pleases me,' she said softly.

A violent tremor went through him. He was resting his forehead against her, his eyes closed while he fought to subdue himself. She held him with passionate tenderness, waiting, wondering what was happening behind his eyelids, and half-convinced that she knew.

At last he drew away and spoke in a shaking voice.

'Then let us make the arrangements quickly.'

He led her back to the table, took out his phone, and in a few brief calls changed her flights, booked her into his hotel in Xi'an, and just managed to grasp the last available place on the Yangtze cruise.

Then a silence fell. Both suddenly felt embarrassed, as though the emotion that had brought them thus far had abandoned them, leaving them stranded in alien territory where nothing looked the same.

'Perhaps we should go home and start getting ready,' he said awkwardly.

'Yes—packing.'

Lang had recovered his composure and gave her a mischievous look. 'Don't forget to include that dress you're wearing.'

'Oh, do you like it? I wasn't sure it suited me.'

'Stop fishing. You know exactly what it does for you. And if you didn't know at the start,' he added, 'you do now.'

'Yes,' she said, feeling her heart beat faster. 'I know now.'

'Let's go.'

At her door he said, 'I'll be here for you at midday tomorrow.'

He gave her a brief peck on the cheek and drove away.

She began her packing in a dissatisfied frame of mind and grew more dissatisfied as she lay wakeful overnight. Her mood was nothing to do with Lang and everything to do with the fact that her wardrobe was inadequate. The only really glamorous item she possessed was the *cheongsam*, and something had to be done—fast.

When buying the *cheongsam* she'd lingered over several other items, wanting them but too prudent to spend the money.

But now she was going away with Lang, and to blazes with prudence.

He wouldn't arrive until noon. The shop was three streets away, and a quick dash there and back in a taxi would enable her to collect what she needed and return before him. She took her suitcases down to the front door, and spoke to the tenant of the downstairs apartment.

'If a man calls for me, will you tell him I'll be back in ten minutes? Thanks.'

She called a taxi and waited for it outside, waving cheerfully at a little girl from one of the other apartments who was playing nearby. The taxi was prompt and she took off, managing to be back barely five minutes after midday. With luck, she thought, Lang wouldn't be there yet—but it wasn't really a surprise to find him ahead of her. What did surprise her was the volcanic look on his face.

'Where the devil have you been?' he demanded explosively.

'Hey, cut it out!' she told him. 'I'm a few minutes late. It's not the end of the world. I went to do a bit of last-minute shopping. I left you a message with the woman who lives downstairs. Didn't you see her?'

'The only person I've seen is a child who was playing here. She said you got into a taxi and went away *for ever*. That was her exact phrase.'

Olivia groaned. 'I know who you mean. She saw me get into the taxi but the rest is her imagination. I just went to buy something. I'm here now. Have you been waiting long?'

'Five minutes.'

She stared. 'Five minutes? That's nothing. No need to make a fuss.'

For answer he slammed his hand down hard on the bonnet of the taxi, causing the driver to object loudly. While they sorted it out, Olivia dashed inside to retrieve her suitcases.

She was stunned at what she'd just seen. Lang was the last man she would have suspected of such an outburst. Here was a troubling mystery, but her dismay faded as she emerged from the building and saw his face. It was no longer angry, but full of a suffering he was fighting to hide.

The driver, placated by a large tip, helped them load the bags, and then they were off.

In the taxi Olivia took Lang's hand and rallied him cheerfully. 'We're going to have a great time. Don't spoil it by being mad at me.'

'I'm not. I'm mad at myself for making a mountain out of a molehill. After all, what's five minutes? That's the trouble with being a doctor, you get to be a stickler for time.'

He went on talking, turning it into a joke against himself. But Olivia knew it wasn't a joke really. It wasn't about five minutes; just what it was about was something she had yet to learn. In the meantime, she fell in with his mood, and they went to the airport in apparently good spirits.

The flight took two hours, and they reached the hotel in the evening.

'Is your room all right?' Lang asked as they went down to the restaurant.

'Yes, I'm going to sleep fine. Not that I plan to do much sleeping. I've still got a lot of reading to do about the Emperor.'

'I saw you buried in a book on the plane. Good grief, you've brought it down here with you.'

'He fascinates me. He took the throne of Qin when he was only thirteen, unified all the states into one country, standardised money, weights and measures, built canals and roads. But he only lived to be fifty, and he seems to have spent the last few years of his life trying to find a way to avoid death.'

'Yes, he dreaded the idea of dying,' Lang agreed. 'He sent court officials all over the world with orders to find a magic elixir. Most of them simply vanished because they didn't dare go back empty-handed. He tried to prolong his life by taking mercury, but that's probably what killed him so soon.'

'Which makes it all the more ironic that he had over half a million men building his tomb for years.'

'That was the convention. The pharaohs in Egypt used to

do the same thing—start building their pyramids as soon as they ascended the throne.'

'And in the end all those poor, innocent women were trapped in there with him.' She sighed. 'What a pity we can't see inside.'

So far the tomb had not been excavated, although radar investigations had suggested many things of interest, including booby traps and rivers of mercury. Olivia knew that it would probably be several years before visitors could go into the tomb and see the place where Jaio would have died if Renshu hadn't rescued her.

In the meantime there was the other great sight to be seen, the terracotta warriors, buried nearly a mile away from the tomb and discovered thirty-five years earlier by farmers who'd happened to be digging in a field. The inspiration for these statues had been the men who protected the Emperor, of whom Renshu was one.

'I wonder how they met,' she mused now. 'Weren't the concubines kept strictly away from other men, except eunuchs?'

'Yes. The story is that Renshu was part of a group of soldiers who escorted her from the far city where she lived. Even so, he wasn't meant to see her face, but he did so by accident. The other story is that he was on duty in the palace one evening and caught a glimpse of her.'

'But could that be enough?' Olivia asked. 'They see each other for just a moment and everything follows from that?'

'Just a moment can be more than enough,' Lang mused. 'You never know when it's going to happen, or how hard it's going to hit you. You don't get to pick the person, either. She's just there in front of you, and it's her. She's the one.'

He gave a faint smile, aimed mainly at himself.

'Sometimes you might wish that she wasn't,' he said softly. 'But it's too late for that.'

'Oh, really? And why would you wish that she wasn't?'

'Lots of reasons. She might be really awkward. She might get you in such a state that you didn't know whether you were coming or going. You could go to bed at night thinking, "I don't need this. How can I get her out of my hair?" But the answer is always the same. You can't.

'And you come to realise that whichever one of the deities decides these things isn't asking your opinion, just giving you orders…"There she is, she's the one. Get on with it".'

Olivia nodded. 'You say deity, but that voice can be more like a nagging aunt.'

'You too?' he asked slowly.

'Yes,' she said in a low voice. 'Me too. You try to explain to the aunt that she's got it all wrong—you weren't planning for anything like this guy—and all she says is, "Did I ask what you planned?"'

Lang laughed at her assumed hauteur. His eyes were warm as they rested on her.

'It's like being swept along by an avalanche,' Olivia continued. 'And sometimes you just want to go with it, but at other times you think—'

'Not yet?' Lang supplied helpfully.

'Yes. Just a little longer.'

She wished she could explain the sweet excitement he caused within her, and the caution she still had to overcome. But he came to her rescue, saying, 'I imagine Renshu felt the same when he fell in love with Jaio. He probably had a fine career in the army, and falling for the Emperor's concubine just spelled big trouble. He must have fought it, and maybe he kidded himself that he was succeeding, until her life was threatened, and then nothing else mattered. He knew he had to save her, and then he knew he had to be with her for ever—to love her, protect her, have children with her.'

His voice became reflective, as though he was just realising something.

'When he finally faced it, he was probably relieved. However hard the way ahead, he'd be at peace, because the big decision was made.'

'And yet he gave up so much,' Olivia mused. 'It was easier for her, she had nothing to lose, but he lost everything.'

'No, he gained everything,' Lang said quickly. 'Even though they didn't have very long together, she fulfilled him as nothing else ever could have done. And he knew that she would, or he'd never have gone to such lengths to make her his.'

'And yet think of how they must have lived,' Olivia said. 'On the run for the rest of their lives, never really able to relax because they were afraid of being caught.'

'I expect it was more than just being afraid,' Lang said. 'They probably knew for certain that one day they'd be caught and pay a heavy price. And, when it came, they were ready. The story is that when the soldiers found them Renshu tried to make Jaio escape while he held them off, but she went to stand beside him and they died together.'

'But what about their son?' Olivia asked. 'Shouldn't she have tried to live for his sake?'

'Her son had been rescued by the family. If she'd gone after him she would only have led the soldiers to him. Her choice was either to die in flight, or die at Renshu's side. To her there was really no choice at all. They knew what was coming. That's why they left those writings behind. They wanted to tell the world while there was still time.'

Olivia gazed at him in wonder.

'You speak as though you knew them, as though they were real people here with you this minute.'

'Sometimes that's just how it seems,' he confessed. He

gave her a wry smile. 'No doubt you think that's ludicrously sentimental, you being such a practical person!'

'But you're a practical person too,' she pointed out. 'How could a doctor not be?'

'Yes, I'm a doctor, but that doesn't mean I only believe in things that can be proved in a test tube.'

'So a doctor can be as daft as anyone else?' she teased.

'Emphatically, *yes*. More so, in fact, because he knows what a false god scientific precision can be, and so he's wiser if he—'

He broke off abruptly and she guessed the reason. He was moving faster than her, so fast that perhaps he even alarmed himself.

But her alarm was fading. With every minute that passed the conviction was growing in her that this was right. She didn't know what was lying in wait for them, but whatever it was she was ready, even eager, to find it.

CHAPTER SEVEN

AT LAST he said, 'If you've finished eating I think we should go upstairs. We need plenty of sleep.'

At her door he bid her goodnight with a brief kiss on the cheek before hurrying away, leaving her wishing he'd stay the same person for five minutes at a time.

She went to bed quickly and read some more of the book until finally she put it down and lay musing. After their talk that evening Renshu and Jaio seemed strangely real, and she had the feeling that tomorrow she was going to meet them. Face to face she would hear their story, about their life, about the love that was stronger than death. And perhaps she would understand a little more about the man whose existence had sprung from that love at a distance of two-thousand years.

Olivia turned out the light and went to the window. Opening it, she stood gazing out at the mountains that were just visible in the moonlight, and a thin line of silver where a river followed a curving course.

In the room beside hers, Lang's window was closed. She could see that his light was still on and, by leaning out, she could just see his shadow coming and going. She was about to call out to him when his light went off. She hurried back to bed and was soon asleep.

She awoke early, going to sit by the open window to breathe in the cool air and enjoy the view over the mountains now bathed in early-morning light. On impulse she took out her laptop and set up the connection with Norah. In England it would be mid-afternoon, not their usual time, but she might still make contact.

She was in luck. Almost at once Norah's face appeared on the screen. When the greetings were over, Olivia said, 'We're going to see the terracotta warriors.'

'I've heard of them. They're very famous.'

'Yes, but we have a special reason.'

Briefly she told the tale of Jaio and Renshu. As she'd expected, Norah was thrilled.

'So Lang is descended from a warrior and a concubine. What fun!'

'You're incorrigible,' Olivia said, laughing. Then something made her stop and peer more closely at the screen. 'Are you all right? You look a bit pale.'

'I've been out doing some shopping. It was nice, but very tiring.'

'Hmm. Come closer, so that I can see you better.'

'Stop fussing.'

'I just want to take a look at you.'

Grumbling, Norah moved until Olivia could see her better.

'There,' she said. 'Now stop making a fuss.'

Suddenly there came a knock on Olivia's bedroom door.

'Don't go away,' she said, drawing the edges of her light bathrobe together and heading for the door.

Lang was standing outside in a towel robe. He too pulled the edges together when he saw her.

'Are you all right?' he said. 'I heard you talking, and I wondered if anything's wrong.'

'I'm talking to Aunt Norah by video link. I promised her I'd stay in touch. Come and meet her.'

She showed him to the window chair and made him sit where the camera could focus on him.

'Here he is, Aunt Norah,' she said. 'This is Dr Lang Mitchell.'

'How do you do, Dr Mitchell?' Norah said formally.

'Please, call me Lang,' he said at once, giving the old woman his most charming smile. She responded in kind and they beamed at each other across five-thousand miles.

'And I'm Norah.'

'Norah, I can't tell you how I've looked forward to meeting you.'

'You knew about me?'

'Olivia talks about you all the time. At our very first meeting she told me that you said if she ever shut up she'd learn something.'

Olivia gaped, outraged, and Norah beamed.

'And I have to tell you,' Lang continued confidentially, 'that after knowing her only a short time I realise what a good judge of character you are.'

The two of them rocked with laughter while Olivia glared.

'You can leave any time you like,' she informed him coolly.

'Why would I want to leave? I've just made a new friend.'

He and Norah chatted on for a few minutes and Olivia regarded them, fascinated by the way they were instantly at ease with each other.

At last Lang rose, saying, 'It was delightful meeting you, and I hope we talk again soon.' To Olivia he said, 'I'll see you downstairs for breakfast.'

He left the room quickly. He needed to be alone to think.

The Chinese had a saying: 'it is easy to dodge a spear thrown from the front, but hard to avoid an arrow from behind'.

In Lang's mind the spear from the front had been the

moment he'd arrived to collect Olivia and found that she'd already left, 'for ever'. For a few blinding, terrible minutes he'd been convinced that she'd changed her mind and left him, even fled the country, and that he would never see her again.

The moment when she'd appeared was burned into his consciousness with searing force. She hadn't left him. Everything was all right. Except that now he'd glimpsed a future that didn't contain her, and it appalled him.

He'd coped. He'd known already that his feelings for her were running out of control. It was only their extent that shocked him, and which had made him ultra-cautious in their talk over dinner the night before.

Harder to cope with were the arrows that struck unexpectedly. One had come out of nowhere earlier, giving him a bad fright.

He'd heard Olivia's voice as soon as he'd opened his window, and had smiled, thinking she was on the telephone. But the words, 'you look a bit pale' had told him this was no phone call. And while he'd been trying to take in the implications she'd added, 'Come closer, so that I can see you better.'

The idea of a video link hadn't occurred to him. He'd tried to stay cool, not to jump to the conclusion that she had a man in the room, but no power on earth could have stopped him knocking on her door to find out. Now he was feeling like the biggest fool of all time. Yet mixed in with embarrassment was delight that he'd been wrong. All was well.

The arrows would keep coming when he least expected them. He knew that now. But nothing could stop his mood rioting with joyful relief, and in the shower he gave vent to a yodelling melody. When he joined her downstairs, he was still lightheaded.

'I can see that Norah and I are going to be the best of friends,' he told her.

'Ganging up on me at every turn, I suppose.'

'Of course. That's half the fun. Did she say anything about me after I'd gone?'

'Not a word,' she declared loftily. 'We dismissed you from our minds.'

'As bad as that?' he said, nodding sympathetically.

'Worse. I couldn't get any sense out of her. She just wittered on endlessly about how handsome you are. Where she got that idea, I couldn't imagine.'

'The video quality is never very strong on those links.'

'Well, she likes you enormously.'

'Good. I like her too. Now, let's have a hearty breakfast and get revved up for the day.'

An hour later the coach called to collect them, plus several others from the hotel, and soon they were on the road to the warrior site.

'The thing I loved about it,' Lang said, 'was that they didn't build a separate museum and transport everything to it. They created the museum on top of the actual site of the dig where the figures were found.'

She saw what he meant as soon as they entered. The museum was divided into three huge pits, the first of which was the most astonishing. There in the ground were hundreds of soldiers standing in formation as though on duty. A gallery had been built all around so that the visitor could view them from every angle. This was exactly the place where they had been discovered and, as Lang had said, it made all the difference.

Not only men but horses stood there, patient unto eternity. After burial they had had only a short existence, for less than five years after the Emperor's death they had been attacked, many of them smashed and the site covered in earth. For over two-thousand years they had remained undiscovered, waiting for their time to come, silent and faithful in the darkness.

Now their day had dawned again. Some had been repaired and restored to beauty, although thousands still remained to be unearthed. Now they were world-famous, proud and honoured as they deserved to be.

Although Lang had been here before he too was awed as they walked around the long gallery.

'We've only seen a small part,' he said as he left. 'When we visit the rest you can study some of them close up. It's incredible how they were created so skilfully all that time ago—the fine details, the expressions.'

When Olivia saw the figures that were displayed in glass containers she had to admit that he was right. Not one detail had been skimped on the armour, and the figures stood or crouched in positions that were utterly natural. No wonder, she thought, that historians and art experts had gone wild about them.

But she wasn't viewing them as a professional. It was as men that they claimed her attention, and as men they were awesome, tall, muscular, with fine, thoughtful but determined faces.

'It's incredible how different they all are,' she mused. 'It would have been so easy to give them all the same face, but they didn't do it the easy way. How many of them are there?'

'Something like eight thousand when they've finished excavating,' Lang said. 'And I don't think they're all precisely individual. If you hunt through them you'll find the same face repeated now and then, but it's a long hunt.'

Their steps had brought them to a glass container with only one figure. He was down on one knee, but not in a servile way. His head was up, his back straight, his air alert, as though his whole attention was devoted to his duty.

'Whoever this was based on had a splendid career ahead of him,' she murmured. 'And he gave it all up.'

'You've decided that this was Renshu?' Lang asked, fondly amused.

'Definitely. He's by far the most handsome.'

Before finishing the tour, they went to the pavilion where there was a teahouse to refresh them.

'It's so real,' she said. 'I hadn't expected to find them so lifelike. You could almost talk to them and hear them talk back.'

'Yes, that's how I felt.'

'You know that story you told me—how he might have seen her when he was escorting her, or later in the palace—well, I've been thinking, and they could both be true. Renshu saw her face accidentally on the journey, and after that he knew he had to see her again, so connived to get assigned to palace duty.'

'That's a very romantic suggestion,' Lang exclaimed. 'I'm shocked!'

'All right, I've weakened just a little. Now I've seen what a fine, upstanding man he must have been, I can understand why she fell in love with him.' Olivia laughed at the sight of Lang's expression. 'It's this place. Somehow the whole story suddenly seems so convincing. I can't wait to go back in.'

They spent the afternoon going over everything again, fascinated by the semi-excavated parts in pit one, where broken figures lay waiting to be reclaimed, and the places where they could study the work in progress. The day finished in the shop that sold souvenirs, and Olivia stocked up on books and pictures. Lang also was buying extensively.

'But you've got that book,' she said, pointing. 'I remember seeing it in your room.'

'It's not for me. It's a gift for my friend Norah.'

'That's lovely. She'll be so happy.'

Some of the other tourists were from their hotel and they all made a merry party, exchanging views on the way back.

It was natural to join up again over the meal, and the evening passed without Lang and Olivia having a moment alone.

'When will you talk to Norah?' he asked later.

'Early tomorrow morning.'

'Make sure you call me so that I can talk to her.'

'Can I tell her you've bought her a present?'

'Don't you dare! I want to do that myself. Goodnight.'

'Goodnight.'

She contacted Norah early next morning and found her bright-eyed with anticipation.

'Where's Lang?' was her first question.

'Good morning, Olivia, how nice to speak to you,' Olivia said ironically. 'I gather I don't exist any more.'

'Let's say he rather casts you into the shade, my darling.'

'All right, I'll go and knock on his door.'

'Knock on his—? Do you mean he's in a different room?' Norah sounded outraged.

'Yes, we have separate rooms,' Olivia said through gritted teeth.

She hurried out, unwilling to pursue this subject further. After the way passion had flared between herself and Lang, it seemed inevitable that they would take the next step. But suddenly he seemed in no hurry, and hadn't so much as hinted that he might come to her at night.

Perhaps she had mistaken him and he wasn't as deeply involved as her, but both her mind and her heart rejected that thought as unbearable.

He returned with her and she witnessed again the immediate rapport between he and Norah as he showed her the gifts he'd chosen. For most of the conversation she stayed in the background.

'It's not like you to be lost for words,' he teased her when they had finished.

'I didn't want to spoil it for you two,' she teased back. 'You get on so well, I'm beginning to feel like a gooseberry.'

'Can you give me her address so that I can mail her present before we leave?'

She did so, and they parted, not to meet again until it was time to leave for the airport.

On the flight to Chongqing they fell into conversation with passengers on the other side of the aisle who were headed in the same direction, and before long several more joined in. Olivia brought out the catalogue showing *The Water Dragon*, the boat that would carry them down the Yangtze. It was a gleaming white cruise-liner, but smaller than an ocean vessel would be. It was ninety metres long and took one hundred and seventy passengers.

'That sounds just right,' somebody observed. 'Big enough to be comfortable, small enough to be friendly.'

'Yes, it's going to be nice,' Olivia agreed. She showed the catalogue to Lang. 'What do you think?'

'I think the restaurant looks good,' he said prosaically. 'I hope we get there soon. I'm hungry.'

When they landed a coach was waiting to take them the few miles to the river. Lang had fallen into conversation with an elderly lady who could only walk slowly, and he held back to assist her onto the coach, then sat beside her. Olivia settled down next to a young man who knew all about the river and talked non-stop.

At last the coach drew up at the top of a steep bank, at the bottom of which was the river, and *The Water Dragon*.

Olivia was first off and found herself swept forward by the crowd. Looking back, she saw that Lang was still helping the old lady. He signalled for her to go on without him, so she headed down the steps to the boat and joined other passengers milling around the chief steward. He gave them a smiling welcome, and declared that he was always at their service.

'Now I am going to show you to your cabins,' he said. 'You will find them all clean and comfortable, but if any of you should want something of a higher standard we have two upgrades available. Follow me, please.'

Out of the corner of her eye Olivia saw Lang, still with the old lady, giving her his kindest smile. She waved and turned away to follow the steward.

The cabins were, as he'd said, clean and comfortable, but on the small and spare side. Olivia sat on her narrow bed, looking around at her neat, efficient surroundings, and felt there was something lacking. Wasting no more time, she went looking for the steward.

'Can I see the upgrades, please?'

'I'm afraid only one is left.'

It was a luxurious suite with a living room, bathroom and a bedroom furnished with a huge bed that would have taken three. From the corridor outside came the sound of footsteps approaching. Someone else was going to inspect the place and she had one second to decide.

'I'll take it,' she told the steward.

He too had heard the footsteps and moved fast, whipping out a notepad and writing down her details. By the time the door opened, the transaction was complete.

'It's taken,' he sang out.

The newcomers, a man and a woman, groaned noisily and glared at Olivia.

'Can't we come to some arrangement?' the man demanded of Olivia. He was an oafish individual, built like an overweight walrus.

'Sorry, it's mine,' she told him.

'Aw, c'mon. You're on your own. What difference can it

make to you?' he demanded belligerently. 'Here.' He flashed a wad of notes. 'Be reasonable.'

'Forget it,' she said firmly.

'Let me show you out,' the steward urged.

The man glared but departed. As he left she heard him say to his companion, 'Damned if I know what a woman alone needs with a place like this.'

It was a good argument, she thought wryly. Just what did she need with a huge double bed? She should stop being stubborn, admit that her own cabin was adequate and give up this delightful palace, possibly even take the money. That was what a sensible woman would do.

But suddenly she couldn't be sensible any more.

Lang, having been shown to his cabin, was also regarding it with dismay. When he'd suggested joining Olivia on the cruise, this functional little room wasn't what he'd had in mind. He considered taking an upgrade, but how was he to explain this to her? She would immediately suspect his motives, and the fact that her suspicions would be correct merely added to his problems.

But at last, annoyed with himself for dithering, he approached the steward, only to discover that he was too late. Both upgrade suites were taken.

'Surely there must be something?' he pleaded with the steward.

But this achieved nothing. He was left cursing himself for slowness, and generally despairing.

'You too?' said a man's voice behind him.

Lang turned and saw a large, belligerent-looking man scowling in frustration.

'They shouldn't give those upgrades to just anybody,' he snapped. 'We went for the top one—nothing but the best for the missus and me—but it had already been taken by some silly woman who didn't need it.'

'Maybe she did need it,' Lang said.

'Nah, she was on her own, so why does she want to bother with a double bed? Hey, that's her over there in the green blouse— All right, all right.'

His wife was tugging his arm. He turned aside to squabble with her, leaving Lang in a daze.

Olivia was watching him across the distance, a slight smile on her face. He returned the smile, feeling delight grow and grow until it had stretched to every part of him. She began to move forward until she was standing in front of him, looking up, regarding him quizzically.

'I'm not sure what to say,' he told her.

'Don't tell me I've made you speechless?' she said, teasing and serious together.

'You do it often.'

The oaf had seen her and turned back to resume battle.

'Look, can't we talk…?' He fell silent, realising that neither of them was aware of him. They had eyes only for each other.

'Oh, well,' he mumbled at last. 'If it's like that.'

He let his wife drag him away.

Lang didn't speak, but he raised an enquiring eyebrow as though the question was too awesome to be spoken aloud.

Olivia nodded.

'Yes,' she said softly. 'It's like that.'

From somewhere came the sound of footsteps, calls, engines coming to life, and there was a soft lurch as the boat began its journey.

'Let's go and watch,' he said.

She nodded, glad of the suggestion. The time was coming, but not quite yet.

Up on deck they watched as the boat glided gently into the middle of the river and started its journey downstream between the tall hills on either side. After a while they went to the rear where a blazing-red sun was beginning to set, sliding slowly down the sky.

To Olivia's eyes that setting sun seemed to be prophetic, marking the end of one thing and the beginning of another. Now she could no longer equivocate about her feelings for Lang, either to herself or to him. By seizing the chance of the upgrade, she'd given herself away, and she was filled with gladness.

No more pretence, no more hiding behind barriers that offered no real protection, no more denial that he had won her heart. She wanted to sing for joy.

'Isn't it wonderful?' she murmured.

He was standing behind her, his hands on her shoulders. 'Wonderful,' he said. 'And you know what would be even more wonderful?'

She leaned back. 'Tell me.'

He whispered softly in her ear. 'Supper.'

She jumped. 'What did you say?'

'I told you I was ravenous, and that was hours ago. They must be opening the restaurant about now.'

The joke was on her. She'd thought they were going to float away in misty romance, and all he cared for was his supper. But it wasn't really a delusion; the tenderness in Lang's face as he gazed down at her told her that.

'Let's go and eat before I fade to nothing,' he said.

'We'll do anything you want,' she vowed.

At that moment she would have promised him the earth.

The restaurant was a cheerful place with large tables where six people could crowd, calling cheerfully across at each other. But in one corner it was different. Olivia and Lang sat at a table small enough for only themselves, speaking little, sometimes looking out of the window at the banks gliding past in the gathering darkness.

He really was hungry, and ate as though his last meal had come. She left him to it, content to sit here in a haze of happiness thinking no further ahead than the night.

'I meant to get that upgrade too,' he said after a while. 'But it took me too long to pluck up the nerve.'

'Nerve? I always thought of you as a brave man.'

'About some things. Not everything.'

He poured her some wine before adding, 'You've always kept me wondering and I—don't cope with that very well. In fact, I'm beginning to think I don't cope with anything very well.'

She smiled at him tenderly. 'Do I look worried?'

'I don't think anything worries you, Dragon Lady. You're the most cool, calm and collected person I know.'

'It's an act,' she said softly. 'I'm surprised you were fooled.'

'Sometimes I was. Sometimes I hoped— Well, at first I was afraid to ask for the upgrade in case you felt I was rushing you.' He gave her a teasing smile. 'After all, we've only known each less than two weeks.'

Less than two weeks? Had it really only been over a week? Yet a lifetime.

'So maybe *I'm* rushing you?' she mused.

He didn't reply in words, but he shook his head.

As the diners came to the end of the meal the steward announced that they might like to gather in the bar where entertainment would be provided. The others hurried out leaving Lang and Olivia together. The steward approached, meaning to remind them cheerfully that they were missing the fun, but the words died unspoken as he became aware of the silence that united them.

Realising that they would never hear him, he moved quietly away. Neither of them knew he'd been there.

CHAPTER EIGHT

ALONE now, Lang and Olivia drifted up to the top deck. Darkness had fallen completely and the brilliant moon overhead showed the stark outline of the river.

Olivia had read about the Yangzte River; it was nearly four-thousand miles long and the third-longest river in the world. But nothing had prepared her for the reality.

Used to English waterways, where the sides were either gently sloping or completely flat, she was stunned by the height of these banks that loomed up almost like sheer cliffs on either side.

'They seem to go up for ever,' she said, leaning back against Lang. 'And they blot out everything. It's like a separate world.'

'Do you mind that?' he murmured against her hair. 'Do you want to go back to the other world where everything's in the right place?'

'And always the same place every time,' she supplied. 'Until it isn't the right place any more. No, I don't want to go back to that.'

She sighed and raised her arms up to the moon that seemed to glide in a narrow river between the high cliffs.

'This is the world I want!' she cried. 'The one where I belong—but I never knew it.'

Lang dropped his head and she felt his lips against her neck. Yes, this was what a part of her had always known would happen. She'd thought herself safe in the tight little box she'd constructed to protect herself from feelings. And all the time the truth had been waiting for her, ready to pounce out of the darkness, catch her off-guard and fill her with joy.

Slowly she turned in his arms and looked up into his face, which she could just see in the ghostly light. Then he lowered his head and she forgot everything as his mouth touched hers, filling her with a delight that transcended anything she'd known before. All her life had been a preparation for this moment.

Their first proper kiss in his family's home had been thrilling, but it had contained a hint of performance for an audience. Their embrace in the teahouse garden had been sweet, but still they had lacked total privacy, and it hadn't been quite perfect.

Now they were alone with the moon, the sky and the mountains, alone in the universe, and the truth that was flowering between them was for no other eyes.

His kiss was gentle, his lips moving softly over hers, awaiting her response, then growing more urgent as he sensed her eagerness. She answered him in kind, exploring to see how much she tempted him, then relaxing as the answer became gloriously plain.

He kissed her mouth for a long time before moving to her eyes, her cheeks, even her chin. He was smiling.

'What is it?' she whispered.

'You've got such a pretty chin. I've always thought so. I promised myself that one day I'd kiss it.'

She laughed softly and felt his lips move down her neck to the base of her throat. The sensation was so pleasurable that she gave a long sigh of satisfaction and wrapped her arms about him, drawing him as close as possible.

They held each other in silence for a long time, then he stepped back, took her by the hand and together they went below deck.

The door into the suite opened noiselessly, and Olivia locked it behind them without turning on the light. For now they needed only the moonlight that streamed in through the window just behind the bedhead.

This man wasn't like other men. Even in the bedroom he didn't rush things, but took her into his arms again, kissing her slowly, giving her time to be ready for the next step. When he deepened the kiss she was ready, opening up to him from deep inside, eager for what they would exchange.

Slowly he drew her down onto the bed. She felt his fingers moving on the buttons of her blouse until it fell open and he was helping her remove it. When her breasts were free, he touched them almost reverently before dropping his head to caress them with his lips.

Olivia sighed with satisfaction and laid her hand on his head, letting her fingers run gently through his hair, tightening them slightly as the pleasure mounted then arching against him, inviting him to explore her further. He did so, starting to pull at the rest of her clothes, but not fast enough for her. She undid her own buttons, then his, opening his shirt wide and running her hands over his chest.

She had to discern it by touch and everything she found delighted her—the smoothness, the slight swell of muscles, the faint awareness of his heart beating.

'Tell me what you're thinking,' he murmured.

'I want you,' she said simply.

'I've always wanted you—is this really happening?'

'Yes. We can have anything—everything.'

As though the words were a signal, he hurriedly removed the last of his clothes and she did the same. They had known

each other such a little time, yet they were both moved by the
thought that they had been kept apart too long. Later they
might talk about this, try to analyse it, but now there was only
the urgency of leaping barriers, closing the distance, becoming one.

She opened her arms and he fell into them like a man coming home, loving her body and celebrating it with his lips and
his hands, teasing and inciting her into an ecstasy of anticipation. Her head was spinning, her flesh thrumming with desire until at last they were united in one powerful movement,
and she was claiming him as urgently as he claimed her.

She wanted it to last for ever, and for a few glorious moments anything seemed possible, but then it ended suddenly
in an explosion of light and force that consumed her then
threw her back to earth, gasping, reaching out into the darkness, no longer sure where she was or what was happening.

'Olivia...' Lang's voice reached her from a thousand miles
away.

'Where are you?' she cried.

'Open your eyes, my love. Look at me.'

She did so, and found his face close to her. Even in the
darkness she could sense his profound joy, feel the smile on
his lips as he pressed them against her cheek.

She lay there, breathing hard, trying to come to terms with
what had happened to her. It was a loving beyond anything
that she'd known in her life before, something that possessed
her completely, but only because she was willing to be possessed.

'Don't go away,' she whispered, tightening her arms about
him.

'I'm always here, if you want me.'

'I want you,' she said passionately. 'I want you. Hold me.'

He did so, keeping her against him while they both grew

calmer. She was suffused by a sense of well-being such as she had never known before, as though everything in the world was right. She was where she was always meant to be, in the arms of the man who had been made for her, as she had been made for him. Of that she had not the slightest doubt.

'Do you remember what you said?' he asked softly. 'That we could have everything?'

'Wasn't I right?'

He shook his head. 'No, I've just found out that it isn't possible. Because, when you think you have everything, you discover that there's something more and you'll never reach the end. There will always be something more in you for me to find. And I will always want to find it.'

She nodded slowly. 'And I'll always want you to.'

He moved back carefully, looking down, trying to read her face in the moonlight. She smiled, and something in that smile seemed to reassure him, for he relaxed.

'I wondered how it would be,' he murmured. 'I knew we belonged together from the first moment we met.'

She raised an eyebrow and surveyed him with a touch of mischief.

'Really? You were very sure of yourself.'

'No, I was never that. You scared me. I wanted you so much that I was haunted by the fear of not winning you. I thought maybe there was another man, and when I found that there wasn't I couldn't believe my luck. I waited for you outside the school and pretended I was there as a doctor.

'I tried to be sensible. You'd have laughed if you could have seen my mental contortions. I didn't call you for several days because I was trying not to be too obvious, but you must have seen right through me.'

'Not quite,' she said with a memory of herself growing frustrated because he hadn't phoned.

'I did it all wrong. I left it so long to call you that the school term came to an end and I thought you might have gone.'

'So that's why you came and haunted the gate?'

'And I practically kidnapped you. Didn't you notice?'

'I can't really remember. I was too busy for distractions.'

He regarded her in dismay. 'Really?'

She just laughed. Let him wonder.

'I thought you might have left early,' he resumed, 'and I'd have lost you through my own carelessness. I nearly fainted with relief when I saw you coming out of the school. After that, I did everything to make sure of you—asking you home to dinner—'

'*Asking?*'

'Yes, I didn't give you much chance to refuse, did I?' He grinned. 'But how could I? You might really have refused, and I couldn't chance that.'

'Then you were quite right not to take any risks. And when you *asked* me to go to Xi'an, and joined me on this boat, you didn't take chances about that, either. I barely had time to catch my breath.'

'That was the idea. I thought I'd got it all sewn up. I was insufferably pleased with myself, so I suppose I was really asking for fate to sock me on the jaw.'

'This I have to hear. How did it do that?'

'I arrived to collect you and you'd gone, "for ever".'

'It was just an accident.'

'I didn't know that. I thought you'd had enough of me and decided to get out fast. You might have left the country and vanished into thin air. I didn't know how to contact you in England, and I couldn't ask the school until term started weeks later. I nearly went mad.'

'You could have texted my mobile phone.'

'Not if you'd turned it off and blocked my calls,' he

said glumly. 'Which you'd do if you were running away from me.'

She stared at him, astonishment at his vulnerability mingling with happiness that she affected him so strongly.

'You've really got a vivid imagination, haven't you?' she said.

'You arrived just in time to stop me going crazy.'

Light dawned. 'Is that why you slammed your hand on the taxi?'

'I had to do something. It was that or a heart attack. I'm not usually violent, it's just—I don't know—it mattered. And until then I hadn't faced how *much* it mattered.

'But I could tell you didn't like me getting so worked up, so after that I backed off, played it cool, so as not to alarm you.'

'I thought you were having regrets,' she whispered.

He shook his head and said in a slow, deliberate voice, 'If there is one thing I will never regret, it is you. If I live to be a hundred I shall still say that this was the supreme moment of my life. If you leave me tomorrow, I'll still remember this as the greatest joy I ever knew. I say that with all my heart and soul. No, don't speak.'

He laid his hand quickly over her lips, silencing what she would have said.

'Don't say anything now,' he urged. 'I don't want you to be kind, or say what you think I want to hear. I'll wait gladly until your feelings prompt you to speak. Until then, silence is better.'

She could have said everything at that moment, gladdening his heart with a declaration to match his own. But instinct warned her that his reticence sprang from a deep need, and the kindest thing she could do for him was to respect that need.

So she merely enfolded him in her arms, drawing him close in an embrace that was comforting rather than passionate.

'It's all right,' she whispered. 'It's all right. I'm here.'

In a moment they were both asleep.

She awoke in the early hours to find him still lying across her in the same position. Everything about him spoke of blissful contentment.

Then he opened his eyes, looking at her. The same contentment was there, like a man who'd come home. It became a joyous, conspiratorial smile, the meaning of which they both understood. They had a shared secret.

Light was creeping in through the curtains over the window behind the bed. She pulled herself up in bed and drew the curtains back a little, careful in case they were passing another boat. But the river was empty. There was nobody to see her nakedness, so she moved up further. He joined her and they sat together at the window, watching a soft, misty dawn come up on the Yangtze, drifting slowly past.

It was like a new day in which the shapes were ill-defined, changing from moment to moment, but always beautiful, leading them on to more beauty and happiness.

Could you really start a new life like this? she wondered. Or was it nothing but a vague dream, too perfect to be true? And did she really want to know the answer just yet?

She slid down into the bed again, stretching luxuriously, and he joined her, laughing. Then he saw something on the side table that made him stare.

'Hey, what's this? Ming Zhi?' He took the little panda in his hand. 'You brought her with you?'

'I like to have her near as a reminder not to get carried away,' Olivia said.

He raised eyebrows. 'What happened last night?'

'I gave her time off.'

He set Ming Zhi down again and lay back, wrapping Olivia in his arms.

'If she's still off-duty, perhaps I should make the most of it.'

He didn't wait for her to answer, but covered her mouth forcefully and proceeded to 'make the most of it' in a way that left her no chance to argue even if she'd wanted to.

It was a riotous loving, filled with the sense of discovery that two people know when they have answered the first question and are eager to learn the others. This was an exploration, with more sense of adventure than tenderness, and when it was finished they were both gasping.

'I need my breakfast,' Lang said in a faint voice. He was lying flat on his back, holding her hand. 'Then I think I'll come back to bed.'

'Nonsense!' she declared in a hearty voice that made him wince. 'When the boat makes its first stop we're going to get out and do some sensible sight-seeing.'

'Not me. I'm staying here.'

'All right. You stay and I'll go. It'll give me a chance to get to know that very tall young man who came aboard in the same group as us.'

'You're a cruel woman. Help me up.'

They became conventional tourists, joining the crowds to see the sights, but always chiefly aware of each other. They were the first back on board, declaring themselves exhausted and badly in need of a siesta. Then they vanished for the rest of the afternoon.

'What shall I wear tonight?' she mused as they were dressing for dinner.

She held up the figure-hugging *cheongsam* and, to her surprise, he shook his head.

'I thought you liked it.'

'I do,' he said. 'When we're alone. But if you think I want every other man in the place gawping at you…'

'Fine, I'll wear it.'

From this he could not budge her. The ensuing argument came close to being their first quarrel, but the knowledge that he was jealous was like heady wine, driving her a little crazy.

When she was dressed, he growled, 'Don't even look at anyone but me,' clamping his arm around her waist to make his point.

'I wasn't going to,' she assured him. 'Unless, of course, I get up onstage.'

'Why should you do that?'

'They're having a talent contest for the passengers. I thought I'd do a striptease.'

'Try that and I'll toss you over my shoulder and carry you off caveman-style.'

'Mmm, is that a promise?'

'Wait and see.'

The boat was equipped with a tiny nightclub, with a stage just big enough for modest entertainment. One by one people got up and sang out of tune, to the cheers of their friends.

'Hey!' A young man tapped Lang on the shoulder. 'There's a group of us going to sing a pop song. Want to join us?'

'Thank you, but no,' Lang said. 'I can't sing.'

'Neither can we, but it won't stop us. Aw, come on. Don't you know how to have a good time?'

'I am having a good time,' Lang said, polite but unmoved.

The young man became belligerent. He had a good-natured, if slightly oafish face, but had drunk rather too much.

'You don't look it to me. It's supposed to be a party. Come on.'

Lang made no reply but merely sat with an implacable

smile on his face. At last the oaf gave up and moved away, but not before one parting shot to Olivia.

'I feel sorry for you, luv, know what I mean? A wimp, that's what he is.'

Olivia could have laughed out loud at such a total misreading of Lang. But she only looked the man in the eye, smiled knowingly and shook her head. He understood at once and backed off.

'More to him than meets the eye, eh?' he queried.

'Much, much more,' she said significantly.

'Ah, well, in that case…'

He took himself off.

Lang eyed her. 'Thank you, dragon lady, for coming to my defence.'

'Don't give me that. You don't need me or anyone defending you.'

'True, but it's nice to know that you don't consider me a wimp. Our vulgar friend can think what he likes.'

'Well, you know exactly what he's thinking.'

He grinned. 'Yes, thanks to you he believes I'm a cross between Casanova and Romeo.'

'He's not the only one. Look.'

Their tormentor had joined his fellows on the stage and was whispering to them urgently, pointing in Lang's direction.

'Oh, no!' Lang groaned. 'What have you done?'

'Given you a really impressive reputation.' She chuckled. 'You should be grateful to me.'

'Grateful? Let's get out of here.'

He hastily set down his glass, grabbed her hand and drew her away with more vigour than chivalry. By now the entire audience seemed to be in the know, and they were pursued by whistles of envy and appreciation.

Lang almost dragged her down the corridor and into their suite, where he pulled her into his arms and kissed her fiercely, both laughing and complaining together.

'Olivia, you wretch! I'll never be able to show my face again.'

'Nonsense, you'll be a hero.' She chuckled, kissing him between words.

'Come here!'

He drew her firmly down on the bed and lay on top of her, pinning her down, his eyes gleaming with enjoyment.

'Perhaps we should discuss this,' he said.

'Mmm, I'd like that. But you know what?'

'What?' he asked with misgiving.

'You're acting in exactly the kind of he-man style that they're imagining.'

'Oh, *hell*!'

He rolled off her but she immediately followed until she'd rolled on top of him, thanking her lucky stars that the bed was wide enough for this kind of frolicking.

'Now it's my turn to be the he-man,' she informed him.

'I didn't think it worked that way.'

'It does when I do it.'

He gave her his wickedest look. 'I'm at your mercy, dragon lady,' he said with relish.

'You'd better believe it.'

She began to work on his shirt buttons, opening them swiftly until she could run her hands over his chest. By the violent tremors that went through him she could tell that he loved it, but he made no move to do the same for her.

'Are you going to just lie there?' she demanded indignantly.

'What else can I do? I am but a mere wimp, awaiting orders.'

'Well,' she said, breathing hard, 'my orders are for you to go into action.'

'Right!'

One swift, forceful movement was enough to demolish the front of her dress. Then she was on her back, having the rest of her clothes ripped away.

'To hear is to obey,' he murmured, tossing aside his own clothes and settling on top of her.

They fought it out, laughing, loving, challenging, bickering amiably, then doing it all again until they fell asleep in each other's arms, happy and exhausted.

It was a good night.

Now and then the boat stopped and everyone went ashore for an excursion to a temple, or to view one of the famous Three Gorges dams. Lang and Olivia joined these expeditions but they were always glad to get back on board.

In the privacy of their suite they could enjoy not merely love-making but talk. To both of them it was a special joy that their pleasure in each other was not confined to passion. Huddled close, they could explore hearts and minds in sleepy content.

Olivia found herself talking about her fractured life as she'd never done before, except with Norah.

'You said once that I was my mother's mother, and you were right. My parents are just like a couple of kids. It can seem charming, until you see all the people they've let down.'

'Mostly you,' Lang said tenderly.

'Yes, but there's a queue that stretches behind me—Tony, my mother's second husband, her step-children by that marriage, her child by Tony—my half-brother. He's about fourteen now and beginning to realise what she's like. He calls me sometimes for advice. I do my best, but I've never told him the worst she's capable of.'

She fell silent. At last Lang said, 'Tell me, if you can.'

'I was about twelve. It was December and I was getting all excited about Christmas. I was staying with Norah, but Dad and I were going to Paris together. I got ready, everything packed, and waited for him. When he was late I went outside and sat on the wall, looking for his car to appear at the end of the road, but he didn't come.

'Norah called him, but all she got was the answer machine. We tried his mobile phone but it was switched off. I suppose I knew in my heart that he wasn't coming, but I wouldn't face it. At last, hours later, he called to see if I was having a great time with my mother. I said, "But I'm supposed to be with you." Then it all came out about Evadne, his new girlfriend. She'd begged him to take her to Paris instead of me, and been very persuasive, so he'd left a message on my mother's phone to say she'd have to have me. He seemed terribly surprised that she hadn't turned up.'

Lang swore violently and rolled over away from her, his hands over his face. Then he rolled back and took her in his arms. 'I will kill him,' he muttered over and over. 'Don't ever let me meet your father or I will kill him. Hold onto me— hold me.'

It felt so good to embrace him, to bury her head against his shoulder and blot out everything else, as though he had it in his power to put the world right.

'So you had to spend Christmas with your mother?' he said at last.

'Oh, no, she didn't get his message until she'd left to spend Christmas with her new boyfriend—at least, she said she didn't. So neither of them came for me and I spent Christmas with Norah.'

He seized her again and this time it was he who hid his face in her shoulder, as though her pain was unbearable to him.

'How did you survive?' he murmured.

'Part of me didn't. I learned not to trust people, especially when they talked about their feelings. I thought Andy was different, but he was just the same.'

'Was he the only one?'

'You mean, have I had other boyfriends? Oh, yes. I dipped my toe in the water a few times, but only my toe. I always got cautious before I went too far. It doesn't take much to turn me back into that little girl sitting on the wall, watching for someone who never appeared. In my heart—' she shuddered '—I always know that's going to happen.'

'Never,' he said violently. 'Never, do you hear me? I'm yours for life. Or at least for as long as you want me. No, don't answer.' He laid a swift hand over her lips. 'You can't promise life, not yet. I know that. But I'll be patient. Just remember that I'm always here.'

'Always,' she murmured longingly.

Always? queried the voice in her head. If only.

But held in his arms she could believe in anything, and she clung to him in desperate hope.

CHAPTER NINE

SOMETIMES he teased her about her preference for good sense.

'If I really believed in good sense I'd never have come anywhere near you,' she said indignantly.

'You're trying to reform me. I realised that ages ago.'

'I'm not having much luck, am I? Sometimes I doubt myself. You know those marvellous roofs you see on old buildings, the ones that curve up at the corners? I read that it dates back to a Buddhist belief about evil residing in straight lines, so they should be avoided if possible.

'But another book talked about architecture and rainfall, and how the curve was precisely calculated to give maximum benefit to the building. I hated that. I like the Buddhist interpretation much better.'

Lang's response was to lift Ming Zhi from beside the bed, and address Olivia severely. 'You're slipping. That kind of sentimentality isn't what I engaged you for.'

They laughed, cocooned in the safe refuge they offered each other. Their laughter ended in passion.

Another time Olivia recalled the night she'd met the Langs, and had seen him in the context of both his families.

'They say a picture's worth a thousand words,' she murmured. 'You told me how out of place you felt with your

English family, but it only became real when I saw the photograph of you all together. You looked exactly like them, but
I could still see you were a fish out of water.'

'That's putting it mildly,' he said. 'But, looking back, I feel
sorry for them.'

'Sorry for *them*?'

'I know I was difficult. In some ways I'm not a very nice
character. You said I looked like a misfit with them, and that
was how I felt. But in my mind it was they who were the
misfits, and I was the one who'd got it right, which isn't very
amiable in a fifteen-year-old boy.'

'No, but it *is* very typical of fifteen-year-old boys,' she
riposted. 'So you were a grumpy adolescent—join the club.'

'That's one way of looking at it,' he said with a self-
mocking smile. 'The other way is that I'm stubborn, inflexible
and set on my own way. Once I want something I won't give
up. Everyone else becomes the victim.' He tightened his arms
around her. 'As you have cause to know.'

'Mmm, I'm not complaining.'

'Good, because I've got you and I'm going to keep you.'

'Do I get a say about that?' she teased.

'Nope, you have nothing to say about it. You belong to me,
understand?'

She couldn't resist saying, 'You mean, like Jaio belonged
to the Emperor Qin?'

'No way. She escaped. You'll never escape me.'

'What, no gallant warrior to ride to my rescue?'

'The man who could take you away from me hasn't been
born.'

'What happened to being patient and letting me decide in
my own time?'

'That was then. This is now.'

She chuckled. 'That's all right, then. I'll forgive you if

you're a bit overbearing, or even a lot overbearing. Which you
most definitely will be. Anything else you want to warn me
about?'

He kissed her, adding thoughtfully, 'Plenty. Take my
career—I want to be the best. I have to be the best, whatever
it means.'

'This job that's coming up?'

'Yes. I've set my heart on it.'

'But you've only been here three years. Aren't you rushing
it?'

'I know the other likely candidates and they don't worry
me. Besides, the present incumbent hasn't retired yet, and
probably won't for another year. I'll be patient until then.'

The unconscious arrogance of that 'I'll be patient' told her
he was speaking the truth about himself. He was still the man
who'd won her heart, gentle, charming, humorous. But she
was learning that his apparent diffidence masked a confidence and determination so implacable that he himself was
made uneasy by it. He flinched from it, tried to disguise it,
but it was the unalterable truth.

As long as he was determined to keep her with him, she
was happy to live with it.

Life wasn't entirely smooth. On the night after the talent
contest there was a dance for the passengers. Wanting to dazzle him, Olivia did herself up to the nines, including wearing
one of the dresses she'd bought at the last minute before their
departure. It was another *cheongsam*, this time in black satin
embroidered with silver, and even more alluring than the last,
which made Lang eye her wryly.

'You wouldn't be trying to make me jealous by any chance,
would you?' he murmured.

'Think I couldn't?'

'We'll have to see.'

She soon realised her mistake. The events of the night before had given Lang a reputation guaranteed to fascinate everyone there. The girls lined up to dance with him. Their men lined up to prevent them. When they couldn't do that they danced with Olivia instead, hoping to aggravate him.

But they had mistaken their man, as Olivia could have told them. Lang seemed oblivious to everything except the succession of women in his arms, which was obviously the clever way to react, even if she did find it personally aggravating.

Watching him from a slight distance, she could admire his graceful, athletic movements. With her imagination heightened to fever pitch she mentally undressed him, feeling those same movements against her, not dancing but loving her powerfully. Her own dancing became more erotic, something she couldn't have controlled if she'd tried. And she wasn't trying.

Just once he looked directly at her and their gazes locked in the perfect comprehension that so often united them. He was doing the same as she, teasing and enticing until they were ready to haul each other off the floor and into bed. Excitement streamed through her, making every nerve tingle with anticipatory pleasure. If only he would make his move soon.

Meaning to urge him along, she allowed herself a little extra wiggle. The result was all she hoped. Lang bid his partner a hasty goodbye, made it across the floor at top speed and hoisted her into his arms.

'You've gone too far,' he said firmly.

'I hope so. Better too far than not far enough,' she said, reminding him of his own words in the zoo.

By this time they were halfway down the corridor. When they reached the door of their suite, Olivia opened it and

Lang kicked it shut behind them. When he tossed her onto the bed she reached up to undo the *cheongsam*.

'No,' he said, removing her hands. 'That's my job.'

'Then get on with it,' she ordered him, edgy with frustration.

He needed no further urging. By the time he'd finished the dress was in tatters on the floor, followed by her underwear. When they were both naked he drew back, breathing heavily, kneeling beside her on the bed. His arousal was hard, almost violent, yet he had the control to stop there, looking down at her with a glint in his eyes that was new.

'You promised to throw me over your shoulder,' she reproached him. 'What happened?'

'I'm a gentleman,' he said in a rasping breath.

'Nah, you're a coward. If you'd kept me waiting any longer, I'd have thrown you over *my* shoulder.'

'That's because you're no lady.' He lay down beside her until his lips were against her ear. 'I watched you dancing all night, and believe me you are *no* lady.'

She gave a sigh of deep contentment. 'I'm glad you realise that.'

His hands were touching her, but differently from before. The movements were fiercer, more purposeful, as though something that had been holding him back had disappeared, releasing him. Now he loved her with a driving urgency, with power, as well as skill, conquering and taking where once he would have waited for her to give.

At the end she was exhausted but triumphant. She'd always suspected that this forceful arrogance was one of the mysteries that lay behind his mild manners, and there was deep satisfaction in having tempted it out at last.

'Are you all right?' he asked quietly. 'I hadn't meant to be quite so—adventurous.'

The other Lang was back, the quiet one with perfect manners. But she'd seen beyond him now, and she liked what she'd discovered.

'Perhaps we should try it that way a few more times,' she said with a contented smile. 'I rather enjoy not being a lady.'

He laughed. 'Were you actually trying to make me jealous tonight?'

'I suppose I was,' she said in a pensive voice. 'But you did quite a bit yourself.'

'You couldn't expect me to ignore your challenge.'

'But it's not fair. I have so much more to be jealous of than you.'

'You think I'm not jealous of Andy?'

'Who? Oh, him. You shouldn't be. You know all about him, and I know nothing about your love life—unless you expect me to believe you've lived like a monk.'

She thought he paused a little before saying lightly, 'Certainly not. I told you about Becky Renton—perhaps not everything, but—'

'Spare me the details of what happened behind the bicycle sheds at school. I don't even want to know about the girls you took to the Dancing Dragon.'

'I explained.'

'Yes, I remember your explanation—very carefully edited, which was probably wise of you.'

He regarded her wryly. 'Do you want chapter and verse?'

Warning bells went off in her mind. This was straying into dangerous territory.

He was lying on his back with Olivia on her stomach beside him with a clear view of his face and its suddenly withdrawn look. Two instincts warred within her. She was curious about his life yet reluctant to sound like a jealous nag.

Let it go, she thought. She'd just had the clearest demonstration of what she was to him.

'Of course I don't want chapter and verse,' she said firmly. 'I know you must have played the field. It would worry me more if you hadn't.'

She put an arm about his neck and lay over him, her face against his shoulder, feeling him curve his arm to hold her more closely.

'There is one I'd like to tell you about,' he said at last. 'So that there are no secrets between us.'

'All right. Go on.' Now the moment was here she only wanted to back away, but it was too late.

'I was like you for a long time,' he said. 'I never let myself get too far into a relationship. I knew where I was heading and I didn't want anything to get in the way. But a few months before I left England I fell in love with a girl called Natalie.

'Everything seemed perfect. We planned to get married and come to China together. But one day I found her looking through advertisements for houses, hoping to buy one for us to live in. When I reminded her about China, she laughed and said, "Isn't it time to be realistic?"

'I understood then that she'd never really meant to come with me. She'd thought of it as nonsense that I'd get over. When she realised that I was serious, she became angry. She forced me to choose between her and China, and so—' He paused. 'And so we said goodbye.'

Olivia had raised herself so that she could look down at him. He turned his head to look at her, and now she wished she could read what was in his eyes.

'Did you ever regret letting her go?' She had to ask, although she feared the answer.

'She'd been deceiving me all that time, keeping a distance between us when I'd thought we were so close. Our minds would always have been apart.'

'But if you loved her—it's not just minds, is it?'

He glanced at her naked body leaning over him, the beautiful breasts hanging down so that the nipples touched him, and he caressed them gently.

'No,' he said softly, 'it's not just minds. But you and I have everything—minds, as well as hearts and bodies. Have you not felt that?'

'Yes, from the first moment.'

'You would never hide your thoughts from me, or I from you. I didn't tell you about Natalie before because I was afraid you would misunderstand and think it had more importance than it has.'

'And how much does it have?'

'Some, for a while. But now none at all. She married someone else last year, and I'm glad for her. If we'd married it would have been a disaster, because we would each have wanted something the other could never give. There's nothing there to make you jealous. The wisest thing I ever did was to wait for you.'

She lay down against him, reassured and content. It wasn't until the last moment that it occurred to her that there was something ominous in the story, but before she could think of it she was asleep.

Only one person was welcome in their secret world, and that was Norah.

The boat had a computer link-up and Olivia had brought her laptop. Now they both enjoyed going online to her. She and Lang would embark on a chat as though taking up where they'd left off only a few minutes before. Norah liked him as she had never liked Andy, Olivia realised.

He talked about the Yangtze, describing the view from the deck until her eyes shone.

'Oh, that must have been so marvellous!' she exclaimed. 'What a sight!'

'Perhaps you'll see it yourself one day,' he suggested.

'That would be lovely, but I'm old now. I don't think there are any long journeys for me.'

'Who knows what the future holds?' Lang said mysteriously.

Listening to this, Olivia wondered if she was reading too much into a few words, but they seemed to lead in only one direction. If she and Lang were to choose a life together, she would have to move permanently to China. His life here was too settled to allow any doubt.

For just a little longer they could live in this private universe where the real world was set at a distance. But soon the practical decisions would have to be made.

They said goodnight and hung up. Lang was regarding her with a question in his eyes.

'Something troubling you?'

'I was just wondering about Norah. She's very old, and when you talk of her coming here…'

'She's not too old for China. Old people get treated very well here, better than in many other countries.'

'Yes, I know, but that long air-journey.'

'Can be made a lot more comfortable with an upgrade.' He gave her a conspiratorial smile, reminding her that the word had a special significance for them. 'We just buy her a ticket in business class, where she can travel in comfort, stretch out and go to sleep. I think she'd like it here.'

'Lang, what are you saying?'

'I'm just looking ahead, down many different roads, but they all lead to you, my love. Let it happen as it will.'

Yes, she thought, that was the way. Fate, something she'd never believed in before, but which now seemed the only way.

Yet the flight arrangements he'd mentioned showed that he'd been thinking about this in detail, planning for the day.

He partially explained the mystery as they lay together later.

'It comes from belonging to two different cultures,' he said sleepily. 'One side of me believes in fate and destiny, good luck, bad luck, being touched by another world we can't control. The other side makes graphs and looks up flight timetables.'

'Which side of you is which?'

'They're mixed up. Both cultures have both aspects, but they speak with different accents. Sometimes I tell myself how completely I belong here. I love my Chinese family.'

'And they love you dearly too. Biyu talked of you being "a little bit English" as though that bit doesn't matter at all next to your Chinese quarter. It must be wonderful to be so completely accepted.'

A slight shadow came over Lang's face.

'What is it?' Olivia asked. 'Have I said something wrong?'

'No, it's just that you speak of them accepting me.'

'But they do, that's obvious.'

'I know it looks like that, and I'm probably imagining that the acceptance isn't complete. I simply have this feeling that they're holding back just a little.'

'But why?'

'I don't know. All I can tell you is that I feel they're waiting for me to do something, or say something. But I don't know what it is.'

'I think you're wrong. They're not holding back at all. They're so proud of you, and they're especially proud that you came here and chose them. Biyu did this.' She tapped her breast. 'And she said, "In here, he is one of us".'

'She actually said that?' There was something touchingly boyish in his eagerness.

'She actually said that. So doesn't that prove you're accepted?'

'Maybe, but I don't think even they know that something doesn't fit.'

'Then you have to be patient,' Olivia said. 'It'll happen naturally, and you'll all know by instinct.'

'I didn't think you believed in trusting your instinct.'

'But it's not *my* instinct we're talking about.'

'Perhaps it is. I think that whatever we seem to be talking about we're also finding out about each other—and about ourselves.'

'Yes, it's alarming when you start to discover that you're not the person you thought you were,' she agreed.

'What have you learned about yourself?' he murmured, his mouth close to hers.

'Things that alarm me. Things that I'm not sure I want to learn.'

'Tell me about them.'

'I'm just not the person I thought I was—but, if I'm not, then who am I?'

'Does it matter?'

'Of course it matters. What a question!'

'I'm serious. Why do you have to know who you are? It's enough that you *are*. And, besides, I know you. You're a dragon lady—wild, brave, inventive, everything that's powerful and good.'

'To you, yes. But that would mean putting myself entirely in your hands.'

'Don't you trust me that much?'

'It's not that, it's just—I don't know.'

'Believe me, I know what it's like to put yourself in the hands of the woman you love and to realise that, if she understands you, it doesn't matter whether you understand yourself because she's wiser than you are.'

He might have been talking about Natalie, but the warmth in his eyes told her what he really meant.

'Perhaps you should be careful,' she whispered. 'Who knows if I can really be trusted that much?'

'I do,' he said at once. 'I'd trust you with my life, with my heart, soul and all my future.'

'But we've known each other such a little time.'

'We've known each other for over two-thousand years,' he said. 'Ever since the moment I caught a glimpse of your face and knew that I'd gladly give up everything else in my life in order to be with you.'

'Is that you talking?' she asked in wonder. 'Or Renshu?'

'Ah!' he said with satisfaction. 'I said you understood me. Yes, I'm Renshu, and so is every man who's ever loved as much as I do. And I know one thing—I can't be without you. You must stay with me for ever or my life will be nothing.

'I know you can't abandon Norah, but I don't ask you to. She has been your mother, and from now on she will be mine too. She'll be happy in China, I'll make sure of that. Don't you think I can?'

'I think you can do anything you set your mind to,' she said in wonder.

'Does that mean yes?'

'Yes, yes, *yes*!'

Flinging her arms about him, she hugged him with wild joy and he hugged her back powerfully. When they drew back to behold each other's faces she saw that his was full of mischief.

'I was so afraid you'd refuse me,' he said meekly.

'Liar, liar! You never thought that for a moment,' she cried, thumping him. 'You're the most conceited devil that ever lived.'

'Only because you make me conceited,' he defended himself, laughing. 'If you love me, how can I not have a good opinion of myself? I merely bow to the dragon lady's superior good sense. Ow! That hurt!' He rubbed his thigh where she'd landed a lucky slap.

'I never said I loved you,' she riposted. 'I'm marrying you out of pity. No— Ah, wait!' Her laughter died as something occurred to her. 'You never actually mentioned marriage, did you?'

'I didn't think it needed mentioning. It has to be marriage. Of course, I'd really prefer to keep you as a concubine— No, no, I give in!' He fended off a renewed attack, securing her arms and keeping her close for safety. 'You don't think Tao and Biyu and the others would let me deprive them of a wedding, do you?'

'Shall we go back to Beijing and tell everyone?'

'Not just yet. Let's go off on our own for a while. You once mentioned Shanghai? Let's go there. But, in the meantime, let's dress for dinner. Put on your glad rags because you're going to enjoy tonight.'

CHAPTER TEN

As THEY were having dinner he explained what he'd meant. 'After this we'll go back to the little theatre,' he said.

'Not another talent contest, please!'

'No, they're doing a play with music. It's based on a fable that goes back centuries, and it's known as the Chinese *Romeo and Juliet*.'

'Star-crossed lovers?'

'That's right. He was poor, her family was rich. When they couldn't marry, he died of a broken heart, but she went to his tomb and— Well, wait and see.'

When dinner was over they slipped into place, securing a table near the stage. Gradually the lights went down and plaintive music filled the air. Zhu Yingtai, a beautiful young girl, appeared with her family, pleading with them for the right to study. They were shocked at this unladylike behaviour, but finally let her go to college disguised as a man. She sang of her joy:

'Other women dream of husbands,
But I do not seek a husband.
I choose freedom.'

As the scene changed Lang whispered provocatively to Olivia, 'She's looking forward to a life of learning and independence, with no male complications. I know you'll approve.'

She smiled. It seemed such a long time since she'd been that woman, and the man who'd released her from her cage was sitting so close that she could feel his warmth mingling with another kind of warmth that was part memory, part anticipation.

In the next scene Zhu Yingtai, now dressed as a man, met Liang Shanbo and they became fellow students. They grew close, singing about their deep friendship.

'Our hearts beat together.
All is understood between us.'

'And yet he doesn't suspect that she's a woman?' Olivia mused.

'Perhaps friendship is also part of love,' Lang murmured. 'If they'd been able to marry, the fact that they could confide in each other might have sustained them through the years, making them strong while other couples fell apart.'

His face was very close to hers, his eyes glowing with a message he knew she could understand without words. She nodded slowly.

At last Zhu Yingtai revealed her true identity and they declared their love, but it was in vain. Liang Shanbo was poor. Her parents betrothed her to a rich man.

He sang a plaintive ballad, full of heartbreak, saying that his life was nothing without his beloved. Then he lay down and quietly died.

The day of Zhu Yingtai's wedding dawned. She too sang, longing for death to reunite her with the man she loved. On the way to the ceremony she stopped beside her lover's tomb, crying out her longing for them to be together.

Olivia held her breath. For some reason what would happen next mattered to her.

The music swelled. The tomb doors opened. Zhu Yingtai threw up her arms in ecstatic gratitude and walked triumphantly inside.

The lights dimmed, except for one brilliant beam over the tomb. From somewhere overhead a hologram was projected into the light, and two large butterflies came into view. They hovered for a moment before flying off together into the darkness.

These were the souls of the lovers, now united for ever. The audience gasped, then applauded ecstatically. The lights came up and Olivia hastily dried her eyes.

All about them people were exclaiming with appreciation. Lang and Olivia quietly slipped away and went up on deck.

'Did I understand the end properly?' she asked as they strolled hand in hand. 'The butterflies were the lovers, and now they'll always be together?'

'That's right.'

She stopped and looked up at the moon. No full moon tonight, but a crescent hanging in the sky. Lang followed her gaze.

'According to Meihui,' he said, 'the two butterflies didn't only signify reunion in death, but eternal fidelity in life also. She said there were so many different stage versions all over China that one or other was always being performed. When I came here, almost the first thing I did was to find a performance, to see if it spoke to me in her voice, and it did. I was so glad it was on here tonight, so that I could show it to you.'

'Butterflies,' she mused. 'Flying away together for eternity. What a lovely thought!'

'Eternity,' he echoed. 'That's what I want with you, if it's what you want.'

'It's all I shall ever want,' she told him passionately.

'Then we have everything. Let's go inside.'

'We can go on travelling for another couple of weeks,' Lang said next morning. 'And then it'll be back to Beijing to plan the wedding.'

'And that's going to take a lot of planning,' Olivia mused.

'Nonsense, we just give Biyu the date and leave everything to her. In fact, why don't we just let her choose the date?'

'Good idea. She'll be better at planning it than I will.'

Biyu thought so too. In a feverish telephone call, she tried to make them return at once and plunge into arrangements. It took all Lang's strength to resist, and when he hung up Olivia had to take drastic steps to restore his energy. That distracted them so long that they got behind with their packing and nearly weren't ready when the boat docked at Yichang.

From there they took a plane to Shangai on the coast. During the flight, they planned out the rest of their trip.

'We could go to Chengdu and see the panda sanctuary,' he said. 'I've got some more relatives up there, and I'd like them to meet you. But let's enjoy Shanghai first.'

It was a revelation, an ultra-modern, bustling city where almost every inch seemed to be neon-lit. On the first night they took a boat down the river, gazing up at the skyscrapers adorned with multi-coloured lights. Then they escaped to their hotel room on the thirty-fifth floor and watched from the window.

'I'm dizzy being up so high,' she murmured, leaning back against him.

'I'm dizzy too,' he whispered against her neck. 'But it's not from the height.'

She chuckled but didn't move, even when he drew his lips across the skin below her ear, although it sent delicious tremors through her.

'Come to bed,' he urged.

'Can't you just let a girl enjoy the view?'

'No,' he said firmly, sweeping her up and carrying her to the huge bed, where she forgot all about skyscrapers and neon lights.

They slept late, rose late and sauntered out, meaning to do some serious educational sightseeing. They ended up in a theatre where motorbike riders diced with death, crossing each other's path within inches at high speed.

'Well, I've learned something,' she remarked as they walked slowly back to the hotel. 'I've learned never to get on a motorbike.'

They had the elevator to themselves and kissed all the way to the thirty-fifth floor, their minds running ahead to the pleasures to come.

But as they reached their room Lang's mobile phone began to buzz. Groaning, he answered, and Olivia saw him grow instantly alert. The next moment he swung away from her, as though she had no part of what was happening, and went to stand by the window.

He was talking too rapidly for her to follow, and his whole body was alive with excitement. When he hung up, he looked as though he was lit from within.

'That's it!' he cried. 'I knew it must happen some time.'

He hurled himself on the bed and lay back with his hands behind his head, the picture of triumph. Then he saw her regarding him, puzzled, and opened his arms to her. She went into them and nearly had the breath squeezed out of her.

'What's happened?' she gasped, laughing.

'That vacancy for a consultant has come up at the

hospital!' he cried exultantly. 'It's a brilliant opportunity. Just what I've been waiting for.'

'That's wonderful. Who called you?'

'Another doctor, a friend who knows how badly I want this. He's put my name forward, and he called to tell me when the interviews start.'

'So we have to go back now,' she said, trying not to sound too disappointed.

'No, nothing's going to happen until next week. We can have another couple of days. And then...' He sighed. 'Back to the real world.'

'But the real world is going to be wonderful,' she reminded him. 'You're going to be a great consultant, and in a few years you'll be in charge of the whole hospital.'

'I hope so. If you only knew how much I hope so. I want it so much it scares me.'

That night was different. They made love and slept close as always, but when Olivia awoke in the small hours she saw him standing at the window looking out, so preoccupied that he never once looked back at the bed.

She wondered where he was now, inside his mind, and concluded that wherever it was she wasn't there with him. It was the first shadow on their relationship, only a tiny one, but perceptible.

Next day he seemed preoccupied over breakfast, and she said little, understanding that he would wish to mull over the situation that was opening up to him. They went out on a brief shopping-expedition, but over lunch he suddenly left her alone and was away for nearly an hour. Returning, he apologised profusely, but didn't say where he'd been. Sadly, she realised that part of him was already returning to 'the real world', where she seemed to live on the margins.

Or did she live anywhere at all? Had she, in the end, been

nothing but a holiday romance? Lang had spoken of marriage and eternity, but that was before he'd been offered the chance of the thing he admitted he wanted more than anything in the world.

Suddenly she was in darkness, stumbling about an alien universe. She had survived Andy's betrayal. She knew she wouldn't survive Lang's.

But the moment of doubt passed, and that evening her fears were eased when Lang suggested talking to Norah.

In a moment they were online, and there was Norah's face, beaming at them.

'Hello, darling! And, Lang—is that you I see?'

'Hello, Norah,' he said, seating himself on the bed next to Olivia, before the little camera. 'How are you?'

'Better than ever since my gifts arrived. Look.'

She held up the tiny figurine of a terracotta warrior in one hand, and a book in the other.

'The postman delivered them this morning,' she bubbled. 'It was so kind of you.'

He told her about Biyu and the wedding plans.

'As soon as we've set the date we'll arrange your flight out here,' he told her.

For a moment Olivia thought a faint shadow crossed Norah's face, but it was gone too quickly for her to be sure. It might have been a trick of the camera.

'What kind of a wedding are you going to have?' Norah wanted to know.

Lang talked at length, describing in detail what would probably happen and the part he expected her to play in it. She giggled and called him a cheeky young devil, which seemed to please him.

'Hey, can I get a word in edgeways?' Olivia protested. 'How about saying something about my new dress?'

'It's very pretty, dear.'

'I chose it,' Lang put in.

'Of course you did. Olivia's dress sense was always a little wayward.'

'Oi!' Olivia cried.

'Well, it's true, darling. But Lang has wonderful taste. You should always listen to him.'

'I'll remind her of that,' Lang said gravely.

'Oi!' Olivia said again, nudging him in the ribs with her elbow. He gave an exaggerated wince, which made Norah laugh more than ever.

'I'm so glad you're having a wonderful time,' she said. 'You look ever so much better. I was becoming afraid for you, but not any more.'

'Don't be afraid for her,' Lang said, suddenly serious. He slipped his arm around Olivia in such a way that Norah could see it.

'I never will again,' she said. 'Darling, you be good to him. He's one in a million.'

'I know,' Olivia replied, gazing back at the old woman with love. Norah beamed back, their understanding as perfect as ever.

'Now I've got some marvellous news to tell you,' Lang said.

'More marvellous news? As well as your marriage? Tell, tell.'

'I've had a call from—'

He stopped as a terrible change came over Norah. Her smile faded abruptly and she gave a choking sound. Aghast, they watched as she clutched her throat and heaved in distress.

'Norah!' Olivia cried, reaching out frantically to the screen. But Norah was five thousand miles away. 'Oh, heavens, what's happening to her?'

'I think she's having a heart attack,' Lang said.

'A heart attack?' Olivia echoed in horror. 'Oh, no, it can't be!'

'I'm afraid it is,' he said tersely, not taking his eyes from the screen. 'Norah—can you hear me?'

Norah couldn't speak, but she managed to nod.

'Don't fight it,' Lang told her. 'Try to take deep, slow breaths until the ambulance reaches you.'

Olivia was dialling her mobile phone.

'I'm calling her neighbour in the apartment downstairs,' she said. 'Hello, Jack, it's Olivia. Norah's having a heart attack—can you—? Norah, Jack says he's on his way.'

'Can he get in?' Lang asked.

'Yes, they've each got a key to the other's place so that they can keep an eye on each other. There he is.'

They could see Jack on the screen now, an elderly man but still full of vigour. He reached for Norah's phone, dialling for the ambulance.

'It's on its way,' he said at last to Olivia.

'Thank you,' she wept.

By now Norah was lying back on the pillow, not moving. They saw Jack try to rouse her, but she lay terrifyingly still.

'She's passed out,' Jack said desperately. *'What can I do?'*

'Don't panic,' Lang said firmly. 'I'm a doctor, do as I say. Place two fingers against her throat to check for a pulse.'

Jack did so, but wailed, 'I can't feel anything, and she's stopped breathing. Oh, dear God, she's dead!'

'No!' Olivia screamed.

'Don't panic, either of you,' Lang said sternly. 'She isn't dead, but she's had a cardiac arrest. Jack, we've got to get her heart started again. First raise her legs about eighteen inches, to help blood flow back to the heart.'

They both watched as Jack put a couple of pillows under

Norah's feet, then looked back at the screen for further instructions.

'Place the palm of your hand flat on her chest just over the
lower part of her breast bone,' Lang continued. 'Then press
down in a pumping motion. Use the other hand, as well, to
give extra power—that's it! Excellent.'

'But is it working?' Olivia whispered.

'Don't disturb him,' Lang advised.

As they watched, Norah made a slight movement. Jack
gave a yell of triumph.

'The medics should be here soon,' he said. 'I left the main
door open so that they could— Here they are.'

Two ambulance crew burst in, armed with equipment, con-
fidently taking over. One of them asked Jack what he'd done,
then nodded in approval.

'Well done,' he said. 'She was lucky to have you.'

As they moved Norah onto the stretcher, Jack addressed
the screen.

'I'm going to the hospital with her,' he said. 'I'll call you
when I know something.'

'Give her my love,' Olivia begged. 'Tell her I'll be there
soon. And, Jack, thank you for everything.'

'It's not me you should thank, it's him,' he said gruffly, and
the screen went dead.

'He's right,' she whispered. 'If she lives, you did it.'

'Of course she will live,' Lang insisted.

'I shouldn't have left her. She's old and frail. I've stayed
away too long.'

'But she wanted you to. Every time I've seen her she's been
encouraging you, smiling.'

'Yes, because she's sweet and generous. She must have
smiled on purpose to make me think she was all right. She
was thinking of me, but I should have been thinking of her.'

'Olivia, my darling, stop blaming yourself. You're right, she is generous. She knew that you needed your freedom and she gave it to you. Accept her generosity.'

'I know you're right, but—'

She could say no more. Grief overwhelmed her and she sobbed helplessly. Lang's arms went around her, holding her close, offering her all the comfort in his power.

Many times in the past he'd held her with passion, letting her know that she could bring his body alive, as he could hers. But now there was only strength and tenderness, giving without taking, all the warmth and compassion of his nature offered in her service.

She stopped weeping at last, because the strength had drained out of her. Normally so decisive, she now found herself floundering.

'Start your packing,' he told her gently, 'and I'll call the airport.'

An hour later they were on their way. Lang had found a flight to London for her, and one to Beijing for himself. When she had checked in, they sat in silence, holding hands, trying to come to terms with what had happened. One moment their joyous life had seemed set to last for ever. The next, without warning, it was all over. The speed with which light had turned to darkness left her reeling.

And yet, what had I expected? she asked herself. *We were always fooling ourselves about bringing Norah to China. I have to go to England and his life is here.*

How bitter was the irony! The woman who'd been so sure she could command her own fate had been swept away by a tide of love whose strength she was only beginning to appreciate now that it was slipping away from her.

'I've got something for you,' Lang said. 'I bought it to give you as a symbol of our coming marriage.'

'Oh, no,' she begged. 'Don't say that. I can't bear it. How can we ever marry?'

'I don't know,' he said sombrely. 'I only know that somehow we must. Don't you feel that too?'

'Yes. Yes, I do. But how can we?'

'I had hoped that we might make our home in China and Norah could come here and live with us. I still hope for that. She will recover in time, and all will be well. We have only to be patient.'

She looked at him with desperate eyes, longing to believe that it could be that easy, but she was full of fear.

'We must never give up hope,' Lang persisted. 'Don't you know that whatever happens some day, somehow, we must be together?'

'I want to think so, but how can we? I don't know how long I'll be gone, perhaps always.'

'However long it is,' he said, taking her hands between his, 'it will happen at last. There will be nobody else for me. So in the end we must find each other again, because otherwise I shall spend all my life alone. Now I've known you, there could never be anyone else.'

'You make it sound so simple,' she said huskily.

'No, I make it sound possible, because it is. That's why I want you to take this.'

He drew out a small box and placed it in her hands. Opening it, Olivia saw a brooch in the shape of a dainty, silver butterfly: the sign of eternal love and lifelong fidelity.

'I bought it yesterday, when I was gone for that time,' he said. 'I've been waiting for the right moment to give it to you, but I never thought it would be like this. Wear it and never forget that we belong together.'

'I will wear it always,' she promised.

Overhead a loudspeaker blared.

'They're calling your flight,' he said. 'Goodbye—for now.'

'For now,' she repeated.

He took her into his arms. 'Remember me,' he begged.

'Always. Just a few more moments…' She kissed him again and again.

'You must go—you must go.' But still he held onto her.

The call came again.

'Oh, God, it's so far away!' she wept. 'When will we see each other again?'

'We will,' he said fiercely. 'Somehow we'll find a way. We must hold onto that thought.'

But even as he said it there were tears on his cheeks, and now she could see that his despair was as great as her own.

The crowd was moving now, carrying her away from him. In agony she watched him grow smaller, fading, until the distance seemed to swallow him up and only his hand was still visible, faintly waving.

The flight from Shanghai to London was thirteen hours. During the interminable time Olivia drifted in and out of sleep, pursued by uneasy dreams. Norah was there sometimes, laughing and strong as in the old days, then lying still. Lang was there too, his face anguished as he bid her farewell.

She managed to get a little restless sleep, but it was tormented by ghosts. There was Norah, as she'd seen her on-screen only a few hours ago, looking dismayed at the thought of the flight to China. Now Olivia realised that she hadn't imagined it. Norah had known she wasn't well, and she'd hidden it.

From beneath her closed eyes, tears streamed down Olivia's face.

Jack was waiting for her at the airport, his face haggard.

'She's in Intensive Care,' he said. 'She was alive when I left her an hour ago, but she's bad, really bad.'

'Then I'll get there fast.'

'Shall I take your bags home with me?' he offered. 'I expect you'll want to move into Norah's place.'

Until that moment it hadn't dawned on her that she had nowhere to go. She thanked him and hurried to the hospital.

Once there, she ran the last few steps to Intensive Care, her fear mounting. A nurse rose to meet her, smiling reassurance.

'It's all right,' she said kindly. 'She's still alive.'

Alive, but only just. Olivia approached the bed slowly, horrified at the sight of the old woman lying as still as death attached to a multitude of tubes.

'Norah,' Olivia said urgently, hurrying to the side of the bed. 'It's me. Can you hear me?'

The nurse produced a chair for her, saying, 'I'm afraid she's been like that since she was brought in.'

'But she will come round soon, surely?' Olivia pleaded.

'We must hope so,' the nurse said gently.

Olivia leaned close to Norah. It was hard to see her face through the tubes attached to aid her breathing, but the deathly pallor of her skin was frighteningly clear. She seemed thinner than before, more fragile and lined. How could she have gone away from Norah knowing that she was so frail?

But she hadn't known, because Norah had been determined to prevent her knowing. During their talks she'd laughed and chatted, apparently without a care in the world, because to her nothing had mattered but that Olivia should be free to go out and explore.

Now she was dying, perhaps without regaining consciousness, and she might never know that the person she'd loved most had returned to her.

'I'm sorry,' Olivia said huskily. 'I shouldn't have stayed away so long. Oh, darling, you did so much for me and I wasn't there for you.'

Norah's hands were lying still on the sheet. Olivia took hold of one between both of hers, hoping by this means to get through to her, but there was no reaction. Nothing. Norah didn't know she was there, and might never know.

'Please,' Olivia begged. 'Don't die without talking to me. *Please*!'

But Norah lay so still that she might already have been dead, and the only sound was the steady rhythm of the machines

Olivia laid her head down on the bed in an attitude of despair.

CHAPTER ELEVEN

SHE must have lain there for an hour, holding Norah's hand and praying desperately for a miracle.

When it finally came it was the tiniest, most fragile of miracles, just a faint squeeze, but it was enough to make Olivia weep. Somehow, through the dark mists, Norah had sensed her. She *must* believe that. She must—she must.

She awoke to the feeling of someone shaking her shoulder.

'I'm sorry,' she mumbled. 'I didn't mean to go to sleep, but jet lag...'

'I know,' the nurse said sympathetically. 'Do you mind waiting outside while we attend to her?'

Olivia almost sleepwalked into the corridor and sat down, leaning back against the wall, exhausted. Inside her head there was a howling wilderness of grief, desolation and confusion. It felt as though that was all there would ever be again.

She forced herself to think clearly. She should call her mother.

Melisande answered at once. As briefly as possible, Olivia explained what had happened and that she was at the hospital.

'Norah could die at any moment. How long will it take you to get here?'

'Get there? Oh, darling, I don't think— Besides, she's got

you. Since you went to China she's talked about nothing else. You're the one she wants. Keep in touch.'

She hung up quickly.

Well, what else did I expect? Olivia asked herself bitterly.

The nurse appeared, signalling for her to come back in.

'She's opened her eyes,' she said. 'She'll be glad to see you.'

Norah's eyes were just half-open, but they lit up at the sight of Olivia.

'You came,' she whispered.

'Of course I came.'

Norah closed her eyes again, seemingly content. Olivia sat there, holding her hand for another hour until the nurse touched her on the shoulder.

'You should go home and get some rest. She's stable now. Give me your number and I'll call you if anything changes.'

Norah's apartment was dark and chilly. Olivia stared at her suitcases which Jack had left there for her. She knew that she should make an effort to unpack, but it was too much.

With all her heart she yearned for Lang, yearned for his voice, his comforting presence, the feel of his body close to hers. He was so far away—not just in miles but in everything that counted. Suddenly it seemed impossible that she would ever see him again.

She began to wander aimlessly around the apartment, trying to understand the depths of her isolation. Less than twenty-four hours ago she'd been the happiest woman on earth. Now the ugly silence sang in her ears, perhaps for ever.

He'd promised love eternal, but what was in his mind now—her or the all-important interview for the job? She was suddenly convinced that he must have forgotten her as soon as they'd parted, drawn back to his 'real' life.

She should call him, but what was he doing at this moment? With her mind fuzzy, she couldn't work out the time difference. He might be talking to somebody vital to his career and resent her interrupting.

She took out her mobile phone and sat staring at it, feeling stupid. After a while she put it away again.

Then it shrilled at her.

'Where have you been?' came Lang's frantic voice. 'I've been waiting and waiting, thinking you'd call me as soon as you had news. When you didn't, I nearly went crazy. I started checking the flights to see if anything had happened to your plane.'

'Oh, heavens!' She wept.

'Darling, what is it? Is she dead? Tell me.'

'No, she's alive and holding on.'

She told him about her journey—her arrival and the moment when Norah had seemed to become aware of her. She hardly knew what she said. She was almost hysterical with relief that he'd reached out to her.

'So it's good news,' Lang said. 'If she's survived the first twenty-four hours, then her chances are fine. She'll be well in no time.'

'What's been happening to you?' she asked.

'I'm back in Beijing.'

'Have you done anything about the job?'

'No, it's still only dawn here. When the day starts properly I'll get to work. Then I'm going to get myself a video link so that we can talk face to face.'

'You can call me on Norah's. I'm living there for the moment.'

'Go and get some sleep now. You must be in need of it. I love you.'

'I love you,' she said wistfully.

She hung up and tumbled into bed, trying to tell herself that

Norah would soon be well; Lang had seemed sure. After all, he was a doctor. But she knew in her heart that he was being too optimistic too soon. If Norah made only a partial recovery they would be faced with huge problems and she guessed that he didn't want to think about them just yet.

She went to the hospital early next day. Norah was still unconscious, but after an hour she opened her eyes. Her smile as she beheld Olivia was full of happiness.

'I thought I'd only dreamed that you were here,' she murmured.

'No, I'm here, and I'm staying to look after you until you're all right.'

'What about Lang?'

'He's fine. I've talked to him.'

'What was the marvellous news he was going to tell me?'

'There's a big job coming up and he reckons he's in line for it. He's very ambitious.'

She went on talking softly until Norah's eyes drooped again and she drifted into a normal sleep.

'Is she going to make it?' Olivia asked the nurse softly.

'The doctor thinks so. Despite her age, she's very strong. It's too soon to be certain, but it'll probably work out.'

She went home feeling more cheerful than she'd dared to hope. Norah would recover and their plans could go on as before. She *must* believe that.

The next day Lang hooked up online and she saw his face for the first time since their goodbye. The sight gave her heart a jolt. He was so near, yet so far. She gave him the nurse's words.

'What did I tell you?' he said cheerfully. 'Biyu will be delighted. She'd actually pencilled in a date for our wedding— the twenty-third of next month. When I explained about the delay, she was very put out. So was Hai. He was practically lining the fish up to be caught.'

Olivia laughed shakily.

'Tell them I'm sorry to disappoint them, and I'll be back when I can.'

How hollow those words sounded to her own ears.

'They'll be glad to hear that. Wei's fiancée is writing a new song to sing at the wedding. I've got an interview for the job next week, and someone has dropped me a private hint that my chances are good.'

'Darling, I'm so thrilled for you. It'll be everything you always wanted.'

'You know better than that,' he told her.

'Yes, I do. It's just that things look different now that we're so far apart.'

'But we aren't far apart,' he said at once. 'In here—' he tapped his breast '—you're still with me, and you always will be. Nothing has changed.'

When he talked like that it was easy to believe that things would work out well. But when they had disconnected there came the time, which she dreaded. Then the distance became not merely real but the only reality.

Inch by inch she slipped into a routine. In the morning she was a housekeeper, shopping and cleaning. In the afternoon she visited Norah, now out of Intensive Care.

In the evenings she linked up to wait for Lang to appear on-screen. It occurred to her that she was following much the same timetable Norah had followed while waiting for her to call from China. When the connection finally came it marked the beginning of her day. When it was over, she counted the hours until the next one.

With a heavy heart she realised that this was how it must have felt for Norah years ago, waiting for news of her lover overseas, until finally there was nothing left to hope for.

* * *

One day Lang didn't appear at the usual time. When he finally came online he apologised and said he'd been helping out at the hospital.

'There was an emergency and they called in all hands. I've decided to abandon the rest of my vacation and go back to work. It could be useful to be on the spot—just in case.'

'I think that's very wise,' she said cheerfully.

'It means I don't know exactly what time I'll be calling,' he said.

'It doesn't matter. I'll stay hooked up permanently so that I'm always ready.'

Which was exactly what Norah had done for her, she remembered, and the similarity made her shiver.

On the day of his interview she waited by the computer for hours and knew, as soon as she saw him, that things had gone well.

'I'm through to the next stage,' he said triumphantly. 'I have to meet the whole board next week.'

That meeting too went well, and Lang confided that several board members had spoken in complimentary terms of his work at the hospital over the last three years. He said it without apparent conceit, but she was certain that he knew exactly how good he was.

Then a problem developed. His name was Guo Daiyu, and he was brilliant, Lang told her despondently.

'He didn't hear of the job at first, but someone told him recently and he hurried to apply. He has an excellent reputation, and he's the one person who could take it away from me.'

She comforted him as best she could, but she could see that the thought of losing the prize at the last minute was appalling to him.

It was ironic, she thought as she lay staring into the darkness in the early hours. Lang talked romantically, he spoke of his family's legend of love, but beneath it he was a fiercely ambitious man who knew the value of practical things.

She still believed in his love, but she also knew that the coming struggle was going to reveal each one of them to the other in a way that might destroy them.

Now she found herself remembering the story of Natalie, the woman he'd loved but had given up because she'd threatened to divert him from his chosen path. That path had included China and his professional ambition, and nothing would be allowed to stand in the way. Nothing. That was the message, clear and simple.

Then something happened. It was stupid, incongruous and even amusing in a faintly hysterical way, and it cast another light on the turn her life was taking.

After some nagging on Olivia's part, her parents visited Norah in hospital. They giggled a lot, said the right things and left as soon as possible.

Her father seemed faintly embarrassed to see her, but that was par for the course. He muttered something about how she must be short of money, pressed a cheque into her hand and departed, confident of having done his fatherly duty.

The cheque was large enough to make Olivia stare, and since she was indeed short of money she accepted it thankfully, if wryly. But she wondered what was going on.

She found out when her mother telephoned that evening.

'Darling, I have the most wonderful news. You'll be so thrilled—but I expect you've guessed already.'

'No, I haven't guessed anything.'

'Daddy and I are going to get married.'

'Married?'

'Isn't it wonderful? After all these years we've discovered that our love never really died. We were always meant to be together, and when that's true nothing can really keep you apart. Don't you agree?'

'I don't know,' Olivia whispered.

Luckily Melisande was too wrapped up in herself to hear this.

'We've both suffered so much, but it was all worth it to find each other again. The wedding is next Friday and I want you to be my bridesmaid.'

She should have been expecting this, but for some reason it came as a shock.

'Melly, I really don't think—'

'Oh, but, darling, it'll be so beautiful. Just think of it—true love rediscovered, and there, as my attendant, is the offspring of that love. Now, come along, don't be a miserable old grumpy. Of course you'll do it.'

'So I said yes,' Olivia told Norah next day. 'At least, she said yes, and I didn't have the energy to argue. Somehow I just can't take it seriously.'

'Oh, it's serious, all right,' Norah said caustically. 'You can't blame your mother. Time's getting on, and it was a very big win.'

'What was?'

'Your father had a win on the lottery some time back.'

'So that's where the cheque came from.'

'I'm glad he had the decency to give you some, even if it was just a way of shutting you up. He's rolling in it at the moment, which explains a lot about "love's young dream". Or, in their case, love's middle-aged dream.'

'Oh, heavens,' Olivia said, beginning to laugh.

She attended the elaborate wedding and endured the sight of her parents acting like skittering young lovers. At the reception almost everyone made speeches about the power of eternal love, and she wanted to cry out at the vulgar exhibition of something that to her was sacred. Afterwards Melisande embraced her dramatically.

'I'm so sorry you're here alone. Wasn't there some nice young man you could have brought? Well, better luck next time. We don't want you to be a miserable old maid, do we?'

'I suppose there are worse things than being alone,' Olivia observed mildly.

'Oh, no, my darling, I promise you there aren't.'

'I'm very happy for you, Mother.'

'You did promise not to call me that.'

Olivia's sense of humour came to her rescue.

'If I can't call my mother "Mother" on the day she marries my father, well, when can I?'

'Pardon?'

'Never mind. Goodbye, Mother. Have a happy marriage.'

Soon it would be the twenty-third of the month, the day on which Biyu had wanted her and Lang to marry. They had laughed at her determination, but now Olivia's heart ached to think of it.

'She's consoling herself with Wei's wedding,' Lang told her. 'He and Suyin were going to wait until autumn, but she ordered them to make it the twenty-third, so they did as they were told.'

Olivia dreaded the arrival of the day but it started with a pleasant surprise. Opening a parcel delivered by the postman, she discovered a butterfly brooch that exactly matched the one Lang had given her. On the card he'd written,

Do you need me to tell you that it's all still true? Call me as soon as this arrives, any time.

It was midnight in Beijing but he was there waiting for her.

'Thank heavens!' he said fervently. 'I've been praying I wouldn't miss your call.'

'You should be getting some rest,' she chided him fondly. 'You look tired.'

'I can't rest until I've talked to you. Tell me that you like it.'

'It was exactly what I needed.'

'Tell me that you still love me.'

'Yes, *sir*,' she said, giving him a mocking salute. 'I obey.'

'I'm sorry.' He grinned. 'I don't change, do I? Still giving orders.'

'Giving direct orders isn't really your way. You're better at pulling strings from behind. I guess you're just practising an autocratic manner for when you get the job. Has anything happened?'

'It'll be any day now. Darling, you still haven't told me that you love me.'

She was feeling lighthearted for the first time in weeks. 'Well,' she teased. 'Let me see…'

She was interrupted by the sound of his phone. He snatched it up, and immediately became angry.

'What, *now*? All right, I'm coming.' He turned back to the screen. 'That was the hospital. I have to go. We'll talk again tomorrow.'

'Lang, I—'

But he had gone.

She sat very still for a while, looking at the blank screen. Then she went to bed.

Next morning the doctor said to her, 'Norah can't be left on her own, but if you're going to live with her then I think we can send her home.'

'Yes, I'll always be there,' Olivia assured him quietly.

Norah was sent home that very afternoon. They hugged each other joyfully and settled down to chat, but almost at once Norah was too tired to continue. Olivia put her to bed and sat with her for a while, feeling the responsibility settle around her shoulders.

Lang came online early that night. One look at his beaming face told her everything.

'You got it!' she exclaimed.

'Yes, they confirmed it today. I now have a three-year contract at more money than I was earning before. I can afford a really nice home for you.'

Out of this only one thing stood out.

'You've already signed the contract?'

'I took the first chance before they changed their mind. I only wish you could have been there with me to make everything perfect.'

So that was it. He'd committed himself finally and, by a cruel irony, he'd done it on the day Norah's return home had made her frailty even clearer than before. If anything more was needed to confirm that their feet were set on two different paths, this was it.

She smiled and congratulated him, told him of her happiness and then of her love. His look of joy was the same she'd seen before, as though nothing could ever change.

'I love you so much,' he told her. 'I can't wait for our life together to start.'

He parted with the words, 'Give Norah my love. Tell her to get well soon.'

'I will,' she promised.

To her relief, the connection broke. In another moment he would have seen that she was weeping, but he didn't see it, nor the way she reached out to touch the screen as though he were really there, then drew away quickly because he would never be there.

An hour later she looked in on Norah, who'd just awoken and was cheerful.

'Come and sit with me,' she said, patting the bed.

As Olivia sat down the light from the bedside lamp fell on the silver butterfly pinned to her shoulder.

'That's such a pretty brooch. I've noticed that you always wear it, so I guess it must be special.'

'Yes, it's very special,' Olivia said.

'Did *he* give it to you? Don't worry, I won't pry if it's a secret.'

'When have I ever kept secrets from you? Yes, Lang gave it to me at the airport when we said goodbye.'

She removed the butterfly and laid it in Norah's hand. The old woman drew it close and studied it intently.

'It's so beautiful,' she whispered. 'It must have a special meaning.'

'Butterflies are a symbol of eternal love, because of an old Chinese legend.'

She told the story of Liang Shanbo and Zhu Yingtai, how they had loved each other and been forced apart.

'When she stood before his tomb, it opened and enfolded her. A moment later two butterflies flew up and away into the sunset, together for ever.'

'Together for ever,' Norah whispered. 'Even death couldn't divide them. Oh, yes, that's how it is.'

'How have you endured all these years without him?' Olivia whispered.

'But, my dear, I haven't been without him. In my heart he has been with me always, waiting for me as Shanbo waited for Yingtai. When my time comes I shan't be afraid, because we will take wing together. You're very lucky to have Lang. He's a man of great understanding.'

'But what can come of it? How can I ever marry him? How could I have engaged myself to a man I'd known only a week or two? Of all the people to do such a daft thing, how could I?'

'But you mustn't give up hope. You've got your whole future ahead of you. I couldn't bear it if you sacrificed it for me. Please, my darling, don't spend your life in bitter regrets, as I have, always thinking how different it might have been if I'd only—' She broke off.

'But you couldn't have changed anything,' Olivia protested. 'He died in the army.'

'Yes, but...' Norah was silent a long time, but then she seemed to come to a resolution. 'I've told you so much about my love for Edward, but there's one thing I've never spoken of to you or anyone. Things were different fifty years ago. Couples were expected to wait for marriage before they made love.

'I loved Edward so much, and when he wanted us to make love I wanted it too, but I was afraid that he'd despise me afterwards. So we didn't. I was *sensible*. I could tell he was hurt, afraid I didn't love him enough. I told myself that I'd make it up to him when we were married.

'But in those days we still had National Service, and he had to finish his time before we could marry. He was sent abroad suddenly. It should just have been a short tour of duty but he was killed by a sniper, and the world ended for me. Night after night I wept, but it was too late. He'd died without really knowing how much I loved him. Oh, Edward, Edward, *forgive me*!'

Suddenly it might have happened yesterday, and she sobbed without restraint. Olivia gathered the old woman into her arms and her own tears fell. For years she'd thought she understood Norah's feelings, but now she realised she'd never guessed the yawning chasm of grief that had turned her life into a nightmare of emptiness.

When Norah's sobs had subsided Olivia controlled her own feelings and managed to say, 'But things are different these days. Lang and I have made love.'

'Then you know what you mean to each other, and you mustn't take any risks with that. Don't let me see you wishing every day that you could turn the clock back.'

'I've been thinking. I'm going back to China to clear out my apartment and talk to Mrs Wu. I'll see Lang again, talk to him. Maybe we can come to some arrangement with me dividing my time between China and here. If not, well...'

'Oh, no. You mustn't finish with him.'

'I'm not leaving you alone.'

'I'm not alone. There's the rest of the family.'

'Oh, yes, Mum and Dad prancing around like the world's their stage. The others who send you the occasional Christmas card. I have to be here at least some of the time. He'll understand.'

'Perhaps he'll return to England.'

'No.' Olivia set her jaw stubbornly. 'I'd never ask him. Besides, he's already signed a contract.'

She didn't mention the other reason; the story he'd told her about the woman he'd left rather than change course had carried a hidden warning.

'I fixate on something,' he'd said on another occasion, 'and I stick with it. It doesn't make me a nice person.'

She hadn't seen the warning then, but it was clear enough now.

She clung to the thought that they might still be together, that somehow life could be arranged so that she could divide her time between China and England. It was a wildly impractical idea, but it was all that stood between her and the abyss.

At night she slept with Ming Zhi in her arms, gripping her more tightly, more frantically every time, as though hoping to recover the caution and wisdom by which she'd always lived.

She'd prided herself on those qualities, but in the end they had failed to save her from falling in love so deeply that she belonged to him body and soul, for ever. She could almost have laughed at herself, but the laughter would be terrible and bitter.

She knew that Lang loved her. But he was the man he was, a man made of granite beneath a gentle surface.

His face came into her mind as she'd last seen it in real life, not merely on the screen: the sadness as they'd parted, the yearning look that had seemed to follow her. Then she thought of how he'd beamed when he'd told her he'd got the job. He would survive their parting—if there had to be a parting—because he had something else. And she would survive knowing that all was well with him.

That was as far as she dared to let herself think. But the temptation to see him once more, to lie in his arms one last time, was too great to be resisted. From it she would draw the strength to live a bleak life without him.

She hired an agency nurse, a pleasant young woman who got on well with Norah from the first moment. She moved into the apartment at once, leaving Olivia's mind at ease.

The only problem now was what to say to Lang when they next talked, but he solved that by texting her to say he would be at the hospital all night.

She texted back, informing him that she was coming to China.

That was how they communicated now.

CHAPTER TWELVE

THE taxi seemed to take for ever to get from Beijing Airport to the apartment, and Olivia had to pinch herself to stay awake. When at last she was in her room, she left a message on Norah's answer machine, saying that she'd arrived safely. Then she lay down, promising herself that it would be just for a moment, and awoke five hours later.

Soon she must text Lang. He would text back, telling her the first moment he could spare from his busy schedule. Somehow they would meet, she would put her plan to him and perhaps they would have a kind of disjointed future. Or perhaps not.

Exhausted from the flight, she could see only the dark side. He would refuse. He had another life now. He didn't need her.

One part of her—the common-sense part—reckoned it would have been wiser not to come here. They could have talked online and decided their future for good or ill.

But common sense—such a reliable ally in the past—failed her now. The yearning to be with him again was intolerable. To part without holding him just once more, without feeling his body against hers, inside hers, loving her as only he could love—this would have been more than she could bear.

She put her hands up over her face and a cry broke from her at the thought.

But she was a dragon lady, strong and resolute, one who faced whatever life threw at her no matter how painful. If love failed her she would have the memory of love to carry her through, and this one final night that she had promised herself.

There was a knock on the door. Throwing on a light robe, she hurried to it and called softly, 'Who's there?'

'It's me, Lang.'

She had the door open in a second. Then he was in the room, holding her fiercely, covering her face with passionate kisses, murmuring her name over and over.

'Olivia, Olivia, it's really you. Hold me—kiss me.'

'Yes, yes, I came because—'

'Hush,' he whispered. 'Don't let's talk, not yet.'

She couldn't reply. His mouth was over hers, silencing everything but sensation. He was right; this wasn't the time for words. She wanted to belong to him again, and it was happening fast. He had the robe off in a moment, and then there was only the flimsy night dress, which suddenly wasn't there any more.

She tried to help him off with his clothes but there was no need. He was already moving faster than she could follow, and when he was naked she could understand why. His desire for her was straining his control. He almost tossed her onto the bed and fell on top of her, loving her with a fierce vigour that would have made her think he was a man staking his claim if she'd been capable of thought.

She'd forgotten how skilled he was with his mouth, his hands, his loins. But he reminded her again and again, demanding without mercy, but giving with no holding back.

Their final moment was explosive, leaving them both too drained to do anything but clasp each other and lie still.

Lang's eyes were closed, and he might have fallen asleep. She tightened her arms about him in a passion of tenderness.

'I love you,' she whispered. 'You'll never know how much I love you because I don't think I can find the words. And perhaps you wouldn't believe me, because how can I explain it?'

'No need,' he murmured. 'Don't talk.'

He was right. No words now. She was back in her dream, where only he existed. Nothing else in the world. She slept.

She knew something had gone wrong when she awoke to find Lang sitting by the window. She'd dreamed of awakening in his arms, seeing his face looking down tenderly at hers. After their passionate love-making, he should have found it impossible to tear himself away.

But he sat there, seemingly oblivious to her, absorbed in a conversation on his mobile phone.

She lay back on the bed, stunned and disillusioned. It had never occurred to her that she was already on the fringe of his life.

At last he finished the call, turned and looked at her, smiling when he saw she was awake. He returned to the bed to take her eagerly into his arms.

'Thank you,' he said. 'Thank you for coming back to me. Let me look at you. I still can't believe you're actually here. Kiss me, kiss me.'

She did so, again and again.

He was the one to break the embrace, laughing and saying, 'If we don't stop now I'll have to make love to you again, and then I won't be able to give you my news.'

'What news?' she whispered.

'I'm coming back to live in England with you.'

'But—you can't. Your new job—'

'That was my boss at the hospital I was just talking to. I spoke to him yesterday, asking him to help me get out of the job. I knew it wouldn't be easy, so soon after signing a contract, but he said he'd do his best. It was between me and Guo Daiyu, and Guo might still be available.

'He just called me to say it's good news—Guo can start almost at once. I wanted to tell you last night but I didn't dare. There was still a chance that it wouldn't work out and I wanted to be sure first.

'In a couple of weeks I'll be free and we can leave together. We'll stay with Norah and look after her. And when—when she no longer needs us, we'll return to China.'

'But you'll lose the job when it means everything to you!' she cried.

'No, it is you that means everything to me. I'll do anything rather than risk losing you.'

'But you said—when you told me about Natalie—and how you couldn't put her first.'

'Of course I couldn't. Because she wasn't you. I parted from her because there was something I wanted more. But I can't part from you, because there is *nothing* I want more. Nor will there ever be. Do you remember I told you that first a man needs to understand himself? Through you I came to understand myself. I'd believed that no woman could ever mean so much that she could divert me from my path. But then I met you, and found that I was wrong. Only you mattered. We must get married at once. I won't take no for an answer.'

'Get married?' she whispered.

'I can't go on any longer without being married to you. If you don't become my wife, then my life will be empty and meaningless until its last moments. Don't you feel the same?'

'Oh, yes, *yes*! But you never said anything about coming to England before, and—'

'You never asked me,' he said, with a touch of reproach. 'But that's my fault. I talked so much about myself and what

I wanted that I left you no space. The fact is that nothing matters to me except being with you. We'll come back one day, and there will be other jobs.'

'Not this one. You'll have to start again among strangers and lose what you've built up.'

He drew her close so that his lips hovered just over hers.

'Shut up!' he said, lowering his mouth.

It was a kiss full of tenderness, not passion. They had all they needed of passion, but for now it was a promise for the future that counted, and the peace that flooded them both.

There was a knock on the door. Lang released her and went to open it. Olivia heard murmuring for several minutes. When he returned, he was holding a paper.

'That was your landlord,' he said. 'I told him you were leaving this apartment today.' He showed her the paper.

'It's my final rent bill,' she said. 'Receipted.'

'I've just paid it. He wants you out fast, because he's got someone else ready to move in.'

'You've arranged all this?'

'Yes, so let's hurry up with your packing so that I can deliver you before I have to go to work.'

'And where exactly are you going to deliver me to?'

'To the family. You'll have my room until we're married in two weeks' time.'

'Now you're giving orders again. None of this new man stuff, respecting my right to make my own decisions?'

Gently he took hold of her shoulders. 'Olivia, darling, that's what I've been doing up until now, and look where it got us. No, this time I'm taking no risks. The family will keep their beady eyes on you and make sure you don't escape. Now, let's hurry so that I can deliver you into the hands of your gaolers and get to work.'

They found the family leaning out of the windows watching for his car, and by the time it drew up they were on the step, opening their arms to her, waving and cheering. Lang had to hurry away at once, pausing merely to tell them, 'Don't let her out of your sight, whatever you do.'

The women promptly formed a guard about Olivia, laughing to indicate that they were all sharing a joke. Yet it wasn't entirely a joke; Olivia knew. Lang had endured the loss of her once, but he couldn't endure it again, and now he was nervous when he was away from her.

'We have so much to do before the day,' Biyu said as they drank tea. 'We must talk about the big plans to be made.'

'Lang told me you'd already have everything planned down to the last detail,' Olivia told her.

'He's a cheeky devil,' Biyu said serenely. 'What does he know about anything important? Now, down to work. This is an album of pictures we took of Suyin's wedding. It was very traditional, very beautiful, and yours will be the same.'

'You think a traditional wedding would be right for me?' Olivia asked.

'Of course. What else?'

Leafing through the album, Olivia had to agree with her. Both bride and groom wore long satin robes of deep red, the symbol of joy. She was suddenly seized by the desire to see how handsome Lang would look in this wedding garb, which had an air of stately magnificence.

'Now, we have lots of shopping to do,' Biyu declared.

'You mean, you're actually going to let me out of the house?' Olivia joked. 'I thought you promised Lang that you wouldn't risk my running away.'

Biyu's eyes twinkled. 'Oh, but four of us will be with you at all times.'

'Why didn't I think of that?'

One of the little girls named Ting, who was about twelve

years old, confided, 'If you escape we have to give Uncle Mitch his money back.'

'He's *paid* you to guard me?'

'Of course,' Ting declared. 'Twenty yuan a day. Each.'

'That's about two pounds. You're definitely being underpaid.'

'Also some sweet buns,' Ting admitted. 'If you escape we have to give them back—but we've eaten them, so please don't escape.'

Olivia doubled up with laughter. After her recent misery everything that was happening felt like a happy dream, one from which she prayed never to awaken.

In the end eight of them went out, since nobody was going to pass up a shopping expedition. There were gifts and favours to be bought for all the guests, most of whom would be family members making a special trip in from the country.

'Will there be many?' Olivia asked when they paused for tea.

'About a hundred,' Biyu said casually.

'There were only eighty for me,' Suyin said with a giggle. 'You're *much* more interesting, ever since the day he brought you home.'

'One thing I've always wanted to know,' Olivia said. 'When I was there with him that night, you were all so wonderful to me. I know you were being courteous to a guest—'

'But you sensed something more?' Biyu helped her out. 'It's true. Not every guest would have been shown the temple and told the things that you were. But we knew you were his future bride.'

'He *told* you that?'

'Not exactly. It was the way he spoke of you—with a note in his voice that had never been there before. He'd only known you a few days, but something was very different. He sounded a little shy, tentative—for the first time in his life, I'll swear. I don't think even he knew what he was giving away.

'We honoured you as his future wife so that you would know you were welcome in the family. These last few weeks, we've been holding our breath, hoping that things would come right.'

She became suddenly serious. 'You were able to walk away from him, but he wasn't able to walk away from you. That makes you the strong one.' She added quietly, 'Dragon Lady.'

'He told you about that?'

'Of course. If you only knew how proud of you he is! He is a strong man in every way but one—you are his weakness. Never forget that his need is greater than yours. It gives you power, but we all know you will never misuse that power, and we can give him into your hands with easy hearts and minds.'

'Thank you,' Olivia said softly, so deeply moved that she could hardly speak. 'I promise that I won't betray that trust.'

Biyu smiled. 'You didn't need to tell us that,' she said.

Arriving home, they plunged into a discussion of details. Biyu insisted that everything must be done properly.

'So we must first seek and obtain your parents' consent.'

'At my age?' Olivia said, scandalised. 'Besides, they're on their honeymoon in the Bahamas. They won't be back for ages.'

'But there is your great-aunt Norah, whom Mitchell says is like a mother to you. He tells me that she likes him.'

'She certainly does.'

'Then she'll say yes when we talk tonight. You must show me how to work this video link he talks about.'

Biyu was fascinated by the reality of it later. Norah was up and waiting, and she crowed with delight at the news. Olivia introduced her to the family members who were at home, and Biyu explained about the ceremony of consent that would take place that evening.

'Then I'll catch up on my sleep and be ready,' Norah said.

By eight o'clock that evening they were all gathered around the screen for her appearance. The first thing she did on seeing Lang was to raise her thumb triumphantly in the air. He responded with the same gesture, which made everyone else do the same.

Lang introduced Grandfather Tao, who greeted her solemnly, and embarked on a formal speech in which he praised the bride and groom—but especially the bride—finishing with, 'Do you give your consent to this marriage?'

Norah smiled and inclined her head, saying, 'I do give my consent, with all my heart. And I want to say how proud I am to be connected with such an honourable family.'

Everyone bowed to her. She was one of them now.

As Lang had said, Olivia was installed in his room. He hadn't thought much further ahead than that, and it came as a shock to him when the young women of the house, determined to protect the bride's virtue, gathered outside her door, barring his entry.

'Very funny,' he said wryly to Olivia, who was doubled up with laughter.

'Well, we must do everything in the proper way,' she reminded him.

'And where am I supposed to sleep until the wedding? I have to move out of my own apartment in two days.'

'We can find you a couch somewhere in the north house,' Biyu promised him. 'It won't be for long. Now, you may kiss your bride a chaste goodnight and leave.'

Conscious of his family's eyes on him, he kissed her and departed hurriedly.

Had they been planning to remain in China, there would

have been the ceremony of the bed, when a newly purchased matrimonial bed was installed. This had happened at the wedding of Wei and Suyin a few weeks earlier, and they were making their own bed available for the bridal couple on their wedding night.

The result was a modified version of the ceremony in which the bed was moved a few inches to symbolise installation, after which it was covered with various fruits, and the children of the family, symbols of fertility, scrambled to seize them.

These days Hai was in his element, conjuring fish from all directions, while Biyu took care of the rest of the banquet. Because the words for *eight* and *good luck* were similar it was customary to have eight dishes, not including dessert. Shark's fin soup, crab claws and as many fish as he could find formed the basis of the feast.

On the last night before the wedding Lang came to bid Olivia goodnight, and they strolled in the dark garden.

'When we next see each other it'll be at the wedding,' he said. 'No regrets?'

'Not if you have none.'

'None at all. Are you still worrying about the job?'

'How can I help it? You may have lost the chance of a lifetime.'

'There'll be other jobs,' Lang said.

'As good as the one you've given up?'

He frowned a little, troubled that she couldn't understand what was so simple to him.

'It doesn't matter,' he said. 'I made my choice, and it was the right one. While I have you, I have everything. Without you I have nothing. There was never really a choice at all.'

'That's what *he* said,' came a voice from the darkness.

They hadn't seen Biyu there. Now she came closer.

'He?' Olivia asked.

'Renshu,' Biyu replied. 'Those must have been his very words.'

'"While I have you, I have everything",' Lang repeated slowly. '"Without you, I have nothing". Yes, that's what he said to Jaio when he went to rescue her. And she understood that he meant every word and she could trust him never to have any regrets.'

He was looking at Olivia as he said this, a slight question in his eyes.

'Yes,' she said joyfully. 'She understood. It took her too long, but in the end she really understood.'

Biyu touched Lang's cheek.

'Congratulations,' she said. 'You are truly a son of Renshu.'

She drifted away into the darkness.

'That was it,' Olivia said. 'That's what you were waiting for, the moment of complete acceptance. It came in its own time.'

'As you said it would. You were right, as you are right about everything. I can safely put my fate in your hands, and tomorrow that is what I will do.'

He drew her close, not in a kiss but a hug. Their bodies pressed tightly together so that in the darkness they looked like one person. Looking back at them, Biyu smiled in satisfaction.

Because there were so many guests the wedding could not be held at home, and a hall had been booked two streets away.

Norah was with her as soon as she rose. Suyin made the connection and kept the camera on Olivia as they prepared her in her red-satin gown and dressed her hair in the style of a married woman, as she would soon become.

Norah watched it all in ecstasy. She had rested all day so that she would be fresh enough to stay up overnight, and now she and her nurse sat together, eyes fixed on the screen.

The groom, accompanied by the sound of drums and gongs, arrived in a sedan chair to collect his bride and take her to the place of the marriage. Olivia was pleased to see that he looked as splendidly handsome in traditional attire as she had known he would.

At this point there was a small delay. The groom requested that the bride appear but the bride's attendants, in accordance with tradition, refused to produce her until mollified by gifts. Since the attendants were the children of the house, there was a good deal of horse trading, led by Ting, and the price rose higher and higher.

'How are they doing?' Olivia asked Suyin from behind the window.

'Ting is driving a hard bargain,' Suyin chuckled. 'At this rate, you'll be lucky to be married today.'

At last Biyu intervened, declaring that enough was enough. The children seized their prizes and scampered away, squeaking with satisfaction.

Then it was time for the bride to get into her sedan chair for the journey to where the ceremony was to take place. All around her firecrackers exploded as she began her journey.

As they travelled she couldn't help thinking about Zhu Yingtai going to her wedding in a similar sedan, stopping it beside Liang Shanbo's grave and leaving it to join him for ever. It was in memory of this that Lang had given her the silver butterflies, and now she wore them both on her dress.

The wedding itself was simple. In the hall they approached

the altar and spoke the words of homage to heaven and earth and the ancestors. There followed the declaration of homage to each other, expressed formally, but saying so much more than mere words could ever convey.

One of Lang's young cousins had undertaken to care for the laptop with the camera, and he did his duties so well that Norah saw everything close-up.

When the little ceremony was over the bride and groom bowed to each other. Now it was time for the feast. An elaborate paper dragon bounded into the room and performed a dance to loud applause. Then Suyin sang the song she had written in their honour:

'Now our family is happy
Because you are a part of us.
This you will always be,
Near or far.'

Hidden by the heavy red satin, Olivia reached out her hand for Lang's and felt him seize her in return. They both understood the message: near or far.

There was an extra touch that she hadn't expected but which filled her with happiness: Suyin went to stand before the camera and sang directly to Norah, repeating in English the words she had already sung, welcoming Norah as one of them.

Everyone saluted Norah, and she in turn raised a glass.

At last it was over. The crowds faded, the noise was silenced, darkness fell and they were finally alone.

'Are you happy?' Lang asked as they lay together.

'If this is the only happiness I ever know for the rest of my life,' she replied softly, 'it will be enough. I have everything.'

'And I shall give you everything in my power,' he vowed. 'All I ask is your love and your eternal presence.'

Her lips answered him silently, and after that nothing more was said.

They lingered two more days, paying visits of respect to those who had come in from distant places to be at their wedding. Then it was time to go. Everyone came to see them off at the airport.

Lang was very quiet, but sometimes his eyes rested on Olivia's shoulder where she had pinned the two butterflies, symbols of eternal love and fidelity. He was content.

At last the goodbyes were finished and they were on the aircraft, gliding down the runway, taking off.

Higher they climbed, and higher, with the ground falling away beneath them until they were in the clouds. Then the clouds too disappeared and they were up in the clear, brilliant air, still climbing. Olivia watched through the window, entranced by the beauty. But then...

She blinked and gave herself a little shake. She was dreaming; she must be. Because otherwise she could have sworn she saw two butterflies flying together.

That was impossible. No butterfly could climb this high. When she looked back, the illusion would have disappeared.

But it persisted: two bright, darting creatures fluttering here and there, until at last they turned and winged their way towards the sun, blended with the air and vanished as if they had never been.

Full of wonder, she turned to Lang and found that he too was looking out of the window. Then he smiled at her and nodded.

* * *

Norah lived another eighteen months, finally dying peacefully with Olivia and Lang holding her hands.

She was cremated, and when they returned to China they took her ashes and laid them in the little temple with the ashes of Meihui.

Her photograph is there today, with one of Edward close by. They stand opposite the pictures of Meihui and John Mitchell.

Beside them are more pictures, of Lang, Olivia and their baby son.

Above them on the wall are written the words of the faith by which Jaio and Renshu lived two-thousand years ago, and which still survive in their descendants:

Love is the shield that protects us from harm.

A Trip with
the Tycoon

NICOLA MARSH

Nicola Marsh has always had a passion for writing and reading. As a youngster she devoured books when she should have been sleeping and she later kept a diary, which could be an epic in itself!

These days, when she's not enjoying life with her husband and son in her home city of Melbourne, she's at her computer doing her dream job – creating the romances she loves. Visit Nicola's website at www.nicolamarsh.com for the latest news of her books.

**There's more Nicola Marsh at
www.millsandboon.co.uk – don't miss
One Indian Summer, your free online read!**

Dear Reader,

Travel is in my blood. I first flew at two months of age and haven't stopped since! I love the different cultures, the food, the sights and the people of our big, wide world and I have been lucky enough to visit many places.

For me, India evokes images of spices, saris, sun and sand. The people are as diverse as the delicious cuisine, their monuments steeped in centuries-old tradition. It is a land of contrast and mystique. What better place to set a romance novel?

Such a spectacular setting is the perfect backdrop for Tamara and Ethan's story. Tamara, of Indian descent, is on a journey of self-discovery. Travelling on the majestic "Palace on Wheels" train through Rajasthan, and later Goa, she never expects to find romance. Suave, sexy Ethan has other ideas and the corporate pirate sweeps Tamara off her feet.

There's nothing like a holiday romance – but what happens when these two return to Melbourne? Turn the pages to find out!

I hope you enjoy this magical journey through India.

Happy reading!

Nicola

For Uncle Ian and Rayner, who kindly shared
their recent memories of the "Palace on
Wheels" as I wrote this. Thanks for the photos,
the anecdotes, the laughs – and for bringing
the trip alive.

CHAPTER ONE

TAMARA RAYNE'S high heels clacked impatiently against the cobblestones as she strode towards Ambrosia, Melbourne's hippest restaurant, a gourmet's delight and the place where she was trying to get her life back on track.

Her favourite butterscotch boots, patent leather with a towering heel—impractical yet gorgeous—never failed to invoke the stuff of her surname as plump drops splashed down from the heavens and lashed her in a stinging sheet.

With her laden arms and no umbrella, she needed a mythical knight in shining armour. She'd thought she'd had him once in Richard. How wrong she'd been.

Blinking back futile tears—wasted tears, angry tears—she pushed on Ambrosia's door with her behind, staggering with her load, almost slamming into her knight.

More of a pirate, really, a corporate pirate in a designer suit with rain-slicked dark hair, roguish blue eyes and a devilish smile.

'Need a hand?'

Definitely devilish, and used to great effect if the constant parade of women traipsing through Ethan Brooks's life was any indication.

'You're back.'

'Miss me?'

'Hardly.'

She hadn't meant to sound so frosty but then, what was he doing? Flirting? She barely knew him, had seen him three times in the last year out of necessity, so why the familiarity?

'Too bad.' He shrugged, his roguish smile widening as he pointed to the bundle in her arms. 'Do you want help with that?'

Quashing the urge to take her load and run, she nodded. 'Thanks.'

He grunted as she offloaded the bag perched precariously on top of the rest. 'What's in here? Bricks for the new tandoori oven I've ordered?'

'Almost as heavy.'

Her voice wobbled, just a tad, and she swallowed, twice. It was the mention of the tandoori oven that did it.

Her mum had loved tandoori chicken, had scored the chicken to let the spices and yoghurt marinate into it, had painstakingly threaded the pieces onto skewers before grilling, while lamenting the loss of her real oven back in Goa.

Her mother had missed her homeland so much, despite living in Melbourne for the last thirty years of her life. It had been the reason they'd planned their special trip together: a trip back in time for her mum, a trip to open Tamara's eyes to a culture she'd never known even though Indian blood ran in her veins.

Thanks to Richard, the trip never happened and, while her mum had died three years ago and she'd come to terms with her grief, she'd never forgiven him for robbing her of that precious experience.

Now, more than ever, she needed her mum, missed her terribly. Khushi would've been her only ally, would've been the only one she trusted with the truth about Richard, and would've helped her reclaim her identity, her life.

Hot, bitter tears of regret stung her eyes and she deliberately glanced over Ethan's shoulder, focusing on anything other than the curiosity in his eyes.

'Can you take the rest? My arms are killing me.'

She knew he wouldn't push, wouldn't ask her what was wrong.

He hadn't pushed when she'd been detached and withdrawn following Richard's death while they'd sorted through the legal rigmarole of the restaurant.

He hadn't pushed when she'd approached him to use Ambrosia six months ago to kick-start her career.

Instead, he'd taken an extended business trip, had been aloof as always. There was a time she'd thought he disliked her, such was his distant demeanour whenever she entered a room.

But she hadn't wasted time figuring it out. He was Richard's mate and that was all the reason she needed to keep her distance. Ethan, like the rest of the planet, thought Richard was great: top chef, top entertainer, top bloke.

If they only knew.

'Sure.' He took the bulk of her load, making it look easy as he held the door open. 'Coming in?'

She didn't need to be asked twice as she stepped into the only place she called home these days.

Ambrosia: food of the gods. More like food for her soul.

It had become her refuge, her safe haven the last few months. Crazy, considering Richard had owned part of it, had been head chef since its inception, and they'd met here when she'd come to critique Melbourne's latest culinary hot spot.

For that alone she should hate the place.

But the welcoming warmth of Ambrosia, with its polished honey oak boards, brick fireplace and comfy cushioned chairs that had drawn her here every Monday for the last six months was hard to resist and what better place for a food critic determined to return to the workforce to practise her trade?

Throw in the best hot chocolate this side of the Yarra and she couldn't stay away.

As she dumped her remaining load on a nearby table and

stretched her aching arms, her gaze drifted to the enigmatic man lighting a match to kindling in the fireplace.

What was he doing here?

From all accounts, Ethan was unpredictable, blew hotter and colder than a Melbourne spring breeze. His employees enjoyed working here but never knew when the imperturbable, ruthless businessman would appear.

She'd been happy to have the place to herself the last six months, other than the skilled staff and eager patrons who poured through the door of course, had been strangely uncomfortable the few times she and Ethan met.

There was something about him…an underlying steeliness, a hard streak, an almost palpable electricity that buzzed and crackled, indicative of a man in command, a man on top of his game and intent on staying there.

He straightened and she quickly averted her gaze, surprised to find it had been lingering on a piece of his anatomy she had no right noticing.

She'd never done that—noticed him as a man. He was Richard's business partner, someone who'd always been distantly polite to her the few times their paths had crossed, but that was it.

So why the quick flush of heat, the flicker of guilt?

It had been a year since Richard's death, two since she'd been touched by a man, which went a long way to explaining her wandering gaze. She may be numb on the inside, emotionally anaesthetised, but she wasn't dead and any woman with a pulse would've checked out Ethan's rather impressive rear end.

'If I get you a drink, will you tell me what's in the bags?'

Slipping out of her camel trench coat, she slung it onto the back of a chair. She didn't want to tell him, didn't want to show him the culmination of half a year's work.

She'd come here for privacy, for inspiration, and having him here intruded on that. Ridiculous, considering he owned the

place and could come and go as he pleased, but something about
his greeting had rankled, something about that damn smile.

'I'd kill for a hot chocolate, thanks.'

'Coming right up.'

His gaze lingered on the bags before meeting hers, challenging. 'I won't give up until I know what's in there so why
don't you just tell me?'

He stared at her, unflinching, direct, his persistence indicative of a guy used to getting his own way, a guy who
demanded nothing less.

She fingered the hessian holding her future, *mind your own
business* hovering on her lips. His authority niggled, grated,
but he'd given her the opportunity to relaunch her career by
using this place and she should be civil if nothing else.

'If you throw in a side of marshmallows, I'll show you.'

'You're on.'

With a half salute and a twinkle in his eyes, he strode
towards the bar.

Ah…the pirate was in top form today. Full of swagger,
cheek and suave bravado. She was immune to his charm, of
course, but for a split second it felt good, great, in fact, to be
on the receiving end of some of that legendary charm.

While he headed for the espresso machine behind the bar
she plopped onto a chair, stretched her legs and wiggled her
toes. She loved these boots, she really did, but they were
nothing but trouble for the weather, her feet and her back,
which gave a protesting twinge as she sat up.

Though that could be more to do with the ten-ton load
she'd hefted up the street, but she'd had no choice. She held
her future in her hands—literally—and, despite the gut feeling
she was ready for this, it wouldn't hurt to get Ethan's opinion
on it. If anyone knew this business inside out, he did.

'Here you go. One hot chocolate with a double side of
marshmallows.'

He placed the towering glass in front of her, a strong Americano in front of him, and slid into the chair opposite, fixing her with a half-amused, half-laconic tilt of his lips.

'I've kept my side of the bargain, so come on, what's in there?'

'A girl can't think without a sip of chocolate first.'

She cradled the mug, inhaled the rich chocolate-fragrant steam, savoured the warmth seeping into her palms and, closing her eyes, took a deep sip, letting the sweet lusciousness glide over her taste buds and slide down her throat.

Ethan made a strange sound and her eyes flew open, confused by the flicker of something darker, mysterious in his eyes before he quickly masked it.

'Right. One sip, you said.' He tapped the nearest bag. 'Now, let's have it.'

'You hotshot businessmen are all the same. Way too impatient.'

She placed her mug on the table, unzipping the first bag and hauling out a folder.

He tilted his head on an angle to read the spine. 'What's that?'

'A list of every restaurant in Melbourne. The new list I've been compiling over the last six months.'

Her tummy quivered as she glanced at the folder, at what it meant for her future.

'I'm ready.'

His eyes sparked with understanding and she wondered how he could do that. He'd read her mind, whereas Richard hadn't a clue what she'd been thinking after three years of marriage. Then again, considering what he'd been up to, he probably hadn't cared.

'You're going back to work?'

'Uh-huh. Thanks to your chef whipping up those amazing meals and letting me get my hand back into critiquing, I reckon I'm finally ready.'

She gnawed on her bottom lip, worrying it till she tasted the gloss she'd swiped on this morning.

'Think I'm crazy?'

His eyebrows shot up. 'Crazy? I think it's brilliant. Just what you need, something to focus on, get your mind off losing Rich.'

She hated the pity in his eyes, hated the fact she still had to fake grief, still had to pretend she cared.

She didn't.

Not since that first incident four months into her marriage when the man she'd married had given her a frightening glimpse into her future.

She'd thought Richard was the type of guy to never let her down, the type of guy to keep her safe, to give her what she'd always wanted: stability, security—something she'd never had since her dad had died when she was ten.

But Richard hadn't been that guy and, from the accolades of his adoring public and coworkers, she was the only one who knew the truth.

That Richard Downey, Australia's premier celebrity chef, had been an out-and-out bastard. And it was times like this, when she had to pretend in front of one of his mates, that an all-consuming latent fury swept through her.

If he hadn't upped and died of a heart attack, she would've been tempted to kill him herself for what he'd put her through, and what she'd discovered after his death.

'This has nothing to do with Richard. I'm doing it for me.'

Her bitterness spilled out in a torrent and she clamped her lips shut. He didn't deserve to bear the brunt of her resentment towards Richard. She'd wasted enough time analysing and self-flagellating and fuelling her anger. That was all she'd been doing for the last year since he'd died—speculating, brooding over a whole lot of pointless 'what-ifs'.

What if she'd known about the affair?

What if she'd stood up to him and for herself, rather than keeping up appearances for the sake of his business?

What if she'd travelled to India with her mum when Khushi had first asked her years ago? Would any of that have changed her life for the better?

'I didn't mean to rehash any painful stuff for you.'

Shaking her head, she wished the simple action could wipe away her awful memories.

'Not your fault. It's not like I don't think about it every day anyway.'

He searched her face for—what? Confirmation she wasn't still grieving, wasn't so heartbroken she couldn't return to the workforce after wasting the last few years playing society hostess to a man who hadn't given a damn about her?

What he saw in her expression had his eyes narrowing in speculation.

'You should get away. A break, before you get sucked back into the full-time rat race. Take it from me, a certified workaholic, once you hit the ground running you won't have a minute to yourself.'

She opened her mouth to protest, to tell him that as a virtual stranger he could stick his advice, but he held a finger to her lips to silence her, the impact of his simple action slugging her all the way to her toes. It had to be the impulse to tell him to shut up rather than the brush of his finger against her lips causing her belly to twist like a pretzel.

'A piece of advice. Seeing you six months ago, seeing you now, you've held together remarkably well considering what you've been through, but it's time.'

He dropped his finger, thank goodness.

'For what?'

'Time for *you*. Time to put aside your grief. Move on.'

He gestured to the stack of folders on the table between them. 'From what I've heard, you're a damn good food critic, one of Melbourne's best. But honestly? The way you are right now, the tears I saw when I made a simple flyaway comment about an oven, what you just said about thinking about Rich every day, holding down a regular job would be tough. You'd end up not being able to tell the difference between steak tartare and well-done Wagyu beef, let alone write about it.'

She should hate him for what he'd just said. It hurt, all of it. But then, the truth often did.

'You finished?'

She knew it was the wrong thing to say to a guy like him the instant the words left her mouth, for it sounded like a challenge, something he would never back away from.

'Not by a long shot.'

Before she could blink, his mouth swooped, capturing hers in a heartbeat—a soul-reviving, soul-destroying, terrifying kiss that stirred her dormant body to life, setting it alight in a way she'd never dreamed possible.

She burned, swayed, as he changed the pressure, his lips coaxing a response—a response she couldn't give in her right mind.

But she wasn't in her right mind, hadn't been from the second his lips touched hers and, before she could think, rationalise, overanalyse, she kissed him back, an outpouring of pent-up passion from a shattered ego starving for an ounce of attention.

Her heart sang with the joy of it, before stalling as the implication of what she'd just done crashed over her in a sickening wave.

Ethan, the practised playboy, Richard's friend, a guy she barely knew, had kissed her.

And she'd let him.

Slivers of ice chilled her to the bone as she tore her mouth from his, staring at him in wide-eyed horror.

She couldn't speak, couldn't form the words to express how furious she was with him.

Though her anger was misplaced and she knew it. She was furious with herself for responding; worse, for enjoying it.

'Don't expect me to apologise for that.'

His eyes glittered with desire and she shivered, petrified yet exhilarated to be the focus of all that passion for a passing moment in time.

'That should show you you're a vibrant woman who needs to start living again. You should start by doing one thing you've always wanted to do before you return to work.'

He made sense, damn him, prove-a-point kiss and all. And while her body still trembled from the impact of that alarming kiss and her astounding response, at least it had served a purpose. If she'd been prevaricating about taking a trip before, he'd blasted her doubts sky-high now.

She had to go, had to leave Ambrosia, for facing him in the future would be beyond mortifying.

Mustering a haughty glare that only served to make his eyes gleam more, she shook her head.

'I can't believe you just did that.'

Shrugging, he sat back and crossed his ankles, the supremely confident male and proud of it. 'Many people can't believe a lot of the stuff I do, so don't sweat it. Let's talk about this trip of yours.'

'Let's not,' she snapped, annoyed by his persistence, more annoyed by the glimmer of anticipation racing through her.

She'd already been thinking about a trip herself. Specifically, the trip she'd booked with her mum. The itinerary they'd planned was tucked away in her old music box at home, the one her dad had given her when she'd been three, the one with the haunting tune that never failed to make her cry when she thought of all she'd lost.

She'd contemplated taking the trip on her own for all of two seconds before slamming the idea. The trip would've been emotional enough with her mum by her side but without her?

Her eyelids prickled just thinking about it and she blinked, wishing Ethan would put that devilish smile to good use elsewhere and butt out of her business.

'Think sun, sand and surf. Somewhere hot, tropical, the opposite of blustery Melbourne at the moment.'

Considering her toes were icy within her boots and she couldn't feel her fingers, the thought of all that heat was tempting.

India would be perfect, would fit the bill in every way. Buoyed by an urge to escape, she rummaged through the top folder, wondering if a brochure was still there. She'd had hundreds of the things when they'd been planning the trip, immersing herself in India, from the stone-walled city of Jodhpur—home of the Mehrangarh Fort and the grand palaces of Moti Mahal, Sheesh Mahal, Phool Mahal, Sileh Khana and Daulat Khana—to Ranthambhore National Park, India's best wildlife sanctuary, to see the majestic tigers, eager to see as much of the intriguing country as possible.

She'd kept them everywhere, hiding them from Richard when he'd first expressed his displeasure at letting her out of his sight, tucking them into books and magazines and her work stuff.

Suddenly, she really wanted to find one, wanted to see if the tiny flame of excitement flickering to life could be fanned into her actually doing this.

Flicking to the front of the folder, she dug her fingers into the plastic pocket and almost yelled for joy when she pulled out a glossy brochure featuring the Taj Mahal and the legendary Palace on Wheels train on the front.

'You're one of those incredibly annoying, painfully persistent guys who won't give up, so here. Take a look.'

She handed him the brochure.

His eyes widened. 'India?'

'I planned to visit a few years ago but it never happened.' She stared at the brochure, captivated by the exoticism of it all.

She should've thrown this out ages ago, but as long as she hung onto it, as long as the promise of her mum's dream trip was still a reality, albeit a distant one, it was as if she were keeping alive her mum's spirit.

Every time she found a brochure tucked away somewhere she felt connected to her mum, remembering the day she'd picked them up as a sixtieth birthday surprise and they'd pored over them during an Indian feast of spicy, palate-searing beef vindaloo, masala prawns, parathas and biryani, her favourite spiced rice, rich in flavoursome lamb.

They'd laughed, they'd cried, they'd hugged each other and jumped up and down like a couple of excited kids heading away on their first camping trip.

She'd wanted to explore the part of her history she knew little about, wanted to take the special journey with her mum.

Richard may have put paid to that dream and, while she'd love to take the trip now, it just wouldn't be the same without Khushi.

'Guess I should explore all my options first.'

She fiddled with the brochure, folding the ends into tiny triangles, absentmindedly smoothing out the creases again.

'Uh-uh.' He snapped his fingers. 'You're going to take the trip.'

Her eyes flew to his, startled by his absolute conviction, as a lump of sorrow lodged in her throat and she cleared it. 'I can't.'

She'd find another destination, somewhere she wouldn't have a deluge of memories drowning her, missing her mum every step of the way.

He stabbed at the brochure. 'You can. Clear your head, make a fresh start.'

She shook her head, using her hair to shield her face. 'I can't do this trip alone. I'd planned to take it with my mum. This was her trip—'

Her voice cracked and she slid off her chair and headed for the fireplace, holding her hands out to the crackling warmth, wishing it could seep deep inside to the coldest, loneliest parts of her soul.

'You won't be alone.'

He came up behind her, the heat from the fire nothing on the warmth radiating from him—a solid, welcoming warmth she wished she could lean into before giving herself a swift mental slap.

Stepping around in front of her, he stared at her, direct, intense, the indigo flecks in his blue eyes gleaming in the reflected firelight.

'You won't be alone because I'm coming with you.'

'But—'

'No buts.'

He held up a hand. 'I'm going to India anyway, to lure Delhi's best chef to work here.'

One finger bent as he counted off his first point.

'You need company.'

The second finger went down.

'And, lastly, I've always wanted to do the Palace on Wheels trip and never got around to it so, this way, you're doing me a favour.'

Her eyes narrowed. 'How's that?'

'I hear it's an amazing journey, best shared with a beautiful companion.'

His smile could've lit the Arts Centre spire, damn pirate, and in that second she snapped to her senses.

What was she doing? He'd be the last person she'd take a trip with, the last guy to accompany her anywhere considering he'd just kissed her and turned some of that legendary charm onto her. Beautiful companion, indeed.

'Your mum would've wanted you to go.'

Oh, he was good.

Worse, he was right.

Khushi would've wanted her to go, to visit Goa and the

beach where she'd met her father, to take a magical train journey through India's heartland, to visit the Taj Mahal, something her mum had craved her entire life.

She wanted to rediscover her identity. Maybe a link to her past was the best way to do it?

Staggered by her second impulse in as many minutes—she determinedly ignored the first, foolishly responding to that kiss—she slapped the brochure against her opposite palm, mind made up.

'You're right, I'm taking the trip.'

She fixed him with a glare that lost its impact when her lower lip wobbled at the enormity of what she was contemplating.

'That's great. We'll—'

'I'm taking the trip. *Alone.*'

'But—'

'I don't even know you,' she said, wishing she hadn't stayed, terrified how that incredible kiss had made her feel for a fleeting moment.

It had obviously given him the wrong idea. What sort of a guy went from a cool acquaintance to kissing her to thinking she'd go away with him?

Maybe she was overreacting, reading more into the sudden twinkle in his sea-blue eyes and his scarily sexy smile?

Leaning forward a fraction, invading her personal space with a potent masculinity she found disconcerting, he lowered his voice. 'That's what the trip is for. Loads of time to get to know one another.'

She wasn't overreacting. He was chatting her up!

Sending him a withering glance that would've extinguished the fire at her back, she headed for the table and slipped her trench coat on.

'Thanks for the offer but I like being on my own.'

When he opened his mouth to respond, she held up a hand. 'I like it that way.'

Before he could protest any further, she slung her bag over her shoulder and pointed to the stack of folders. 'I'll come back for these tomorrow.'

His knowing gaze followed her towards the door and she knew he'd get the last word in.

'Going solo is highly overrated.'

Halting with her hand on the door, she glanced over her shoulder, startled by the ravenous hunger in his greedy gaze.

'Someone like you would think that.'

Rather than annoying him, a triumphant grin lit his face, as if she'd just paid him a compliment.

'Next to business, dating is what I do best so I guess that makes me qualified to pass judgement.'

'Overqualified, from what I hear.'

His grin widened and she mentally clapped a hand over her mouth.

What was she doing, discussing his personal life? It had nothing to do with her and, while she valued the opportunity he'd given her in using Ambrosia as a base to relaunch her career, what he did in his spare time meant diddly-squat to her.

Propped against the bar, he appeared more like a pirate than ever: all he needed was a bandanna and eye patch to complete the overconfident look.

'You sure you wouldn't like me to tag along?'

'Positive.'

She walked out, somewhat satisfied by the slamming door.

Take a trip with a playboy pirate like Ethan Brooks?

She'd rather walk the plank.

CHAPTER TWO

'WHAT the hell are you doing here?'

Ethan grinned at Tamara's shell-shocked expression as he strolled towards her on the platform at Safdarjung Station.

'You mean here as in New Delhi or here as in this station?'

Her eyes narrowed, spitting emerald fire. 'Don't play smart with me. Why are you here?'

'Business. I told you I'm a workaholic. The Delhi chef wasn't interested so there's a chef in Udaipur I'd like to lure to Ambrosia. Rather than commute by boring planes I thought I'd take the scenic route, so here I am.'

By her folded arms, compressed lips and frown, she wasn't giving an inch.

'And this *business trip* just happened to coincide when I'm taking the trip. How convenient.'

'Pure coincidence.'

He couldn't keep the grin off his face, which only served to rile her further. That smile may well have seduced every socialite in Melbourne, but she wasn't about to succumb to its practised charm. He laid a hand on her arm; she stiffened and deliberately stepped away.

'If it makes you feel any better, it's a big train and the trip only lasts a week.'

'It doesn't make me feel better.'

If the Tamara he'd seen all too infrequently over the last few years was beautiful, a furious Tamara was stunning—and vindicated why he'd booked this trip in the first place.

It was time.

He was through waiting.

'Why don't we stop quibbling and enjoy this fanfare?'

He thought she'd never relent but, after shooting him another exasperated glare, she turned towards their welcoming committee.

'Pretty impressive, huh?'

She nodded, maintaining a silence he found disconcerting. He preferred her annoyed and fiery rather than quiet and brooding.

Only one way to get her out of this huff. Turn on the charm.

'Just think, all this for you. Talented musicians playing tabla as you board the train, young Indian girls placing flower garlands around your neck, being greeted by your own personal bearer for your carriage. Nothing like a proper welcome?'

The beginnings of a smile softened her lips as a bearer placed a fancy red turban on his head as a gift.

'Looks like I'm not the only one getting welcomed.'

He wobbled his head, doing a precarious balancing act with the turban and she finally laughed.

'Okay, you can stay.'

He executed a fancy little bow and she held up a hand.

'But remember I like being on my own.'

He didn't. Being alone was highly overrated and something he'd set about compensating for the moment he'd had his first pay cheque or two.

He liked being surrounded by people, enjoyed the bustle of a restaurant, thrived on the hub of the business world and relished dating beautiful women. Most of all, he liked being in control. And, finally, this was his chance to take control of his desire for Tamara.

He'd kept his distance while Rich was alive, had respected

his friend's marriage. But Rich was gone and his pull towards this incredible woman was stronger than ever.

He wanted her, had wanted her from the first moment they'd met and had avoided her because of it.

Not any more.

That impulsive kiss had changed everything.

He'd forfeited control by giving in to his driving compulsion for her, hated the powerlessness she'd managed to wreak with her startling response, and he'd be damned if he sat back and did nothing.

Having her walk away had left her firmly in charge and that was unacceptable. He was here to reclaim control, to prove he couldn't lose it over a woman, beautiful as she may be.

Seduction was one thing, but finding himself floundering by the power of a kiss quite another.

Clawing his way to the top had taught him persistence, determination and diligence. When he wanted something in the business world, he made it happen by dogged perseverance and a healthy dose of charm.

Now, he wanted Tamara.

She didn't stand a chance.

Tapping his temple, he said, 'I'll try to remember. But, you know, this heat can play havoc with one's memory and—'

'Come on, let's board. Once you're safely ensconced in the lap of luxury, maybe that memory will return.'

'You make me sound like a snob.'

'Aren't you? Being Australia's top restaurateur and all.' She snapped her fingers. 'Oh, that's right. You're just the average run-of-the-mill billionaire who happens to rival Wolfgang Puck and Nobu for top restaurants around the world. Nothing snobby about you.'

'Come on, funny girl. Time to board.'

She smiled and, as he picked up their hand luggage and followed the porter, he could hardly believe the change in Tam.

Sure, there was still a hint of fragility about her, the glimpse of sorrow clinging to her like the humidity here, but it looked as if India agreed with her. After she'd finished berating him, she'd smiled more in the last few minutes than she had in the odd times he'd seen her.

'You know I have my own compartment?'

She rolled her eyes. 'Of course.'

'I wouldn't want you compromising my reputation.'

She smiled again and something twanged in the vicinity of his heart. She'd had the ability to do that to him from the very beginning, from the first time he'd met her—an hour after she'd met Richard, worse luck.

She'd been smitten by then, with eyes only for the loud, larger-than-life chef, and he'd subdued his controlling instincts to sweep her away.

Neither of them had ever known of his desire for the woman he couldn't have; he'd made sure of it. But keeping his distance was a thing of the past and the next seven days loomed as intriguing.

'Your reputation is safe with me. I'm sure all those society heiresses and vapid, thin models you date on a revolving-door basis are well aware this boring old widow is no competition.'

'You're not boring and you're certainly not old.'

As for the women he dated, there was a reason he chose the no-commitment, out-for-a-good-time-not-a-long-time type. A damn good one.

The smile hovering about her lips faded as fast as his hopes to keep it there.

'But I am a widow.'

And, while he'd hated the pain she must've gone through after Rich died, the struggle to get her life back on an even keel, he couldn't help but be glad she was now single.

Did that make him heartless? Maybe, but his past had taught him to be a realist and he never wasted time lying to himself or others. Discounting the way he'd kept his attraction for Tam a secret all these years, of course.

'Maybe it's time you came out of mourning?'

He expected her to recoil, to send him the contemptuous stare she'd given him after he'd kissed her. Instead, she cocked her head to one side, studying him.

'Are you always this blunt?'

'Always.'

'So you'll ignore me if I tell you to butt out, just like you did by gatecrashing my trip?'

He feigned hurt, smothering his grin with difficulty. 'Gatecrashing's a bit harsh. I told you, I'm here on business.'

He only just caught her muttered, 'Monkey business.'

She fidgeted with her handbag, her fingers plucking at the leather strap as she rocked her weight from foot to foot, and he almost took pity on her before banishing that uncharacteristic emotion in a second.

He had to have her, was driven by a primal urge he had no control over and, to do that, he needed to get her to look at him as a man rather than a bug in her soup.

With a bit of luck and loads of charm, he intended to make good on the unspoken promise of their first kiss—a promise of so much more.

'You're not still hung up over that kiss, are you? Because, if you are—'

'I'm not. It's forgotten.'

Her gorgeous blush belied her quick negation and had him itching to push the boundaries. But he'd gained ground by having her accept his presence so quickly and he'd be a fool to take things too far on the first day.

'Forgotten, huh? Must be losing my touch.'

'There's nothing wrong with—'

He smothered a triumphant grin. He may have lost his mind and kissed her to prove she needed to start living again but her eager response had blown him away. And fuelled his need for her, driving him to crazy things like taking time off work, something he rarely did, to pursue her.

'Let's put it down to a distant memory and move on, shall we?'

To his horror, her eyes filled with pain, which hit him hard, like a slug to the guts, and he tugged her close without thinking, enveloping her in his arms.

'Hell, Tam, I'm sorry. I shouldn't have mentioned memories.'

She braced herself against his chest, her palms splayed, and his body reacted in an instant, heat searing his veins as he cradled a soft armful of woman.

She sniffled and he tightened his hold, rather than his first instinct to release her in the hope of putting an instant dampener on his errant libido.

His hand skimmed her hair, thick and dark like molten molasses, soothing strokes designed to comfort. But, hot on the heels of his thoughts of how much he wanted her, his fingers itched to delve into the shiny, dark mass and get caught up in it. He could hold her like this all night long.

'You okay?'

Ethan pulled away, needing to establish some distance between them, not liking her power over him. He didn't do comfort. He never had a hankie in his pocket or a host of placating platitudes or a shoulder to cry on. He didn't do consoling hugs; he did passionate embraces.

So what had happened in the last few minutes? What was it about this woman that undermined him?

'Uh-huh.'

She managed a watery smile before straightening her shoulders and lifting her head in the classic coping pose he'd seen her exhibit at Rich's funeral and his admiration shot up another few notches.

How she'd handled her grief after the initial shock of Rich's heart attack, burying herself in the business side of things, sorting through legalities with him, only to approach him several months later for the use of Ambrosia to get her career back on track, had all served to fuel his respect for this amazing woman.

Quite simply, she was incredible and he wanted her with a staggering fierceness that clawed at him even now, when he was left analysing how he'd let his control slip again in her intoxicating presence.

'I can see you're still hurting but if you ever want to talk about Rich, remember the good times, I'm here for you, okay?'

Maybe, if she opened up to him, he could encourage her to get it all out of her system and move on. Highly altruistic but then, when was he anything but?

To his surprise, she wrinkled her nose and he knew it had little to do with the pungent odours of diesel fumes, spices and human sweat swirling around them.

'Honestly? I don't want to talk about Richard. I'm done grieving.'

A spark of defiance lit her eyes, turning them from soft moss-green to sizzling emerald in a second. 'I want to enjoy this trip, then concentrate on my future.'

He'd never seen her like this: resolute, determined, a woman reborn.

He'd seen Tam the society wife, the perfect hostess, the astute businesswoman, the grieving widow, but never like this and a part of him was glad. Releasing the past was cathartic, would help her to move on and he really wanted her to do that on this trip. With him.

'Sounds like a plan.'

Her answering smile sent another sizzle of heat through him and he clenched his hands to stop himself from reaching out and pulling her close.

Plenty of time for that.

* * *

Tamara lay down on the bed, stretched her arms over her head and smiled.

The rocking motion of the train, the clickety-clack as it bounced its way out of Delhi, the aroma of marigolds and masala chai—the delicious tea, fragrant with cardamons—overloaded her senses, lulled her while making her want to jump up and twirl around from the sheer rush of it.

For the first time in years, she felt free. Free to do whatever she wanted, be whoever she chose. And it felt great. In fact, it felt downright fantastic.

While she'd once loved Richard, had desperately craved the type of marriage her folks had had, nothing came close to this exhilarating freedom.

She'd spent months playing the grieving widow after Richard had suffered that fatal heart attack, had submerged her humiliation, her bitterness, her pain.

Yet behind her serene, tear-stained face she'd seethed: at him for making a mockery of their marriage, at herself for being a gullible fool and for caring what people thought even after he was gone.

She hadn't given two hoots about social propriety until she'd married him, had laughed at his obsession with appearances. But she'd soon learned he was serious and, with his face plastered over every newspaper, magazine and TV channel on a regular basis, she'd slipped into the routine of being the perfect little wife he'd wanted.

While his perfect little mistress had been stashed away in a luxurious beach house at Cape Schanck, just over an hour's drive from Melbourne's CBD where they'd lived.

Damn him.

She sat bolt upright, annoyed she'd let bitter memories tarnish the beginning of this incredible journey, her gaze falling on the single bed next to hers. The single bed her mum should've been occupying while regaling her with exotic tales of Goa and its beaches, Colva beach where she'd met her dad, her love at first sight for a scruffy Aussie backpacker with a twinkle in his eyes and a ready smile.

Tales of the Taj Mahal, the monument she'd always wanted to see but never had the chance. Tales of an India filled with hospitable people and mouth-watering food, imparting recipes in that lilting sing-song accent that had soothed her as a young girl when the nightmares of losing her dad would wake her screaming and sweat-drenched.

Khushi should've been here. This was her trip.

Instead, Tamara swiped an angry hand across her eyes, dashing her tears away.

She wasn't going to cry any more. She'd made herself that promise back in Melbourne when she'd decided to take this trip.

And while she knew her heart would break at every turn on the track, at every fabulous place she visited, wishing her mum was here to share it with her, she should be thankful she'd taken another positive step in getting her life in order.

She was through cringing with shame and humiliation at what Richard had put her through, done feeling sorry for herself.

This was *her* time.

Time for a new life, a new beginning.

So what the heck was Ethan Brooks doing here, muscling in on her new start?

Ethan, with his smiling eyes and that deadly smile. Where was the famed hard-ass, hard-nosed businessman? Instead, Ethan the pirate, the player, the playboy, had swaggered along on this trip and while every self-preservation instinct screamed for her to stay away, she couldn't be that rude.

He'd helped her with the legalities surrounding Ambrosia after Richard's death, had smoothed the way for her to re-enter the workforce by allowing her to use Ambrosia as a base. She owed him.

But he had her rattled.

She preferred him business-oriented, juggling a briefcase, a laptop and barking instructions on a mobile phone at the same time, barely acknowledging her presence with an absentminded nod as he strutted into Ambrosia.

He'd practically ignored her when their paths had crossed while Richard had been around, his head always buried in financial statements and yearly projections, and that had been fine with her.

He made her uncomfortable and it had nothing to do with the fact that they didn't really know each other. The shift had happened when they'd met to sort out Ambrosia's ownership, those two times when she'd noticed things: like the way he cracked pistachio nuts way too loudly, flipping them in the air and catching them in his open mouth, how much he loved Shiraz Grenache and sticky date pudding and the North Melbourne Football Club.

Trivial things, inconsequential things that meant little, but the fact that she'd noticed and remembered them annoyed her.

As for that kiss…she picked up a pillow and smothered a groan, hating how it haunted her, hating how she'd dreamed of it, hating how the dream had developed and morphed into so much more than a kiss, leaving her writhing and panting and sweat-drenched on waking.

She didn't want to remember any of it, didn't want to remember his expertise, his spontaneity, his ability to dredge a response from her deepest, darkest soul, better left untouched.

But she did remember, every breathtaking moment, and while her head had slammed the door on the memory of her temporary insanity, her body was clamouring for more.

Now this.

Him being here, all suave and charming and too gorgeous for his own good, was making her nervous. Very nervous.

She didn't need anyone in her new life, least of all a smooth tycoon like Ethan Brooks.

As for her wayward thoughts lately in the wee small hours of the morning when she lay sleepless, staring up at the ceiling and trying to regain focus to her meandering life, she'd banish them along with her anger at Richard.

Wondering what would've happened if she'd gone for Ethan rather than Richard that fateful night she'd entered Ambrosia four years earlier was a waste of time.

Now was her chance to put the past to rest and concentrate on her future.

CHAPTER THREE

'TELL me you're not working.'

Ethan pointed at the small blue notebook tucked discreetly under her linen serviette—obviously not discreetly enough.

Ignoring him, Tamara sliced a vegetable pakora in two and dipped it in the tamarind sauce, her taste buds hankering for that first delicious taste of crispy vegetables battered in chickpea flour and dunked in the sour, piquant sauce.

'Fine, I won't tell you.'

He shook his head, laughed, before helping himself to a meat samosa from the entrée platter between them.

'You're supposed to be on holiday.'

'I'm supposed to be getting back to work soon and I need the practice.'

Resting his knife and fork on his plate, he focused his too-blue gaze on her.

'You're an expert critic. One of Australia's best. Skills like that don't disappear because you've had a year or so off.'

'Two years,' she said, quelling the surge of resentment at what she'd given up for Richard. 'Despite the last six months at Ambrosia, I'm still rusty. The sooner I get back into it, the easier it'll be.'

She bit down on the pakora, chewed thoughtfully, knowing

there was another reason she had her trusty notebook within jotting reach.

The minute she'd opened her compartment door to find Ethan on the other side in charcoal casual pants and open-necked white shirt, his gaze appreciative and his smile as piratical as always, she'd had to clamp down on the irrational urge to slam the door in his face and duck for cover.

It had been her stupid thoughts earlier of *what if* that had done it, that had made her aware of him as a man—a gorgeous, charming man—rather than just her…what was he? A business acquaintance? A travelling companion? A friend?

She didn't like the last two options: they implied a closeness she didn't want. But they'd moved past the acquaintance stage the moment he'd kissed her and there was no going back.

She didn't want to have these thoughts, didn't want to acknowledge the sexy crease in his left cheek, the tiny lines at the corners of his eyes that added character to his face, the endearingly ruffled dark hair that curled over his collar.

She'd never noticed those things before or, if she had, hadn't experienced this…this…*buzz* or whatever the strange feeling coursing through her body was that made her want to bury her nose in her notebook for the duration of dinner and not look up.

That might take care of day one, but what about the rest of the week as the Palace on Wheels took them on an amazing journey through Rajasthan?

Ethan was Richard's friend, reason enough she couldn't trust him, no matter how much he poured on the charm.

She'd fallen for Richard because he'd been safe and look at the devastation he'd wreaked. What would letting her guard down around a powerful, compelling guy like Ethan do?

Inwardly shuddering at the thought, she reached for the notebook at the same instant that he stilled her hand. Her gaze flew to his, her heart beating uncharacteristically fast.

He'd touched her again. First that hug on the station and now this. Though this time her pulse tripped and her skin prickled as determination flared in his eyes, while fear crept through her.

Fear they'd somehow changed the boundaries of their nebulous relationship without realising, fear they could never go back, fear she could lose focus of what she wanted out of this trip and why if she was crazy enough to acknowledge the shift between them, let alone do anything about it.

'This is the first holiday you've taken in years. Don't be so hard on yourself.'

He squeezed her hand, released it and she exhaled, unaware she'd been holding her breath.

'You'll get back into the swing of things soon enough. Once I coerce the super-talented Indian chef to leave the Lake Palace and work at Ambrosia, critiquing his meals will keep you busy for months.'

'You're too kind.'

She meant it. He'd never been anything other than kind to her, helping her with Richard's business stuff, arranging a special table for her at Ambrosia away from the ravenous crowd so she could sample the food and write her critiques in peace.

But kind didn't come close to describing the hungry gleam in his eyes or the subtle shift that had taken place between them a few moments ago—dangerous, more like it. Dangerous and exciting and terrifying.

He screwed up his nose, stabbing a seekh kebab from the entrée platter and moving it across to his plate. 'You know, *kind* ranks right up there with *nice* for guys. Something we don't want to hear.'

'Fine. You're a cold, heartless businessman who takes no prisoners. Better?'

'Much.'

His bold smile had her scrambling for her notebook,

flipping it open to a crisp new blank page, pen poised. 'Now, take a bite of that kebab and tell me what you think.'

He cut the kebab—spiced lamb moulded into a sausage shape around a skewer and cooked to perfection in a tandoor oven—and chewed a piece, emitting a satisfied moan that had her focusing on his lips rather than her notebook.

'Fantastic.'

He screwed up his eyes, took another bite, chewed thoughtfully. 'I can taste ginger, a hint of garlic and cumin.'

He polished off the rest with a satisfied pat of his tummy, a very lean, taut tummy from what she could see of it outlined beneath his shirt.

Great, there she went again, noticing things she never normally would. This wasn't good—not good at all.

Pressing the pen to the page so hard it tore a hole through to the paper underneath, she focused on her scrawl rather than anywhere in the vicinity of Ethan's lips or fabulous tummy.

'Not bad, but that's why you're the guy who owns the restaurants and I'm lucky enough to eat in them and write about the food.'

He smiled, pointed at her notebook. 'Go ahead, then. Tell me all about the wonders of the seekh kebab.'

She glanced at her notes, a thrill of excitement shooting through her. She loved her job, every amazing moment of it, from sampling food, savouring it, titillating her taste buds until she couldn't put pen to paper fast enough to expound its joys, to trying new concoctions and sharing hidden delights with fellow food addicts.

As for Indian food, she'd been raised on the stuff and there was nothing like it in the world.

'The keema—' he raised an eyebrow and she clarified '—lamb mince is subtly spiced with an exotic blend of garam masala, dried mango powder, carom seeds, raw papaya paste, with a healthy dose of onion, black pepper, ginger, garlic and a pinch of nutmeg.'

'You got all that from one bite?'

She bit her lip as she pushed the notebook away, unable to contain her laughter as he took another bite, trying to figure out how she did it.

'My mum used to make them. I memorised the ingredients when I was ten years old.'

Her laughter petered out as she remembered what else had happened when she was ten—her dad had dropped dead at work, a cerebral aneurysm, and the world as she'd known it had ceased to exist.

She'd loved listening to her parents chat over dinner, their tales of adventure, the story of how they'd met. She'd always craved a once-in-a-lifetime romance like theirs. Richard hadn't been it. Now she'd never find it.

'Hey, you okay?'

She nodded, bit down hard on her bottom lip to stop it quivering. 'I still miss my mum.'

He hesitated before covering her hand with his. 'Tell me about her.'

Tell him what?

How her mum used to braid her waist-length hair into plaits every day for school, never once snagging the brush or rushing her?

How she'd concocted an Indian feast out of rice, lentils, a few spices and little else?

How she'd loved her, protected her, been there for her in every way after her dad had died?

She couldn't put half of what she was feeling into words let alone articulate the devastating sadness reaching down to her barren soul that she was here on this train and Khushi wasn't.

Besides, did she really want to discuss her private memories with him? Revealing her innermost thoughts implied trust and that was one thing she had in short supply, especially with a guy hell-bent on charming her.

'Tell me one of the favourite things you used to do together.'

'Watch Bollywood films,' she said on a sigh, reluctant to talk but surprised by his deeper, caring side, a side too tempting to ignore.

The memory alleviated some of the sadness permeating her thoughts as she remembered many a Sunday afternoon curled up on the worn suede couch in the family room, a plate of jalebis, milk burfi and Mysore pak—delicious Indian sweets made with loads of sugar, milk and butter—between them, as they were riveted to the latest Shah Rukh Khan blockbuster— India's equivalent to Hollywood's top A-list celebrity.

They'd laugh at the over-the-top theatrics, sigh at the vivid romance and natter about the beautiful, vibrant saris.

Raised in Melbourne with an Aussie dad, she'd never felt a huge connection to India, even though her mum's Goan blood flowed in her veins. But for those precious Sunday afternoons she'd been transported to another world—a world filled with people and colour and magic.

'What else?'

'We loved going to the beach.'

His encouragement had her wanting to talk about memories she'd long submerged, memories she only resurrected in the privacy of her room at night when she'd occasionally cry herself to sleep.

Richard's sympathy had been short-lived. He'd told her to get over her grief and focus on more important things, like hosting yet another dinner party for his friends.

That had been three years ago, three long years as their marriage had continued its downward spiral, as her famous husband had slowly revealed a cruel side that, to this day, left her questioning her own judgement in marrying someone like that in the first place.

He'd never actually hit her but the verbal and psychological abuse had been as bruising, as painful, as devastating
as if he had.

Ethan must've sensed her withdrawal, for he continued
prodding. 'Any particular beach?'

She shook her head, the corners of her mouth curving
upwards for the first time since she'd started reminiscing
about her mum.

'It wasn't the location as such. Anywhere would do as
long as there was sand and sun and ocean.'

They'd visited most of the beaches along the Great Ocean
Road after her dad had died: Anglesea, Torquay, Lorne,
Apollo Bay. She'd known why. The beach had reminded
Khushi of meeting her dad for the first time, the story she'd
heard so many times.

Her mum had been trying to hold on to precious memories,
maybe recreate them in her head, but whatever the reason
she'd been happy to go along for the ride. They'd made a great
team and she would've given anything for her mum to pop
into the dining car right now with a wide smile on her face
and her hair perched in a plain bun on top of her head.

'Sounds great.'

'It's why I'm spending a week in Goa after the train. It was
to be the highlight of our trip.'

She took a sip of water, cleared her throat of emotion. 'My
folks met on Colva Beach. Dad was an Aussie backpacker
taking a year off after med school. Mum was working for one
of the hotels there.'

She sighed, swirled the water in her glass. 'Love at first
sight, apparently. My dad used to call Mum his exotic princess
from the Far East, Mum used to say Dad was full of it.'

'Why didn't she ever go back? After he passed away?'

Shrugging, she toyed with her cutlery, the familiar guilt
gnawing at her. 'Because of me, I guess. She wanted me to

have every opportunity education-wise, wanted to raise me as an Australian, as my dad would've wanted.'

'But you're half Indian too. This country is a part of who you are.'

'Honestly? I don't know who I am any more.'

The admission sounded as lost, as forlorn, as she felt almost every minute of every day.

She'd vocalised her greatest fear.

She didn't know who she was, had lost her identity when she'd married Richard. She'd been playing a role for ever: first the dutiful wife, then the grieving widow. But it was all an act. All of it.

She'd become like him, had cared about appearances even at the end when she'd been screaming inside at the injustice of being abused and lied to and cheated on for so long while shedding the appropriate tears at his funeral.

Ethan stood, came around to her side of the table and crouched down, sliding his arm around her waist while tilting her chin to make her look him in the eye with his other hand.

'I know who you are. You're an incredible woman with the world at her feet.' He brushed her cheek in a gentle caress that had tears seeping out of the corners of her eyes. 'Don't you ever, ever forget how truly amazing you are.'

With emotion clogging her throat and tears blinding her, she couldn't speak let alone see what was coming next so when his lips brushed hers in a soft, tender kiss she didn't have time to think, didn't have time to react.

Instead, her eyelids fluttered shut, her aching heart healed just a little as her soul blossomed with wonder at having a man like Ethan Brooks on her side.

His kiss lingered long after he pulled away, long after he stared at her for an interminable moment with shock in the indigo depths of his eyes, long after he murmured the words, 'You're special, that's who you are.'

A small part of her wanted to believe him.

A larger part wanted to recreate the magic of that all-too-brief kiss, as for the second time in a week she felt like a woman.

The largest part of her recoiled in horror as she realised she'd just been kissed—again—by the last man she could get close to, ever.

Ethan sprang to his feet and catapulted back to his chair on the opposite side of the table, desperate for space.

She'd done it again.

Left him reeling with her power to undermine his control.

Those damn tears had done it, tugging at nonexistent heart-strings, urging him to kiss her, to comfort her, making him *feel,* damn it.

He'd been a fool, urging her to talk about her mum. He should've known she'd get emotional, should've figured he'd want to play the hero and help slay her demons.

'You're good at that.'

His gaze snapped to hers, expecting wariness, thrown by her curiosity, as if she couldn't quite figure him out.

'At what?'

'Knowing when to say the right thing, knowing how to make a girl feel good about herself.'

'Practice, I guess.'

If his offhand shrug hadn't made her recoil, his callous comment did the trick.

He'd just lumped her in with the rest of his conquests—something she'd hate, something he hated.

But it had to be done.

He needed distance right now, needed to slam his emotional barriers back in place and muster the control troops to the battlefront.

'Lucky me.'

Her sarcasm didn't sock him half as much as her expression, a potent mix of disappointment and derision.

He had to take control of this situation before it got out of hand and he ended up alienating her completely, and all because he was furious at himself for getting too close.

'Before I put you off your food with any more of my renowned comforting techniques, why don't we finish off this entrée? I've heard the lentil curry to come is something special.'

She nodded, her disappointment slugging him anew as she toyed with the food on her plate.

Establishing emotional distance was paramount. He'd come close to losing sight of his seduction goal moments before but steeling his heart was one thing, carrying it through with a disillusioned Tam sitting opposite another.

'What do you think of the potato bondas?'

An innocuous question, a question designed to distract her from his abrupt turnaround and get them back on the road of comfortable small talk.

However, as she raised her gaze from her plate and met his, the accusatory hurt reached down to his soul, as if he were the worst kind of louse.

For a moment he thought she'd call him on his brusque switch from comforting to cool. Instead, she searched his face, her mouth tightening as if what she saw confirmed her worst opinion of him.

'They're good.'

Hating feeling out of his depth, he pushed the platter towards her. 'Another?'

'No, thanks.'

They lapsed into silence, an awkward silence fraught with unspoken words—words he couldn't bring himself to say for fear of the growing intimacy between them.

Being here with her wasn't about establishing an emotional connection, it was about seducing the one woman he'd wanted for years and couldn't have.

He needed to keep it that way, for the other option scared the life out of him.

CHAPTER FOUR

ETHAN focused on the tour guide as he droned on about Hawa Mahal, the Palace of the Winds.

Structurally, the place was amazing, like a giant candy-floss beehive with its tiers of windows staggered in red and pink sandstone.

Architecture usually fascinated him—every restaurant he purchased around the world was chosen for position as well as aesthetics—but, while the guide pointed out the white borders and motifs of Jaipur's multi-layered palace, he sneaked glances at the woman standing next to him, apparently engrossed in what the guy had to say. While he, Ethan, was engrossed in her.

As the train had wound its way from New Delhi to the 'Pink City' of Jaipur overnight, he'd lain awake, hands clasped behind his head, staring at the ceiling.

For hours. Long, endless hours, replaying that comfy scene over dinner and cursing himself for being a fool.

He'd overstepped with the cosy chat about her mum, had panicked and back-pedalled as a result.

The upshot? Tam's barriers had slammed down, shutting him out, obliterating what little ground he'd made since she'd forgiven him for crashing her trip.

Stupid, stupid, stupid.

Ever since he'd boarded the train he'd been edgy, unfocused, displaced. And he hated feeling like that, as if he had no control.

Everyone said he was a control freak and, to some degree, he was. Control gave him power and impenetrability and confidence that things would work out exactly as he planned them, at total odds with his childhood, where no amount of forethought could give him the stability he'd so desperately craved.

When he'd first landed in this cosmopolitan, jam-packed country, he'd had a clear goal: to seduce Tam.

He wanted her—had always wanted her—but had stayed away for business reasons. Richard had been the best chef in the country and he'd needed him to cement Ambrosia's reputation.

Nothing got in his way when his most prized possession was at stake, not even a beautiful, intelligent woman. He hadn't needed the distraction at the time, had been hell-bent on making Ambrosia Melbourne's premier dining experience.

He'd succeeded, thanks to Richard's flamboyance in the kitchen and a healthy dose of business acumen on his part. Now, nothing stood in his way. Discounting his stupid over-eagerness, that was.

He sneaked another sideways glance at Tam, wondering if her intent focus was genuine or another way to give him the cold shoulder.

She wasn't like the other women he'd dated: everything, from her reluctance to respond to his flirting to the lingering sadness in her eyes, told him she wouldn't take kindly to being wooed.

He hoped to change all that.

'Some structure, huh?'

She finally turned towards him, her expression cool, her eyes wary.

'Yeah, it's impressive.' She pointed at one of the windows. 'Don't you think it's amazing all those royal women of the palace used to sit behind those windows and watch the ceremonial processions without being seen?'

He squinted, saw a pink window like a hundred others and shook his head.

'Sad, more like it. Having to stay behind closed doors while the kings got to strut their stuff. Don't think many women would put up with that these days.'

She stiffened, hurt flickering in the rich green depths of her eyes.

'Maybe some women find it's easier to give in to the whims of their husbands than live with callous coldness every day.'

Realisation dawned and he thrust his hands in his pockets to stop from slapping himself in the head. Had she just inadvertently given him a glimpse into her marriage to Richard?

He'd seen Rich like that at work. All smiles and jovial conviviality but if things didn't go his way or someone dared to have a different opinion to King Dick, he'd freeze them out better than his Bombe Alaska.

Would he have ever treated his wife the same way?

He hated thinking that this warm, vibrant woman had been subjected to that, had possibly tiptoed around in order to stay on his good side, had put a happy face on a marriage that would've been trying at best.

She didn't deserve that, no woman did, and the least he could do now was distract her long enough so she forgot his unintentional faux pas and enjoyed the rest of their day in Jaipur.

'I've seen enough palaces for one day. How about you and I hit some of those handicraft shops the guide mentioned earlier?' He bent towards her ear, spoke in an exaggerated conspiratorial whisper. 'By your different footwear for breakfast, lunch and dinner, I'd say you collect shoes on a weekly basis so I'm sure the odd bargain or two wouldn't go astray.'

She straightened her shoulders, flashed him a superior

smirk while her eyes sparkled. 'I'll have you know I only buy a few pairs of shoes a year, mainly boots. Melbourne's winters can be a killer on a girl's feet.'

'I'll take your word for it.'

He smiled, thrilled that his distraction technique had worked when she returned it. 'So, you up for some shopping?'

'I'm up for anything.'

Their gazes locked and for a long, loaded moment he could've sworn he saw a flicker of something other than her usual reticence.

'Come on then, let's go.'

As she fell in step beside him, his mind mulled over her revelation. He had no idea what sort of a marriage Rich and Tam had shared; he'd barely seen them together, preferring to make himself scarce whenever she'd appeared.

He'd cited interstate or overseas business whenever she'd hosted a party and had avoided all contact if she dropped into Ambrosia to see Rich on the odd occasion.

In fact, he'd rarely seen the two interact, such had been his blinding need to avoid her at all costs.

Maybe he was reading too much into her comment about tolerant wives and their private battle to keep the peace? Probably a passing comment, nothing more.

Then why the persistent nagging that maybe there was more behind her fragility than ongoing grief for a dead husband?

Jamming his hands into his pockets, he picked up the pace. The sooner they hit the shops, the sooner she'd be distracted and the sooner he'd lose the urge to bundle her in his arms, cradle her close and murmur soothing words again. Last night had been bad enough and he had no intention of treading down that road again.

He shouldn't get involved.

Her marriage was her business and the less he thought about it the better. Remembering she had once loved another man enough to marry him didn't sit real well considering how much he wanted her.

Besides, it would be dangerous—very dangerous—for Tam to become emotionally attached to him and that was exactly what would happen if he started delving into issues that didn't concern him and offering comfort.

He didn't do emotions, hated the wild, careening, out-of-control feelings they produced, which was why he dated widely and frequently and never got involved.

Never.

Better off sticking to what he knew best: work. He understood work. He could control work. He could become the man he'd always wanted to be through work. That suited him just fine.

As for Tam, he'd concentrate on keeping things light and sticking to his original plan.

These days, what he wanted he got and he had his sights firmly fixed on her.

She was no good at this.

Her plan to freeze Ethan out had hit a snag. A big one, in the shape of one super-smooth, super-charming, super-likeable pain in the butt.

She wanted to maintain a polite distance between them to ensure he didn't get the wrong idea—that she was actually starting to enjoy his flirting.

A long camel ride across the sand dunes of Jaiselmar had been perfect for her plan. Little opportunity for conversation, lots of concentration required to stay on the loping dromedaries.

But she hadn't counted on arriving at this romantic haven in the middle of the desert for an early dinner, nor had she counted on the persistent attention of one determined guy.

She'd been so close to seriously liking him last night, when he'd encouraged her to talk about her mum. To trust him enough to do that alarmed her, for it meant she was falling under his legendary spell.

Thankfully, he'd retreated quicker than she had at the sound of Richard's footfall after work and, while she'd been hurt at the time, she was now grateful.

Smooth, charming Ethan she could handle—just.

Caring, compassionate Ethan had the power to undo her completely.

So she'd retreated too, limiting their time spent together by taking breakfast in her carriage rather than the dining car, making boring, polite small talk at lunch.

Now, forced to be in his company on this tour, she'd maintained her freeze but, despite her monosyllabic responses, her deliberate long silences and her focused attention on the horizon, he persisted.

For some reason, Ethan was determined to get her to respond to him as a man. Why? Why here, why now?

They'd crossed paths infrequently over the last year and he'd been nothing but super-professional, almost aloof. So what was with the charming act?

He'd gone from teasing to full-on flirting and, try as she might, she couldn't maintain her freeze much longer. Under the scorching Indian sun, there was a serious thaw coming.

'Pretty spectacular, huh?'

With a weary sigh, she turned to face him, instantly wishing she hadn't when that piercing blue-eyed gaze fixed on her with purpose.

'Sure is.'

Her gaze drifted back to the beautiful tent city silhouetted against a setting sun, the sky an entrancing combination of indigo streaked with mauve and magenta where it dipped to the horizon, a sweep of golden sands as far as she could see.

A tingle rippled through her and she shivered, captivated by the beauty of a land she felt more for with each passing day.

This was why she'd come—to reconnect with herself, with her past. When she'd first booked this trip she'd envisioned shedding tears, letting go of some of her anger and discovering that missing part of herself tied up in this mystical country.

Never in her wildest dreams had she anticipated feeling like this. Not that she could verbalise what *this* was.

But every time Ethan had glanced at her she felt overwhelmed, dizzy, off-kilter, *alive*.

It was more than his inherent ability to coax a smile to her face, to make her laugh despite the unrelenting bitterness weaving a constricting net around her heart

No, there was more—much more than she could handle. An off-guard glance, a loaded stare, a little current of something arcing between them like the faintest invisible thread— intangible, insubstantial, yet there all the same.

And it terrified her.

This journey had been about self-discovery. Well, she'd certainly discovered more about herself than she'd anticipated in the startling, frightening fact that she was attracted to a man totally wrong for her.

'Let's get something to eat.'

She forced herself to relax as Ethan helped her down from the camel by holding her hand and placing his other in the small of her back, a small gesture which meant nothing.

So why the heat from his palm through her thin cotton sundress, the little tingle skittering along her skin, making her wish he'd linger?

She could blame this new awareness on India, its wild, untamed edge bringing out the same in her. But she'd be lying, and if there was one thing she'd learned through her fiasco of a marriage it was never to lie to herself again.

As he held open a tent flap for her and gestured for her to enter, his enquiring gaze locked onto hers and she swallowed at the desire she glimpsed.

He knew she was trying to avoid him and he didn't care.

So much passed in that one loaded stare: challenge, intent and heat—loads of heat that sizzled and zapped and had her diving into the tent for a reprieve.

She was crazy. Playing it cool with Ethan had been a monumental error in judgement. A guy like him would now see her as a challenge and she'd be darned if she sat back and watched him try to charm his way into her good graces. She wasn't interested in anything remotely romantic and, even if she was, he'd be the last guy she'd turn to.

'You can't keep up the silent treatment for ever.'

The amusement in his voice only served to irk more.

'Watch me.'

She swivelled on her heel and he grabbed her arm, leaving her no option but to face him while trying to ignore the erratic leap of her pulse at his innocuous touch.

'So I kissed you again? It was nothing. Surely we can get past it?'

Ouch, that hurt.

Of course a kiss would mean nothing to a playboy like him and, while she should be glad he was brushing it off, a small part of her hurt. She'd done her best to forget it, but she couldn't.

The kiss last night had been different from the impulsive, passionate kiss in Ambrosia the day he'd returned.

This kiss had been filled with tenderness and compassion and understanding, his gentle consideration in stark contrast to the powerful man she knew him to be and thus so much more appealing.

This kiss had unlocked something deep inside, the touch of his lips bringing to life a part of her assumed long dead.

That something was hope.

'Come on, Tam. What do you say we put it behind us and enjoy this lovely spread?'

He waved towards the linen-covered tables covered in a

staggering array of mouth-watering dishes she normally would've pounced on if her stomach wasn't tied in knots, the hint of that pirate smile tugging at his mouth.

How could a woman resist?

'Okay. But, just so you know, I'm not interested in anything…er…what I mean to say is…'

'It was just a kiss.' He ducked down to murmur in her ear and she gritted her teeth as a surge of renewed lust burst through her at his warm breath fanning her cheek. 'An all too short one at that.'

'I've heard that one before.'

'About it being just a kiss? Or me not apologising for it?'

'Yeah, that. It's a catchphrase of yours.'

He laughed, released her arm, and headed for the table, leaving her torn between wanting to shake him and admiring him for not backing down.

She sank into the chair he held out for her as a waiter bearing several silver-domed platters bore down on their table, deposited their meal, whipped off the domes and retreated with a small bow.

The fragrant aromas of spicy curries never failed to set her salivating but tonight her stomach clenched as she realized, no matter what she said to him, he'd continue to do exactly what he liked—and that was flirt with her.

'I'd like to propose a toast.'

He picked up his champagne flute, waited for her to do the same.

'To new beginnings and new experiences. May this journey bring us everything we could possibly wish for.'

Tam stared into her flute, watching the effervescent bubbles float lazily to the surface.

New beginnings, new experiences…hadn't she wanted all that and more on this trip? So why was she getting hot and bothered over a little harmless flirtation?

She knew Ethan's reputation, that flirting would come as easily as his millions. It meant nothing to him, he'd said so. She was so out of practice dealing with a charming man she'd lost perspective. Time to chill out.

'To new beginnings.'

She lifted her glass, tapped his, before raising it to her lips, wondering if the slight buzz was from the bubbles sliding down her throat or his mischievous smile.

'Let's eat.'

Silence reigned as they tucked into Jaipuri Mewa Pulao, a spiced rice packed with dried fruit, Rajasthani Lal Maas, a deliciously spiced lamb and Aloo Bharta, potato with a chilli kick, with relish.

As each new flavour burst on her tongue the words to describe them flashed through her mind in the way they'd always done when she'd worked full-time, vindication that the time was right to get back to the workforce on her return. Rather than being nervous, she couldn't wait.

As Ethan licked his lips and moaned with pleasure, she laughed. 'I take it you're enjoying Rajasthani cuisine.'

'Can't get enough of it.'

Popping another ladle of potato onto his plate, he nodded. 'Want to hear a fascinating fact I heard from our tour leader?'

'Uh-huh.'

'Rajasthan is an ancient princely state and it gave rise to a royal cuisine. The Rajas would go on hunting expeditions and eat the meat or fowl they brought back, which is why their feasts flaunt meat.'

'It all sounds very cavemanish.'

He glanced around, as if searching for something. 'Where's my club?' Accompanied by a ludicrous wiggle of his eyebrows. 'Fancy checking out my cave?'

She chuckled, glad she'd made the decision to lighten up. Sharing a meal with a charismatic dinner companion was enjoyable and definitely more fun than dining alone, something she'd honed to a fine art in the last year.

Though, in reality, she'd been alone a lot longer than that, Richard's long absences put down to work or media appearances or travelling to promote his latest book. Oh, not forgetting the time he'd spent holed away with his mistress.

Before she could mull further, he shot her a concerned glance and pushed the platter of potato towards her. 'More?'

Grateful for his distracting ploy, she nodded and ladled more food onto her plate.

'How did you get your start as a food critic?'

Another distraction and she silently applauded his ability to read her moods. Though it wouldn't take a genius to figure out her expression must've soured at the thought of Richard and his girlfriend.

'I've always been passionate about food and I loved telling a good story at school. So I worked in a professional kitchen for a while, cultivated my palate outside of it, immersed myself in all things food, then spent a year as a hostess at Pulse.'

'You must've learned a lot there. That place was big— before Ambrosia opened, of course.'

She smiled. 'Of course.'

She'd loved her experience in the industry: being able to give an in-depth description of an entire meal, the restaurant, its décor, how the service contributed to the dining experience. Work had never been a chore for her and, thanks to Ethan and the opportunity he'd given her at Ambrosia for the last six months, she now had the confidence to get back to it.

'Can I ask you a stupid question?'

'Sure.'

'Does all that writing spoil the fun of eating for you?'

She shook her head. 'Uh-uh. I love to eat, I love what I do. It's as simple as that.'

And as they made desultory small talk over dessert,

Churma Laddoos—sweet balls made from flour, ghee, sugar, almonds and cardamoms—she pondered her words.

As simple as that.

Were things simple and she was complicating them?

She'd wanted to expand her mindset on this trip, wanted to explore a side of her long quashed, away from the sour memories dogging her, away from Richard's malevolent presence still hanging over her.

While she had no interest in romance, maybe she could explore the side of her long ignored?

She was a woman—a woman who'd had her self-esteem battered severely, to the point where she didn't trust her judgement any more.

Maybe Ethan could help reaffirm the woman she'd once been—a woman who'd loved to smile and laugh and flirt right back.

She longed to be that woman again.

But would she have the courage to try?

CHAPTER FIVE

'It's beautiful.'

They stood inside Udaipur's Jag Niwas, the stunning Lake Palace that rose out of the blue waters of Lake Pichhola like an incredible apparition, looking out over the rippling, murmuring waves lapping the foreshore.

When Tamara had been planning this trip with her mum, she'd wanted to stay in this dreamlike marble palace with its ornately carved columns and tinkling fountains and clouds of chiffon drapes, now a grand heritage hotel.

Now, with Ethan by her side, she was glad she wasn't. The last thing she needed was to stay in some exquisitely romantic hotel with a man putting unwanted romantic ideas into her head.

She turned away from the picture-perfect view, gestured to the silver-laden table behind them. 'You ready to eat?'

He nodded, dropped his hand, and she clamped down on the instant surge of disappointment. 'Business all done. The chef signed the contract in front of me.'

He pulled out her chair in a characteristic chivalrous act she loved. If Richard had ever done it, he'd plonked his own selfish ass in it before she could move.

'He's one of India's best. And, considering my other choice in Delhi wouldn't budge, it's a coup getting this guy on board. Can't wait for him to start at Ambrosia.'

She sat, smiled her thanks. 'If you can't wait, neither can I. Just think, I get to sample his Chicken Makhani and crab curry and sweet potato kheer for nothing, all in the name of work.'

He chuckled, sat opposite her and flicked out his pristine white linen napkin like a troubadour before laying it in his lap.

'It's a hard life but somebody's got to do it, right?'

'Right.'

Hope cradled her heart, warming it, melting the band of anguish circling it. This was one of those moments she'd grown to crave yet fear, a poignant moment filled with closeness and intimacy.

A moment that said she was a fool for thinking she could start testing her flirting prowess and come out unscathed—or, worse, wanting more.

He broke the spell by picking up the menu, scanning it. 'Let me guess. You've already studied this in great depth and have your trusty notebook at the ready.'

She tossed her hair over her shoulder, sent him a snooty stare that lost some of its impact when her lips twitched.

'My trusty notebook is safe in my bag.'

He raised an eyebrow and sent a pointed look at her favourite patent black handbag hanging off the back of her chair.

'No notes today?'

'Not a one.'

The corners of his mouth kicked up into the deliciously gorgeous smile that had launched this crazy new awareness in the first place. 'Well, well, maybe you're starting to like my company after all.'

'Maybe.'

She picked up a menu, ducked behind it to hide a faint blush. 'Want to know what I think?'

He leaned forward, beckoned her with a crook of a finger, leaving her no option but to do it.

'You're going to tell me anyway, so go ahead.'

He murmured behind his hand, 'I think that notebook is like Bankie.'

'Bankie?'

'The security blanket I had when I was a toddler. I couldn't say blanket, so called it Bankie. A frayed, worn, faded blue thing that went everywhere I did.'

Her heart turned over, imagining how utterly adorable he would've looked as a wide-eyed two-year-old clinging to his blanket.

He'd never spoken of his family but she assumed he had one tucked away somewhere; probably parents who doted on their wonder-boy son and a proud sibling or two.

'Why do you think I need a security blanket?'

'Because of what's happening between us.'

Her belly plummeted. She didn't want to have this conversation, not here, not now, not ever.

Darn it, until now she could've dismissed the awareness between them as a figment of her imagination.

Now it was out there.

Between them.

Larger than life and more terrifying than anything she could've possibly imagined.

She could ignore it, try and bluff her way out of it. But this was Ethan. The guy who'd helped her with the legal rigmarole after Richard's funeral, the guy who'd given her a chance at getting her career back on track. She owed him her thanks if not the truth.

'Seeing as you keep kissing me, what do you think is happening between us?'

He paused, shifted his plate and cutlery around before intertwining his fingers and laying his hands on the table and leaning forward.

'Honestly? I like you.'

He leaned closer, lowered his voice, and she had no option

but to lean closer too. 'I like that you've changed since we've arrived here.'

This she could handle. She could fob him off with the real reason behind her change: her journey of self-discovery, her awakening to being her own person, her enjoyment of answering to no one but herself. All perfectly legitimate reasons to satisfy his curiosity and hide the real reason behind her change.

She shrugged, aiming for nonchalance. 'India's in my blood. Maybe my inner self recognises it on some subconscious level.'

He shook his head. 'I think there's more to it.'

'Like?'

'Like you opening your mind. Like you contemplating maybe there could be a spark between us.'

'I'm not contemplating anything of the sort!'

It sounded like the big fat lie it was.

He merely smiled, a captivating, sexy smile that made her feel a woman and then some.

'Come on, Tam. Admit it. You're as attracted to me as I am to you.'

She pushed away from the table, stood abruptly. 'I'm going for a walk.'

He let her go but she knew it wouldn't be for long. While he'd been surprisingly relaxed and laid-back on this trip, she'd seen his underlying streak of steel that had taken him to the top of the restaurant game around the world.

He'd made every rich list the year before, had women clamouring after him. So what the heck was he doing harassing a boring, sad-case widow like her?

She headed for the lake, head down, sandals flapping against the ancient stone path, eager to be anywhere other than sitting opposite the man she *was* attracted to in a palace restaurant in one of the most romantic settings on earth.

'Hey, wait up.'

His shout had her wanting to pick up the pace and flee. Futile, really, because she'd be stuck on the train with him for another few nights regardless if she outran him now.

Slowing her steps, she reached the edge of the lake, staring into the endless depths, searching for some clue to her problem, the problem of opening her heart to trust again, only to find the guy she liked was the one most likely to break it.

She knew when he reached her, could sense his body heat behind her, and she turned slowly, no closer to answering him now than she had been a few moments earlier.

He reached for her, dropped his hands when she frowned.

'You know I'm blunt. I call it as I see it and, deny it all you like, but something's happening between us.'

'Nothing's happening.'

A sudden breeze snatched her defiant whisper, making a mockery of her feeble protestation.

'If that's what you want to believe…' He shrugged, turned away, stared out over the lake to the island in the middle housing an entertainment complex where they'd have afternoon tea later, giving her time to concoct more excuses, more repudiation.

As if time would help.

She could protest all she liked but it wouldn't change the fact that everything had shifted and she didn't have a clue what to do about it.

How could she tell him that acknowledging the attraction between them, let alone giving in to it, was beyond frightening? How could she make him understand what a big deal this was for her?

It came to her as she glanced at his profile: so rugged, so handsome, so strong. She needed his strength, needed someone in her corner.

She'd never felt so alone as this last year, the last few years, despite being married and the implicit promise of safety it provided. And, while Ethan was the last guy she'd turn to for safety, having him here, every enigmatic, enthralling, enticing inch of him, being more honest than Richard had ever been, went a long way to soothing her fear that this crazy, burgeoning physical need for him was totally wrong.

She laid a hand on his arm, dropped it when he turned towards her.

'Want to know what I believe? I believe you're a good guy. You make me laugh when you tell those horrible corny jokes. You make me smile with your outrageous flirting. But, most of all, you've made me believe I can have a fresh start.'

Some nebulous emotion bordering on guilt shifted in his eyes before he blinked. 'Good guy? Far from it.'

He glanced away, rubbed the back of his neck. 'I think you're amazing and I'm attracted to you, but don't go thinking I'm some prince because I'm not.'

'I gave up expecting a prince to rescue me a long time ago,' she said, annoyed she'd let slip another indication that Richard had been anything other than the guy Ethan thought him to be.

He searched her face—for answers, for the truth?

'You want me to drop this? Pretend it doesn't exist?'

That was exactly what she wanted but, for one tiny moment, the faintest hope in her heart that there could ever be anything more between them snuffed out like a candle in the breeze.

'Yes,' she breathed on a sigh, wishing there could be another way, knowing there wasn't.

She'd lost her mother, her husband and her identity over the last few years and she'd be darned if she lost the chance at a new start.

Falling for Ethan would be beyond foolish, destined to shatter what little of her trust remained and there was no way she'd put herself through something like that ever again.

A new hardness turned his eyes to steely blue as he nodded. 'Fine, have it your way. But know this. Pretending something doesn't exist won't make it disappear.'

He turned on his heel and strode towards the palace, leaving her heart heaving and her soul reaching out an imaginary hand to him, grasping, desperate, before falling uselessly to her side.

He wouldn't give up.

It was a motto that had got him through a horror childhood, the nightmare of his teens, and had taken him to the top of the restaurateur game.

Right now, what was at stake was just as important as scavenging for the next food scrap to fill his howling belly or opening a new restaurant in New York.

Tam had blossomed, had become a woman who smiled and laughed and raised her face to a scorching Indian sun. She ran through ancient forts. She sampled the spiciest dishes and called for more chilli. She played with the little children who dogged their steps when the train stopped, bestowing smiles and hugs and her last rupees.

This was the woman he wanted with an unrelenting fierceness that constantly tore at him, an overwhelming need out of proportion to anything he'd remotely felt before.

Now she'd let down her guard, was attracted to him. He could see it in the newly sparkling eyes, the quick look-away when he captured her gaze, the smile never far from her lips, which had been constantly downturned until recently.

And, no matter how much she wanted to pretend, this attraction wasn't going away. Not if he had anything to do with it.

In the business arena, he was notorious for his ruthlessness, his take-charge and take-no-prisoners attitude. He didn't have much time left with Tam and, the way he saw it, he needed to make something happen—now.

He just hoped she'd still talk to him after she discovered what he'd done to help them along a little.

She stood at the bow of the boat, a vision in a white dress scattered with vivid pink and red flowers, her hair loose and flowing around her shoulders, fluttering in the breeze.

He'd never seen anything so beautiful, so vibrant, so stunning, and his desire for her slammed into him anew.

Yeah, he was through waiting. He'd waited years already and now there was nothing standing in his way.

She glanced up at that exact moment, sending him a tentative smile, and he strode towards her, needing little invitation to be right by her side.

'You sure we've got time to cruise the lake and check out the entertainment complex on the island?'

He glanced at his watch, noting the time with satisfaction.

'Plenty of time.'

The glib lie slid from his lips and he didn't regret it, not for a second.

Udaipur's Lake Palace was one of the most romantic hotels on earth and if he couldn't convince her to confront their attraction here, it wouldn't happen anywhere.

She smiled and he instantly quashed his yearning to slip a possessive arm around her waist as his heart slammed against his rib cage and his blood thickened with the drugging desire to make her his.

'You sure? We wouldn't want to miss the train and be stuck in this place.'

She waved towards the tranquil lake, the Palace on the far shore. 'I mean, staying in the hotel wouldn't be a hardship, but stuck with you? Now, that'd be tough.'

Ignoring the flicker of guilt that he was instigating just such an outcome, he propped his elbows on the railing and leaned back.

'Are you actually teasing me?'

She glanced at him from beneath lowered lashes and he could've punched the air with elation that she was lightening up enough to spar with him.

'Maybe.'

'Well, if this is the reaction I get for suggesting a simple boat ride, I'm going to do it more often.'

The light in her eyes faded as her gaze left his to sweep the horizon.

'I'll be busy relaunching my career when we get back to Melbourne and you'll be too busy being the hotshot businessman so I think any boat rides down the Yarra are wishful thinking.'

Was that her way of saying what happened in India stayed in India? That, even if she eventually capitulated and acknowledged their attraction or, as he was hoping, did something about it, things would come to an abrupt end when they got home?

'In that case, let's make the most of our time cruising here.'

'Okay.'

He didn't push the issue and it earned him a grateful glance, but he didn't want her gratitude, damn it. He wanted her to look at him with stars in her eyes and hope in her heart—hope that they could be more than friends.

'Speaking of Melbourne, can I ask you a question?'

She could ask him to take a flying leap and he'd ask how high. 'Sure, shoot.'

'You and Richard were mates. Why didn't I see you at the dinner parties he was so fond of? And, when we did cross paths, it was almost like you avoided me.'

Her question hit too close to home and dread settled like overcooked Beef Wellington in the pit of his stomach, solid and heavy with discomfort assured.

Since he'd started pursuing her he'd known they'd have this

conversation one day, surprised it'd taken her this long to ask and wishing it wasn't here, now, when he was making serious headway in his quest to have her.

'I wasn't avoiding you.'

'No?'

What could he say?

That he'd wanted her so badly he'd kept his distance for fear it'd distract him from his job? Or, worse, cause a serious problem between him and Rich, thus affecting their business?

That he'd wanted her so badly he'd dated a few look-alikes?

That he'd been so envious of Rich he'd taken a month off from the restaurant when they'd married?

That he'd been unable to look at the two of them together without wanting to hit something in frustration?

'I guess we moved in the same social circles occasionally, but I was busy schmoozing or courting business deals at those events to make chit-chat. Business, you know how it is.'

He avoided her shrewd stare by looking over her shoulder at the Palace shimmering in the distance. 'Never enough hours in the day.'

'Yet, by all accounts, you have plenty of time to date. Hmm…'

She tapped her bottom lip, drawing his attention to its fullness; as if he needed reminding. 'I guess what the rumour mill says about you is true.'

'What's that?'

'You're a seasoned playboy and Melbourne's number one eligible bachelor.'

'Playboy, huh?'

Her teasing smile surprised him, warming him better than the fiery vindaloo he'd sampled at lunch. 'Bet you're proud of it too.'

He pretended to ponder for all of a second before shrugging, feigning bashfulness.

'That's some title. Care to help me live up to my reputation?'

He expected her to leap overboard at what he was suggesting but once again she surprised him, merely quirking an eyebrow, her smile widening.

'What? And become yet another statistic?' She shook her head. 'Nope, sorry, no can do. But don't worry, I'm sure you'll have loads of dewy-eyed, stick insect bimbos lining up when your plane touches down at Tullamarine.'

He chuckled, only slightly disconcerted by the fact that she'd described his usual dates to a T.

'Are you implying I'm shallow, Miss Rayne?'

'I'm not implying anything. I'm stating a fact.'

She joined in his laughter and he marvelled at the transformation from reserved widow to relaxed woman. He'd always thought her beautiful but when she was like this—laughing, laissez-faire—she was simply stunning.

'Lucky for you, the boat's about to dock. I don't think my ego could take much more of your kid-glove treatment.'

'There's plenty more where that came from.'

'I stand duly warned.'

As they disembarked, Ethan didn't have a care in the world. The woman he wanted was definitely warming to him and they'd have several days together away from the train to get to know each other much better.

He was making things happen, was back in control—exactly where he wanted to be.

'What do you mean, we missed the train?'

Tamara stared at Ethan in open-mouthed shock, his calm expression only serving to wind her up. 'You said we had plenty of time.'

He shrugged, checked his watch again. 'I made a mistake. Sorry.'

'*Sorry?* Is that all you can say?'

As the concierge glanced their way, she lowered her voice with effort. 'This is ridiculous.'

'Look, it's no big deal. We get a couple of rooms for the night, make arrangements to catch the train at the next stop.'

'It's not that easy.'

She sank into the nearest chair, tired after their long day, annoyed he'd made them miss the train and afraid—terribly afraid—of spending the night in this romantic hotel with Ethan.

There was a difference between not acknowledging the simmering attraction between them, the newly awakened awareness that shimmered between them hotter than the Indian sun, and trying to ignore it in a place like this.

'We'll miss the next stop tomorrow and that leaves the last day, the most important of the whole trip.'

'Because of the Taj?'

She nodded, a tiny pinch of latent grief nipping her heart. 'And the birds. My mum was obsessed with birds. She collected figurines of anything from geese to cranes and she always wanted to visit Bharatpur's bird sanctuary.'

He must've caught the hint of wistfulness mingled with sadness in her tone, for he pulled his mobile out of his pocket and leapt to his feet.

'I'll handle this. We'll stay here tonight and tomorrow we'll head to Bharatpur, then Agra.'

Before she could respond, he was already punching numbers on his phone. 'Don't worry, you won't miss a thing.'

'But all my clothes are on board. I don't have—'

'I'll sort everything out. Trust me.'

He held up a finger as someone answered on the other end and she snuggled into the comfortable lobby sofa, grateful to be stuck with someone so commanding.

She was tired of making decisions over the last year: when to return to work, what to do with the house, with her stock in Ambrosia, to take this trip. Sure, she'd appreciated the independence, especially since she'd been robbed of it for so long, but here, now, with Ethan taking charge, she was happy to sit back and go with the flow.

Strangely, she did trust him—with their travel arrangements, at least. He'd make things happen, he was that kind of guy.

'Right, all taken care of.'

He snapped the phone shut, thrust it into his pocket and dusted off his hands, mission accomplished.

'With one phone call?'

He grinned and held out a hand to help her up from the sofa. 'My PA's handling all the arrangements. In the meantime, let's grab a room.'

Her heart stuttered, her pulse skipped and she broke out in a cold sweat before realising it was just a figure of speech. He meant two rooms; he'd said as much earlier.

'Or we could get the honeymoon suite if you're feeling particularly adventurous.'

Her shocked gaze flew to his, only to find his too-blue eyes twinkling adorably.

With a shake of her head, she waved him away. 'As tempting as that sounds, I've already told you I'm not another statistic.'

His mischievous grin had her wishing she could throw caution to the wind and become just that.

'Too bad, my bedpost needs a new notch.'

'You're—'

'Adorable? Endearing? Growing on you?'

Biting the inside of her cheek to stop herself from laughing out loud, she said, 'Pushing your luck. I'm beat. How about we get a *couple* of rooms?'

She only just caught his muttered, 'Spoilsport,' under his breath as he proceeded to charm the check-in staff as easily as he did everyone else.

Glancing around at the pristine marble floor, the majestic

columns, the sweeping staircase and the glistening chande-
liers, she couldn't help but be glad.

She was spending the night in a beautiful palace on a world
famous lake with the most charming man she'd ever met.

And while she could vehemently deny her insane attraction to a guy so totally wrong for her, it didn't hurt to let some
of the romance of this place soften the edges of her hard
resolve. Right?

Oh, boy.

There was a difference between softening her resolve and
it melting clean away, and right now, staring at Ethan in her
doorway, with champagne in one hand and a glossy Taj
brochure in the other, she knew her resolve wasn't softening,
it was in tatters.

'Mind if I come in?'

Yeah, she minded, especially since she'd rinsed her dress
and underwear and was in a fluffy complimentary hotel robe.

If she felt vulnerable to him in her clothes, what hope did
she have naked?

Oh, no, she couldn't think about being naked under her
robe, not with him staring at her with those twinkling cobalt
eyes, and the mere thought had a blush creeping into her cheeks.

'I come bearing gifts.'

He waved the champagne and brochure to tempt her. As if
he wouldn't be enough to do that. The thought had her clutching the door, ready to close it.

'Actually, I'm pretty tired.'

And confused and drained and just a tad excited.

He'd showered too and, with his slicked-back wet hair, persuasive sexy smile and magnetic indigo eyes, he looked more
like a pirate than ever.

Ethan was dangerous: too glib, too smooth, too gorgeous.

At that moment, she knew exactly why she found him so

attractive. She'd married Richard because he'd made her feel safe. The older guy who loved her, took care of her, made her feel special, and while it may not have lasted, that hadn't stopped her from cherishing the feeling of security he'd temporarily brought to her life.

Which explained why she suddenly found Ethan so appealing. That edge of danger, of unpredictability, was something she'd never experienced and, while she wouldn't want someone like him in her life, for someone who'd played it safe her entire life, she could understand the allure.

He held up the brochure, cleverly honing in on her weak spot. 'Share one drink with me, whet my appetite for the Taj Mahal and I'm out of here. Promise.'

Her instincts screamed to refuse but he'd been nothing but helpful in organising their rooms, transport for tomorrow and entry to the bird sanctuary and the Taj. The least she could do was appear grateful rather than churlish.

'Okay.'

Besides, it was only one drink. Barely enough time to make small talk, let alone anything else happening. Not that she wanted anything to happen.

Great, there went another blush. She quickly opened the door further and ushered him in.

'Room okay?'

'Are you kidding?'

When she'd wanted to stay here, she'd had no idea the rooms would be this gorgeous: the cusped archways, the carvings, the Bohemian crystal lights and the miniature paintings. It was like living in a fairy tale, being a princess for a night.

As long as there was no pea under the mattress, and no prince on top of it.

'It's fantastic.'

'Good. For a while there, I thought you'd behead me for making us miss the train.'

'Wasn't like you did it on purpose.'

Guilt tightened his features as he turned away to uncork the champagne and pour it into the exquisite crystal flutes which were standard room supplies, but it disappeared as he handed her a glass, joined her on the sofa; she must've imagined it.

'Here's to the rest of the trip being as eventful.'

He raised his glass to hers, tapped it and drank, his eyes never leaving hers for a second.

There was something in his stare—something resolute, unwavering and it sent a shiver through her. She had to look away, had to break the spell cast over her the moment he'd walked into the room.

Was she kidding? He'd cast a spell on her the moment he'd landed in India and railroaded her trip.

Lowering his glass, he placed it on a nearby table and did the same with hers before leaning forward, way too close.

'Tell me. Is my being here making you uncomfortable?'

'A little.'

She settled for the truth, hating how gauche and floundering and out of her depth he made her feel. She hadn't asked for this, hadn't fostered this attraction or encouraged it but it was there all the same, buzzing between them, electrifying and alive, no matter how hard she tried to ignore it.

'Why?'

He didn't back away. If anything, he leaned closer and her skin tingled where his shirt cuff brushed her wrist.

'Because you're the type of guy any woman in her right mind should stay away from,' she blurted, silently cringing at her brusque outburst.

Rather than offending him, he laughed, the rich, deep chuckles as warm and seductive as the rest of him.

'You keep coming back to that playboy thing. Don't believe everything you hear.'

She raised an eyebrow. 'So you're not a ladies' man?'

'Let's just say my reputation may be embroidered somewhat.'

His laconic response drew a smile. While Ethan was trying to downplay his reputation, she had little doubt every word was true. She'd seen his passing parade of women, either in the tabloids or at the restaurant, and while she should be the last person to judge who he paired up with—look at the monumental mistake she'd made in marrying Richard—the vacuous women didn't seem his type.

'It really bothers you, doesn't it? My past?'

She shrugged. 'None of my business.'

'I'd like it to be.'

He was so close now, his breath feathered over her cheek and she held her breath, wanting to move away, powerless to do so with her muscles locked in shock.

If she turned her head a fraction, he'd kiss her. His intent was clear—his words, his closeness, his body language—and she exhaled softly, her body quivering with the need to be touched, her heart yelling *no, no, not him!*

Rivers of heat flowed from her fingertips to her toes, searing a path through parts of her she'd forgotten existed. Her body blazed with it, lit up from within and in that instant her resolve was in danger of going up in flames.

'Tell me what you want, Tam.'

The fire fizzed and spluttered and died a slow, reluctant death as reality hit.

She knew what she wanted: to build a new life, to move forward, without the encumbrance of a man.

Yet she was wavering, seriously contemplating giving in to her irrational attraction for a man—not just any man, a man totally wrong for her.

That thought was enough to snap her out of the erotic spell he'd wound around them and she leaned back, forcing a laugh to cover the relief mingled with regret that she'd come to her senses in time.

'I want to take a look at that gorgeous brochure. So hand it over.'

He let her get away with it, but not before she saw the glitter of promise in his eyes.

This wasn't the end of it—far from it.

Ethan waved the brochure at Tam, snatching it away as she reached for it, laughing at her outrage.

He'd wanted her to say those three magical words—*I want you*—three little words that would've given him the go-ahead to seduce her in this exquisite room, a memory to last her a lifetime.

He wasn't a romantic, far from it, but he wanted her first time with him to be special, something she'd remember when they parted back in Melbourne.

After what she'd been through, she deserved special. Hell, she deserved the world on a plate and then some.

'Give me that!'

He raised the brochure higher. 'Uh-uh. Not until you ask nicely.'

She made a grab for it, leaning over far enough that the front of her robe parted and gave him a glimpse at heaven, her breasts lush and free and begging to be touched.

He swallowed, the game he was playing taking on new meaning as she leaned closer, reaching further, his lust skyrocketing as her tantalising exposed skin came within licking reach...

'Hand it over.' Laughing, she added, 'Pretty pleeeease,' before making a frantic lunge at his arm stretched overhead.

That last grab was her undoing, and his, as she teetered on her knees, precariously balanced, before tumbling against him and knocking him flat on his back on the sofa.

'Oops, sorry.'

Staring up at her, propped over him, her palms splayed against his chest, her mouth inches from his, her eyes wide and luminous and darkening with desire, she didn't look sorry in the least.

The brochure fluttered to the floor, forgotten, as she poised over him, hovered for an endless tension-fraught moment before lowering her head and slamming her mouth on his, eager, hungry, desperate.

He didn't know what shocked him more: the sheer reckless abandon with which she kissed him or the yearning behind it as her lips skidded over his, craving purchase, demanding he respond.

He didn't need to be asked twice, opening his mouth, the thrill of her tongue plunging in and exploring him tearing a groan from deep within.

How many times had he fantasised about having her?

But never in his wildest dreams had he envisioned her like this: crazy with passion, commanding, on top and totally in control.

Realisation slammed into him as she eased the kiss, lifted her head to stare at him with adoration in her glistening green eyes.

He wasn't in control any more, had lost it the second she'd pinned him down and initiated the kiss, demanding a response he was all too willing to give, but at what cost?

If losing control wasn't bad enough, the clear message in her eyes was.

She cared.

Too much.

He should've known a woman like her wouldn't respond physically to him unless she made an emotional connection and, by his own foolishness in encouraging deeper conversations, she had, damn it.

He wanted her so badly his body throbbed with it but this was all wrong.

It had to be on his terms, with her fully aware of what she was getting into, without hope in her heart and stars in her eyes.

Placing his hands around her waist, he lifted her so he could sit up, releasing her when they sat side by side.

Confusion clouded her eyes, with just a hint of hurt, but he couldn't acknowledge that, otherwise he'd find himself right back where he'd started, offering comfort when he shouldn't, giving her the wrong idea.

'What's wrong?'

'Nothing.'

He stood and strode to the door, needing to retreat before she pushed for answers he wasn't willing to give.

'I thought that's what you wanted.'

Her voice trembled, giving him another kick in the guts and he clenched his hands, thrust them into his pockets to stop himself from heading back to the sofa, sweeping her into his arms, carrying her to that tempting king-size bed and showing her exactly what he wanted.

'What about what you want?'

'That's pretty obvious. At least, I thought it was. Maybe I've been out of practice too long.'

He jammed his fists further in his pockets, rocked by the relentless urge to go to her.

She sounded so sad, so confused, and it was his fault.

He needed to get out of here. Now.

Spinning to face her, he strode back to the sofa, picked up the brochure lying at her feet and placed it on her lap when she didn't make a move to take it.

'Here's what you want.' He stabbed a finger at the glossy image of the Taj Mahal. 'I'm just a pushy guy bustling in on your dream.'

Her accusatory glare cut deep and he hated himself for putting her—them—in this position.

'I don't understand.'

Unable to resist dropping one last swift kiss on her lips, he muttered, 'Neither do I,' as he headed for the door.

CHAPTER SIX

TAMARA still didn't understand the next day when they reached Bharatpur.

She'd spent a sleepless night, analysing the moment Ethan had pulled away, over and over, replaying it until she'd turned over and stuffed her face into the pillow to block out the memory.

She'd kissed him, he'd pulled away.

No matter how many times she went over it in her head, it all came back to that.

It didn't make any sense. The way he'd been flirting, the way he'd been charming her from the moment she'd walked into Ambrosia and found him there, the way he'd been kissing her, repeatedly…

Something wasn't right and, in the wee small hours of the morning, she'd come to a decision.

Forget the humiliation, forget the embarrassing kiss, forget she'd made a fool of herself.

This trip was too important to let one cringe-worthy moment tarnish it. She'd waited too long to take it, was finally discovering her old self beneath layers of battered esteem.

And she liked what she was discovering: that she could feel again, that being with a man could be pleasurable rather than horrifying, that she liked feeling like a desirable woman rather than an ornamental wife brought out of her box to perform on cue at dinner parties and shelved the rest of the time.

If that scared Ethan, tough.

Maybe the guy was too used to getting his own way, was one of those strong guys who preferred to do all the chasing? Well, he could keep chasing, for that was the first and last time she showed him how amazing she found this irrational, incongruous attraction.

She should be glad he'd back-pedalled today, had made urbane small talk and eased off the flirting on their trip here, had made it perfectly clear he didn't want to discuss his about-face last night.

Instead, she found herself darting curious glances at him, trying to read his rigid expression—and failing—somewhat saddened by their long lapses into silence.

'Your chariot…'

Ethan gestured at the rickshaw he'd hired to take them around Keoladeo Ghana National Park, Bharatpur's famous bird sanctuary, and she smiled, relieved, when he responded with one of his own.

Buoyed by the first sign of anything other than irresolute self-control, she said, 'Chariot, huh? Does that make you Prince Charming?'

He shook his head, but not before she glimpsed his familiar rakish smile, her heart flip-flopping against her will in response.

'What is it with girls and princes?'

She could've elaborated on the whole 'being swept off their feet, rescued and living happily ever after' scenario girls loved from the moment they could walk. But considering her fantasy had evaporated quicker than Richard's love for her, she shrugged and stepped up into the tiny rickshaw. Her relief at being sheltered from the relentless sun instantly evaporated as he swung up beside her and she realised how small these rickshaws really were.

'Let's get moving. I don't want to spend too long here when we've got the Taj this afternoon.'

She agreed, though his brisk tone implied he couldn't wait to get to the end of this trip, couldn't get away from her quick enough.

She wasn't going to overanalyse this, remember? Wasn't going to waste time trying to read his mind or figure out his motivations.

'Can't wait.'

After instructing the driver to go, he leaned back, his thigh brushing hers, his arm wedged against hers as she wished her fickle body would stay with the programme.

This was a transient attraction, a natural reaction of her hormones considering she hadn't been with a man for almost two years. Richard hadn't touched her during that last year of their marriage, and she hadn't wanted him to. It made her skin crawl just thinking about where he'd been at the time, who he'd been with.

Silence stretched taut between them and she needed to say something—anything—to distract from her skin prickling with awareness where it touched his.

'My mum talked about the Taj constantly. About its inception, its history, but she never got to see it. This was going to be her first time...'

Her breath hitched on a part sob and she clamped her lips shut, wishing he'd sling an arm across her shoulders and cradle her close. He'd been nothing but comforting the last time she'd spoken about Khushi, had encouraged her to do so.

But, despite the momentary flicker of compassion in his eyes, the flash of understanding, he remained impassive, jaw clenched so hard the muscles bulged.

'You'll get to see it through her eyes, through her stories. You may be the one standing before it today but she'll be the one bringing it alive for you.'

She raised her gaze to his, emotion clogging her throat, tears stinging her eyes, but he glanced away, leaving her torn between wanting to hug him for saying something so perfect and throttle him for cheapening it by looking away.

'Thanks, I needed to hear that.'

'My pleasure.'

Empty words, considering there was nothing remotely pleasurable about the barrier he'd erected between them, the severing of an emotional connection no matter how tentative.

She'd been frozen inside for years, emotionally frigid as she'd shut down to cope with Richard's psychological abuse, numbing her feelings to stop the constant barrage of verbal put-downs and criticism.

She'd thought she was incapable of feeling anything again, yet Ethan had given her that gift.

Despite the urge to go running and screaming in the opposite direction, the more he charmed her, despite the fear that her body was responding to him and overthrowing her mind, despite the paralysing terror of feeling anything for a man ever again, she'd allowed him to get close enough to melt the icy kernel surrounding her heart and, for that, she was eternally grateful.

Her lower lip wobbled at the thought of how far she'd come and she blinked, inhaled sharply, her senses slammed by his sandalwood scent from the hotel's luxurious selection of complimentary toiletries, as she savoured the illicit pleasure of being this close to him.

With a small shake of her head, she pulled a guidebook from her bag and rattled open the pages, desperate for a diversion from her thoughts, her emotions and the uneasy silence.

'It says here this place is a bird paradise, with over three hundred and eighty species, including some rare Siberian cranes.'

He turned, leaned over her shoulder, peered at the book and

she held her breath, unprepared for all that hard male chest to be wedged up against her.

'What else have they got?'

Forced to breathe in order to answer him, she inhaled another heady lungful of pure male tinged with sandalwood, momentarily light-headed. Her palms were clammy, her body on fire and her head spun with the implications of how she was reacting to him, despite all her self-talk that she shouldn't.

Peering at the guidebook as if it had all the answers to questions she shouldn't even be contemplating, she cleared her throat.

'Hawks, pelicans, geese, eagles among countless other species, and they also have golden jackals, jungle cats, striped hyenas, blackbuck and wild boar.'

'Great.'

Yeah, great. He'd hired the rickshaw driver for an hour and in that time she'd be stuck here, nice and tight, unable to breathe without his tantalising scent assailing her, unable to move without encountering way too much firm muscle, unable to think without rehashing reasons why this could be better if he opened up and she shed her inhibitions.

As a pelican flew at the rickshaw in an indignant rage, the driver swerved, throwing her flush against Ethan and all that glorious hard muscle.

Righting her, he smiled, a warm, toe-curling smile that reached down to her heart, the type of smile that made resistance futile, the first genuine smile he'd given her all day.

Desperate to prolong the moment now she'd finally seen a glimpse of the old Ethan, she said, 'No need to throw myself at you, huh?'

Her hands splayed against his chest, the rhythmic pounding of his heart proof that he was as affected by their proximity as her.

'You don't hear me complaining.'

He held her gaze and she couldn't speak, couldn't breathe,

the distant screech of an eagle as hauntingly piercing and achingly poignant as the sudden yearning to stay like this, touching him, secure in his arms, for more than a brief moment.

She wanted to push him for answers, to ask why he'd gone cold on her but, as much as her foolhardy heart urged her, she couldn't do it.

She'd taken a risk on a man once before and her judgement had been way off. She'd thought Richard had been a safe bet, she'd trusted him and look how that had turned out. Trusting Ethan would be tantamount to handing him her heart on a serving platter complete with carving knives.

As she tried to muster a response, he straightened her, putting her away from him with strong yet gentle hands. 'You know what you look like?'

'What?'

'A worm surrounded by the entire population of this bird sanctuary.'

He tucked a strand of hair behind her ear, allowed his fingers to linger, brushing the soft skin of her neck. 'I'm not going to bite, Tam. So quit looking at me like I'm the big bad wolf.'

Before she could respond, he ducked his head, captured her mouth in a swift, urgent kiss that barely lasted a second, leaving her dazed and stunned and more baffled than ever.

'Though I have to say, you'd look great in red.'

With that, he turned to watch a gaggle of geese take flight as she sat there, bracing her feet to stop herself from rocking against him any more than necessary, absolutely speechless, thoroughly perplexed, and touching her trembling lips with a shaky hand.

He confounded, mystified and thoroughly bamboozled her, blowing hot and cold just like his employees said and, right now, she wanted to be like those geese. Free to take off, free to expand her wings, free to be whoever she wanted to be.

She wanted to feel carefree and light-hearted and unbur-

dened for the first time in years, wanted to have the courage
to explore outside her comfort zone, to let the winds of chance
take her wherever.

Darting a quick glance at Ethan, still staring resolutely out
the other side, she knew with the utmost certainty that he was a
part of that yearning to explore the unknown, the craving to take
a chance, no matter how much his behaviour bewildered her.

She was so used to repressing her true feelings, so used to
playing a part, that she didn't know who she was any more, let
alone how to be the carefree, happy woman she'd once been.

Ethan could help her.

He could help her rediscover her zing, could nurture their
spark towards something exciting, something beyond her
wildest dreams.

But she had to take a chance.

Was she willing to take a risk for a fleeting happiness
that would dissolve when Ethan stepped on a plane bound
for Melbourne?

Some choice and, as the rickshaw bumped and rocked and
swayed through the sanctuary, she knew she'd have to make
up her mind and fast. They had half a day and one night left
together. Not a heck of a lot of time to make a decision.

Chance. Risk. Gamble. Venture.

Things she'd never done when married to Richard, content
in the security he'd provided, when she'd been the dutiful wife
so in love with her husband she'd been blinded to his faults
until it was too late.

But that part of her life was over, her dreams of happily
ever after shattered by a selfish egomaniac, and for the first
time in years she could do as she damn well pleased.

Stakes were high.

Make a mistake and she'd lose the tentative friendship
she'd developed with Ethan, something she'd grown to
depend on over the last week.

Make it work and they could shoot to the moon and back.

With a heartfelt sigh she sat back, braced against the rocking, and watched the geese fly higher and higher, reaching for the stars.

Maybe she should too.

CHAPTER SEVEN

'YOU ready?'

Tamara nodded, took a deep breath and opened her eyes, the air whooshing out of her lungs as she caught her first un-forgettable glimpse of the Taj Mahal.

The incredible monument shimmered in the early dusk, its white marble reflecting in the long moat in front of it, casting a ghostly glow over the magical gardens surrounding it.

'It's something else.'

She glanced at Ethan, too choked to speak, grateful he knew how much this moment meant to her.

Sliding an arm around her waist, he hugged her close. 'Your mum's here with you. She'd want you to enjoy this, to be happy.'

Gnawing on her bottom lip to keep from blubbering, she searched his eyes, wondering if he knew how much of an integral part he played in her happiness these days.

All she saw in those fathomless blue depths was caring, compassion and a tenderness that took her breath away.

Thankfully, they'd broken the ice following the rickshaw ride and, while he hadn't slipped back into full-on flirting just yet, she had hopes that their last kiss hadn't ruined their friendship for ever.

For no matter how many logical, sane reasons she'd pondered as to why they couldn't be anything more than

friends, they all faded into oblivion the second she caught her
first breathtaking glimpse of the Taj.

There was nowhere else she'd rather be this very moment
than right here, with this man.

Placing a hand on his cheek, she caressed the stubble,
enjoying the light prickle rasping against her palm.

'I hope you know that sharing this with you is beyond special.'

Surprise flickered in his eyes—surprise tinged with wariness.

'I'm a poor stand-in for your mum but I'm glad I can be
here for you.'

He semi-turned, forcing her to drop her hand, and she
followed his line of vision, blown away by the fact that she
was standing in front of one of the new Seven Wonders of the
World, the River Yamuna flowing tranquilly nearby, surrounded by fellow tourists yet feeling as if she were the only
woman in the world to have ever felt this incredible in the face
of such beauty.

'It's stood the test of time, hasn't it?'

She followed his line of vision, taking in the curved dome,
the archways, the exquisite ornamentation. 'Considering it
took twenty-two years to build, I guess they made it to last.'

He did a slow three-sixty, taking in the gardens, the fountains, before fixing his gaze on the Taj again. 'I knew it'd be
impressive but I didn't expect anything like this.'

'I know,' she breathed on a sigh, closing her eyes for a
second, savouring the moment, elated that when she opened
them again she'd see the same incredible sight. 'Do you know
the story behind it?'

He held up his hand; it wavered from side to side. 'A little.
Shah Jahan, a Mughal Emperor, had it constructed in memory
of his beloved wife Mumtaz Mahal. Took about twenty
thousand workers, a thousand elephants to haul materials and
used about twenty-eight precious and semi-precious stones to
do the inlay work.'

She smiled. 'Someone's been reading their Lonely Planet guide.'

He raised an eyebrow. 'Okay, Miss Smarty Pants. Why don't you tell me what you know?'

'My version reads like a romance novel.'

'I'm a sensitive New Age guy. Go ahead. Try me.'

'Okay, but you'd better sit down. This could take a while.' She sank onto the ground, clasped her hands around her knees and rested her chin on her knees, waiting until he sat to begin.

'Shah Jahan was the son of the fourth Mughal emperor of India. He was fourteen when he met Arjumand Banu Begum, a Muslim Persian princess, who was fifteen. It was love at first sight.'

She sighed, wondering what it would be like to be swept away like that, to know in an instant you were destined to be with that person.

Richard had charmed and blustered and cajoled his way into her affections, offering her the safety of marriage, a safety she'd craved since her dad had died. Yes, it had been quick and, yes, she'd fallen hard but nothing like locking eyes with a person and knowing with the utmost certainty he was *the one*.

'But they were kids! That's not even legal.'

She waved away his protest. 'Different times. We're talking about the early sixteen hundreds. Do you want to hear the rest or not?'

'Go ahead. I can see you're busting to tell me.'

Sending him a mock frown, she continued. 'After meeting the princess, Shah Jahan went back to his father and declared he wanted to marry her. They married five years later. When he became emperor eleven years later, he entrusted her with the royal seal and gave her the title Mumtaz Mahal, which means "jewel of the palace". Though he had other wives—'

'That's not romance, that's bigamy.'

She rolled her eyes. 'That's allowed in his religion. Any-waaaay—'

He grinned at her obvious annoyance at his constant interruptions.

'She was his favourite, accompanied him everywhere, even on military campaigns. But when she was giving birth to their fourteenth child—' Ethan winced and she couldn't blame him '—there were complications and she died. Apparently, legend has it that she secured a promise from him with her last breath to build a beautiful monument in her memory.'

She gestured to the Taj Mahal. 'And he did.'

Her glance roved over the towering dome, the intricate archways, the cypress trees nearby, as she pondered the depth of that kind of love, captivated by the spellbinding romance of it all.

'That's some story.'

He stared at the monument, the sudden tension in his shoulders alerting her to the fact that something bothered him, before swiftly turning to her and fixing her with a probing stare.

'Do you believe in love at first sight?'

At that moment, with his intense blue eyes boring into hers, his forearm brushing hers, his heat radiant and palpable and real, she wished she did.

'My parents did. They took one look at each other on Colva beach and fell in love.'

He didn't let her off that easily. 'I didn't ask about them. I'm asking you.'

Here was her chance to tell him she'd been thinking about pushing the boundaries, possibly seeing where it could take them.

But the reservations of a lifetime dogged her. She'd always done the right thing, been the dutiful daughter, the good little wife. She didn't like rocking the boat, changing the status quo. She'd tried it once before, was still dealing with the consequences.

Drawing a harsh, shaky breath, she forced her fingers to relax rather than leave welts from digging into her hands.

'I don't know what I believe any more.'

He shook his head, disappointment clouding his eyes. 'That's a cop-out.'

'Pardon?'

'You heard me. You're a strong, resilient woman. You've coped with losing your husband. You've made decisions to move forward with your life. Plans to return to work.' He jerked his head towards the Taj Mahal. 'Coming here.'

He laid a hand on her arm and she started. 'All major decisions—but see that? The way you just jumped when I touched you?' He shook his head, his mouth twisting with disappointment as he released her. 'You're selling yourself short there. You're not being honest.'

She leaped to her feet, needing space, a continent's worth to flee the truth of his words and the reckless pounding of her heart.

'This isn't about honesty. It's about taking a risk and I hate taking risks.'

When a passing couple stared, she ran a weary hand over her face, lowered her voice.

'I'm not like you. You're brave. Fearless. Take charge. Everything so clear in black and white. While I feel like I've been living in some alternate grey universe and I'm finally coming out the other side.'

He stood, reached for her but she held him away. 'No, let me finish. I need to say this. You're successful, accomplished, but you know what I envy the most? You know who you are. You know your place in the world and, right now, that's something I don't have a clue about...'

Her declaration petered out on a whisper, a taut silence

stretching between them until she wished he'd say something—anything—to fill the tense void.

Finally, he slid an arm around her waist, pulled her close, and she let him.

'I didn't know.'

'That I'm such a sad case?'

Her attempt at humour fell flat.

'That you felt like that. I'm sorry.'

'Don't be. It's something I have to work through.'

Something she was determined to do. Everything seemed much easier here, away from the memories of Richard, of discovering the truth.

'You've had a rough trot. You know you deserve to be happy, right?'

She'd spent years pretending she was happy when she was anything but: pretending Richard's passive-aggressive barbs didn't hurt, pretending his criticism was well-intended, pretending she still loved him when inside she'd died a little every day.

The pretence had extended following his death, playing the grieving widow for appearance's sake when deep down she'd felt like screaming at his treachery, at his selfishness in making her life miserable while he had a ball with another woman behind her back.

'I want to be happy…'

'Then let go.'

She knew what he was implying, could read it in every tense line of his body.

Meeting his unwavering stare, she suppressed her inner voice screaming, *no, no, don't do it.*

'With you?'

He nodded slowly, his eyes never leaving hers. 'Want to know why I came on this trip?'

'I thought it was all business?'

He smiled at her soft sarcasm, his expression inscrutable.
'Because of you.'

He gripped her arms, his fierceness so overwhelming she
would've taken a step back if he wasn't hanging on to her.

'Then why do you keep pulling away? It's like you get too
close and then—wham, nothing.'

He shook his head, his hands tightening their grip as he
hauled her closer. 'I barely knew you before this trip and
spending time with you changed everything. Yeah, I'm a red-
blooded male and I want you. But now—'

He searched her eyes for—what? Approval? Some sign
that she wanted to see this through until the end?

'What do you want from me now?'

'This.'

Before she could make sense of his words, before she
could push him for an explanation, his mouth swooped and
captured hers in a hungry, rash kiss, blindingly brilliant in its
savage intensity.

Her senses reeled as he deepened the kiss, as she let him,
stunned by the ferocity of her own response as she grabbed
frantically at his T-shirt, clung to him, dragged him closer.

If he'd slowed down, been tender and gentle rather than
commanding and masterful, she would've had time to think,
time to dredge up every rational reason why she shouldn't be
doing this after the way he'd rebuffed her last night.

Instead, she let go, became herself, not some mouse-like
woman worried about what other people would think of her
for staying in a loveless marriage with a heartless tyrant if they
knew.

Her knees wobbled as he pulled her closer, his hands
strumming her back, his lips playing delightful havoc with
hers as he challenged her with every tantalising sweep of his
tongue, with every searing brush of his lips.

It was the kiss of a lifetime.

A kiss filled with promise and excitement and wonder, without a shade of grey in sight.

A kiss memories were made of.

An eternity later, when the initial blistering heat subsided and their lips eased, lingered, before releasing, the reality of the situation rushed in, the old self-doubts swamping her in a crushing wave.

'Don't do that.'

He tipped her chin up, caressed her bottom lip with his thumb. 'Don't go second-guessing yourself or what just happened.'

'I'm not—'

His mouth kicked up into the roguish smile she loved so much. 'This is me you're talking to.'

'That's what I'm afraid of,' she murmured, smoothing his T-shirt where she'd gripped it so hard she'd wrinkled it to the point where it needed a shot of steam or two to de-crease.

'Just take that kiss at face value, as a first step.'

She was almost too afraid to ask. 'A first step to what?'

Brushing a soft, barely-there kiss across her lips, he said, 'That's something we're about to find out.'

CHAPTER EIGHT

As far as first dates went, Ethan couldn't fault this one. He leaned back on outstretched arms and looked up at the monstrous India Gate in the centre of New Delhi.

In reality, he could've been in a dingy alleyway in the back of Timbuktu and the date would've been amazing all the same, courtesy of the stunning woman by his side, looking happy and more relaxed than he'd ever seen her.

'What are you thinking?'

Tamara smiled up at him from her vantage point, stretched out on the grass on propped elbows.

'I'm thinking if I see one more monument or fort or palace I'll go cross-eyed.'

He laughed, reached out to pluck a blade of grass stuck to her hair. 'But this is the Arc de Triomphe of India. It commemorates the seventy thousand Indian soldiers who died fighting for the British Army in World War One and is inscribed with the names of over thirteen thousand British and Indian soldiers killed in the 1919 Afghan war.'

She shook her head. 'There you go again, swallowing another guidebook. You know, all those facts will give you indigestion.'

He winked, ducked his head for a quick kiss that left her blushing. 'Just trying to impress you.'

'You've done that already.'

Her praise, the easy way she admitted it, warmed his heart, before stabbing doubt daggers into it again.

He'd tried his best to back off, to subdue his panic, to alienate her.

It had worked for a while; he'd regained control but it hadn't eradicated the fear.

The fear that he was already feeling way too much, the fear that what was happening between them was beyond anything he'd ever felt before but, most of all, the fear that no matter what he did, how hard he tried to stay in command, his overwhelming need for this woman would engulf him anyway.

He wanted this—right? Then why the constant nagging deep in his gut that this was more than he could handle?

During his relentless pursuit, he hadn't actually spelled it out that he wasn't interested in a relationship. He hoped to date for a while, have some fun together, explore the underlying spark simmering between them.

But that was where things ended. Would Tam want more? He doubted it, considering she'd talked about new beginnings, a fresh start. Believing her only encouraged him to indulge their attraction, guilt-free.

If things got too heavy, he knew what he had to do: run, just like his mum.

He'd loved her, had been secure she returned the sentiment until his childish delusions had been ripped from under him, leaving him a homeless orphan with a mother who'd rather be on her own than stuck with a five-year-old.

'What's wrong?'

He blinked, wrenched back to the present by her tentative question, her hand on his arm, and he mentally dusted himself off.

Today wasn't a day for sour memories.

Today was a day for creating brilliant new ones.

'Just thinking about where we go from here.'

It wasn't a lie exactly. He'd been stewing over their future since they'd opened an emotional Pandora's Box at the Taj yesterday.

He wanted this, wanted more than friendship with this incredibly special woman. Then why couldn't he rid himself of the faintest mantra stuck on rewind in the back of his mind, the one that chanted *be careful what you wish for?*

He'd always been ambitious, driven to succeed, craving control to stave off the darkness that crept into his soul at the oddest of times—a darkness filled with depressing memories of physical abuse and living on the streets and starving to the point of desperation.

Being one hundred per cent focused on business had served him just fine. Until now, when his legendary control was smashed like a soup tureen by a temperamental chef by taking the next step with Tam.

He half expected her to balk at the question, to shirk it. Instead, she fixed him with those mesmerising green eyes, eyes he could happily get lost in for ever.

'Honestly? I have no idea. I'm in Goa for the next week. You're here on business.'

She idly plucked at the grass beneath her hands, picking blades and letting them fall. 'I guess we wait until we're back in Melbourne and see what happens.'

For some strange reason her answer filled him with relief when he should be pushing her, ensuring she wouldn't back off once their journey together ended today.

What the hell was happening to him?

Sure, he enjoyed the thrill of the chase as much as the next guy but usually didn't tire of something once possessed—until the woman in question wanted to possess him. So why was he feeling like this? So uncertain, so uneasy, so unhinged.

His goal had been to seduce her and he was almost there. Then why the unrelenting fear he'd got more than he'd bargained for?

'You're not happy about that?'

He forced a smile, tension sneaking up the back of his neck and bringing on one of the classic headaches reserved for day-long meetings.

'We've come a long way in a week. Maybe things will be different when we get home.'

A tiny frown puckered her brow as she pushed up to a sitting position. 'That's not like you. You're the optimistic one. I'm the confirmed pessimist.'

What could he say?

That he didn't want a full-blown relationship? That he didn't trust what they had? That he didn't trust easily, period?

Reaching out, she draped a hand over his, squeezed softly. 'There's more. Tell me.'

If he looked for excuses long enough he'd find them and at that moment a veritable smorgasbord flooded his mind, leaving him to choose the juiciest one.

'The press hounded you for weeks after Richard's death. What do you think they'll do when they discover we're dating?'

Her frown intensified as her hand slid off his. 'They'll probably say I'm some kind of trumped up tart who waited until her dearly beloved husband was cold in the ground for a year before moving on from the chef to the billionaire res-taurateur where he worked. So what? It's all nonsense. Who cares what they say?'

But she was worried. He saw it in the telltale flicker in her eyes, in the pinched mouth.

If Tam had put up with the constant publicity barrage being married to Rich entailed, she had to care about appearances and, no matter how much she protested now, he knew the first hint of scandal in the tabloids back home would send her scut-tling for cover.

Where would that leave him? Content to sit back and watch from the sidelines? He'd be damned if he settled for that again.

'As long as you're sure—'

'Of course I'm not sure!'

She jumped to her feet, eyes flashing, hands clenched, more irritated than he'd ever seen her.

'But you wanted this—*you*. You pushed me. You chased and pulled back several times, confusing the heck out of me until I couldn't think straight but I'm still here.'

She stabbed a finger in his direction, glared at him, all bristling indignation and fiery righteousness, and he'd never seen anything so beautiful.

'Now I'm ready to take a chance on us, you start hedging. What's with that?' She ended on a half sob and he leaped to his feet and reached for her.

'Don't, just don't.'

She held up her hands to ward him off and he couldn't blame her.

He was still a screwup. No matter how far he'd come from that lonely, desperate, filthy street kid who'd scrounged food scraps to survive, no matter how rich or successful, he was still the same wary guy who wouldn't let anyone get too close, let alone a woman.

But he had to fix this, and fast, before he not only ruined any chance they had of dating but shot down their new friendship too.

'Tam, listen to me. I—'

'Why should I? Give me one good reason why I should listen to you?'

She folded her arms, glared, her stoic expression at odds with her trembling mouth, and it took every ounce of self-control not to bundle her into his arms.

He held his hands out to her, palms up, and shrugged. 'Because I care about you.'

She wrinkled her nose. 'Care, right. Well, you know what? If you cared, you wouldn't say you want one thing, act another when you get it. I'm sick of it.'

Tears glistened in her eyes, turning them a luminous green and slugging him harder than his first shot of alcohol as a shivering fourteen-year-old squatting in a Melbourne hovel, desperate to stay warm.

Shaking her head, she swiped a hand over her eyes, sniffed. 'I don't need this. I didn't ask for it, I didn't want it, but at least I had the guts to take a chance, so I'll be damned if I stand here and let you play me for a fool.'

'I'm not—'

'You are.'

If she'd shouted, ranted, abused him, he might've stood a chance at convincing her otherwise but her soft, empty words, frigid with contempt, reached icy fingers down to his soul, freezing what little hope he had left.

'You've got a week to figure out what you want.'

He reached for her hand, briefly capturing her fingertips before she snatched it away.

'Tam, don't do this.'

She straightened, fixed him with a superior glare at odds with her shaky hands. 'Do what? Stand up for myself? Speak my mind?'

Her mouth twisted into a wry grimace. 'This is *my* time now. Time I start looking after number one, and that's me.'

She shook her head, gathered her hair, piled it into a loose bun on top of her head before letting it tumble around her shoulders again. He loved watching her do it, an absent-minded habit she did when thinking or uptight.

'I just want to make sure you know what you're getting yourself into. As far as I know, I'm the first guy you've dated since Rich and that's got to be a big step for you.'

'But it's my step to take!'

He'd never seen her so irate and for a moment he wondered if there was more behind her flare-up. Was she nervous and covering it with bluster? Or was she as crazy for him as he was for her and had no idea how to control it, just like him?

'You know, for the first time in forever, I felt safe yesterday. At first I thought it was the Taj, the overwhelming sense of calm that flowed through me when I stepped inside. But it wasn't just that.'

She raised her wide-eyed gaze to his, her unguarded expression beseeching him to understand. And he did, all too well. Tam needed a man to make her feel secure, to cherish her, to spoil her, to do all the things Rich had done.

But he couldn't be that man.

He couldn't relinquish control of anything, let alone lose it over a woman, no matter how special. However, now wasn't the time to get into all that. The way things were heading, it looked like their first date may also be their last.

'It was you, Ethan. You being there with me, sharing it, treating me like a woman…'

She trailed off, shrugged and took a step backwards. 'Maybe it was just the monument, after all.'

'Tam, look—'

She raised her hand—to ward him off? To say goodbye?

'I'll see you in Melbourne.'

While his heart urged him to follow her, to tell her the truth, to make her understand, his feet were rooted to the spot as he watched the woman who'd captured his heart without trying walk away.

CHAPTER NINE

TAMARA slid her sunglasses into place, tucked the latest crime novel under her arm, slung her towel over her shoulder and headed for the beach.

She'd been in Goa two days—two long days when she'd spent every waking moment touring around, filling the hours with sights and sounds of her mum's birthplace.

'Prawns today, missie?'

Smiling, she stopped at one of the many food vendors scattered along the roadside leading to Colva Beach. She'd been starving when she'd arrived here her first day and the tantalising aroma of seafood sizzling in garlic and turmeric had led her straight here.

'Two, please.'

She held up two fingers for reinforcement, knowing the wizened old man would give her four, just like he had the previous times she'd stopped here. Not that she was complaining but the waistbands of her skirts sure were.

His wide toothless grin warmed her heart as she handed over the rupees and juggled the hot prawns, waving the skewer around and blowing on them before biting into the delicious crispy flesh, savouring the freshness of the seafood drenched in spicy masala.

She devoured the first prawn in two bites, saliva pooling

in her mouth at the anticipatory bite of the next as she strolled past another vendor selling a fiery fish vindaloo that smelled as good as the prawns.

'Tomorrow,' she mouthed to the hopeful guy whose face fell when she didn't stop.

Not that she wasn't tempted but at that moment her new friends caught sight of her and were busy hopping from one foot to the other in some bizarre welcoming dance that never failed to bring a smile to her face, and she had no option but to stop.

'You build?'

The eldest of the group of five kids, ranging from three to six, pointed to a makeshift bucket made from an old ghee tin while the rest dropped to their knees and started digging in the sand with their hands.

'Sure.'

She knelt, picked up the tin and started scooping, enjoying the hot sand beating down as she fell into a rhythm: scoop, pat, dump, scoop, pat, dump, listening to their excited chatter, unable to understand a word of the rapid Hindi but returning their blinding smiles as their castle grew.

Today, like the first day they'd beckoned her to join in their fun, she took simple pleasure in doing something associated with her childhood, the repetitive activity as soothing now as it had been then.

She'd built monstrous sandcastles after her dad had died, had poured all her energy into the task in an attempt to block out the pain. But, as the castles had grown, so had her resentment until she'd kicked them down, one crumbling turret at a time.

Yet she'd started building the moment her mum had taken her to the beach the next time, painstakingly erecting the towering castles, complete with shell windows and seaweed flags.

Until it hadn't hurt so much any more and she'd stopped kicking them down, happy to watch the sea gently wash away her creation.

It had taken time to release her resentment—at losing her dad, the unfairness of it—and now, with the sand trickling through her fingers, calmness stole over her, soothing the discontent gnawing at the edges of her consciousness since she'd arrived.

She'd tried ignoring it, had even tried meditating as darkness descended each evening and she sat in a comfy cane chair on her veranda looking out over peaceful Colva beach, her beach hut the perfect spot away from the madding crowds.

While the deliberate relaxation had gone a long way to soothing her weary soul, to banishing some of the anger and acrimony that had dogged her incessantly for the last year, it had also served to tear a new wound in her already bruised heart.

Thanks to Ethan.

Even now, she had no idea what had happened in the interim between their first kiss and her walking away from him in Delhi.

She'd often felt like that with Richard—lonely, as if floating on a sea of anonymity despite being constantly surrounded by his business acquaintances and friends. She'd been a part of his life, a fixture, like part of the furniture, smiling and chatting and playing the perfect hostess while inside she'd been screaming.

She hadn't told her mum about it. Khushi had lived through enough trauma of her own, had lost a husband, a country. Her mum had fussed over her enough when she was growing up, overprotective to the point of stifling at times. She'd understood it, her mum's need to hang on to the only family she had, and in her own way she'd wanted to return the favour.

She'd never spoken an ill word against Richard, despite her growing despair that her husband had morphed from a strong, steady man to a controlling, spoiled tyrant with a penchant for wine and women.

Losing her mum had been devastating but, considering what she'd learned about Richard when he'd died, a small part of her had been glad her mum hadn't been around to see it.

Bitterness had plagued her for the last year, yet over the last week it had ceased seeping into her soul and sapping her energy.

Because of Ethan.

Ethan, who by encouraging her to open her heart to him, only to hand it straight back to her, had now left her unhappier than ever.

He'd been relentless in his pursuit of her ever since they'd started this trip—discounting the occasional withdrawal—yet when she'd finally given in he'd retreated faster than a lobster sighting a bubbling bisque.

And she'd overreacted. Boy, had she overreacted and the memory of how she'd berated him made her knock over a turret or two as her hands turned clumsy.

The kids frowned as one and she shrugged in apology, intent on smoothing her side of the castle, wishing she could smooth over her gaffe with Ethan as easily.

She'd picked a fine time to rediscover her assertiveness and, while it had felt great standing up for herself and verbalising exactly how she was feeling, she'd chosen the wrong place, the wrong time, the wrong man.

He hadn't deserved her outpouring of anger any more than she'd deserved any of Richard's callous put-downs.

Shame she wouldn't get the chance to tell him, for she was under no illusions that, once they returned to Melbourne, Ethan would move onto his next challenge, relegating her to what? Distant acquaintance again? Friend?

Considering they hadn't been anything remotely near friends before this trip, she should be grateful. Instead, she couldn't help but wish she'd had a chance to rediscover another part of her identity: that of a desirable woman with needs desperate to be fulfilled.

Dusting off her hands, she stood, surveying their creation. The kids imitated her and she pointed at the lopsided castle and applauded them, charmed by their guileless giggles and high-fiving.

Everything was so simple for these kids: they had little, lived by the sea in makeshift shanties, shared a room with many siblings, had few toys, yet were happier than any kid she'd ever seen rollerblading or skateboarding in Melbourne.

Another lesson to be learned: keep things simple. She had once, content to curl up with a good romance novel, soft jazz in the background, a bowl of popcorn.

Living the high life, living a lie with Richard, had changed all that but it was time to get back to the basics. Her few days in Goa had taught her that if nothing else.

Waving goodbye to the kids, she set off for the shade of a nearby tree, throwing down her towel, smoothing it out and lying down, watching a couple stroll hand in hand down the beach.

She wanted to warn them that the first flush of love didn't last, that it soured and faded, no matter how committed the other person was to you.

She wanted to caution the beautiful young woman against giving too much of herself all in the name of love, wanted to alert her against loving too much to the point she risked losing herself.

She wanted to rant at the injustice of being a loyal, loving wife, only to have it all flung back in her face in the form of a six-foot Dutch ex-model with legs up to her neck and a dazzling smile.

But she didn't do any of that.

Instead, she slapped on her sun hat, flipped open her book and buried her nose in it. A much safer pastime than scaring young lovers and wasting time wishing she could change the past.

Ethan had enough business meetings to keep him busy for the next month.

This trip had been a success: he'd secured the chef he'd wanted and had put out feelers for a new flagship restaurant in Mumbai. He'd flown the length and breadth of India over the last two days, from Delhi to Mumbai to Chennai.

However, as he sat in the plush surrounds of the InterContinental Hotel in Chennai, he couldn't concentrate on business. Thoughts of Tam consumed him, as they had since she'd walked away from him in New Delhi.

He'd reached for his mobile phone numerous times, desperate to call her, to see how she was doing, to simply hear her voice. But he'd stopped each and every time, all too aware that ringing her would prove what he'd suspected for a while now—his legendary control was slipping.

Slipping? More like shot.

During their journey on the Palace of Wheels he'd dreamed of surprising her in Goa, of spending a leisurely week getting to know each other in every sense of the word.

So much for that dream.

'Ethan, my boy, good to see you.'

Dilip Kumar, his Indian representative in business matters, appeared out of nowhere, slapped him on the back as he stood. 'This is Sunil Bachnan, the investor we discussed on the phone last week.'

'Pleased to meet you.' He shook Sunil's hand, a giant of a man with a rounded belly protruding over his trousers, testament to a lifetime's worth of chappatis and dosais, the crispy rice pancakes filled with spicy potato he'd become addicted to.

'Likewise. I hear you're looking to open a restaurant here?'

He nodded, resumed his seat along with the other men, grateful to be back doing what he knew best. Business.

This he could manage. Unlike the rest of his life, which had spiralled dangerously out of control since he'd landed in this mystical country.

'Actually, I was thinking Mumbai. The growth there is staggering.'

Sunil gestured to a waiter for menus, nodded. 'The entire country is an economic boom. Pick a city, any city and your famous Ambrosia will do big business.' Patting his ample gut, he chortled. 'We love our food here in India.'

'You and me both.'

Though his appetite had vanished the last few days, a shame considering the array of amazing food on offer every-where he went. For a guy who made his life out of food, he'd landed smack bang in food paradise.

'Right. Let's talk business as we eat.' Sunil rattled off an order in rapid Hindi to the hovering waiter as Dilip raised his beer. 'Cheers, my friend. And how is your travelling companion?'

'Good.'

He sculled half his beer in two gulps, wishing he hadn't opened his big mouth and mentioned Tam, not wanting to discuss her. The less he said the better, considering the constant repetition buzzing around his brain: replaying every scene of their trip, every hand touch, every smile, every kiss...

'You must bring her to dinner. My wife Sireesha will be thrilled to have you both—'

'Tamara's in Goa.'

Dilip's black eyes widened at his snapped response. 'I see.'

'Glad someone does,' he muttered into his beer glass, grateful that Sunil had answered a call on his mobile and wasn't privy to this conversation.

Trying to present a professional front to an investor sure as hell didn't involve discussing his non-existent love life.

'You and your lady friend are having problems?'

'Nothing I can't handle.'

Yeah, right, which was why he was on the east coast of India and Tam was on the west.

Dilip shook his head, steepled his fingers on his chest and

wobbled his head from side to side in a gesture he'd seen many times in India.

'If you permit me to be so bold, I have a story for you, my friend.'

Darting a frantic glance in Sunil's direction in the hope his phone call had ended, his heart sank as the investor held up a finger at him, pushed away from the table and headed for the foyer to continue his conversation.

'Look, Dilip, I'd rather focus on business—'

'Patience, my friend, patience.' He squeezed his eyes shut, as if trying to recall the story, before his bulging eyes snapped open and fixed on him. 'When I met my Sireesha, I was a penniless student and she was engaged to the son of a prominent doctor. Our paths crossed at university one day, when she dropped her books and I helped pick them up, and from that moment I knew she was the one for me.'

'And you're telling me this because?'

Dilip frowned, waggled a finger at him. 'Because I never wavered from my pursuit of her, no matter how unlikely it was we would ever be a couple. I was determined to have her and all the obstacles in our way were inconsequential.'

Ethan rubbed the back of his neck, shook his head. 'That's great but we're different. There are complications—'

'Complications, pah!'

Dilip waved his hand like a magician waving a wand. If only he could make all his problems disappear.

'The only complication is up here.' He tapped his head like an overzealous woodpecker. 'You think too much, you over-analyse, you lose.'

He pointed to his heart. 'You need to think with this. Let your heart rule your head. I know you are a brilliant businessman, so this will be foreign to you, yes?'

Hell, yeah. He never let his heart rule his head, not any more. His mum was the only woman who'd ever had a piece of his heart and she'd taken it with her the second she'd walked out of his life and left him to fend for himself, a bewildered five-year-old with no family, no money, no home.

'If you want her, this—' he tapped his heart '—needs to rule this.' He pointed to his head. 'Simple.'

Was it that simple?

Was he thinking too much, overanalysing everything, obstinately refusing to relinquish control despite the potentially incredible outcome?

What could be a greater incentive to lose control just a little than dating Tam?

Dilip snapped his fingers, jerked his head towards the door. 'Sunil is returning. For now, we do business. But later, my friend, you remember what I've said.'

He'd remember. But would he do anything about it?

Tamara needed a walk.

Her mum's cooking had been amazing but the authentic Goan cuisine she consumed way too much of at every meal was sublime.

She was particularly partial to bibinca, a rich sweet made from flour, sugar, ghee, coconut milk and about twenty egg yolks, baked and flavoured with nutmeg and cardamom.

Rich, delicious, addictive.

Exactly like Ethan, though his sweetness had evaporated around the time he'd stolen her hard-fought trust in him and flung it into the Ganges.

Picking up the pace, she headed for the water's edge, where the ocean tickled the sand, the only sound being the waves breaking gently on the shore.

Colva Beach was tranquil, lazy, the type of place to hang out the 'do not disturb' sign and just chill out. Her mum had said it was special but she'd always attributed her partiality to the fact she'd met her dad here. But mum had been right.

This place had an aura, a feeling, a sense that anything was possible, as she stared out over the endless ocean glowing turquoise in the descending dusk.

She slowed her pace, hitched up her peasant skirt and stepped into the waves, savouring the tepid water splashing about her ankles.

As a kid, she used to run through the shallows at St Kilda beach, jumping and splashing and frolicking, seeing how wet she could get, her folks strolling hand in hand alongside her, smiling indulgently.

They'd head to Acland Street afterwards, trawling the many cake shops, laughing as she'd pressed her face up to each and every window, trying to decide between melt-in-the-mouth chocolate éclairs or custard-oozing vanilla slices.

And later, much later, when her tummy was full and her feet dragging, she'd walk between them, each parent holding her hand, making her feel the luckiest little girl in the world.

A larger wave crashed into her legs, drenching the bottom half of her skirt and she laughed, the sound loud and startling in the silence.

How long since she'd laughed like that, truly laughed, totally spontaneous?

Ethan had made her laugh last week, several times... Shaking her head, she resisted the temptation to cover her ears with her hands.

Ethan, Ethan, Ethan—couldn't she focus on a new topic rather than the same old, same old?

With her skirt a dripping mess, she trudged up the beach, heading for her hut. Maybe a nice long soak in that killer tub filled with fragrant sandalwood oil would lull her into an Ethan-free zone?

As she scuffed her feet through the sand, a lone figure stepped onto the beach near her hut.

She wouldn't have paid much attention but for the breadth

of his shoulders, the familiar tilt of his head… She squinted, her pulse breaking into a gallop as the figure headed straight for her, increasingly recognisable with every determined stride.

It couldn't be.

It was.

In that instant, she forgot every sane reason why she should keep her distance from Ethan and ran towards him, sprinting, her feet flying across the sand as she hurtled herself into his open arms.

CHAPTER TEN

'Is THIS real?'

Ethan smoothed back her hair, caressed her cheek, his other hand holding her tight against him. 'Very.'

'What are you doing here?'

Tamara touched his face, her fingertips skimming his cheek, his jaw peppered in stubble, savouring the rasping prickle, still not believing this was real.

'I came to be with you.' He brushed his lips across hers—soft, tender, the barest of kisses that had her breath catching, along with her heart. 'There's nowhere else I'd rather be.'

She couldn't comprehend this. One minute she'd been alone and confused, the next he was here. For her.

'But after what happened in Delhi—'

'I was a fool.'

He clasped her face between his hands, his beseeching gaze imploring her to listen. 'I owe you an explanation.'

Her response of *you don't* died on her lips.

Considering the retreat and parry he'd been doing and the way they'd parted, he owed her that at least.

'Come on. I'm staying in that hut you just passed. We can talk there.'

She stepped out of his embrace but he swiftly pulled her

back into his arms, hugged her so fiercely the breath whooshed out of her lungs.

'Tam, I missed you.'

'Me too,' she murmured against his chest, her cheek happily squashed against all that lovely hard muscle.

Stroking her hair, he held her, their breathing in sync with their beating hearts, and for that one brief moment in time she understood the incredible power of the emotion that had drawn her mum and dad together on this very beach all those years ago.

There was something magical about this place, something transcendental and, as the first stars of the evening flickered overhead and the faintest tune of a soulful sitar drifted on the night air, she wondered if it was time to take a chance on love again.

'Any chance this hut of yours has a fully stocked fridge?' He patted his rumbling tummy. 'Feels like I haven't eaten in days.'

'Better than that. The hut is part of a resort so I put in an order for my meals first thing in the morning and they deliver.'

'Great. So what's for dinner?'

She laughed. 'You can take the boy out of the restaurant but you can't take the restaurant out of the boy.'

'Too right.' He slipped his hand in hers, squeezed. 'So, what's on for tonight?'

For an insane moment she could've sworn he wasn't talking about food as his steady blue-eyed gaze bored into hers, questioning, seeking, roguish. And, for the life of her, she couldn't remember what she'd ordered that morning.

Chuckling at her bemused expression, he fell into step beside her. 'Never mind, whatever it is I'll devour it.'

He paused, sent her a significant look. 'Happiness does that to a man. Gives him an appetite.'

'You're happy?'

He stopped, pulled her close again. 'Considering you didn't

run the opposite way when you first saw me, you're still talking to me and you've invited me to dinner, I'm downright ecstatic.'

Joy fizzed in her veins, heady and tingling and making her feel punch-drunk. Sure, they needed to talk but, for now, she was happy too. Happier than she'd been in days. Heck, happier than she'd been in years.

This last week with Ethan, she'd found a surprising peace. She didn't have to pretend to be someone she wasn't, to fake a smile, to be poised and elegant and refined all in the name of appearances.

He saw her for who she was—a woman out to make a new start, a woman happiest with no make-up, no artifice and no platitudes.

'I've never seen you like this.'

He tucked a strand of hair behind her ear, twisting the end around his finger, brushing the delicate skin beneath her ear.

'What? With my hair frizzy from sea water and wearing a kaftan from a local market?'

His gaze searched her face, her eyes, focusing on her lips.

'I've never seen you so relaxed. You're truly happy here, aren't you?'

She nodded, filled with a sense of serenity she'd never had elsewhere.

'Maybe it's a mental thing, knowing my mum spent half her life here and I feel more connected to her here than anywhere.'

'It's more than that.'

He was right. It was the first time in a long time she'd been on her own, content in her own company.

She'd been alone in Melbourne since Richard's death but that had been different. There'd been the whirlwind of the funeral, countless trips to the solicitors, endless paperwork to tidy up and the personal fallout from Richard's little bomb-shell in the form of his girlfriend, Sonja.

Here, there was none of that. She could finally be true to herself, true to *her* needs.

She smiled. 'You've got to know me pretty well, huh?'

'Enough to know I've never seen you so at ease.'

'It's this place.'

She waved at the endless stretch of sand, the shimmering azure sea, the purple-streaked sky scattered with diamond-like stars.

'Not just the tranquillity, the pace of life, but everything about it. I can just be myself, you know.'

'I'm happy for you, Tam, I really am.'

He was, she could see he was genuine, which made her like him all the more.

'But a part of me can't help but wish I'd found you with unwashed hair and chewed-to-the-quick fingernails and pale and sallow from pining away for me, rather than the picture of glowing health.'

She'd pined all right. She'd struggled to sleep the first night, moped around while sightseeing, dragged her feet through this sand on more long walks than she'd ever taken.

Nothing had soothed the hollow ache in her heart, the anxiety gnawing at her belly that she'd lost her chance at exploring something new, something exciting, something that could potentially be the best thing to ever happen to her.

Yet here he was, in the flesh, wearing his trademark rakish pirate smile, khaki shorts and a white T-shirt setting off his newly acquired tan.

He was gorgeous, every tantalising, delectable inch of him, and by coming here, she was hoping he'd made the statement that he was ready to explore this spark between them.

'You're staring.'

She raised an eyebrow, fought a blush. 'Am I?'

'Uh-huh.' He ducked his head for a quick kiss. 'And I like it. That gleam in your beautiful eyes tells me I still have a chance.'

'Only if you're lucky.'

Laughing at his wounded expression, she slipped out of his grasp, hitched up her long skirt and sprinted across the sand with him in hot pursuit.

She'd never felt this carefree, this spontaneous, and while Colva Beach may have worked its magic on her, it had more to do with the man rugby-tackling her to the sand as they reached the hut.

'Hey! Don't go trying out for your Kangaroos footy team by practising on me.'

He rolled onto his back, taking her with him so she lay deliciously along the length of him. 'Wouldn't dream of it. Besides, those guys are way out of my league.'

'Am I?'

All too aware of their heated skin being separated by the sheer chiffon kaftan and cotton, she propped on his chest, the teasing smile dying on her lips as she registered the sudden shadows in his eyes.

'Maybe you are.'

'I was kidding, you great oaf.' She whacked him playfully on the chest, disappointed when he stood and hauled her to her feet.

'Yeah, well, my ego bruises easily. You need to take it easy on me.'

She didn't buy his rueful grin for a second, something akin to hurt still lingering in his eyes.

'I'll keep that in mind.'

Eager to restore the playful mood between them, she gestured to the hut. 'Maybe you won't be so sensitive once you get some food into that great bottomless pit of yours.'

He instantly perked up. 'Did you mention food?'

She laughed, opened the door. 'Kitchen's on the left. Dinner's ready to be heated. I'll just take a quick shower before we eat.'

While she preferred the au naturel look here, she felt distinctly grubby in the presence of his sexy casualness. That glow he'd mentioned probably had more to do with a day's worth of perspiration than any inner peace.

'Right. See you in ten.'

She held up one hand. 'Make that five. I'm starving too.'

Before she could move, he captured her hand, raised it to his lips and placed a hot, scorching kiss on her palm and curled her fingers over. 'I'm really glad I came.'

'Me too,' she murmured, his kiss burning her palm as she kept her hand clenched, backing slowly into the bathroom, not breaking eye contact for a second, waiting until she all but slammed the door before slumping against it in a quivering heap, her hormones leaping as high as her heart.

Ethan headed for the tiny kitchen, drawn by the faintest aroma of fish, onions and ginger.

For a guy who hadn't been able to face food in the last forty-eight hours, he was ravenous.

Not just for food.

The instant he'd laid eyes on Tam, the craving was back, so intense, so overwhelming, he wondered how he'd managed to let her walk away from him in the first place.

All his doubts had washed away on the evening tide as she'd run towards him, her incredible green eyes shining, her smile incandescent.

He wasn't a romantic kind of guy—dating arm-candy women who liked to be seen with rich guys took all the gloss off romance—but, if he were prone to it, he'd say their reunion had been picture perfect, the type of moment to relate to their kids, their grandkids.

Whoa!

He stopped dead, backing up a moment.

He'd gone from the possibility of dating to kids?

This hunger must be making him more light-headed than

he'd first thought and, heading for the fridge, he dug out a casserole dish filled with fish curry, a bowl of steamed white rice and a raita made from yoghurt, cucumber, tomato and onion.

Food of the gods, he thought, smiling to himself as he heated the fish and rice, amazed he'd gone a whole day without thinking of his precious Ambrosia.

He spent all day every day in constant touch with the managers of each restaurant around the world, keeping abreast of the daily running, meeting with accountants, conference calling with staff.

Being in control of Ambrosia, seeing his business grow to international stardom status never failed to give him a kick, a solid reminder of how far he'd come.

From loitering around the back door of Ma Petite, hoping for food scraps, to being taken under the wing of the great Arnaud Fournier and given an apprenticeship in his world-class restaurant, to working eighty-hour weeks and scrounging every cent to invest in his first restaurant, to running one of the most famous restaurant chains in the world was heady stuff for a guy who could still remember the pinch of hunger in his belly and the dirt under his fingernails from scrabbling for the last stale bun out of a dumpster.

From bum to billionaire and he couldn't be prouder.

Then why hadn't he told Tam the truth?

They'd discussed her family, her career, but he'd neatly sidestepped any personal questions she'd aimed his way, reluctant to taint her image of him.

Why? Was he ashamed? Embarrassed? Afraid she'd see him as less of a man?

Hell, yeah. The less said about his sordid past the better. She was taking a huge step forward, both career-wise and personally, in letting him get close and he'd be a fool to risk it by giving her a glimpse into the real him.

'Something smells good.'

She stepped into the kitchen, her hair wet and slicked back into a low ponytail, her skin clear and glowing, wearing a simple red sundress with tiny white polka dots, and he slammed the hot rice dish onto the bench top before the whole thing slid onto the floor courtesy of his fumbling fingers.

She had that effect on him, could render him useless and floundering out of his depth with a smile, with a single glance from beneath those long dark lashes that accentuated the unique green of her eyes.

'Now who's staring?'

She sashayed across the kitchen, lifted the lid on the fish and waved the fragrant aroma towards her nose. 'Wait until you try this fish moilee. It's fabulous.'

Thankful she'd given him a chance to unglue his tongue from the roof of his mouth where it had stuck the moment he'd caught sight of her, he quickly set the table.

'How's moilee different from curry?'

'Different spices, different method of cooking.' She gathered a jug of mango lassi, a delicious yoghurt and fruit drink he loved, and glasses and placed them on the table. 'You add a little salt and lime juice to the fish, set it aside for a while. Then you fry mustard seeds, curry leaves, onion, ginger, garlic, green chillies and turmeric before adding the fish, covering the lot with coconut milk and letting it simmer.'

She inhaled again, closed her eyes, her expression ecstatic and he cleared his throat, imagining what else, apart from a tasty curry, could bring that look to her face.

'My mouth's watering. Let's eat.'

Her eyes snapped open at his abrupt response and he busied himself with transporting the hot dishes to the table under her speculative stare rather than have to explain why he was losing his cool.

For a couple who'd chatted amicably during most meals on their Palace on Wheels journey, they were strangely silent as they devoured the delicious fish and rice, darting occasional glances at each other over the lassi, politely passing the raita, focusing on forking food into their mouths.

Tension stretched between them, taut and fraught, as he wished he could articulate half of what he was feeling. Overwhelmed. Out of control. And more attracted to anyone than he'd been in his entire life.

He'd dated many women, most had left him cold. He told himself he liked it that way; he chose fickle women because he didn't want to get emotionally involved.

So what was he doing here, now, hoping this incredible woman would let him into her heart when he knew that would be an irrevocable step down a very dangerous road, a road less travelled for him, a road peppered with emotions he'd rather ignore?

Tam had been grieving, had closed down emotionally, hadn't dated, let alone looked at a guy since Rich's death.

Yet here she was, opening her heart to him, welcoming him back despite how he'd acted like a jerk, first on the train, then in Udaipur, lastly in Delhi. Which could only mean one thing.

She was already emotionally involved with him, was willing to gamble her heart on him.

He had no idea if he deserved it.

'That was delish.' She patted her mouth with a napkin, refolded it, before sitting back and rubbing her tummy. 'I don't think I could move for a week after that, which gives you plenty of time to start talking.'

So much for being let off the hook. She'd lulled him into a false sense of security, yet he'd known it would come to this.

He had to tell her the truth—some of it—if they were to have any chance of moving forward from here.

Wishing he hadn't eaten so much—it now sat like a lump of lead in his gut—he sat back, crossed his ankles, wondering if she'd buy his relaxed posture while inside he churned with trepidation.

Opening up to anyone, let alone the woman he cared about, didn't sit well with him and he'd be damned if he messed this up after what had happened in Delhi.

Folding his arms, he looked her straight in the eye. 'You want to know why I backed off at India Gate.'

'For starters.'

She didn't look angry—far from it if the gentle upturning of her lips was any indication. Yet she had every right to be, every right to kick his sorry butt out of here after the way he'd treated her.

'Did you ever want something so badly as a kid, something you wished for, something that consumed you yet, when you got it, you didn't know what to do with it?'

Understanding turned her eyes verdigris. 'I was a bit like that with my Baby Born doll. Really wanted one, then when I got it for Christmas, didn't know whether I should feed it or burp it or change its nappy first.'

'You're laughing at me.'

'I'm not.'

Her twitching mouth made a mockery of her last statement and he chuckled, shook his head.

'I'll be honest with you, Tam. I came on this trip because I wanted you. Then I started to get to know you—really know you—and it's like…'

How could he explain it? Like being hit over the head with a four-by-two? Like being struck by lightning? Like having the blinkers ripped from his eyes only to see the stunning, vibrant woman he desired was so much more than he could've possibly imagined?

'It's like…?'

Her soft prompt had him saying the first thing that popped into his head.

'It's like finding the person you want most in this world is holding the key to your heart as well.'

No way—had he really said that?

Inwardly cringing at his emotional explosion, he met her gaze, the shimmer of tears in her eyes slugging him harder than the realisation that this had already moved beyond caring for him, that he was already half in love with her.

'Look, that's too heavy—'

'Don't you dare apologise for saying that!' Her head snapped up, her gaze defiant as the tears spilled over and rolled down her cheeks. 'Do you have any idea how I feel, hearing you say that?'

'Like bolting?' he ventured, earning another wide-eyed stare.

'Like this.'

She stood so abruptly her chair slammed onto the floor and she traversed the tiny table in a second, flinging herself onto his lap and wrapping her arms tightly around his neck.

'Well, now, maybe I should blurt my innermost thoughts more often if this is the type of reaction I get.'

Her eyes gleamed with mischief. 'No, *this* is the type of reaction you get.'

She covered his mouth with hers in a desperate, frantic kiss filled with longing and passion and recklessness.

The type of kiss that filled his heart with hope, the type of kiss with the power to teach him this relinquishing control lark wasn't half as scary as he'd built it up to be.

She was warm and vibrant and responsive in his arms, her hunger matching his and, as she shifted in his lap, inflaming him further, he knew he had to put a stop to this before they jumped way ahead of themselves.

He wasn't a Boy Scout and he'd like nothing better than to carry her into the bedroom right this very second and make love to her all night long but he'd botched things with her once; he'd be damned if he made another mistake now.

And that was what sex would be, despite the blood pounding through his body and urging him to follow through—a mistake.

He wanted to take things slow this time. He'd rushed her on the train journey, had almost lost her because of it, and there was no way in Hades he'd make the same mistake twice.

'Tam?'

'Hmm?'

She nuzzled his neck, giving his good intentions a thorough hiding as she straddled him, her breasts pushing deliciously against his chest.

'I can't stay.'

She stilled, raised her head, her eyes glazed, confused. 'Why not?'

Cradling her face in his hands, he brushed a soft kiss across her swollen lips.

'Because I want to do this right.'

He didn't have to add *this time*.

He saw the respect in her eyes, the understanding, and knowing this incredible woman was on the same wavelength as him sent another flood of intense longing washing over him.

'Great, the playboy has morphed into a goody two shoes,' she said, sliding off his lap in a slow, deliberate movement designed to tease as he clenched his hands to stop himself from reaching out and yanking her back down.

'Oh, you'll see how good I really am.'

He stood, pulling her back into his arms, enjoying her squeal of pure delight. 'Soon—very soon.'

'I'll hold you to that.'

'I'm counting on it.'

This time their kiss was slower, exploratory, leisurely, and as he reluctantly slipped out of her arms and raised his hand in goodbye he feared there'd come a time in the not too distant future where he'd find it near on impossible to walk away from her.

CHAPTER ELEVEN

'I THOUGHT Goa was settled by the Portuguese?'

Tamara nodded, browsing the market stall's brightly coloured powders for the Holi festival tomorrow. 'It was. That's why you see so many Portuguese-inspired buildings and a lot of the population are Catholic. Apparently thousands of people make the pilgrimage to see Saint Francis Xavier's body at the basilica here every five years.'

Ethan trailed his fingers through a mound of sunshine-yellow powder and earned a frown from the vendor for his trouble.

'If it's predominantly Catholic, what's with this Holi festival? Isn't that Hindu?'

'Uh-huh. But, like most of India, there are so many different religions and castes living side by side that everyone's pretty tolerant of the different festivals.' She pointed to several piles of powder, smiling at the vendor, who began shovelling mini mountains of the stuff into clear plastic bags. 'I think it's fabulous everyone gets involved. It's such a joyous occasion that you can't help but get swept up in the fun. At least, that's what Mum told me.'

He nodded, pointing to the bags being thrust into her hands. 'So tell me about it. All I know is everyone goes berserk and throws colour on everyone else.'

Upon hearing this, the vendor frowned again and shook his

head, while she handed him rupees and laughed. 'Come on, I'll enlighten you over a cup of masala chai.'

'Sounds good.'

He held out his hand for her carry-all and she gratefully gave it to him. Choosing every colour of the rainbow for Holi mightn't be such a great idea if she had to lug all those kilos back to the hut.

'Do the colours mean anything?'

She nodded, instantly transported back to the first time she'd heard about Holi, sitting on her mum's knee. She'd just learned to make her first chapatti that same day, and had had so much fun rolling the balls of dough into flat breads, standing on a stool next to the stove as her mum had fried them.

She'd been five at the time and her dad had come home after work, scoffed three with jam and pronounced them better than her mum's.

It'd been a magical day, one of those days where her mum was reminiscing about India, eager to tell stories, and she'd lapped it up. Yet another thing she missed.

'Green's for vitality, red is purity, blue is calmness and yellow is piety.'

He squinted through the bag. 'So what happens when you mix the lot together?'

'You'll find out.'

She could hardly wait. Ever since she'd first learned of the festival of colour, she'd been entranced. The freedom to play and dance and sing like a kid, flinging coloured powders and water balloons over anyone and everyone, visiting friends, exchanging gifts and sweets, all sounded like a good time.

'Let's have a cuppa here.'

They stopped at a roadside café, ordered masala chais and relaxed, watching the passing procession of people gearing up for Holi, each weighed down with vibrant magentas, daffodil-yellows, peacock-blues, dazzling emeralds and vivid crimsons.

Ethan gestured towards the passing parade. 'Looks like everyone gets in on the act.'

She nodded, delighting in the infectious excitement of the kids bouncing down the street, laden down with colour-filled bags.

'It's a time where age is irrelevant; everyone joins in. You can get wild and no one will blink.'

It was also a time for lovers, where the application of colour to each other was a sign of their love. Wisely, she kept that gem to herself. It was hard enough handling the swift shift in their relationship, and trying not to dwell on the erotic dreams of the last few nights, without adding to it.

He leaned forward, crooked his finger at her. 'How wild?'

She laughed. 'It's good clean fun. Well, if you discount getting dirty with colours, that is.'

His devilish grin sent heat sizzling through her. 'I'm all for getting dirty.'

'I bet.'

Her dry response had him chuckling as the waiter deposited two stainless-steel mugs filled to the brim with steaming chai in front of them.

'So what does it all mean?'

'There are loads of different legends surrounding it, centring on the ultimate victory of good over evil. Holi helps people believe in the virtue of being honest and banishing evil. It helps bring the country together and the tradition is that even enemies turn into friends during the festival.'

She sipped at her chai, sighing as the burst of cardamom-flavoured tea hit her taste buds. 'And there's no differentiation between rich and poor. Everyone gets in on the fun. It's about strengthening bonds between friends, revitalising relationships.'

'Wow, sounds like the world could do with a good Holi festival every now and then.'

She nodded. 'Wouldn't it be great? A sea of colour and a giant group hug.'

'I could do with a hug myself.' He stared at her over the rim of his mug, his blue eyes mischievous. 'Similar to that one you gave me at your kitchen table the night I arrived.'

She blushed, tried a frown and failed miserably when her lips curved into a secretive smile at the memory.

'Drink your chai. We have about half an hour to get changed before the fun starts.'

'Make that five minutes if we get back to the hut in time.'

She almost choked on her tea. He hadn't flirted so blatantly since he'd arrived, hadn't pushed, despite the increasingly heated kisses they'd shared the last few days.

He wanted to take things slow and while her head and heart were grateful for the fact, her body was way behind in the acceptance stakes.

Something had shifted today. Ever since he'd turned up on her doorstep this morning and all through their stroll around the market he'd been pushing the boundaries, flirting outrageously, hinting at something more than a quick, sizzling kiss at the end of the day.

She'd put it down to infectious Holi madness. Who knew— maybe, just maybe, there would be some revitalising of their relationship happening later tonight?

'This is insane!' Ethan shouted at the top of his lungs, dodging another kid pointing a super-sized water soaker at him, bright blue this time, only to be splattered in the middle of the back by a magenta water bomb from Tam.

'Yeah, isn't it great?' She flung her arms overhead, twirled around, did a defiant jig in front of him, taunting him now he'd used up his colour supplies.

He advanced towards her, pointing at the remaining bags in her hand. 'Give me some of that.'

'No.' She stood on tiptoe, jiggled the bags in front of him. 'Not my fault your aim is lousy.'

'That does it!' He grabbed her around the waist and she squealed, her laughter firing his blood as much as having her wriggling and warm and vibrant in his arms. 'Tam, I'm warning you—'

'You're in no position to warn me. I'm the one holding the ammunition.'

To reinforce the point, she swung one of the bags at his back, where it exploded, drenching him further.

'What colour was that?'

'Red, to match your face for letting a girl beat you at this.'

'That does it.' He hoisted her over his shoulder, growling when she emptied the last few bags on his back, then proceeded to pummel him with her fists.

'Put me down.'

He patted her butt in response. 'Nope, sorry, no can do. This is Holi, remember? Anything goes.'

'I take it back.'

'Too late.'

She stiffened as he slid a hand up her calf, reaching her thigh, all in the name of getting a better grip. That was his excuse and he was sticking to it.

'Are you copping a cheap feel?'

'No, just don't want to drop you and ruin your outfit.'

'But it's already ruined—'

'Gotcha!'

She pummelled harder, he laughed harder and he jogged the last few metres to her hut, deliberately sliding her down nice and slow, her body deliciously rubbing against his.

This was madness—pure and utter madness.

So much for taking things slow.

Every moment he spent in Tam's company, he found it harder to resist her, harder not to say caution be damned and sweep her into his arms and make slow, passionate love to her all night long.

He wanted her. Thoughts of her consumed him every waking moment and most sleeping ones too and now, with her standing less than a foot away, her tie-dyed kaftan plastered to her curvy body, he knew he couldn't hold out much longer.

He wanted to do the right thing, give her time to adjust to their new relationship but his knight in shining armour routine had taken a serious beating since he'd arrived on her doorstep earlier that week and she'd welcomed him with open arms.

'So?'

'So…' His gaze dipped, took in her orange, green and blue spattered face, her purple matted hair and the Technicolor kaftan.

Despite the mess, she'd never looked so beautiful and he clenched his hands to stop himself from reaching out to her and never letting go.

'Time to clean up.' She stepped back, as if sensing his urge. 'Though some of us need more cleaning up than others.'

She pointed to his irredeemable T-shirt. 'Not only can some of us not throw, we're none too crash hot at dodging too.'

'You're asking for it.'

He made a grab for her and they tumbled through the doorway, drenched to the skin and laughing uncontrollably.

'You look like a preschooler's finger-painting.'

'You look worse.'

They stared at each other and laughed again, as Tamara clutched her side. 'I'm sore.'

'From taking my direct hits full on?'

'More like from dodging your average throws.'

He pointed to her powder-spattered kaftan. 'Then how do you explain all that colour?'

She shrugged, put a thumb up to her nose and waggled her fingers. 'Other people.'

He advanced towards her. 'Are you saying my aim is lousy?'

She smiled. 'Oh, yeah. Though you might've landed a few lucky shots. Beginner's luck and all that.'

'Beginner, huh?' He continued to advance, his mouth twitching, his eyes filled with devilry and she backed up, stumbling into the bathroom. 'You going to admit I'm good?'

He halted less than two feet in front of her, close enough to feel his radiant heat, not close enough according to her body, straining towards him.

Tilting her chin up, she tossed her bedraggled hair over a shoulder. 'Never.'

'Never's a long time, sweetheart.'

His hand shot out, captured her wrist, tugging her closer and she laughed when their bodies made a strange squelching sound as they came into contact.

'Ready to concede?'

'Nope.' She shook her head, spraying them with the finest purple droplets, like sparkling amethysts raining from a jewelled sky.

'Well, then, I might just have to make you.'

His eyes glittered with pure devilry as he lowered his head, brushed his mouth across hers in a slow, masterful kiss that had her clinging to his wet T-shirt, her knees wobbling.

'Concede?'

Her tongue darted out to moisten her lips, still tingling from his kiss. 'I think I need more convincing.'

He growled, swept her up in his arms and deposited her on the hand basin, the hard, cold enamel barely registering as he swooped in for another kiss, a fiery, passionate explosion of melding mouths that heated her from the inside out and would've dried her clothes if they'd continued.

But she stopped, uncurled her fingers from where they clung to his T-shirt, all too aware of where this would lead.

'What's wrong?'

How could she articulate half of what she was feeling?

Blinding anticipation at being touched by a man after so long?

Good old-fashioned lust that licked along her veins and made her throb with need?

Crippling uncertainty that she wouldn't live up to his expectations?

Or the mind-numbing fear that, once she took this irreversible step, there'd be no going back?

Making love with Ethan would be just that for her—making love—and it would cement what she'd known the last few days.

She'd fallen in love with him.

Enough to take a chance on love again, enough to want it all—with him.

'Tam?'

He tipped up her chin, leaving her no option but to stare into his glittering blue eyes, those eyes she'd seen clear and sincere, determined and focused at work, currently a smoky gentian with passion.

'I'm scared.'

He cupped her cheek, drawing comforting circles in the small of her back with his other hand. 'I'd never do anything to hurt you.'

'I know, but—'

'But?'

'What if—' *this doesn't work, this makes you pull back again, this makes me fall in love with you even more and you don't feel half as much for me as I feel for you?*

'What if you stop second-guessing this and let me love you?'

She knew he meant it as a physical expression of love, but hearing him say the word out loud banished the last of her lingering doubts.

She'd spent every moment of her marriage carefully weighing and assessing—trying to say the right thing, do the right thing, wear the right thing. And she'd been miserable.

Now she had a second chance, a real chance at happiness and she'd be a fool to let it slip through her fingers.

Her hands slid up his chest, caressed his neck, cradled his face as she wrapped her legs around him. 'What if I show you how much I want this?'

His face creased into an instant smile, the heartrendingly familiar sexy smile that never failed to set her pulse racing.

'Sounds like a plan.'

He sent a pointed glance at their clothes. 'But we're filthy.'

Shocked at her bravado, she met his gaze head-on.

'Let's take a shower, then.'

His eyes, radiating enough heat to scorch her clothes right off her, never left hers as she reached out, her fingers grappling with the hem of his wet T-shirt before peeling it upwards with slow, exquisite deliberation, revealing inch by inch of spectacular hard, bronzed chest.

When she reached his shoulders, he helped shrug it off, leaving his torso deliciously bare, beckoning her fingertips to explore.

And explore she did, smoothing her palms over every hard plane, skating her fingertips over every ridge, every delineation, her breath catching as his hands shot out and captured her wrists.

'My turn,' he gritted out, ducking for a searing kiss before almost tearing her kaftan off. 'I've waited too long for this to take it slow.'

'Fast is good,' she gasped as, with a deft flick of the clasp on her bra, he had her breasts spilling free into his waiting hands.

'Ethan...'

She whispered his name on a sigh, a long, drawn-out, blissful sigh as his mouth replaced his hands until she almost passed out from the blinding intensity.

'You're so beautiful, so responsive,' he murmured, kissing his way down her body as sensation after sensation slammed into her, rendering a simple task like standing impossible.

She sagged against the basin, braced her hands on it as his fingers hovered, toyed with the elastic of her panties.

'I want this to be beyond special for you,' he said, wrenching a low moan from deep within as he set about doing just that.

She'd never been loved like this, never had a man want to please her first, please her so totally before taking his satisfaction and as Ethan brought her to the peak of ecstasy and she tumbled over the edge into an explosion of mind-numbing bliss, she finally came alive.

When he stood, she cradled his face, stared into his eyes, hoping he could read the depth of emotion there.

'Thank you,' she said, gasping as he pressed against her, her desire needing little to reignite.

'The pleasure's all mine.'

His roguish smile brought out the pirate in him and she gladly wrapped her arms around his waist, more than happy to be ravaged.

As the steam rose around them, she lost all sense of time. His shorts joined her discarded clothes, his body melded with hers and he made passionate love to her until she almost cried with the beauty of it.

Later, as he held her close, cocooned in the safety of his arms, the heat from their bodies drying them better than any towels, she knew without a doubt that this man was her destiny.

Ethan groaned, sat back and patted his stomach. 'Okay, now I'm done, are you going to tell me what's in that sorpotel?'

The corners of Tam's mouth twitched, the tiny movement slugging him as he recalled in vivid detail how those lips had explored his body last night. He'd dated widely but never had he felt so connected with a woman in the bedroom.

Though it was more than that and he knew it—knew it with every guarded cell in his body. What he felt for Tam defied description and had him jumpier than a mongoose around a cobra.

If she'd zapped his control before, he didn't stand a chance now; he wanted her more than ever. It was like sampling the finest Shiraz Grenache: one taste was never enough.

'You sure you want to know?'

He pointed to the empty bowl, where he'd mopped up every last bit of gravy with a paratha. 'Considering I've just devoured the richest curry I've ever had without leaving a drop, I think I can handle it.'

'It's made from pork, beef and pig's blood.'

Ignoring the smallest tumble of revolt his belly gave, he reached for his coconut milk and raised it to her.

'Nothing like those magic secret ingredients.'

She leaned across the table, giving him a delectable view of her cleavage and, to his credit, he managed to keep his gaze on her face.

'You don't have to pretend with me.'

His belly griped again but this time it had nothing to do with the thought of eating pig's blood.

He *was* pretending with her, living a fantasy—one he'd craved a long time. But fantasies didn't mesh with reality and if there was one thing he'd come to respect, it was reality.

He lived the reality every day—of trusting no one but himself, of staying on top in business, of never losing control.

Yet here, now, with Tam staring at him with a new sparkle in her eyes and a permanent smile on her face, he wasn't just in danger of losing control. He was in danger of losing his mind.

Seeing curiosity creep into her gaze, he clanked his coconut against hers. 'I couldn't come to a Goan institution like Souza Lobo's and not try the sorpotel. So, whatever's next, bring it on.'

Her eyes twinkled as she lowered her coconut. 'Brave words from a guy who got obliterated during Holi.'

He shrugged, thankful they'd safely navigated back to playful. 'I just wanted you to think you had the upper hand.'

'Didn't I?'

'I'll let you in on a little secret.'

He crooked his finger at her, laughing when she twisted it. 'I was lulling you into a false sense of security.'

The twinkle faded, replaced by a flicker of fear that had him cursing his poor choice of words.

Of course she'd be insecure with how fast things had developed between them. In effect, he was her rebound guy, the first guy she'd allowed near her after the love of her life, and having her questioning whether it was the right thing to do was a dumb move, however inadvertent.

Placing a finger under her chin, he tipped it up. 'I'm kidding.'

'I know.'

But he'd shattered the light-hearted mood and, considering he had no idea how to deal with emotion, was having a damn hard time getting it back.

'I know.' He snapped his fingers. 'Let's go haggle for some of those handmade Kashmiri scarves you were admiring on the way over here.'

Her mouth twisted in a wry grin. 'That's the second time this trip you've tried to distract me with the inducement of shopping.'

'Is it working?'

'I'll let you know when you've bought me a scarf or two.'

Happy to have the smile back on her face, he held out his hand. 'Me?'

'Yeah, don't you tycoons like flashing your cash around?'

'Only to impress.'

'Well, I'm ready to be impressed. Lead the way.'

As she slipped her hand into his, it hit him how truly lucky he was.

Despite her joking around, Tam wasn't remotely interested in his money. With the type of women he usually dated that meant a lot to him, but here, with the pungent aromas of frying spices and fresh seafood in the air, the hot sand squelching between his toes and the relentless sun beating down, it merely added to the unreality of the situation.

He was in a tropical hot spot with a gorgeous woman, they'd become lovers and grown closer than he'd dared imagine.

Was any of this real?

Would it evaporate as quickly as the steam off flavoursome mulligatawny when they returned to Melbourne? Did he want it to?

He liked Tam—a lot. But did he like her enough to give up the habits of a lifetime and relinquish control of his tightly held emotions?

'Come on, I see a flea market over there with my name written on a few dozen scarves.'

He groaned, delighting in her wide grin while trying to hide his inner turmoil.

Tamara leaned back against Ethan, secure in the circle of his arms. These days, there was no place she'd rather be.

'Comfortable?'

Turning her face up, her breath caught at the beauty of his face, shadows from the fire flickering over his cheekbones, highlighting his strong nose, the curve of his lips.

He was gorgeous and, for now, he was hers.

'Very.'

She wriggled back slightly, enjoying the sudden flare of heat in his eyes, the wickedly sexy smile.

'When you first mentioned a full moon party at Arjuna Beach, I envisaged a bunch of hippies drinking and having a full-on rave complete with bubbles. Nothing like this.'

He cuddled her closer, sweeping a kiss across her lips before resting his chin on her shoulder, content to just hold her as they stared at the bonfire one of the revellers had lit not far from the water's edge.

The stubble peppering his jaw brushed her cheek, the tiny

prickles strangely comforting. Gone was the slick, smooth, clean-shaven corporate pirate; in his place was his laid-back, easygoing, constantly smiling counterpart.

And she liked this guy much better.

How had she ever thought him distant and ruthless and aloof? The Ethan she'd got to know the last two weeks, the Ethan she'd fallen for, was warm and spontaneous and generous. He made her laugh, made her forget every sane reason why she shouldn't be losing her heart to him.

But what if it was too late? For, no matter how attentive and carefree he was here, she knew once they returned to Melbourne he'd revert back to type and she'd be left with nothing but memories.

She'd known it from the start, had held him at bay because of it, but no amount of self-talk could withstand a barrage of Ethan at his best: charming, gregarious and able to make her feel one hundred per cent female.

That was most seductive of all, for she hadn't felt this way in a long, long time.

Not only had Richard sapped her identity, he'd battered her self-esteem and, thanks to Ethan, she'd rediscovered another part of herself she'd thought lost—she was still a desirable woman, capable of instilling passion in a man and, right now, that made her feel like a million dollars.

'You've heard pretty much anything goes at these full moon parties, right?'

'Yeah.' His soft breath caressed her ear, sending a shiver of delight through her. 'So what do you have in mind?'

Tilting her face up to see him, she said, 'Dance with me.'

'Here?'

His dubious glance flicked to the couples surrounding the fire, some of them entwined, some holding hands, some lying back and staring at the stars, and she laughed at his doubtful expression.

'I love dancing and haven't done it for ages.'

His reticence melted away at her wistful tone and he stood, tugging her to her feet in one fluid movement, pulling her close until her breasts were squashed against his chest and her pelvis snuggled in his.

'How's that?'

'Perfect.'

And it was, not just the way their bodies fitted but the way he held her, as if she was something precious, something he never wanted to let go.

While logic said she was kidding herself in thinking that even for a second, her heart was going with the flow, caught up in the magic of the moment with soft sand still warm from the day's sun under her feet, Ethan's sandalwood scent enveloping her and his body speaking to her on some subconscious level.

They didn't speak, her head resting on his shoulder as they swayed in time to the sultry strains of a sitar, the drugging beat of a tabla. Closing her eyes, everything faded: the other couples, the fire, the music, the waves lapping at the water's edge.

She wanted to remember every second of tonight, imprint every incredible moment in her memory, for this was the night.

The night she admitted she'd fallen in love.

While she might not be ready to admit it to Ethan yet, the knowledge that she'd come so far—opening her heart again, learning to trust, taking a chance—was beyond empowering.

As the sitar faded, Ethan pulled away and she looked up, wondering if he could read the exultation in her eyes.

Cupping her cheek, he said, 'You're glowing.'

Smiling, she stood on tiptoe and kissed him. 'Thanks to you.'

'So I'm forgiven for muscling in on your holiday? And for deliberately making us miss the train in Udaipur?'

'Why, you—'

She whacked him on the chest and he laughed, swooping

in for a quick kiss. 'I had this stupid notion you'd fall for me surrounded by all that romance.'

'I don't need all those trappings.'

Sliding her arms around his waist, she snuggled into him again. 'You've kind of grown on me.'

'Good. You know why?'

'Why?'

'Because we only have a few days left and I intend to spend every second by your side. Think you can handle that?'

Ignoring the flutter of panic at the thought of what they had ending in a few days, she nodded. 'Yeah.'

'Then what are we waiting for? Let's head back and start making the most of our time together.'

His mouth captured hers again, his kiss searing as she melted against him, powerless to do anything other than want him, no matter how much her inner voice warned her their time together would soon be coming to an end.

'You sure you don't want me to come with you? I can always postpone this meeting.'

Tamara waved Ethan away. 'Go take care of your business. I'll meet you back at the hut later.'

'Not too much later.'

He pulled her in for a swift scorching kiss that sizzled all the way to her toes, leaving her breathless as he winked and waved, heading for the nearest five star hotel.

She watched him until he was a tiny speck in the distance, a tall figure striding down the dusty road with the long, determined steps of a man with things to do, places to be.

But he wasn't running from her and that was a bonus—a big one.

Since they'd made love two nights ago, they'd spent every waking moment together. All the things she'd planned on doing, like eating at Souza Lobo's and attending a full moon party, had been much more special with Ethan by her side, sharing the experience.

As for the nights…exploring each other's bodies, pleasuring each other…had surpassed any expectations she'd ever had.

Richard had been selfish so it figured he'd been a selfish lover too. But Ethan… Just thinking about the ways he gave her joy brought a blush to her cheeks.

Their time together had been beyond special. They were good together—really good. You couldn't fake what they had.

An unexpected chill ran down her spine as she remembered how she'd faked a lot during her marriage, how easy it was to act one way while feeling another.

Ethan may be a player but surely he didn't treat all his women this way? Surely his actions spoke louder than words in the way he'd cherished her in Goa?

While she hadn't gone into this expecting him to love her, now she'd fallen for him she couldn't help but wish they could explore this further.

He'd barrelled into her life when she'd least expected or wanted it but, now he was here, she hoped he'd stay.

She stopped in front of a sari shop, pressed her hands to the dusty glass and peered inside. Her mum had always wanted her to wear a sari, just once, but she'd never had the occasion or the inclination. Besides, Richard would've had a fit if she'd paraded her ethnicity around in front of his posh friends.

She'd overheard him once, boasting about her royal heritage or some such guff, implying she descended from a line of exotic East Indian princesses. She'd confronted him later and in typical fashion he'd laughed off her concerns, saying he had standards to live up to in the public eye and people liked that sort of thing.

She hadn't, though. She'd hated it and, while she'd toed the line in the vain hope of making her marriage work, the lies he'd told had never sat well with her.

Lies far more poisonous and extending further than she'd ever thought possible, considering what had come to light after his death.

Making an impulsive decision to buy one more souvenir of her memorable time here, she pushed open the door and stepped into the welcome coolness of the shop.

'*Namaste*. Can I help you, madam?'

The older woman placed her palms together and gave a little bow, her sightless eyes honing in on Tamara with unerring accuracy as she wondered how a blind woman could assist customers in a shop filled with so much vibrant colour.

'Yes, thanks, I'm looking for a sari.'

Duh! Not unlikely, considering she'd entered a sari shop.

'Anything in particular?'

She shook her head, belatedly realising the woman couldn't see her. 'I've never worn a sari before.'

'But it is in your blood.'

Her eyebrows rose at that. How could the woman know her background? Even if she could see, her light olive skin, green eyes and black hair could be any nationality.

'You are after something like this.'

It was a statement rather than a question as the woman ran her hands along countless silk, chiffon saris until she hovered over one, in the palest of mint-greens.

Her breath caught as the woman held it up, the exquisite length of material catching the sunlight filtering through the front window, the sari shimmering like the iced peppermint milkshakes she'd loved as a kid.

It was perfect, something she'd never imagine wearing; yet, with the shop filled with so many dazzling combinations, she should have a look around rather than grab the first thing on offer. Probably the most expensive sari in the shop and the woman thought she'd be foolish enough to pounce on it.

'Actually, I'm not sure what I want.'

The sari slid through the woman's fingers like quicksilver as she turned her head towards her.

'I think you do.'

A ripple of unease puckered her skin as she registered the woman wasn't talking about the sari.

She knew India was a country big on legends and myths and superstitions. Her mum had told her many stories of ghosts and ghoulies and mysterious happenings but, as far as she was concerned, her superstitious nature extended to a quick glance at the daily horoscope in the morning newspaper, and only then for a laugh.

But here, now, standing in this ancient shop, the heady fragrance of neroli and saffron in the air, surrounded by the soft swish of silk as the woman continued to run her hands over the saris, she could almost believe there was something 'otherworldly' at play.

'The sari is beautiful but—'

'You are searching. For many things. For love. For a home. For yourself.'

Another shiver ran through her. Okay, this was getting too spooky.

The woman was scarily accurate, though her predictions had been pretty generic. What tourist wouldn't be on a quest, searching for something, if only a good time?

'You have love. But all is not as it seems.'

She'd got that right. Since when was anything in her life simple?

'You will face many obstacles on your path to true happiness.'

More generic stuff and she'd had enough.

'Actually, that sari's perfect.' Checking out the price tag, she sagged with relief. 'I'll take it.'

She thrust money towards the woman, somewhat chastened when she shook her head, sadness creasing her face.

Great, she'd offended the soothsayer. Who knew what fortune she'd get now?

'You will face trials, recross oceans, to find true happiness.'

Giving the woman money and all but yanking her purchase out of her hands hadn't stopped the predications so she'd better make a run for it.

'Thank you.'

She had her hand on the door handle, eager to leave, when the woman stopped her with a low groan that raised the hackles on her neck.

'Take care, my dear. You will need to be on the lookout for false happiness.'

Okay, enough was enough.

She bolted from the shop, wishing she could outrun her doubts as fast as the blind woman. As if she wasn't filled with qualms already, she had some crazy fortune-teller fuelling her insecurities.

This was why she didn't pay attention to superstitious nonsense. Yet, no matter how hard she tried to forget the woman's predictions on the walk back to the hut, she couldn't help but feel she'd voiced some of her own concerns.

Was her relationship with Ethan too good to be true?

Was it all just a mirage, a *false happiness* that would fall down around her ears once they returned to Melbourne?

She'd talked herself into believing what they had was real. She was good at that. Convincing herself to see things in a positive light, no matter how dire they were. She was an expert considering she'd done it for most of her marriage.

There was a huge difference between faking happiness and experiencing the real thing and, while this last week with Ethan had shown her the difference, she still couldn't banish her doubts.

She'd come so far. Over the past year she would've wallowed in them, let them drag her down. Not now. Taking this trip had not only boosted her esteem, fuelled her confidence and encouraged her to take risks she'd never thought possible, she'd also become an optimist. Looking on the bright side was much more liberating than brooding and, for now, she'd take each day as it came with Ethan.

As for what happened in Melbourne, she'd find out soon enough. They were due to fly back tomorrow.

Back to the real world. Back to a new life for her. She had a new job to find, apartment-hunting and a new beginning with Ethan.

Ethan, the man she'd fallen in love with against her will. Her friend, her lover, her soulmate.

Her mum had been right. Every person had a soulmate and she'd just taken a detour on the way to finding hers.

They could have a future together—a good one.

This time, she wouldn't settle for anything less.

CHAPTER TWELVE

'LET me guess. You have business to take care of.'

Ethan leaned over, brushed a kiss across her lips. 'You know me too well.'

'I do now.'

Tamara placed a possessive hand on his arm, scraped her fingernails lightly across the skin, enjoying his slight shudder before he clamped his hand over hers, blatant hunger in his eyes.

'I promise I'll make it the fastest investors meeting on record.' He glanced at his watch, grimaced. 'I have to run. How about I meet you at Ambrosia afterwards?'

'Only if you make me a hot chocolate.'

'Over your chai addiction already?'

'No, but I remember that fabulous hot chocolate you made the day you came back and have a real hankering for it.'

He paused, his expression inscrutable and for a split second a finger of unease strummed her spine. 'So much has changed since that day.'

'For the better.'

He nodded, his tight-lipped expression not inspiring her with confidence. 'I've been doing a bit of thinking.'

The shiver increased. 'About?'

'About making up for lost time. About how much time I wasted not being around this last year, not seducing you earlier.'

That surprised her. She'd been anticipating many responses but not that one.

'Maybe I wasn't ready to be seduced?'

He smiled at her hand-on-out-thrust-hip defiance. 'Lucky for me you are now.'

'You think you've got me wrapped around your perfect little finger, huh?'

'Hey, I'm not perfect. Pretty tarnished, in fact.'

'Not to me.'

She wound her arms around his neck, snuggled close, breathing in his fresh, just-showered scent, wishing he didn't have to dash off.

They'd barely been back in the country six hours and it was business as usual for him. Not that it surprised her. His dynamic go-get-'em attitude was one of the things she loved about him.

While Richard had been good at his job—the best according to the experts—Ethan had a quiet confidence underlined by success.

She'd once been good at her job too, before she'd given it all up for Richard, and she couldn't wait to get back to it.

The restaurateur and the food critic.

People would talk, would say she'd moved on from the chef to the owner, but let them. She'd faced the media barrage after Richard died and, while she'd hated every minute at the time, she'd weathered the storm.

She'd never want to do it again, couldn't face it, but knew the man holding her close would protect her; she'd learned to trust him that much.

Pushing him away, she patted down his collar and smoothed the lapels of his suit jacket.

'Okay, off you go. Go do what you tycoons do.'

He smiled, ran a fingertip down her cheek before tapping her lightly on the nose. 'See you in two hours.'

'If you talk real fast, maybe one?'

'I'll try.'

As she watched him walk out of the door, utterly gorgeous in a charcoal pinstripe suit, she had to pinch herself to make sure this wasn't all a dream.

They'd landed back in Melbourne and the dream hadn't evaporated. Instead, he'd dropped her at the hotel suite she was staying in until she found a suitable apartment to buy, had raced home to get ready for his meeting and had paid a surprise visit back here on the way.

He must've thought she was a grub because he'd found her the way he'd left her—dishevelled and tired and still wearing the clothes she'd worn on the flight home. All his fault; after he'd dropped her off, she'd mooned about, flicking through travel brochures on India, lolling on the couch, lost in memories, remembering every magical moment of their journey.

The trip had exceeded all her expectations.

She'd discovered a part of her heritage that enthralled her, had finally released the last of her residual anger and had put the past—and Richard—behind her.

And she'd discovered a guy who had been on her periphery until now was in fact the love of her life.

Exceeded? Heck, her expectations had been blasted clean into orbit.

But, for now, she had a date with a shower. She wanted to get cleaned up before heading over to her favourite place in the world: Ambrosia, and right by Ethan's side.

Tamara pocketed her keys, grabbed her bag and was halfway out the door when the phone rang.

She paused, glanced at her watch and decided to let the answering machine pick up in case Ethan had finished early and was waiting for her.

With one ear on the garbled voice coming through the machine, she tapped the side of her head, wondering if water from the shower had clogged her ears. She could've sworn the guy was a reporter from a prominent Melbourne newspaper, the same guy who had hounded her relentlessly after Richard's death. What could he want with her now?

Not interested in anything he had to say, especially on the day she'd landed back in the country, she slammed the door, took the lift to the ground floor, strode through the swank foyer and out into a perfect autumn day.

There was nothing like Melbourne in autumn: the frosty weather, the crisp brown leaves contrasting with the beautiful green in the city parks, the fashionable women striding down Collins Street in high boots and long coats.

She loved it all and as she took a left and headed for Ambrosia, she'd never felt so alive. With a spring in her step, she picked up the pace, eager for her hot chocolate fix—her Ethan fix, more precisely.

Smiling to herself, she passed the newsstand she occasionally bought the odd glossy food magazine from. She may not have worked for a while but she'd kept up with the trends, critically analysing her competitors' work, knowing she could do better if she ever got back to it. That time had come and she couldn't be happier.

However, as she slowed to scan the latest cover of her favourite magazine, her blood froze as her gaze fixed on the headlines advertising today's newspapers.

CELEBRITY CHEF'S MISTRESS HAS LOVE CHILD.

She inhaled a sharp breath, let it out, closed her eyes and opened them.

This was silly. That headline could be referring to any number of celebrity chefs around the world.

With legs suddenly jelly-like, she forced her feet to walk forward, past the newsstand. She'd almost made it when the truth hit her.

The reporter's phone call.

The headline.

No, it couldn't be…

With her lungs screaming for oxygen, she turned back and snatched the nearest newspaper with trembling hands.

'Haven't seen you around here for a while, love?'

She arranged her mouth into a smile for the old guy who'd been working here for ever, when all she wanted to do was flap open the paper and see if the horrible sense of impending doom hanging over her was true.

'Been away.'

She thrust a ten dollar bill at him. 'Here, keep the change.'

'But that's way too much—'

She waved over her shoulder and half ran, half wobbled to the nearest wrought-iron bench, where she collapsed, the newspaper rolled tight in her fist.

It's not about him…it's not about him…

However, no matter how many times she repeated the words, the second she opened the paper and saw Richard's face smiling at her, right next to Sonja's, adjacent to that of an adorable chubby baby with her husband's dimples, the life she'd worked so hard to reassemble crumbled before her very eyes.

She had no idea how she made it to Ambrosia, no recollection of the walk as she unlocked the restaurant and relocked the door before falling onto the nearest chair.

She stared blindly around the room, the place that had become a safe haven for her. The pale lemon walls, the honey oak floorboards, the open fireplace along one wall, the glittering bar along the other—she'd spent every Monday here for the last six months, drinking hot chocolate, honing her work skills, putting her life back together.

A life now laid bare for the public to see and scrutinise and judge.

It had been hard enough discovering Sonja's existence,

the evidence that not only had Richard been cheating on her, but he'd done it in a house bought and paid for by him too while he'd imposed ridiculously tight budgets on her.

She'd been humiliated at the discovery of the other woman, had told no one, and now her degradation would be seen by everyone, her hopes for a new start dashed.

She fisted her hands, pushed them into her eyes in the vain hope to rub away the haunting image of that cherubic baby picture in the newspaper.

That should've been her baby, the baby she'd wanted but Richard had always vetoed, the baby he'd been too busy to have, the baby that would've given her the complete family she always wanted.

She'd pushed for a child, had been placated with lousy excuses and now she'd come face to face with yet more evidence of how much her husband hadn't loved her, how little he'd really thought of her.

Damn him for still having the power to annihilate the self-confidence she'd so carefully rebuilt.

She'd handled his infidelity but this…

Deep sobs racked her body as she bundled the paper into a ball and flung it across the room with an anguished scream.

'What the—' Ethan dropped his briefcase near the back door, where he'd entered, and ran for the main restaurant, where he'd heard the most God-awful sound.

He burst through the swinging doors, his heart leaping to his mouth at the sight that greeted him.

Tam, slumped on a chair, her head buried in her arms while great sobs rent the air, her delicate shoulders heaving.

'Tam?'

He raced across the room, pulled up a chair next to her and reached out to touch her.

'Sweetheart, it's me.'

Her head snapped up and the raw pain radiating from her

red-rimmed eyes slammed into him like a cast-iron skillet. He opened his arms to her, wanting to comfort her, desperate to slay whatever demon had driven her to this.

She shook her head, hiccuped. 'He had a baby.'

Who had a baby?

She wasn't making sense.

With tears coursing down her cheeks, she jerked her thumb towards the floor, where he spied a balled-up newspaper.

He reached it in two strides, smoothing it on the bar, the picture painting a shocking scenario before he sped-read the accompanying article.

Hell, no.

White-hot rage slammed through him, quickly turning to blinding fury as he bunched the newspaper in his fist, searched Tam's face, seeing the truth in every devastated line.

That bastard.

That low-life, lying, cheating, no good, son of a— He sucked in a deep breath.

He needed to support Tam, not fuel his anger. An anger that continued to bubble and stew and threatened to spill over as he watched her swipe her eyes, her hand shaky, her lower lip trembling.

He'd never seen her so bleak, even when she'd lost Rich, the jerk he'd like to personally kill at this very moment if he weren't already dead.

'That baby should've been mine.'

He froze. Surely she didn't mean that?

After what he'd just learned about Rich, about their marriage, how could she have wanted a child by that monster?

'I wanted one, you know.'

She scrambled in her bag for a tissue, her fingers fumbling as she finally found one and used it to great effect. 'More than one. I hated being an only child.'

What could he say? That he thought she was crazy for

wanting kids with Rich? That now, a year after his death, she shouldn't be reacting this way to proof that the guy was scum?

Then it hit him.

What he'd been trying to ignore all along.

She still loved him.

He'd kept his distance all these years, had only made a move now because he'd thought she was over him.

But she wasn't and, despite everything Richard had done, clearly stated in that paper for the world to see, she still wasn't over him.

His hands balled into instant fists, frustration making him want to pound the table.

It was the reason why he hadn't rushed her at the start, this fear that she still had feelings for Richard, the fear that he'd just be the rebound guy, no matter how long he waited.

He'd put it down to his own insecurities, had ignored the twinge of doubt, had taken a chance by letting his iron-clad control slip for the first time ever.

He'd made a monumental mistake, just as he'd feared. Losing control, allowing emotions to rule, only led to one thing: disaster.

'I don't believe this.'

Her red-rimmed eyes sought his, her expression bleak. But she didn't reach out to him and he wanted her to. Damn it, he wanted her to need him, to want him, to love him.

As much as he loved her.

The realisation sent him striding from the table to behind the bar, desperate to put something concrete and solid between them.

He'd made enough of an idiot of himself over her without adding an inopportune declaration to the mix.

She didn't need his love. How could she, when she was still pining for Richard?

She wished her late husband's girlfriend's baby was hers.

He couldn't compete with that. He couldn't compete with the memory of a dead guy. He didn't want to.

'I'm sorry you're going through this.' He switched on the espresso machine, needing to keep busy, needing to obliterate the driving need to vault the bar and bundle her in his arms. 'Coffee? Or a hot chocolate?'

She stilled before his very eyes, her hands steadying as she pushed her chair back, her legs firm as she stood and crossed the restaurant to lean on the bar.

Confusion clouded her eyes. 'I thought you'd be more understanding about this.'

'Oh, I understand a lot more than you think.'

Silently cursing his hasty response, he turned away and busied himself with getting cups ready.

'What's that supposed to mean?'

Rubbing a hand across the back of his neck, he swivelled to face her, trying not to slam the cups onto the bar.

'I've never seen you this upset, even after he died.'

He had time to swallow his words, clamp down on the urge to blurt out exactly what he was thinking. But nothing would be the same after this anyway, so why not tell her the truth? Go for broke?

'Yet here you are, wishing that child was yours.'

He shook his head, poured milk into a stainless-steel jug for frothing to avoid looking at her shattered expression.

'I don't get it. I've just learned the guy I thought I knew had a mistress he shacked up with whenever he could and he had a kid with her, yet here you are, still affected by him. Makes me wonder why.'

When she didn't respond, he glanced up, the emerald fire in her eyes surprising him. She'd gone from quivering victim to furious in a second.

'Why don't you go ahead and tell me what you think? You seem to have done a pretty good job until now.'

He didn't deserve her anger—Rich did, and somehow the fact that she'd turned on him when she should've turned to him lit a fuse to his own smouldering discontent.

'Fine. You want to know what I think?'

His palms slammed onto the bar as he leaned towards her. 'I think Richard left a lasting legacy. I think you're so hung up on the guy you can't get past him, maybe you never will. And I think as long as you let your past affect you this way, you won't have the future you deserve.'

Derision curled her upper lip, her eyes blazing, but not before he'd seen the pain as he scored a direct hit.

'What future is that? With you?'

She made it sound as if she'd rather change that baby's diapers for a lifetime than be with him and he turned away, anguish stabbing him anew.

He had his answer.

She'd just confirmed every doubt he'd ever had—that he'd never live up to King Richard in her heart.

'You know, this place has been a safe haven for me lately. Not any more.'

Her heels clacked against the floorboards as she marched to the table, scooped up her bag and headed for the door.

He watched her in the back mirror, his heart fracturing, splintering, with every step she took.

He could've called out, stopped her, run after her.

Instead, he watched the woman he loved walk out of the door.

CHAPTER THIRTEEN

THE drive down the EastLink Freeway passed in a blur. It was as if she'd been on autopilot ever since she'd stormed out of Ambrosia, hell-bent on putting the past behind her, once and for all.

Ethan was wrong. Dead wrong. About everything.

Except one thing: she had no hope of moving forward unless she confronted her past and that was why she was here in the peaceful ocean retreat of Cape Schanck, clutching a crumpled piece of paper in her hand, staring at the address written in a woman's flowing script, her heart pounding as she slowly looked up at the beautiful beach house.

Richard had been careful to hide his infidelity from her while he'd been alive but she'd found this in an old wallet in the back of his wardrobe after he'd died.

She'd been clearing out his stuff, donating his designer suits to charity and had come across it. At the time, she hadn't cared what it meant but later, when she'd discovered his private appointment diary detailing every sordid detail, along with a stack of emails complete with pictures, it had all made sense.

Cape Schanck. Haven for gold-digging mistresses. And their illegitimate babies.

She blinked several times, determined not to cry. This wasn't a time for tears. She had to do this, had to get on with her life before the bitterness and anger threatened to consume her again; there was no way she'd go back to living the way she had been before India.

Taking a steadying breath, she strode to the front door and knocked twice, loudly.

As she waited, she noticed the spotless cream-rendered walls, the duck egg blue trim, the soft grey shingles. The garden was immaculate, with tulips in vibrant pinks and yellows spilling over the borders, the lawn like a bowling green, and she swallowed the resentment clogging her throat at the thought of Richard tending this garden, on his hands and knees in the dirt, with *her*.

She knocked again, louder this time, feeling foolish. She'd driven the hour and a half down here, fuelled by anger and the driving need to forget, yet hadn't counted on Sonja not being here.

As she was about to turn away, she heard footsteps and braced herself, thrusting her hands into the pockets of her trench coat to stop herself from reaching out and wrapping them around the other woman's neck when she opened the door.

The door swung open and she came face to face with the woman who had stolen her life.

Sonja Van Dyke was stunning, a Dutch supermodel who had graced the catwalks for years in her late teens and, even now, couldn't be more than twenty-five.

She'd taken Australia by storm when she'd first arrived and was rumoured to be making her television debut on a reality show any day now.

Considering how she'd just splashed her sordid affair with Richard all over the tabloids with gay abandon, heaven help her, for who knew what gems she'd drop on live TV?

Even though they'd never met, instant recognition lit the redhead's extraordinary blue eyes as she took a step back, her hand already swinging the door shut.

'Wait.' Tamara stepped forward, wedged her foot in the doorjamb.

With a toss of her waist-length titian hair, Sonja straightened her shoulders as if preparing to do battle. 'I've got nothing to say to you.'

'Well, I've got plenty to say to you.'

Her eyes turned flinty as a smug smile curved the mouth that must've kissed her husband's. The thought should've made her physically ill but now she'd arrived, had seen this woman, all she felt was relief.

She'd done it. Confronted her demons. Now all she had to do was slay them and she could walk away, free.

'It's not a good time for me. Little Richie will be waking from his nap soon.'

Just like that, her relief blew away on the blustery ocean breeze, only to be replaced by the familiar fury that one man had stolen so much from her.

Her dignity, her identity, her pride, and she'd be damned if she stood here and let his mistress steal anything else from her.

'Tough. You need to hear what I have to say.'

She drew on every inner reserve of strength, determined to get this out and walk away head held high.

'By making this fiasco public, you've guaranteed a media frenzy for a month at least. Just keep me out of it. Richard owed me that much at least.'

Sonja drew herself up to an impressive five-eleven and glared down at her. 'Who the hell are you to tell me what I can and can't say? As for Richie owing you, you meant nothing to him.'

She ignored the deliberate provocation of the last statement, needing to get through this and slam the door on her past once and for all.

'I don't give a damn what you say as long as I'm left out of it—'

'Did you know I was six weeks pregnant when Richie died? He was so happy. Thrilled he was going to be a daddy.'

Her blue eyes narrowed, glittering with malice. 'He was going to leave you, you know. Over, just like that.'

She snapped her fingers, her cold smile triumphant.

Tamara's resolution wavered as a fresh wave of pain swamped her. Richard had known about the baby, had continued to come home to her every night and play the dutiful husband while preparing to leave her.

Her belly rolled with nausea and she gulped in fresh air like a fish stranded on a dock, willing the spots dancing before her eyes to fade.

'As for little Richie, he's going to be just as famous as his mama and daddy. That's why I waited until now to sell my story and have him photographed.'

Her eyes gleamed with malice. 'He had terrible jaundice for the first eight weeks and would've looked awful. But now, at four months, he's absolutely gorgeous. Ready for stardom, like his parents.'

Just like that, she realised nothing she could say to this woman would get through to her. She'd been a fool to come here, to try and reason with her.

Being confronted by reports and pictures of Richard and herself in the newspapers and glossy magazines every day for a fortnight when he'd died had driven her mad and now the tabloids would have a field day. This could go on for months; she'd hoped by appealing to Sonja she might refrain from fuelling the story.

But she'd been an idiot. There was no reasoning with the woman. She wanted to relaunch her career and was planning on using her affair with Richard and their child to do it.

She'd never be free of them, free of the scandal, free of the whispers and pitying glances behind her back.

She had to get out of here, escape.

Like a welcome oasis for a thirsty desert traveller, the image of Colva Beach, the Taj Mahal, shimmered into her mind's eye.

There was a place she'd never be plagued by her past, continually reminded of her foolishness in trusting a man totally wrong for her.

A place linked to her heritage, a place filled with hope, a place she could dream and create the future she deserved.

A place she would return to as soon as possible.

'Richie trusted me implicitly. He'd back me one hundred per cent on this, as he always did. Nothing like the love of a good man to give a woman courage to face anything, wouldn't you say?'

Sonja's sickly sweet spite fell on deaf ears—until the implication of what she'd said hit her.

She had a guy who backed her one hundred per cent, who'd travelled all the way to India to do it.

A guy who'd given her courage to start afresh.

A guy who deserved to hear the truth, no matter how humiliating for her.

Walking out on Ethan had been a mistake. A rash, spur-of-the-moment action fuelled by that stupid newspaper article.

She'd been living a lie, had thought she'd put the past behind her, only to have it come crashing down around her and, rather than tell him everything, she'd run.

How ironic—it had taken a cheap tart like Sonja to point out what had been staring her in the face.

Without saying a word, she turned on her heel and headed down the garden path towards the car.

'You're just as spineless as Richie said you were.'

The parting barb bounced off her and she didn't break stride. Nothing Sonja could do or say could affect her now.

Coming here might've been stupid but it had been cathartic. She'd soon be free of her past.

And ready to face her future.

Ethan stepped out of the limo in front of Ambrosia and dropped his travel case at his feet.

He'd thrown himself back into business since Tam had walked out on him four days ago, making flying visits to Sydney, Brisbane and Cairns.

Facilitating meetings, presenting figures, convincing investors, he'd done it all in a nonstop back-to-back whirl of meetings but he was done, drained, running on empty.

Earlier that week he'd landed back in the country, had lost the woman he loved on the same day and buried his head in business as usual to cope; little wonder he could barely summon the energy to step inside.

He stood still for a moment, the slight chill of a brisk autumn evening momentarily clearing his head as he watched patrons pack his restaurant to the rafters.

Intimate tables for two where couples with secretive smiles held hands, tables filled with happy families squabbling over the biggest serving of sticky date pudding, tables where businessmen like himself absentmindedly forked the delicious crispy salt and pepper calamari into their mouths while shuffling papers and making annotations.

He loved this place, had always loved it. It was his baby, his home.

Then why the awful, hollow feeling that some of the gloss had worn off?

He should be punching the air. He'd had a lucky escape. Tam had made her true feelings clear before he was in too deep.

Though what could be deeper than falling in love with a woman he could never have?

With a shake of his head, he picked up his bag and headed

in, the warmth from the open fire on the far side instantly hitting him as the fragrant aromas of garlic, bread fresh from the oven and wok-sizzled beef enveloped him.

He was home and the sooner he banished thoughts of his failed relationship with Tam the better.

'Hey, boss, how was the trip?'

He mustered a tired smile for Fritz, his enthusiastic barman. 'Busy.'

'I bet. Want a drink?'

'A double shot espresso would be great.' He patted his case. 'Help me get through these projections. I'll take it upstairs.'

Fritz saluted. 'No worries.'

As he turned away, Fritz called out, 'Almost forgot. Tamara's popping in soon. She came in earlier, asked when you'd be back and I told her. Said she'd come back.'

His heart bucked and he carefully blanked his expression before nodding. 'Thanks. Give me a buzz when that coffee's ready. And throw in a hot chocolate for her.'

'Shall do, boss.'

He trudged up the stairs to his office, too weary for this confrontation. If it had happened a few days earlier, when he hadn't had time to mull over his foolishness, he might've been more receptive to hearing what she had to say.

But now? What could she say that would change any of this?

She was still in love with her dead husband.

He was in love with her.

A no-win situation, something he never dwelled on in business and he'd be damned if he wasted time wishing things were different now.

After flinging his bag down and bumping the door shut with his hip, he headed to his desk and sank into the chair, rubbing his temples.

They'd both been angry that day she'd walked out. They'd probably had a case of mild jet lag, but that didn't explain her reaction to that baby. Strange thing was, she'd been more upset by the baby than her husband's infidelity.

Unless... He sat bolt upright.

She must've known about the affair.

But for how long? Surely a woman of her calibre wouldn't put up with anything like that?

Something niggled at the edge of his thoughts, something she'd said in India... Another bolt of enlightenment struck as he remembered her saying something about wives putting up with their husbands to keep the peace or some such thing...

The ache behind his temples intensified as the impact of what he was contemplating hit him.

He'd thought he'd known Rich: capable, gregarious, master in the kitchen. But while Rich may have been a talented chef, it looked like he'd had another side to him, a side that made him want to knock his teeth in.

A tentative knock had him striding to the door and yanking it open, all his logical self-talk from the last few days fleeing as he stared at Tam, looking cool and composed in a simple black dress, her eyes wide and wary as they met his.

'I needed to see you.'

Stepping back, he gritted his teeth against the overpowering urge to sweep her into his arms. 'Come in.'

'How've you been?'

He gestured towards the stack of paperwork on his desk. 'Busy. Business as usual.'

She didn't glance at the desk, her wide-eyed gaze fixed on him instead. 'Yeah, Fritz told me you'd been away since the day we got back.'

Shrugging, he indicated she take a seat. 'Duty calls.'

'I admire that about you.'

He searched her face for an indication that she was anything but sincere and came up lacking. But there was something in her tone, as if she was judging him for his work ethic.

'Your ability to slot back into the groove as if nothing has happened.'

'Oh, plenty's happened. I just think I'm better suited to business than figuring out what happened with us.'

She winced and he clenched his hands into fists, thrust them into his pockets to stop from hitting himself in the head for letting that slip out.

His legendary control vanished around this woman, shot down, like his hopes of ever being anything more than a holiday romance for her.

'I overreacted the other day. I'm sorry.'

'Hey, you had every right to overreact.'

He paused, hating to dredge up pain for her but needing to know. 'Did you know Rich was cheating on you?'

Her slow nod had his fists bunching, as he wondered for the hundredth time in the last few days what sort of a jerk would screw around on an amazing woman like Tam.

'I had my suspicions and discovered the truth after he died, but I had no idea about the baby.'

'That must've hurt.'

To his surprise, she shrugged, as if it meant little. 'It did at the time. Made me crazy for a while but I'm over it now. I've moved on.'

She perched on the edge of his desk, so close, so temptingly close. 'Thanks to you.'

'Rebound guy.'

The words were out before he could stop them and she frowned, looking more formidable than he'd ever seen her.

'What?'

'You heard me.'

'You think you're my rebound guy?'

'Yeah.'

Her laughter shocked him as much as her quick swivel towards him, leaving her legs dangling precariously close to him, so close they brushed his arm.

'You're not rebound guy. You're *the* guy.'

He had no idea what she meant, was too confused by her nearness to ask.

Was she deliberately trying to provoke him? Get him to touch her? His palms tingled with the urge to do just that and he kept his hands firmly lodged in his pockets.

'The guy I want to have a future with. The guy who has helped me learn to trust again. The guy I'm in love with.'

His gaze zeroed in on hers, searching for some signal that the stress of the last few days had sent her batty.

All he saw were clear green eyes locked on his, eyes brimming with sincerity and tears and love, the latter enough to catapult him out of the chair and reach for her before he could think twice.

'Say it again.'

She smiled, blinked several times. 'I love you. Can't believe I'm actually saying those words to a guy like you, but there you go.'

He gripped her arms, his initial elation dimming. 'A guy like me?'

'The ultimate playboy, remember? Serial dater? Guy voted most likely to break a woman's heart?'

'Who said that?'

Her lips twitched and he itched to cover them with his. 'Okay, so I made that last bit up. But I have to tell you, loving you is the ultimate risk for me.'

'Because of what Rich did to you?'

To her credit, she didn't flinch or react when he mentioned the jerk's name.

'Because I'd sworn never to trust another guy again.'

She cupped his cheek. 'But you're not just any guy, are you?'

She'd put her heart on the line for him. The least he could do was give her a healthy dose of honesty in return.

'No, I'm the guy who doesn't do emotion. I'm the guy who's a control freak, who's so damned scared of letting go that I almost messed up the best thing to ever happen to me.'

'What's that?'

'You.'

He crushed his mouth to hers, devouring her, hungering for this kiss like a starving man being offered a Michelin-starred buffet.

The kiss went on for ever, a fiery union of two people who couldn't get enough of each other.

How he wished that were true.

In reality, he was chary. For while Tam thought she loved him, he couldn't get the image of her reacting to Rich's baby out of his head; the same head that warned him to tread carefully, as always.

He'd had time to think, time to take back control of his uncharacteristically wavering emotions and, whatever happened, he knew he couldn't simply pick up where they'd left off.

As the kiss gentled, their lips reluctant to disengage, he hugged her, tight.

She'd fallen in love with him and, whether it was on the rebound or not, he knew what it must've cost her to come here and tell him.

'I've got something to tell you.'

He pulled back, searched her face for a clue to the sombre edge in her voice.

'I'm going back to India.'

Fear ricocheted through him, a fear he'd long conquered. Fear that no matter how badly he wanted something, when he could almost taste it, it was snatched out of his reach.

He'd battled the fear when on the streets, when first taken

in by Arnaud, when he'd clawed his way to the top, expecting at every turn to have his goal taken away.

With success, he'd expected to lose the fear but here it was, rearing its ugly head and tormenting him anew.

'For another trip?'

She gnawed at her bottom lip, shook her head. 'I'll never be free of the past as long as I stay here. I want to make a fresh start and I can do that over there.'

The fear coalesced, consolidated, pounding in his ears, yelling that he'd lost her before they'd really started.

'I love you but I have to do this, for me.'

His shocked gaze collided with hers, the depth of her feeling evident in the way she looked at him with stars in her eyes.

She loved him.

She was leaving.

So much for being back in control. His wildly careening emotions swung between exaltation that she returned his love to despair that she'd snatched it out of reach before they'd really begun.

'Ethan? Say something.'

Releasing her, he turned away, needing breathing space, needing time to think.

What could he say?

That he loved her so much it'd kill him to see her walk away now?

That he loved her but couldn't contemplate following her for fear of losing ground with the one solid, reliable thing in his life—his business?

That, until recently, being the number one restaurateur in the world was his dream but, thanks to her, his dream had changed?

He could say any of those things. Instead, he had a sinking feeling that his lifelong need to control everything would eradicate his dream.

He'd fought long and hard to conquer the insecurities borne

from being dumped by a mother who didn't love him, of enduring beatings from older step-siblings, from sleeping in doorways and foraging for scraps of food to fill the ache ravaging his empty belly.

Nothing intimidated him any more. In the business arena, he was king.

Yet right at this moment, with Tam's declaration echoing through his head, haunting him, taunting him, he was catapulted back to a time where he felt sick to his stomach with fear.

Fear he'd lose total control and there'd be no coming back.

Dragging a hand through his hair, he turned back to face her, met her eyes, saw his fear reflected there.

'Not very often I'm lost for words, huh?'

'Try never.'

Her bottom lip wobbled, slugging him to his soul, before she squared her shoulders.

'I'm not asking anything of you.' She waved around the office, pointed at the stack of paperwork on his desk. 'I know you've got a business to run but if you take another holiday, you know where to find me.'

'Where will you be?'

'Agra for the first month or two. I'll probably haunt the Taj for the first fortnight. There was so much more I wanted to see. Then back to Goa. I'll base myself there, start looking for a place to live and exploring job opportunities then.'

His heart almost burst with pride as he saw her standing there, confident in what she wanted, in stark contrast to the fragile woman of a few months ago. She'd come so far.

And she loved him.

It all came back to that. Considering what Rich had done to her, for her to trust him enough with her love let alone be honest about it, blew him away.

With her on another continent, damned if he knew what to do about it.

'You're amazing, you know that?'

He slid his arms around her, hugged her close, wishing he could hold her like this for ever.

'I do now.'

Her voice wavered and he cuddled her tighter, wishing he could throw caution to the wind and follow her to the ends of the earth.

She settled into his embrace for a moment before placing her palms against his chest and pushing away.

'I better go.'

He frowned, tipped her chin up, hating the hint of sadness, resignation, in her voice.

'Don't we have time to—'

'My flight leaves tonight.' She held her hand over his lips, pressed lightly, as if imprinting his lips on her palm. 'I have to go.'

He opened his mouth to respond, to tell her to stay, to give them time, to explore the incredible, wondrous love they'd opened their hearts to.

But he couldn't do that to her, couldn't put his needs in front of hers. He'd be damned if he treated her in any way remotely like that bastard Richard.

This was *her* time.

He loved her enough to let her go.

'My Tam.'

He caressed her cheek, his fingertips skating across her skin, imprinting the feel of her into his memory to dredge up at the end of a long day.

Tipping her chin up, his gaze skimmed her face, memorising every detail and, when his gaze collided with hers, the pain in her shimmering eyes took his breath away.

'I'll miss you.'

Before he could move she plastered her lips to his, a swift,

impassioned kiss filled with the yearning clamouring at his
soul, breaking the kiss when he tried to hold on to her.

'Tam!'

'Maybe I'll see you at the Taj some time.'

With wooden legs rooted to the spot, he watched her
hurried yet dignified exit, stifling the urge to chase and beg
her to stay, the dull ache in his chest spreading, gutting him.

He rubbed at his chest, pacing his office like one of the
tigers they'd seen at a National Park.

The ache gnawed at him, eating away a large hole that soon
flooded with a sickening mix of regret and frustration and fear.
Fear that he'd lost her—for good.

Maybe with distance, time apart, he could figure out what
to do. The thought alone made a mockery of his need for time.

Time for what? Time to second-guess himself at every
turn? Time to dredge up every reason why he couldn't do this?
Time to dissociate from the crazy, wild, out-of-control feeling
loving Tam fostered?

The way he saw it, he was all out of time.

She'd had the guts to lay it all on the line for him. So what
was he going to do about it?

Real life was far from rosy and happy endings usually
required a hell of a lot of hard work and compromise. He knew
that better than anyone else.

But he wanted that happy ending, craved it with every
ravenous cell in his body.

His gaze lighted on the phone. He had the resources and
the contacts worldwide to make anything happen.

How hard could it be to organise his life for the next month
or so in order to follow the woman he loved?

Snatching up the phone, he punched in numbers.

Only one way to find out.

CHAPTER FOURTEEN

TAMARA lay back on the wooden massage table, wriggling around to get comfortable while latching onto the skimpy towel in an effort to cover her breasts.

Her mum had extolled the virtues of Ayurvedic therapies at length, a firm believer that all aspects of life, from people to animals to diseases, were combinations of the three energy elements: air, fire and water.

Apparently, her *dosha*—constitution—was predominantly air, which explained why she was prone to worry, anxiety and the occasional bout of nerves.

Right now, she was all three as the therapist, a woman of indeterminate age dressed in a simple white sari, positioned a pot of hot oil directly over her head.

'Relax. This will help rebalance you.'

Easy for her to say. She wasn't the one about to get hot oil dripped onto her forehead.

However, as the first trickle flowed gently onto her forehead, she exhaled in relief and closed her eyes, filled with a serenity she'd been craving for a week.

Coming back to India was supposed to centre her, help her feel safe, and while she'd been more grounded in the last seven days than she had in a while, a strange restlessness still gripped her.

She'd expected an instant fix coming back here. Crazy, considering what she'd been through, but at least she could relax here without fear of opening a newspaper or turning on a television to find evidence of Richard's disregard leering at her.

The oil stream stopped as she squinted through one eye, watching the woman straightening the oil pot before she delved bony fingers through her hair to her scalp.

'Too tense, too tense.' She tut-tutted, digging her fingers deeper until Tamara sighed, determined to ignore her negative thoughts and luxuriate under the expert tutelage of massaging fingers.

'Breathe. Let the oils help you.'

Great, she'd stumbled across another wannabe fortune-teller.

Though, from the tension in her muscles, it didn't take a psychic to figure out she was anxious about something.

'Sandalwood is good for stress, frankincense for fear, gardenia for anger. Breathe, let the oils work for you.'

Yeah, she was stressed. Discovering your husband was a lying, cheating hound and his mistress had just told the world about it led to loads of stress. Not to mention the baby bonus.

And she was scared—scared she'd made the wrong decision in leaving behind the one man who'd brought joy to her life in a very long time.

As for anger, she'd thought she'd left all that behind when she'd walked away from Sonja and all she stood for.

'Your *dosha* needs soothing, many treatments. Abhyanga and aromatherapy today, meditation tomorrow, colour and gem therapy the day after. Yes?'

She could handle abhyanga—this massage really was to die for—and the oils and meditation at a pinch, but she had the feeling that this wise woman was giving her a sales pitch along with the amateur psychobabble.

Mumbling a noncommittal response, she concentrated on relaxing her muscles, blanking her mind.

It didn't work.

Her thoughts zoomed straight back to Ethan.

What was he thinking? Doing? Feeling?

It had taken all her limited supply of courage to see him again after she'd stormed out of Ambrosia the day she'd discovered Richard had a love child by his mistress.

But she'd had to—had to tell him the truth. She loved him, trusted him and, while he hadn't said the words back, she now knew he was a man of action rather than words.

His admission, ripped from somewhere deep within, spoke volumes. He was a control freak and, for someone like him, this powerful yet nebulous emotion gripping her would be terrifying.

She understood. But it didn't make the ache gripping her heart any easier, or eradicate the fruitless wish that he could've come with her. She hadn't expected him to, would've argued if he'd suggested it, but that didn't stop the constant yearning she had.

'No good, no good.'

The woman pummelled her thigh muscles, lifted a leg and dropped it. 'Too tense. You go, come back tomorrow.'

She opened her eyes, sat up, clutching the towel to her chest. 'But I paid for an hour.'

The woman waved her away. 'I will give you two hours tomorrow but today—useless. Your muscles—' she banged the wooden table with a fist '—hard as this. Abhyanga not work for you today.'

She opened her mouth to protest again but the woman floated out of the room on a whirl of sari, leaving her cold and seminaked and ruing her decision to have a massage to unwind.

Maybe she would come back tomorrow.

Then again, she had a feeling that nothing could help release the pent-up tension twisting her muscles into ropes of steel.

Nothing, apart from having Ethan arrive on her doorstep. And that just wasn't going to happen.

He'd been here since daybreak every day for a week, watching the pale dawn bathe the marble monument in translucent light, staying until dusk when the purple streaks turned the Taj luminescent, grateful the law only allowed electric vehicles within ten kilometres of this stunning monument to avoid pollution staining it.

He'd traversed the place from end to end, lingering around the main gateway, oblivious to the beauty of the entwined red lotus flowers, leaves and vines motifs inlaid in semi-precious stones around the niche, always on the lookout.

He'd drifted past the red sandstone mosque on the western side of the Taj and the Taj Mahal Naggar Khana—Rest House—to the east, buoyed by hope.

He'd sat by the tranquil River Yamuna snacking on tiffin packed by the hotel, he'd strolled through the gardens, scanning the crowds for a glimpse of Tam.

Nothing.

An endless week where he'd scoured the Taj Mahal, a shadow to its greatness, drifting to every corner of the magnificent monument with the hope in his heart lending speed to his feet.

He'd walked. And walked. And walked.

Always on the lookout, his gaze darting every which way, following the hordes, desperate for a glimpse of long black hair and sparkling green eyes.

Still nothing.

While the flight details he'd obtained said she'd landed in Delhi, then hopped a train to Agra and hadn't left again, Tam could be anywhere.

Maybe she'd changed her mind about haunting this place, had taken a train, a bus, to goodness knows where. Or she could be holed up in some ashram seeking higher guidance. Or planning a trek up Everest. Or back in Goa already.

Wherever she was, she wasn't here.

He rubbed his eyes, refocused on the crowd heading towards the Taj. This was crazy. A waste of time.

He could spend a lifetime here and she still wouldn't turn up.

This was the last hour.

Come tomorrow, he'd instigate phase two of his plan to track her down. In the meantime, he had one more lap of the grounds to complete.

Tamara's breath caught at her first glimpse of the Taj Mahal, as it did every day she'd come here.

As the sun set the faintest pink blush stole across the marble, the highest dome a breathtaking silhouette against the dusk sky.

Despite the tourists milling around, snapping away, an instant sense of peace infused her and she headed for the back where the river flowed quietly on a familiar path as old as time.

That had been their favourite spot—hers and Ethan's—and, while it may seem foolish, she knew she'd feel closer to him there.

Rounding the corner, she was almost mown down by a pair of rambunctious six-year-olds and, once they'd disentangled themselves, she brushed off her dusty trousers and set off for the river.

A lone figure stood on the banks. A man, dressed in khaki chinos and a white T-shirt. A man whose breadth of shoulders she'd recognise anywhere, whose casual stance, with hands thrust into pockets, heartrendingly familiar and, as the figure sensed her presence, turned, her belly clenched and tumbled with the overwhelming rush of recognition.

A surge of adrenaline urged her to run towards him but

she'd done that before and he, despite her declaration, still hadn't said he loved her.

He could be here for any number of reasons: scoping out another restaurant site, poaching another master chef, a business meeting.

However, as he strode towards her, long, hungry strides rapidly closing the distance between them, she knew he was here for none of those reasons.

The expression on his face told her why he'd come.

And the realisation took her breath away.

CHAPTER FIFTEEN

THEY stopped less than a foot apart, enveloped in uncharacteristic awkwardness.

Tamara didn't know whether to hug him or strangle him—for making her love him, crave him, unable to forget him.

'What are you doing here?'

Ethan smiled, his casual shrug pulling his cotton T-shirt across his shoulders in delicious detail. 'Haunting this place in the hope of finding you.'

He'd come for her and her spirit soared.

'Exactly how long have you been here?'

'About a week.'

'You've been here every day for a week? Are you nuts?'

'Yeah.' He stepped closer, swamping her in warmth and charisma and magic. 'About you.'

Her heart swelled, filled to overflowing with love for this man. But it wasn't that easy. Nothing ever was and she couldn't get carried away because he'd arrived on her doorstep.

He was here but did he love her?

She needed to hear him say it, craved the words more than her next chai fix.

Trying to hide the cobra's nest of nerves twisting and coiling in her belly, she took a step forward, slid her hand into his.

'The feeling's mutual.' She squeezed his hand, knowing his

presence here spoke louder than words ever could but needing to have everything out in the open for them to really move forward. 'Do you know why I chose here to start my new life?'

His fingertips skated over her cheek, lingered on her jaw, before dropping to her shoulder, his touch firm and comforting, as always.

'Because, when we were here, you said it made you feel safe. I get that now, your need for security.'

'Do you? Do you really?' Her gaze searched his, needing reassurance, desperate for it. She wanted to believe him, wanted to believe in him. 'Because I really needed to feel safe when I discovered the baby and you weren't there for me.'

Shadows drifted across his eyes, turning them from startling blue to murky midnight. 'I'm sorry.'

She accepted his apology but it didn't cut it. Not now, after they'd shared so much, been through so much together.

'Why did you shut me out?'

He squeezed her shoulder before releasing it, turning away and dragging a hand through his hair, but not before she'd seen something shocking on his face.

Shame.

Ethan Brooks, the man who had it all, was ashamed.

He dragged in a deep breath, another, before turning back to face her.

'I didn't want to have to tell you this—any of it.'

He was struggling, she could see it in the muscle twitching in his jaw, in his thinly compressed lips. Looked as if she wasn't the only one with enough baggage to bring India's railway system to a screeching halt.

'Tell me. If nothing else, we're still friends.'

His head reared up. 'I want to be more than friends, damn it. I want—'

'Then give us a chance.' She softened her tone, touched his cheek. 'Tell me.'

He raked his hand through his hair again, looking decidedly ruffled and adorable. 'I've never told anyone this.'

She waited, wondering what could rattle him this badly.

'I was jealous that day at Ambrosia, furious you were still hung up over Rich—'

'But I'm not—'

'If you are or aren't doesn't really excuse how I treated you. What really pushed my buttons was not being in control of the situation. And that's something I don't like, not being in control.'

'You've told me. You're a businessman, a successful one, it figures.'

He shook his head. 'That's not the reason.'

He paused and she knew by the bleakness in his eyes that he was leading up to something big.

'I used to be a street kid. Dumped by my mum when I was five, shoved from foster family to family, scrounged on the streets from the age of thirteen.'

Sorrow gripped her heart. 'I had no idea, I'm so sorry.'

A wry smile twisted his mouth. 'We're doing a lot of that—apologising. Not real romantic, is it?'

'This is about honesty.'

As for romance, it would come. Having him open up to her, knowing how much it cost him, told her they had a future—a great one.

'And us.' He scanned her face, searching for reassurance. 'This has always been about us, Tam. I'm not telling you all this for any other reason than to give us a second chance.'

He cupped her chin, tipped it up. 'Do you believe in second chances?'

'You have to ask me that?'

Heck, she was the queen of second chances. She'd given Richard enough of them: after he'd stood her up the first time, after he'd blown her off for a restaurant opening, after she'd caught him groping a waitress within six months of their marriage.

Yet here was this incredibly honest man standing in front of her, his feelings shining bright in his eyes, asking her for a second chance? How loud could she scream yes without getting arrested?

Holding out her hand to him, she said, 'Come on, let's take a walk.'

'That's not exactly the answer I was hoping for.'

She smiled, recognising the instant he glimpsed the love in her eyes—for his eyes widened, all that dazzling blue focused on her.

'I have so much I want to say to you but let's go somewhere quieter.'

He glanced around, puzzlement creasing his brow. 'You can't get much quieter than this. The closest couple is twenty metres away.'

She tapped the side of her nose. 'Trust me, I know somewhere quieter.'

Sliding his hand into hers, she sighed as his fingers intertwined with hers. This felt right, had always felt right from the first moment he'd held her hand at Colva Beach.

Leading him to the furthest corner of the garden, she pointed to a young cypress tree.

'I've come here a few times over the last week. Seems I do my best thinking here.'

His eyebrows shot up. 'You've been here for a week too?'

'I told you I would be. I just didn't expect in my wildest dreams you'd be here too.'

He brushed the barest of kisses across her lips, her eyes welling at his tenderness, but she had to say this, had to make sure he knew where she was coming from.

She slipped her hand out of his, sank down and patted the ground next to her. 'I also came here to think, to figure out some stuff. Seems like every second person in this country is intent on predicting my fortune. I can't even get a massage these days without the therapist giving me a free glimpse into the future.'

He chuckled, sat next to her. 'So what's in the cards?'

She opened her mouth to respond and he held up both hands and waved them in front of her. 'On second thoughts, I don't want to know if they predicted some tall, dark and handsome stranger sweeping you off your feet.'

He winked, his rakish smile so heartrendingly familiar she leaned towards him without realising. 'Unless they mentioned me by name, that is.'

Hugging her knees close, she rested her chin on them, staring at the Taj Mahal, a translucent ivory in the dusk.

'Honestly? I've done so much thinking this last week, I think I can predict my own future pretty accurately.'

She'd sat in this very spot for hours on end, analysing her life, pondering the choices she'd made, knowing she should learn from mistakes of the past in building a better, brighter future.

While she felt safe here, she hadn't quite achieved the peace she'd hoped for, gripped by a relentless restlessness, no matter how many hours she tried meditating.

She knew why.

The reason was staring her in the face with concern in his blue eyes.

'So go ahead. Give it to me straight. What does the future hold for Tamara Rayne?'

Now that the moment of truth had arrived, she balked.

He'd surprised her, turning up when she'd been contemplating some vague, pie-in-the-sky dream, a nebulous idea she'd pondered at great length, debating the logistics of a long-distance relationship, wondering if they could really make it work.

But she couldn't shake off the fear that still dogged her, the fear she'd finally recognised as undermining her relationship with Ethan right from the very beginning.

She shrugged, hugged her knees tighter. 'My future is here. I've put feelers out and loads of the big newspapers are after food critics. Plus I can freelance for some of the glossy magazines and—'

'While it's great your career is back on track, I'm more interested in you. What does the future hold for you?'

Us, was what he really meant.

The unsaid word hovered between them, temptingly within reach if she had the guts to reach out there and grab it.

She took a deep breath and shuffled her bottom around to face him. In the fading light, with the low-hanging branches casting shadows over his face, she couldn't read his expression. And she wanted to, needed to.

He'd come but there'd been no declaration, no emotional reunion, just two people dancing around each other, throwing out the odd bit of truthful information.

Should she put her heart on the line, once and for all? Confront her fear, at the risk of losing the love of her life?

'I guess some of my future depends on you.'

He didn't move a muscle, not the slightest flicker.

'I've done a lot of soul-searching this last week and the only thing I regret in leaving Melbourne is not being completely honest with you.'

'I'm listening.'

She released her arms, shook them out, stretched out her legs, which were cramping as badly as her belly.

'When I ran out of Ambrosia that day, I didn't correct your wrong assumptions. I was too disappointed, too caught up in the moment. I wasn't thinking straight. It wasn't until later, much later, I realised how it must've looked.'

'You still love Richard, I know—'

Her gaze snapped to his, beseeching him to understand.

'No, you don't. I don't love him, I probably never really loved him.'

She bit her bottom lip, knowing she'd sound callous but needing to get this out of her system.

'I'd barely dated before I met him, then suddenly this brash, famous guy is all over me. I was flattered, just a little bit in love and the next thing I know we're married.'

'I always thought you were happy.'

She nodded, slowly. 'We were, for the first few months. I loved being married, loved how safe I felt having a husband who adored me. But then his lies started. And the rest.'

Her heart twisted at the memories of what she'd endured, all in the name of 'for better or worse'.

'He made my life hell. If I wore black, he said I looked too thin. If I wore white, too fat. He belittled my job, saying no one ever read the crap I wrote. He rifled through my handbag and diary to keep tabs on me. He hated what I cooked, threw a chicken Kiev at the wall once.'

'Hell, Tam—'

'He called me a useless bitch too many times to count, used subtle put-downs in front of his friends, demeaned the way I decorated our place, rubbished my friends, disparaged my mum.'

He swore, shook his head but she had to continue now she'd started, had to get this out of her system once and for all.

'Did you know he was a classic passive-aggressive? I started walking around on eggshells, doing the right things, saying the right things, in an effort to avoid the inevitable explosion if things didn't go his way.'

Ethan reached out to her, placed his hand over hers lying on the grass. 'I had no idea.'

'No one did.'

She blinked back tears, swallowed the bitterness. 'How could you, when Richard Downey, Australia's favourite celebrity chef, was all smiles, the life of every party?'

He squeezed her hand. 'Why did you stay?'

She'd asked herself the same question a million times, had come up with different answers.

How could she verbalise her craving for love, for security, for the perfect happily-ever-after scenario her parents had until her dad died?

It sounded so soppy, so stupid, especially after she'd realised Richard could never be that man for her.

'I stayed because I wanted the family I never had after my dad died. I craved it, which is probably half the reason I married him in the first place. As misguided as it sounds, at the time I thought if I could be a good wife, our marriage would stand a fighting chance.'

She wriggled her hand out from under his on the pretext of retwisting her hair into a loose chignon, his touch too painful, too poignant with what she had to say next.

'I became invisible. I lost my identity, my dignity and my self-respect for a man who didn't care about me, no matter what I did. I got caught up in a vicious cycle, trying to convince him I wasn't worthless in order to regain some semblance of self-respect in order to leave him. Round and round I went, trying my guts out, never being good enough, totally helpless. And I'll never forgive myself for that.'

He swore under his breath, bundled her into his arms and she slowly relaxed as he stroked her back in long, comforting caresses. 'It's finished. Over. You're not that person any more.'

But she was the same person, with the same fears dogging her.

Drawing back, he cradled her face in his hands. 'Tam, it's going to be okay.'

'Is it?'

In response, he lowered his head and kissed her, a slow, tender kiss on her lips, a kiss of affirmation and optimism and faith, a kiss filled with promise and hope.

The hope was the clincher.

She had to tell him—all of it.

Reaching up, she trailed her fingertips down his cheek, the familiar rasp of stubble sending a shiver up her arm.

'I know you care about me and you're nothing like Richard. But I've finally found myself again, I'm finally comfortable in my own skin and I don't want to risk losing that. For anyone.'

Wariness crept across his face. 'What are you trying to say?'

'I'm scared to get involved in a relationship again.'

She dropped her hand, wriggled back to put some distance between them. 'I'm willing to date but I can't make any promises.'

'You're wrong.'

Confused, she stared at him.

'I don't just care about you. I love you.'

Her sharp indrawn gasp sounded harsh in the silence and his hand shot out and latched onto her wrist as if he expected her to bolt.

'And I get it. You're scared. Scared to take a chance on a relationship for fear of losing your identity again. But hell, Tam, this is me. Not Richard. Surely you know I'd never hurt you?'

Hot, scalding tears burned the back of her eyes—tears of hope, tears of fear.

If loving Richard and losing herself had been painful, loving Ethan and losing him would be a hundred times worse.

But the fear was still there, still undermining her new-found confidence, whispering insidious warnings that her inner strength could vanish in a second if she made the wrong decision again.

'I know. You just being here is proof enough but I guess the fear has been a part of me so long, it's hard to shake.'

He shook his head, his grip unrelenting. 'Do you think this is easy for me? I've never loved anyone, let alone admitted it. I don't trust easily—'

'Which is why you date those airheads,' she finished for him, the realisation flooring her.

After what he'd told her today—being abandoned by his mum, dumped from family to family—everything suddenly slid into place.

He was just as frightened as her: frightened to love, frightened to get emotionally involved, frightened to lose control.

Yet he'd confronted his fear, overcome it, for her.

'You're as scared as me,' she said in a hushed tone, scrabbling on her knees to get closer to him.

'That's it, isn't it? Why you closed off that day at Ambrosia? You thought I still cared about Richard, about having his baby and you loved me then. You were just hiding your fear, weren't you?'

His slow, reluctant nod had her launching onto his lap and wrapping her arms around his neck. 'Jeez, we're a fine pair. We can read each other's minds, we just don't want to delve into our own.'

He nuzzled her neck, sending a delightful shiver skating across her skin. 'So I take it this means you want to take a risk on an old scaredy-cat like me?'

Laughing, she pulled back, planted a loud, resounding kiss on his mouth.

'You bet.'

She kissed him again—slower this time, much slower—and they came up dragging in great lungfuls of air several long moments later.

'I love you too. The for ever kind of love.'

He smiled, his arms locked firmly around her waist, every ounce of devotion and adoration and love blazing from his guileless blue eyes.

'Is that your prediction?'

'Oh, yeah.'

He jerked his head towards the Taj Mahal, the majestic

monument standing tall and strong, a silent observer of yet another romantic drama playing out in its honour.

'You know, they say this place is mystical. The ultimate dedication to love. So what do you say we live up to its romantic promise?'

She held her breath, her heart racing with anticipation as her mind took a flying leap into the future.

Maybe her predictive powers were developing, for she had a sneaking suspicion Ethan was about to—

'Tam, will you marry me? I promise to love you, cherish you, let you be your own person and do whatever you want.'

His wide smile had her grinning right back at him with elation filling her soul and joy expanding her heart.

'How can a girl refuse a proposal like that?'

'You can't.'

He stole a kiss and she poured all her love for him into it.

'You once asked me if I believed in love at first sight.'

His eyes crinkled adorably, the roguish pirate smile back in place. 'And do you?'

'Whether first sight, short sight or long sight, I believe in loving you.'

As their lips met, the moon rose, casting an enchanting glow over the Taj Mahal and its latest pair of lovers bound by destiny.

* * * *

Look for the sequel to
A Trip with the Tycoon – *available FREE*
on www.millsandboon.co.uk

Honeymoon with the Boss

JESSICA HART

Jessica Hart was born in West Africa and has suffered from itchy feet ever since, travelling and working around the world in a wide variety of interesting but very lowly jobs. All of them have provided inspiration on which to draw when it comes to the settings and plots of her stories.

Now she lives a rather more settled existence in York, where she has been able to pursue her interest in history, although she still yearns sometimes for wider horizons. If you'd like to know more about Jessica, visit her website at www.jessica hart.co.uk.

This one is for Julia, who was there at the start

CHAPTER ONE

'WHERE would you like to go on honeymoon?'

Imogen paused in surprise, her arm still extended in the act of handing her boss a folder of letters across the desk. 'Honeymoon?' she repeated cautiously, wondering if she had heard correctly.

It was unlike Tom Maddison to ask personal questions, let alone one so unexpected. Sometimes on a Monday morning he remembered to ask her if she had had a good weekend, but never as if he cared about the answer and she always said 'Yes, thank you' in reply, even if it had been a disaster—as, frankly, it often was.

'Yes, honeymoon,' said Tom with an edge of impatience. He took the folder and opened it. 'You know, after you get married.'

'Er…I'm not getting married,' said Imogen.

Chance would be a fine thing, she thought wryly. All her friends seemed to be settling down, but she was obviously doomed to remain single—and it wasn't for lack of trying, whatever her best friend, Amanda, might say. Ever since Andrew had announced his engagement, she had thrown herself into the dating game, but no matter how promising her date seemed at first, Imogen always ended up making an excuse to leave early.

'Pretend that you are,' said Tom, skimming the first letter and scrawling his signature at the bottom before looking up at her with the piercingly light eyes that always reminded Imogen of stainless steel, so cool and unyielding were they.

He put down his pen. 'You're a woman,' he said, as if noticing the fact for the first time, which it probably was, Imogen thought. She was resigned now to the fact that, as far as Tom Maddison was concerned, she was little more than a walking, talking piece of office equipment.

'I have it on good authority that most women start planning their dream weddings when they're about six,' he said, 'so you must have given it some thought.'

'That's true, but at six you're only interested in pretty dresses,' Imogen pointed out. 'You're not that concerned about the groom at that stage, let alone the honeymoon.'

Tom frowned as he pulled the next letter towards him. 'So you haven't thought about it since then?'

'Well, I wouldn't say *that*,' she admitted scrupulously, 'but my fantasies have never gone beyond getting married. Sadly, I've never been in a position where there's any point in planning a honeymoon.'

'You are now.' Tom cast a cursory glance over the letter and signed it before reaching for the next one.

'Pardon?'

'I want you to plan a honeymoon,' he said, his pen moving briskly over the paper.

'But…who for?'

'For me,' said Tom, as if it were obvious.

'For *you*?'

Imogen stared at him. She shouldn't be surprised, she realised. Tom Maddison was thirty-six, single, straight and very, very rich. Why wouldn't he get married?

It wasn't as if he was unattractive, either. You couldn't call him handsome exactly, but he was tall and powerfully built and attractive in a way she couldn't quite explain. His stern face was dominated by a strong nose and those strange light eyes under formidable brows. So, no, he wasn't handsome. And yet...

And yet there was something about the line of his mouth that made the breath stick in her throat sometimes, something about the big, square, capable hands and the angle of his cheek and jaw that prickled excitingly under her skin and sent a little shiver snaking down her spine.

Offset against that was the fact that she had worked for Tom Maddison for six months without any indication that he had any emotions at all. Not once had he mentioned his personal life. It was only thanks to her friend Sue in Human Resources that Imogen even knew that he was single.

She knew all about his professional reputation, though. In the City, they called him the Iceman. He was famous for the chilly precision of his negotiations and his cold-blooded approach to the failing companies that he was brought in to turn around. She knew Tom had been in New York for a number of years, transforming the fortunes of a succession of firms familiar from the Dow-Jones Index, and that he had been lured back to London at a reputedly gigantic salary to be CEO of Collocom, which had been struggling in the competitive communications market.

But really, that was all she knew. Imogen had never met anyone so driven and focused. It was like working for a machine.

Maybe that wasn't quite fair, she amended mentally. He was too brusque and impatient to be a machine. He was tough, even ruthless, but he was absolutely straight too. Tom Maddison wasn't a man who played games, and she admired that. With Tom, what you saw was what you got.

Except now it turned out that there was another side to him.

'You're getting married?' she asked him, just in case she had misunderstood. It was hard to imagine Tom unbending enough to even smile at a woman, let alone ask her to marry him. He must have had a conversation about something other than work. Amazing.

'Didn't I tell you?'

'No,' she said with careful restraint, 'you didn't.'

She was only his temporary PA, but he might have told her, she thought. Subsiding onto the chair, Imogen studied him across the desk as he scanned another letter and wondered what his fiancée was like.

Thin, no doubt. And probably beautiful, she decided glumly.

Funny how men with millions to squander never chose to spend them on average-looking girls who could do with losing a few pounds, wasn't it?

'Well…congratulations!' she said brightly. 'When did all this happen?'

'At New Year.' Tom looked uncomfortable with the personal turn of the conversation.

'When you were in New York?' Imogen asked, surprised. He had certainly gone on his own—she knew because she had booked his ticket—and he didn't seem the type to spend a romantic weekend with a stranger, let alone rush into marriage.

'I've known Julia for nearly a year,' said Tom, as if reading her mind. He signed the last letter and sat turning the pen between his fingers with a brooding expression, giving a very bad impression of a besotted lover. 'But we didn't get together until just before I came back to London four months ago.'

'Why didn't you say anything before?'

'There didn't seem to be any need. We weren't going to get married until next year. Julia is a financial analyst, and she

obviously has to sort out what's going to happen about her job
if she moves over here, so I thought we had plenty of time.'

'Oh.' Imogen wasn't sure what else to say. It certainly
didn't sound like a mad, passionate love affair, but perhaps
Tom was different behind closed doors.

With a mouth like that, it would be a shame if he wasn't.

'So when are you getting married?' she asked after a moment.

'In six weeks.'

'Six *weeks*!' Maybe it was a mad, passionate affair after
all! 'Gosh, that's not long.'

'I know.'

Tom could hear the glumness in his own voice, and pulled
himself up. He ought to be sounding more enthusiastic at the
prospect. After all, getting married had been his idea.

It had made perfect sense at the time. Julia was a high-flyer,
like him. She was beautiful, intelligent, successful. *Independent*. To Tom, she had seemed everything he wanted in a
woman. Their relationship had been mutually satisfying, with
neither making any demands on the other, and Tom couldn't
imagine ever meeting anyone who would fit into his life with
so little effort.

But that was before he had asked her to marry him and
wedding fever had gripped her, transforming her in an instant
from a cool, competent businesswoman into a neurotic
fiancée, obsessed with dresses and guest lists and flowers and
fuss. It was all very alarming, and Tom just hoped that once
the wedding was over, Julia would revert to normal.

'Julia has set her heart on getting married at Stavely
Castle,' he told Imogen, who was obviously wondering what
the rush was. 'We just assumed it would be a year before we
could book it, but it turns out that they've had a last-minute
cancellation, so Julia jumped at the opportunity.'

That cancellation had thrown out all Tom's calculations. He had planned his proposal with care, just as he planned everything. He preferred his life under strict control. He didn't do spontaneous. So he had thought it all out, weighed up the advantages and disadvantages and prepared exactly what he would say to Julia. He had expected her to say yes, and she had.

What he hadn't expected was her excitement. He had assumed that they could carry on much as before for a while, with Julia's job in Manhattan and his work in London. There was no hurry. They could have a year or so to get used to being engaged and plan the perfect wedding with precision.

But Julia had thrown his plans into disarray. She had thrown herself into planning the wedding with alarming enthusiasm, her ideas becoming more and more extravagant by the day, and once she had heard that the castle would be available so soon, there was no stopping her.

Tom couldn't understand it at all. He had thought that Julia shared his pragmatic attitude to marriage. She had certainly seemed to agree that they could have a successful relationship based on mutual respect, admiration and attraction. It wasn't as if she was a silly, romantic girl expecting him to start gushing about love and all that hearts and flowers stuff. Which just made her enthusiasm for the wedding all the more baffling.

'It's all very exciting,' said Imogen encouragingly.

'Yes,' Tom agreed, but he knew that he didn't sound very excited. It was all right for Imogen. *Her* life hadn't been thrown into disorder.

'Julia is coming over next week to start planning the wedding,' he told her. 'She'll be dividing her time between here and New York, so she may need your help arranging things.'

'Of course,' said Imogen. 'Whatever I can do to help.'

'You can sort out this honeymoon business for a start,'

said Tom, flicking open a file, evidently having had enough personal interaction. 'Julia's dealing with the wedding, but she tells me it's up to me to organise the honeymoon.'

'It's traditional for the groom to do that,' Imogen agreed, wondering a little at the undercurrent of irritation in his voice. Poor Julia. She wondered if his fiancée had any idea of just how unexcited Tom was about his wedding.

'I don't know anything about honeymoons,' he was grumbling.

'It's not that hard,' said Imogen with just a hint of asperity. 'It's just a holiday. You'll want a chance to relax after the wedding, so all you need to do is find somewhere romantic where you can be alone.'

Tom frowned. 'What do you mean by romantic?'

Imogen only just stopped herself from rolling her eyes in time. 'That depends on you. Everyone's got a different idea of what's romantic. What does romance mean to you?'

'It's no use asking me,' he said unhelpfully. 'I haven't got a clue.'

Well, there was a surprise!

Imogen sighed. 'Just choose somewhere relaxing, in that case.'

'It's got to be "special".' Tom used his fingers to put hooks around the word, barely able to contain his discomfort with the idea. 'I can't just book it as if it were a normal holiday. Julia is obviously expecting me to arrange something fabulous.'

'I expect she is.'

'I haven't got time to research fabulous holidays,' Tom objected.

He studied Imogen with critical grey eyes. When he had first arrived at Collocom Imogen had been assigned as his temporary assistant until he appointed a PA of his own.

At first sight, he hadn't been impressed, Tom had to admit. She was younger and infinitely more casual than any secretary he had had before, and she had no experience of working at a senior executive level. As far as Tom could work out, she had drifted into secretarial work and was utterly lacking in ambition. It was symptomatic of the failing firm that the best assistance they could offer their new Chief Executive was a temp whose only relevant experience was a two-week assignment in Human Resources, he had thought disapprovingly.

With that wayward brown hair and relaxed approach to the dress code, Imogen always seemed faintly messy to Tom. Her desk was an absolute disgrace, for instance, and in spite of her temporary status she appeared to have an encyclopaedic knowledge of every member of staff's social life. If Tom hadn't had his hands full taking over the reins of a company whose shares were plummeting in value on a daily basis, he would have insisted on a more professional PA, but stopping the slide and turning Collocom round was his priority for now.

When he had the time, he would be looking to appoint someone qualified and experienced who would act as a professional PA but, in the meantime, Imogen had proved to be surprisingly competent. Tom might wish that she looked a little sleeker, a little crisper, but she was a more than adequate substitute in most things, so he had postponed the decision about replacing her for now. Her image might be unprofessional, but she got the job done, and for Tom that was what mattered most.

'You're a sensible woman,' he told her. 'I'm prepared to go on your recommendation.'

Sensible? It wasn't exactly a compliment to make the heart beat faster, was it? thought Imogen, disgruntled. Why couldn't he think of her as glamorous, or mysterious, or sexy, or exciting? Anything but *sensible*!

Still, it would amuse Amanda, who was always telling her how very *un*-sensible she was when it came to men.

Tom Maddison might look like the kind of man you yearned to sweep you off your feet, but a girl wanted a *little* romance. A man who thought sensible was a compliment and was clearly baffled by the idea of a romantic holiday wouldn't be that much fun to be with in reality, no matter how toe-curling his mouth, or spine-shivering his hands.

No, some men were better in your fantasies than in real life. In her fantasies, Tom had slowly unbuttoned her blouse and pressed hot kisses to her throat. He had pressed her up against a door and reduced her to a puddle of lust with the merest graze of his fingers. *My God, but you're beautiful!* he had cried as he'd thrown her across the bed.

Not *once* in her fantasies had he told her she was a sensible woman!

It would serve Tom Maddison right if she recommended a B&B in Skegness as the perfect honeymoon destination for sensible people! Not that she could do that to the unknown Julia, who obviously had a lot to put up with from her fiancé. Imogen was beginning to really feel for the poor woman.

'I *did* read about a lovely place the other day,' she told Tom.

It had been a fairly typical evening in the flat; Imogen lay on the sofa, flicking through magazines while Amanda painted her nails, both of them bemoaning their lack of a glamorous social life while secretly relieved that neither of them had to miss the latest episode of *Eastenders*. Imogen had seen the piece about the ultimate romantic getaways and shown it to Amanda, who had sighed enviously and nearly passed out when she saw how much it cost.

'It was terribly expensive, though.' Imogen felt she should warn Tom.

He waved a dismissive hand, as if nothing were too much to pay to save him from having to think about a romantic destination for himself.

It probably wasn't, thought Imogen. She didn't deal with his personal finances, but it was common knowledge that Tom Maddison was worth millions. It wasn't as if he ever spent any of them, either. All he seemed to do was work. She never booked fancy restaurants or theatre tickets or arranged for him to fly in private jets or cruise in luxury yachts.

He went to New York occasionally, but Imogen had always assumed that was for work. She had obviously been wrong about that. Perhaps Tom lavished jewels and expensive gifts on Julia? Imogen couldn't imagine it, but she might be wrong about that too.

'If money is no object, Coconut Island was described as the ultimate place for a romantic getaway,' she said. 'It's tiny, with just one incredibly stylish house and a little jetty, and you can hire the whole island just for yourself. There's a luxury hotel on a bigger island nearby, and they send someone over on a boat every day to service the house and stock the fridge with fabulous food. They'll stay and cook for you if you want, but most people there are honeymooners, and they just want to be on their own.

'I saw a picture of it in this magazine,' Imogen went on, remembering. 'It looked absolutely fabulous! There was this perfect turquoise lagoon with a white sand beach and a hammock under the coconut palms...'

Clutching the pile of papers she still held to her chest, she sighed dreamily at the memory of that picture. 'Honestly, it was paradise! I'd love to go somewhere like that, where there's nothing to do all day but laze and swim and read and...'

About to say *make love*, she trailed off awkwardly, wondering if that might be getting a bit intimate, given that her exchanges with Tom had so far been limited entirely to business matters. He wasn't the kind of boss you could chat to about sex.

'…and…er…well, you know…' she finished uncomfortably.

Tom lifted an eyebrow at Imogen's blush. 'I know,' he agreed in a dry voice and, for the first time ever, she could swear she caught a glint of amusement in the cool grey eyes. It changed his expression in a quite startling way, and Imogen felt her pulse give an odd little kick.

It was amazing what a difference a glimpse of humour made, she reflected. If she had seen *that* look before, her fantasies might have been a lot more dangerous! Just as well he was safely engaged now.

The next moment, though, he had reverted to type. 'It sounds fine,' he said briskly. 'Book it for me.'

Imogen hesitated. This was his honeymoon they were talking about. 'Wouldn't you rather do it yourself?'

'No,' said Tom with emphasis, 'I'd *rather* get on with some work.'

'But a honeymoon is such a personal thing,' she protested.

'Yes, and you're my *personal* assistant,' he pointed out. 'That means you assist me personally, so I suggest that's what you do. Now, the wedding is on…'

To Imogen's amazement, he actually consulted his computer about a date that ought to be engraved on his heart. 'Ah, yes, twenty-seventh of February. Julia is talking about having it at some castle in Gloucestershire, but we can get to Heathrow easily enough from there, so book a flight that night.

'I don't want to know about how much everything costs,'

he added as Imogen opened her mouth. 'I can't be bothered with the details. Just book whatever you think and charge it to my account.'

'Very well,' said Imogen, the perfect PA once more. 'If that's what you want.'

'What I *want*,' said Tom grouchily, 'is not to be distracted. We've got an important contract to negotiate before I can get married, so let's get on with that.'

'And I've booked the honeymoon for you,' Imogen finished after handing Tom the last message. He had been out of the office in meetings all day, and the phone had been ringing constantly.

'Good, good,' said Tom absently, flicking through the messages. He was still wearing his overcoat, and his shoulders still glistened with raindrops in the harsh overhead light.

'Don't you want the details?'

He frowned. 'I suppose I'd better have them,' he decided. 'Julia might ask what I've arranged. Can you put it all in a file for me?'

'I've got it here.' Imogen handed the file over the desk. 'I do hope you'll enjoy it,' she said. 'I can't think of anywhere I'd rather be, especially with the weather the way it is at the moment,' she added, nodding to where the January rain was still splattering against the window.

Tom only grunted as he opened the file and scanned the arrangements that she had typed up. His ferocious brows rose at the cost, Imogen noticed, but to her relief he made no comment. What would it be like to barely blink at spending a hefty five-figure sum on a holiday?

He turned to the next page. 'Leaving on the twenty-seventh…' his voice sharpened '…back on the nineteenth of *March*?'

'You told me to book whatever I thought would be most appropriate,' she reminded him.

'I can't believe you thought it would be appropriate for me to be away from the office for *three weeks*!'

Imogen refused to quail. 'It's your honeymoon,' she said. 'It's a special time. It's important to get your marriage off to the right start if you *can* afford it, as you obviously can.'

'I'm not talking about money,' he said impatiently. 'It's time I can't afford.'

'I'm not talking about money either,' said Imogen. 'Collocom isn't going to fall apart if you're not here for three weeks, so you can afford the time. It's a question of priorities. What matters more, Collocom or your marriage?'

Tom eyed his PA with something close to dislike. He knew how he was supposed to reply to *that*!

He thought wistfully of the days when he and Julia had had a successful long-distance relationship. Their weekends in New York had been mutually satisfying. Julia had her own busy life, and respected his space. He hadn't been expected then to think about all this emotional stuff, or to reassess his priorities.

He hadn't counted on all these changes. If he'd known, would he ever have thought about marriage? Tom wondered with an inward sigh.

It would be fine, he reassured himself. Julia was an incredible woman, and he was lucky to have met her. She would understand about the honeymoon.

'I'll talk to Julia about it,' he told Imogen, closing the file with a snap. 'Then you can rearrange the flights.'

But Julia was thrilled when he told her about Coconut Island. 'Thank you for choosing somewhere so romantic, honey,' she enthused. 'And three weeks alone! I can't wait!

Won't it be wonderful to spend that time together and get to know each other properly?'

Tom thought they *did* know each other. Why else would they be getting married?

He had been hoping that Julia would want to cut the honeymoon short. A drive for success was something they had in common—or, at least, it had been until Julia had gone wedding crazy. Now it appeared she would rather loll around on a beach for three weeks than get back to work! Wouldn't she want to know what was happening in her absence? Wouldn't she be concerned about deals being made without her, or the challenges and opportunities she would miss while she was sitting under some coconut palm?

This was Imogen's fault, Tom thought darkly. If she hadn't booked such a long stay, Julia would have been perfectly happy to return to normal after a week.

When Imogen asked him if he wanted her to rearrange the flights, he snapped at her but had to concede that the dates should stay as she had booked.

'Leave it as it is,' he snarled.

'Oh-kay…good,' said Imogen, eyeing him warily. Being engaged didn't seem to be suiting him at all.

Tom's foul mood continued for the next couple of days. He was so grouchy that Imogen began to wonder if Julia had called the engagement off. If Tom was like this with her, Imogen wouldn't have blamed her!

Not that she had any intention of asking him if everything was all right. She valued her head too much. The only thing to do when Tom was like this was to keep her head down and be glad that she was only a very temporary secretary.

Think of the money, Imogen told herself. She was earning good money here and her travel fund was looking positively healthy. As soon as Tom got round to appointing a new PA she would be off to Australia and someone else could deal with him. Good luck to her!

It appeared, though, that the engagement was very much still on. Imogen was squinting at her shorthand a couple of days later when the phone rang.

'Chief Executive's office.'

'Hi, is that Imogen?' The warm American voice spilled out of the phone. 'This is Julia, Tom's fiancée, here. Tom said you might be able to help me with a few little things.'

Those 'few little things' turned out to be a list of details to check that extended to three pages. Imogen rolled her eyes as she scribbled down notes, but she had to admit that Julia was very friendly and appreciative. Unlike Tom, she was obviously thrilled at the prospect of a wedding.

'I'm having a dress made here,' she told Imogen excitedly. 'It is so-o-o-o beautiful! I knew exactly what I wanted. In fact, I'll email you the design—you're being so helpful, I'm thinking of you as a kind of cyber bridesmaid! Would you like to see it?'

Imogen had little choice but to murmur politely that she would love to.

'Don't show Tom, though! It's unlucky for him to see it before the wedding.'

Imogen tried, and failed, to imagine poring girlishly over a dress design with her boss. Tom must be very different with Julia if she thought he'd have the slightest interest in what anyone wore.

'I won't.'

'Now, I've booked Stavely Castle for the wedding and reception,' said Julia. 'I visited last time I was in England and it was just so romantic. I decided there and then if I ever got married, that's where I wanted the wedding!'

She rattled on, wanting Imogen to book a string quartet, find a supply of fresh rose petals, put her in touch with a cake designer, draw up a list of hotels in the area...

'You're so sweet to help me out like this,' she told Imogen. 'It's difficult to sort out details like this from New York, and I'm just so busy at the moment, what with sorting out everything here before I come over to London. I had no idea how much work organising a wedding would be on top of it all!'

'It's a lot to do at such short notice,' Imogen agreed, reflecting that Julia wasn't the only busy one. Sadly, they didn't all have fiancés with assistants they could fob off with all the time-consuming jobs!

'I know, it's crazy, isn't it?' Julia's laugh sounded a little wild to Imogen. 'But Stavely Castle suddenly had a cancellation and it just seemed *meant* somehow. As I said to Tom, when you know you've found the right person, why wait?'

Imogen murmured something noncommittal. It seemed to her that if you wanted a spontaneous wedding, it made sense to keep things simple and let the rose petals and the string quartets go. Still, it wasn't her wedding, and Julia and Tom had plenty of money to throw at the problem, which always helped.

'How *is* Tom?' Julia was asking.

'Er, he's fine,' said Imogen, wondering if she was expected to report that her boss was working himself into a frenzy of excitement about the wedding. 'Working hard. You know what he's like.'

Julia laughed. 'I know. Isn't he a darling? He's so British sometimes!'

'Absolutely,' Imogen agreed, boggling at the phone. Tom Maddison, a *darling*? Julia must be in love!

'Is he there?'

'Of course. I'll put you through.'

Putting Julia on hold, Imogen buzzed Tom. 'I've got Julia on the line.'

'Julia?' he snapped.

'Your fiancée,' she reminded him.

'What does she want?'

'She didn't say. I imagine she wants to talk to you.'

'I can't talk now,' he said irritably. 'Can't it wait? Tell her I'm in a meeting.'

'I've already said that I would put her through.'

He made an exasperated sound. 'Oh, very well.'

Imogen grimaced as she put down the phone. Some darling!

She felt sorry for Julia. There had been a feverishness to the other woman's voice that boded ill for a measured conversation with her fiancé. A few minutes' conversation had been enough to show Imogen that Julia was a control freak, and already stressed by having to organise the perfect wedding at long distance. Right now, Julia needed calm reassurance, but Imogen was afraid she was unlikely to get it from Tom in his current mood.

Five minutes later, Tom banged out of his office, his mood clearly even worse than she had feared.

'This wedding business is getting out of control,' he snarled. 'I haven't got time to talk about invitations and vows and rehearsal dinners! And *you're* spending far too much time on it, too,' he added accusingly.

'I don't mind,' she said quickly. 'It'll be easier when Julia is here.'

'I hope to God you're right!'

'You have to make allowances.' Imogen was beginning to feel like a counsellor. She certainly seemed to spend more time talking to Tom and to Julia than they were talking to each other. 'A wedding is a big deal for any woman,' she tried to placate Tom. 'Julia's giving up her life in New York to be with you, so it's going to be an even more emotional time than usual for her. I know it seems like a lot of stress at the moment, but it will be worth it when you're married, won't it?'

Tom stopped pacing and imagined a time when he and Julia were safely married. Everything would be calm again, and he would go home every night to a beautiful, accomplished wife who understood what made a successful relationship and who would support him professionally and personally. He could rely on Julia to always say the right thing, and do the right thing. She was neat and orderly and sensible—except when it came to weddings, it seemed.

Perhaps Imogen was right, and it was just the stress of arranging a wedding at short notice that was making Julia so uncharacteristically emotional. Once this damned wedding was over, surely she would go back to the way she had been before?

It had taken Tom a long time to find just the right wife. Julia wouldn't normally expect him to be all lovey-dovey. They had come to a very clear agreement about what they both wanted from marriage, so if it didn't work with her, it was never going to work with anyone.

No, Julia was perfect. He didn't want to lose her now.

He would just have to be more patient, Tom decided. He would try harder to show an interest in the wedding if that was what Julia wanted.

He could feel Imogen's stern eye on him and remembered her question. *It will be worth it, won't it?*

'Of course it will,' he said.

CHAPTER TWO

IMOGEN waved at the girls on Reception and pressed the button to call the lift. This was Tom's last day in the office before the wedding, and the staff had planned a surprise champagne reception later that afternoon to wish him well.

She hoped Tom would appreciate the gesture and manage a smile for them. Most of the staff were terrified of his brusque manner, but they respected him, too. He was tough, but fair, and no one was in any doubt that he had transformed Collocom in the six months he had been there. Their boss's wedding was an excuse to celebrate a much more secure future for them all.

It had been a busy few weeks. Imogen had spent most of them chasing up string quartets and florists and photographers. She was an expert now on everything from the design of the place settings to special licence arrangements, and she was on first-name terms with the staff at Stavely Castle after ringing on a daily basis to change or check endless details. Perhaps when she got back from her travels she could set up as a wedding planner?

There had been no word from Julia for a couple of days now, which was odd. Tom's fiancée had been backwards and forwards between New York and London for the past few weeks, but ten days ago she had arrived, she said, to stay. Imogen had arranged for her to lease a fabulous flat in Chelsea Harbour so that she could prepare for the wedding, but she had still been on the phone several times a day. Imogen just hoped that—finally!—everything was ready and Julia could stop fretting.

Tom's fiancée was very lovely, as slender as predicted, and beautifully dressed. There was a glossiness and a sheen to her that made Imogen feel gauche and faintly shabby in comparison. They were probably much the same age, but Julia was so much more sophisticated she seemed to come from a different world, one where first-class travel and designer clothes were the norm, and a million miles from Imogen's life sharing a chaotic flat in south London.

In spite of the differences between them, Julia was determined to treat Imogen as her new best friend when they'd finally met in the office one day. She was warm and friendly, embarrassingly so at times, but Imogen sensed a tension to her and a frenetic undercurrent to her obsession with wedding arrangements, as if she were wound up like a tightly coiled spring. Imogen hoped she would be able to relax enough to enjoy the wedding.

Julia had brought Imogen a beautiful scarf to thank her for all her work. 'I do hope you'll come to the wedding, Imogen,' she said, kissing her on both cheeks when she first met her. 'It would mean the world to Tom and me if you were there. Wouldn't it, Tom?'

It had clearly never crossed Tom's mind to care one way or another, but he nodded. 'Of course,' he agreed. 'I know how hard Imogen has worked to make sure it all happens.'

There was a very faint edge to his voice. Imogen knew just how often he had been exasperated to find her tied up with wedding arrangements when he needed her to do something else, but she had to admit that he'd been making much more of an effort lately. She wondered if Julia realised quite how hard he was trying.

Julia had confided to Imogen in one of her many phone calls that she had wondered at one time if Tom had been having second thoughts about getting married. 'But he's been so sweet lately that I can see I was silly to have worried,' she said. 'He rings twice a day, and sends me a red rose every morning just so I know he's thinking about me.'

Julia sighed with satisfaction. As well she might, Imogen reflected. She had arranged the delivery of the single roses herself and knew exactly how much it cost. Her mind boggled at the idea of Tom being sweet. He must really love Julia if he was prepared to change to such an extent, she thought wistfully.

She tried hard to be happy for them. It wasn't Julia's fault if she was thin, beautiful, wealthy, glamorous and had a man like Tom Maddison at her feet.

It wasn't her fault if Imogen couldn't stick to a diet, devoured a whole packet of chocolate digestives at a sitting and was reduced to dates with men who explained exactly how a mobile phone worked or who actually thought she would be interested in a detailed account of the intergalactic battles in *Star Wars*.

'Your trouble is that you're too picky,' Amanda was always telling her. 'You're looking for a prince, and he's just not going to turn up. You've got to be prepared to compromise a bit.'

'I don't want to compromise.' Imogen could be stubborn too. 'I want what I had with Andrew.'

Amanda sighed. 'You've got to get over him, Imo.'

'I *am* over him.' She thought she was, anyway. 'I know he's happy with Sara. I know he's not going to come back. But when you've had the perfect relationship, it's hard to settle for anything less.'

'If it had been the perfect relationship, Andrew wouldn't have broken it off,' Amanda invariably pointed out.

It was a good point. Imogen knew her friend was right, and she really *was* trying to meet someone new. It was just that the men she met seemed lacking in even the hint of a spark.

Still, perhaps she should give them more of a chance, Imogen had decided only the week before. Look at how Tom had changed and was trying hard to please Julia. He must be in love with her if he was prepared to make that kind of effort.

Sick of yearning after the unattainable, as Amanda put it, Imogen had vowed to try harder. There was no reason why she shouldn't find someone she could have a real relationship with, perhaps even someone who might like to come travelling with her, but it hadn't been going well. Last night she had let Amanda's boyfriend set her up on yet another blind date, this time with an engineer who had spent most of his time telling her about his multiple allergies.

No wonder she was feeling depressed this morning.

It was nothing to do with the fact that Tom Maddison was getting married in a couple of days.

The lights were on in both offices when she went in. That meant Tom was here already. He had probably been here since at least seven, in fact, the way he usually was. He wasn't the kind of man who would take it easy just because he was getting married.

Imogen tested a smile in the mirror as she hung up her coat. It didn't look very convincing. She tried again, adding a little sparkle to her eyes. Better. She could almost pass for a girl who was genuinely pleased for her boss.

She *wanted* to be. Tom might be grouchy at times, but she admired his self-discipline and integrity. He wasn't the friendliest of bosses, but you always knew where you were with him.

And he never mentioned an allergy or gave the slightest indication he had even seen *Star Wars*. He deserved a beautiful wife like Julia.

'Good morning,' she said brightly, as she knocked and went into his office. 'Your last day before the wedding! Where would you like me to start?'

Tom looked up from the papers on his desk, and Imogen's heart plummeted as she saw that his face looked as if it were carved out of stone.

'You can start by cancelling the wedding,' he said.

There was a catastrophic silence.

'*Cancel* it?' said Imogen, aghast, hoping against hope that she had misheard.

Tom nodded curtly. 'Pull the plug on everything.'

'But…what on earth has happened? Where's Julia?'

'On her way back to New York.' He looked at his watch. 'Probably taking off right now.'

'She'll come back,' said Imogen, thinking that Julia would have to turn round as soon as she landed to get back in time for the wedding. 'It must just be last-minute nerves.'

'She doesn't want to get married,' said Tom flatly. 'No, that's not quite right,' he corrected himself. 'She *does* want to get married, just not to me.'

No matter how hard he tried, he couldn't keep the bitterness from his voice.

Imogen had been standing as if rooted to the spot, but at that she turned to close the door and, without waiting to be invited, sat down across the desk.

'Are you sure there hasn't been some kind of mistake?' she

asked carefully. 'Is it possible you've misunderstood what the problem is?'

Tom gave a harsh, mirthless laugh. 'Oh, no, she was crystal clear. I misunderstood the whole situation, it turns out, but not what she wants to do now.'

He couldn't bear to be pitied. Swinging his chair round so that he wouldn't have to look at the sympathy in Imogen's face, he stared out of the window at the bleak February morning. It suited his mood exactly.

'All of Julia's family and friends are over for the wedding, and she'd arranged to spend the evening with them, so I wasn't expecting to see her. But she turned up at my door at ten o'clock and said that we had to talk,' he told Imogen. 'It wasn't the easiest of scenes. She said that she was sorry, but she couldn't marry me because she was going to marry Patrick.'

'Patrick?' Imogen felt completely lost. This was all so unexpected it was difficult to grasp what he was telling her. 'Who's Patrick?'

'Patrick is Julia's best friend, always has been, ever since they were at college together. I met him in New York, and knew they spent lots of time together, but Julia always said that they had decided long ago not to spoil their friendship by sleeping together. It was always a platonic relationship, and they both dated other people, like me. That was one of the reasons she was always so happy with a long-distance relationship,' Tom remembered. 'When I wasn't there, she had plenty of time to spend with Patrick, just "goofing around", as she called it.'

Imogen could practically hear the quotation marks around the phrase, and she could understand his baffled distaste. Tom probably didn't even know what goofing around was.

'It turns out that Julia was in love with Patrick all along,' he went on. 'She didn't say anything because she didn't want to lose him as a friend, but she wasn't getting any younger and she decided that if she wanted to get married and have a family, as she does, she would have to make a decision to commit to someone else. That's when Muggins here came along.'

Tom couldn't look at Imogen. He was burning with humiliation, furious with himself for not realising the truth, furious with Julia for making a fool of him. She had made such a fuss about the wedding, and invited half the world, so everyone would know that he was the man too stupid to realise his fiancée was in love with someone else, too weak to convince her to stay, too inept to build a successful relationship.

Now they would all know he was a failure.

They would know he hadn't been able to control his own life.

His jaw was clenched, but he couldn't stop the betraying muscle jumping frantically in his cheek. He wanted to bellow with rage, to punch his fist into a wall, but he couldn't do that. Imogen would think he was upset and feel even sorrier for him.

'When I asked her to marry me, she thought it was a good chance to get away from New York and Patrick, and start afresh,' he went on after a moment. 'She liked me, she said, and she liked sleeping with me. She thought we had a lot in common and would make a good team. I did, too,' he remembered with bitterness. 'Once she'd made that decision, she threw herself into the whole idea of getting married.'

'To compensate for the fact that she really wanted to be marrying someone else?' Imogen said numbly. The feverish edge to Julia's planning was beginning to make more sense now. She must have been desperate to get married while she could still convince herself that she was making the right decision. No wonder she had been keen to have the wedding in England and so soon.

'She certainly fooled me.' Tom's mouth twisted as he swung round to face Imogen once more. He would show her that he was in control. 'I had no idea I wasn't the one she really wanted to marry.'

'So what changed?'

'Apparently the prospect of losing her was too much for Patrick and he came to his senses. He realised that he was in love with her, too, and probably always had been. It's quite a touching story, when you think about it.'

Tom smiled without humour. 'Patrick came over for the wedding, but when he saw Julia he told her how he felt, and then of course she realised she couldn't go through with marrying me. She said she was sorry,' he added expressionlessly.

The look in his eyes made Imogen want to cry. 'I don't know what to say. I'm so sorry,' she said helplessly.

'It's probably all for the best,' said Tom briskly. 'Better for Julia to realise that she was making a mistake now than after the wedding. At least it's saved us the hassle—and cost!—of a divorce.'

That would have been an admission of failure too. Either way, Julia would have made him look a loser.

And Tom was a winner. He didn't like losing. He never had.

He picked up his pen, almost as if he intended to get on with some work, but put it down again after a moment. The truth was, he didn't know how to deal with this. He was too angry and humiliated to work, but what else could he do?

Imogen swallowed. Tom wasn't the kind of man who went in for emotional displays but she knew how hard he must be hurting. He had tried so hard to be what Julia wanted.

'What can I do?' she asked.

'I'd be grateful if you would deal with telling everyone who needs to know.' The curtness in Tom's voice didn't quite disguise his gratitude that she was going to stick to practicalities.

'Of course.'

'Here's the key to Julia's apartment. She left it with me last night.'

He pushed a key across the desk. Imogen recognised it from when she had arranged the short-term lease of the flat. Julia had wanted somewhere to stay where she could keep her wedding dress secret from Tom.

At the time, Imogen had rolled her eyes at the extravagance, which seemed to be taking tradition to extremes, but now she marvelled that she hadn't seen the separate apartment as a warning sign. If Julia had been really in love with Tom, she wouldn't have been able to wait to move in with him. It wasn't as if he didn't have the space. Imogen had been to his penthouse flat in the Docklands to collect some papers once, and there had been more than enough room to hide a dozen wedding dresses if necessary.

'The flat is full of presents that will need to be returned. Presumably you've got a list of guests?'

Imogen nodded. 'I'll make sure they all know the wedding has been cancelled.'

'You'd better deal with Stavely Castle first.'

'I'll do that.' She got to her feet and hesitated, looking at him with concern. With anyone else, she would have offered the comfort of a hug, but she didn't think Tom would welcome a gesture like that. He wasn't a tactile man.

Still, this would be a devastating blow for a man of his pride. Imogen wished she could do something to help him, but she sensed the best thing she could do was deal with the practicalities and make as little fuss as possible.

She couldn't go without saying something, though. 'Will you be all right?' she asked after a moment.

'Of course,' he said, as brusque as ever. 'I've got plenty to do.'

'You're not really going to work, are you?'

'What else is there to do?' he said and even he could hear the bleakness in his voice.

Imogen came back a little while later with coffee and a couple of biscuits.

'I never eat biscuits,' said Tom, glancing up from his computer screen as she set them solicitously at his elbow.

'You should have something to eat.'

'I'm not an invalid, Imogen!'

'You've had a shock,' she said. 'You need the sugar.'

'I don't *need* anything!' The suggestion of neediness always caught Tom on the raw and he glared at Imogen. 'I'm perfectly all right,' he snapped. 'There's no need to treat me as if I'm about to faint or burst into tears.'

'Eat them anyway,' said Imogen, who thought it might be better if he did.

Tom Maddison was a difficult man to help. What was the point of pretending that you didn't have feelings? He had re-treated behind an even more ferocious mask than usual, bottling it all up inside, and was clearly going to lash out at anyone who dared to suggest that he might be hurt, or angry, or in need of comfort.

Well, she would just have to be lashed, Imogen decided. She had been spared Tom's public humiliation, but she knew what it was like to realise that the person you loved didn't love you back and never had. It hurt. It hurt a lot and, although no one could endure it for you, it helped to have someone by your side to see you through it.

Tom would never admit that he needed anyone, but he did.

Imogen wished she knew more about his private life. If only there was a friend she could call, *someone* who would come and be there for Tom, the way Amanda had been there for her. But it looked as if it was just her.

She transferred her notebook from under her arm and flicked it open. For now, she would stick with the practicalities.

'I've spoken to the Castle, and cancelled all the arrangements there. I'm afraid that, at this stage, there's no question of any refunds,' she added apologetically.

'God, what a waste of money!' Tom threw himself back in his chair and rubbed the back of his neck as he thought of the cost. He hadn't begrudged paying for Julia's increasingly extravagant ideas, but what had been the point of it all? He had let Julia have whatever she wanted.

He hadn't realised the only thing she really wanted was Patrick.

'Then there's the honeymoon…'

Imogen hesitated about raising the matter of the honeymoon, but that had been booked and paid for too, and Tom would have to make some decision. The cost of Coconut Island was phenomenal. It would make a dent in even Tom's bank account, surely.

'I've been thinking about that,' said Tom, taking a biscuit without quite realising what he was doing. 'You said it was somewhere you'd love to go,' he reminded her.

Imogen squirmed. 'I'm sorry it turned out to be so expensive.'

But really, how was she to know Julia would turn her back on the wedding of her dreams, the holiday of a lifetime and a man like Tom? Julia must really love Patrick to give up all that, she reflected. 'I'll see if it's possible to get some money back, at least.'

If it had been her own holiday, she would have taken out

insurance, but it had never occurred to her to think it would be an issue for Tom.

'I'll get on to the agents and see what the cancellation terms are,' she said.

'Don't do that,' said Tom, brushing biscuit crumbs from his fingers and making up his mind. 'I don't want you to cancel the trip.'

Imogen looked at him in concern. Surely he wasn't planning to go anyway? It would be a disaster. Every time he turned round he would be reminded that Julia wasn't there.

'I'm not sure it's a great idea for you to go on your own,' she said cautiously.

'I'm not planning to go on my own,' he said. 'You're coming with me.'

'*What?*'

'I've wasted enough money on the wedding. I've spent a bloody fortune on that island, and I'm not going to waste that too. You said you'd like to go there. Well, now's your chance.'

'But…it's booked as a honeymoon,' stammered Imogen. 'Everyone would assume that we were married.'

'Who's going to know, or care?' Tom countered. 'They're only interested in my money. It's not as if they're going to ask to see the marriage certificate when we check in.'

'Well, no, but…' Imogen looked at him despairingly. Couldn't he *see* how awkward it would be? 'I booked it as a honeymoon, so they might make a fuss when we arrive.'

'Let them,' said Tom. 'Surely the whole point of the exercise was that we would have complete privacy? This isn't some B&B where we'd have no choice but to share a bed. At least, it had better not be for the price I'm paying for it!' he added caustically. 'OK, we may have to bluff it on arrival, but after that we should have a whole island to ourselves and no one will know that we're not spending our whole time having sex.'

Imogen was mortified to feel her cheeks burning. Honestly, anyone would think she had never heard the word *sex* before! But somehow Tom talking about it made it all too easy to imagine Tom *doing* it.

She forced the image aside, not without some difficulty.

'You make it all sound so reasonable,' she protested.

'Because it is reasonable. It's a practical solution to the problem, and would be a good thing for both of us. What's not reasonable about that?'

Imogen fiddled with her pen and tried to imagine what it would be like to go on holiday with her boss. 'It would still be a bit…intimate,' she said at last.

'I don't see why—' Tom stopped as it occurred to him, somewhat belatedly, that Imogen might have a personal life of her own. He knew that she wasn't married, but there might be a man on the scene, and that might complicate matters.

He frowned. 'Are you worried about what a boyfriend might think?'

'It's not that,' said Imogen. 'There isn't anyone else at the moment.'

'Even better then,' said Tom, relieved. 'That means no one has any excuse to feel jealous or upset.'

'Maybe not, but there'll be plenty of people who'll speculate about why we're going on holiday together.'

Tom scowled. 'Who on earth is going to care?'

'The entire staff of Collocom for a start, I should think.'

'What business is it of theirs what we do?'

'None, of course, but that's not going to stop them wondering. *I'd* wonder what was going on if my boss and his secretary disappeared to a tropical island for three weeks!'

'Tell them it's a business trip,' Tom said indifferently.

'Oh, yes, like they'll believe that!'

'Frankly, I'm not concerned with what they do and don't believe,' he said with a dismissive gesture. 'The fact is that it *will* be a business trip. We'll have a whole island between us. We can take our laptops, and if we've got access to the Internet there's no reason why we shouldn't get on with some work.'

Imogen looked dubious. 'Do you think there'll be an Internet connection?' she asked, even as she realised that she had been lured into discussing details before they had really dealt with the issue at hand.

'At that price there certainly ought to be!'

'I don't know,' she said, still doubtful. 'I can't imagine many people hire a private island to work. It's meant as a romantic hideaway,' she reminded him. 'I don't think the idea is that you spend your time checking email.'

'Then you'd better find out,' said Tom, 'because I have no intention of cutting myself off from work for three weeks. It'll be a good chance to catch up on a few projects without the distraction of endless meetings.'

Pushing back his chair, he got to his feet and prowled over to the window, where he stood looking out at the sleety rain that splattered against the glass. 'We might as well get something out of this whole fiasco.'

Imogen bit her lip as she regarded his back. Silhouetted against the window, he looked massive and solitary. Internet access, or lack of it, wasn't the problem here.

'Are you sure you've thought this through?' she asked carefully.

Tom kept his gaze on the rain. 'What do you mean?'

'Have you considered how painful it's going to be for you if I'm there instead of Julia?'

'Not as painful as forking out however many thousand pounds and having absolutely nothing to show for it,' he said, but he knew that Imogen had a point.

'I suspect it's going to be awkward to be around for a while,' he went on, not without some difficulty. 'It'll be easier for everyone if I'm not here and then they don't have to tell me they're sorry or remember not to mention anything to do with weddings.'

He hesitated, his eyes on the wet pavements far below. The sun would be shining in the Maldives, he thought. What would it be like there? He hadn't really thought about going with Julia but now he let himself imagine being there with Imogen.

It would be easier if he could work, and she could help him to do that. The beauty of modern technology was that you could work anywhere, so why not the Maldives? Imogen could be his PA there as well as here.

And while Tom might try and tell himself that he didn't care what people thought, deep down his humiliation was still raw. It would be bad enough dealing with the sympathy here without having to explain himself all over again when he turned up for a honeymoon on his own.

He could feel Imogen watching him warily.

'I could go to the island on my own,' he said, turning back to face her, his hands in his pockets, 'but then it really would be obvious that something was wrong. There would be fewer explanations if you came too.'

Dammit, he didn't want to beg! 'You've been doing all the work for this wedding, anyway,' he ploughed on. 'You deserve a break.'

'I thought I was going to work?'

'I'll be working,' he said. 'You can do what you like.'

Imogen regarded him a little helplessly. It seemed all wrong to be taking another woman's place on a honeymoon, but she sensed that Tom was too proud to ask her outright. The holiday would probably be a good thing for him, but he would lose face going alone, and she knew that would be difficult for him.

Was it so much to ask? She hated the thought of Tom being on his own at a time like this, and this way she could at least keep him company and offer support if he needed it.

And, when it came down to it, it was February and he was offering her three free weeks in luxurious surroundings in the Maldives. If nothing else, it would get her away from *Star Wars* fanatics and allergy sufferers.

She drew a breath. 'All right,' she said, 'if you really would like me to go, I'll go.'

'Fine' was all he said, but he couldn't quite conceal the flash of relief in his eyes as he sat back down at his desk, and that made her feel better, or at least as if she was doing the right thing.

'Transfer Julia's ticket into your name,' he said, 'and tell anyone who asks that we're going on a business trip.'

CHAPTER THREE

'WELCOME, Mr and Mrs Maddison, and congratulations!' The resort manager himself met Tom and Imogen as they stepped onto the jetty. The light was dazzling and the heat was both a relief and a shock after the air-conditioning on the flight. A flying boat had brought them from the airport on Malé to their base, and their luggage was already being transferred to a sleek speedboat that was waiting to take them on the last leg to Coconut Island itself.

Imogen averted her eyes from her battered old trolley bag. It was perfectly adequate for package holidays to Greece and Spain, but it looked very out of place here amongst the other designer cases and honeymooners' matching luggage sets that were being unloaded from the seaplane.

She must look as out of place as her luggage, she realised. She was very conscious of her crumpled trousers and creased top. February wasn't the best time to buy hot-weather clothes in London, so she had little choice but to bring the clothes she had worn to Greece the year before. They were cheap and cheerful, and had been perfect there, but she could see the other travellers eyeing her askance.

There was nothing cheap about this resort, where all the guests seemed to be beautifully dressed. Everyone seemed to be in couples, and they were uniformly lithe and golden and glowing with happiness.

Imogen shifted uncomfortably. In comparison, she knew she must look pasty, fat and frazzled by the tension of the last few days. There was no way anyone would take her for a radiant bride, that was for sure. They must all be wondering what on earth she was doing with someone like Tom Maddison.

Not that Tom fitted in any better than she did. He was actually wearing a suit! At least he had taken his jacket off now, but his shirtsleeves were still buttoned, his tie still knotted. Imogen wondered if he had ever been on holiday before.

Tom wasn't giving a very good impression of a newlywed either, it had to be said. His expression was as forbidding as ever, but the power of his presence was such that the resort manager had picked him unerringly from all the couples who disembarked from the seaplane as the recently married Tom Maddison, who had hired the most luxurious and expensive accommodation available.

'If you wouldn't mind completing a few formalities…' he said, politely concealing his disbelief at Tom Maddison's new wife, who was clearly not what they had been expecting.

He led them ahead of everyone else to the spectacular reception area, which was all dark wood, lush tropical plants and understated glamour. It practically reeked of money, thought Imogen, trying not to stare. Fabulously expensive hotels would be ten a penny to the new Mrs Maddison.

'As soon as this is done, you'll be taken straight to Coconut Island, where you'll be assured complete privacy during your stay,' the manager went on. He gestured towards a slim young man dressed in pristine white, who was waiting to one side. 'Ali will visit once a day and will make sure you have everything you need.'

Tom merely nodded, but Imogen felt as if she ought to show a little more enthusiasm. 'Thank you,' she said, plastering on a big smile. 'I'm sure it will all be lovely.'

The manager, having obviously decided he wouldn't get much small talk out of Tom, turned to Imogen with a courteous smile.

'I hope you had a happy day for your wedding?'

There was a tiny pause. They had agreed on the plane that it would be easier not to go into complicated explanations, but surely it must be obvious that they weren't actually married. Imogen felt as if there must be a neon sign flashing 'liar' with an arrow pointing down right above her head, but she kept her smile in place somehow.

'Er...yes...thank you,' she said awkwardly, tucking her left hand away so that the manager wouldn't notice the glaring absence of a wedding ring.

Tom glanced up from the form he was signing and, rather to Imogen's surprise, seemed to pick up on her discomfort. Or perhaps he just didn't think she was putting on a very convincing performance, because he reached out and put his arm around her waist, pulling her into his side.

'Imogen's very tired,' he explained her lack of enthusiasm. 'She's had a busy time organising the wedding, and it was a long flight.'

'Of course, of course.' The manager beamed at them both. 'But now you are here, you can be alone together and relax.'

Oh, yes, *sure*, thought Imogen, who had rarely felt less relaxed than she did at that moment. Tom had shaken her hand when they'd first met, but she didn't think he had ever touched her since, and now his arm was warm and strong around her, holding her against a body that was leaner and harder and more solid than she could ever have imagined.

His big hand rested casually, proprietorially, at her waist, exactly as a besotted husband's would, and he seemed astonishingly natural, as if he knew her body as well as his own.

Imogen's heart was pounding and her skin where she was pressed into his side, and beneath his hand, was tingling and twitching with awareness of him, of his warmth and his strength and the clean masculine smell of him. Her knees felt ridiculously weak and she was conscious of a bizarre and disturbing desire to turn into the hard security of his body, to hold him tight and burrow into him.

Her mouth dried at the very thought of it. Relax? Ha!

She managed a weak smile. 'I can't wait.'

'You must let us know if there is anything—anything at all!—we can do to make your stay more comfortable.'

Imogen wondered wildly if she could ask if he would swap Tom for a less unsettling companion, one she could chat away to without her heart thudding and thumping with the memory of what it felt like to be held against him.

She was overreacting, Imogen scolded herself. She could blame it on jet lag. This was *Tom*, for heaven's sake! Her boss.

The boss who had just had his heart broken, remember? Imogen felt a little ashamed to realise that she hadn't given Julia a thought since she'd arrived. It had been such a thrill to fly over the islands. Pressing her nose against the seaplane's window, she had gasped at the heart-stopping beauty of the scene.

They'd flown across islands fringed with dazzling white sand, while the water between them was so intensely coloured it seemed almost unreal: the deep, dark blue of the ocean beyond the reefs; bright aquamarine striped with violet and lilac over the sand bars; the pale, translucent emerald of the shallow lagoons. Far below, the little boats zipping over the sea had been tiny streaks flecking the surface with their wake, while the waves broke silently against the reef in a froth of white.

Caught up in amazement at it all, it wasn't surprising that she had forgotten Julia, but Tom wouldn't have done. How could he?

This must all be so difficult for him, she thought as, to her intense relief, Tom released her to complete the paperwork. How hard would it be to arrive in this beautiful place to spend what should have been three glorious weeks with his bride, knowing that whenever he turned his head, instead of the svelte, gorgeous Julia, he would just see his very ordinary PA? It would be like salt rubbing into the wound every time.

Imogen bit her lip. And here she was getting in a state about a brief hug! It was far, far worse for Tom. He must surely be regretting now that he had asked her to come.

She stood feeling miserably self-conscious as the resort manager outlined the arrangements that had been made for them. It was clear that Tom wasn't listening any more than she was. 'Yes, yes,' he said with a trace of impatience as he signed the last form. 'Whatever's been arranged will be fine.'

'Excellent. In that case, I'm sure you're anxious to be left alone.' The manager waved Ali over and they all trooped back down to the jetty, where the speedboat was already throbbing gently, ready for the off.

Tom put his hand lightly against her back to guide her to the steps leading down to the boat, and Imogen's heart lurched into her throat once more. Telling herself not to be so stupid, she climbed into the boat, barely noticing the hand Ali put out to steady her, but burningly aware of Tom's touch long after he had dropped his hand.

Willing the blush she could feel creeping up her cheeks to fade, Imogen sat stiffly on the luxurious seat as Tom jumped easily down into the boat and took his place beside her. She couldn't let herself get into a state whenever he touched her! The next three weeks were going to be difficult enough as it was.

Three weeks alone with him.

What on earth was she doing here? It had made a warped kind of sense that day in London when she had agreed to come. Tom had needed to get away. She would help him save face. It was a purely business arrangement.

True, Amanda hadn't seemed convinced. 'Business?' she said when Imogen told her that she would be away for three weeks. 'On a tropical island?'

'It'll be just like being in the office,' Imogen said. 'But with better weather.'

'Sure.' Amanda's tone reeked scepticism.

'It will,' she insisted. 'I've got to take my laptop. I'll have to work.'

'And when you're not working and there's just the two of you alone in paradise? It sounds like this Tom Maddison is pretty hot,' said Amanda. 'How are you going to keep your hands off him? And don't tell me you haven't thought about it!'

'I haven't!' And she hadn't. Not since Tom had announced that he was getting married, anyway.

'Honestly, Amanda, the man has just been jilted at the altar,' Imogen went on a little huffily. 'He won't admit it, but he's really hurt. The last thing he needs is me making things awkward for him! Besides, this is my boss we're talking about.'

'So?'

'So there's no question of anything like that. Tom's too churned up about Julia and I've got more sense. OK, he is quite attractive,' Imogen conceded, 'but he's out of my league, I know that.

'Even if he wasn't in love with someone else, I wouldn't consider it,' she went on. 'Tom Maddison doesn't even have a nodding acquaintance with his emotions. Look at how he's suppressing everything now! A relationship with a man like him would be asking for trouble. I'd end up miserable, and I've had enough misery, thank you very much.

'Quite apart from anything else, it would be unprofessional,' Imogen finished primly. 'It's a well-paid job, and if I can stick it for another two or three months I'll have enough money to take off for a year. There's no way I'm risking that for the sake of a quick fling. No,' she told Amanda, 'I don't think I'll have any trouble keeping my hands to myself!'

Now her words rang a little hollowly in her ears. It had been easy to say in London. She had been so confident then, but that was before he had touched her, before the nerves beneath her skin had started jumping and jittering with awareness of him. Before that long flight, sitting right next to him.

They had travelled first-class, of course, and to Imogen, used to cheap package holidays, it had been absolute luxury. She had been thrilled, playing with her chair, opening her free bag of toiletries, accepting a glass of champagne.

Only she would have enjoyed it more if Amanda had been with her, say. Tom wasn't the kind of person you could have a giggle with.

Understandably enough, he was looking forbidding when he'd come to pick her up from her flat in a chauffeur-driven limousine that had whisked them out to Heathrow. Conversation so far had been confined to practicalities about passports and boarding times. There had been no speculation about what to buy in Duty Free, no testing of perfumes or loitering in the bookshops. The First Class Lounge was very comfortable, but it wasn't much fun, Imogen had decided.

Tom had sat down and opened his laptop and, apart from take-off and landing, he had worked steadily. To Imogen, it seemed as if the anger and hurt over Julia's rejection was still buttoned up tightly inside him. She desperately wanted to help him but she didn't know how. With anyone else she would offer a hug, but she hesitated even to lay a hand on Tom's arm.

Which was difficult when it was just *there*. Imogen could see the immaculate cuff of his pale blue shirt, the expensive watch, the square, capable hand, and she'd found herself fixating on tiny details, like the creases on his knuckles, or the fine dark hairs at his wrist.

Afraid that Tom would see her staring, she'd forced herself to look at the magazine she had bought instead, but her eyes kept straying back to him. His gaze had been fixed on the computer screen and, with the piercing grey eyes shielded, it was easier to study his face. He had surprisingly thick, dark lashes, but the uncompromising angles of cheek and jaw offset any suggestion of softness, as did his mouth, which was set in a stern, straight line. Every time Imogen's eyes had come to rest on it, she got a squirmy, fluttery feeling inside.

In the end, it had been a relief to get off the plane and have something else to look at but, as Imogen sat in the boat, the reality of the situation began to sink in. She was about to spend three weeks alone with a man she found unsettlingly attractive, who just happened to be (a) her boss and (b) in love with someone else, and therefore doubly out of bounds.

Imogen adjusted her sunglasses and tried to wriggle the tension out of her shoulders. Perhaps Amanda was right and it was all going to be a terrible mistake.

But how could it be a mistake when the sun was warm on her skin, and the sea so clear that she could see every ripple in the sand beneath the boat? When she could hear the water slapping gently against the hull and smell the bleached wood of the jetty?

She could be in London, making the most of Tom's absence by catching up on her filing. She could be fielding phone calls and dealing with the emails stacked up in her inbox and chasing up those expenses with the Finance department.

Instead, she was here, with Tom, very distinct beside her, his austere profile outlined against the tropical sky. Eyeing him surreptitiously from behind her glasses, Imogen felt as if she had never seen him properly before. He had put on his sunglasses, which made his expression even more inscrutable than ever, but everything else about him seemed preternaturally clear in the light that bounced off the water: the texture of his skin, the line of his cheek, the faint stubble darkening his jaw after the long flight, the edge of his mouth.

She wished it would curl in a smile sometimes.

The boat started slowly, making its way out to the gap between the reef, but once on the open water the throbbing note of the engine deepened to a throaty roar as Ali accelerated and they skimmed over the waves.

The sun glittered on the water and, in spite of the windshield, Imogen's hair blew crazily around her face. It was so exhilarating that she could feel her fretfulness unravelling with every bounce of the boat and, without thinking, she smiled at Tom, who looked startled for a moment until, incredibly, he smiled back.

'OK?' he shouted over the noise of the engine, and she nodded vigorously as she tried to hold her hair back.

'It's wonderful!' she said, trying to ignore the breathless flip of her heart at his smile.

Although it had only taken a matter of minutes to reach the island in the powerful boat, it felt as if they had entered another world, one that made the laid-back resort seem a frenetic metropolis in comparison. When Ali cut the engine, the silence hit them like a blow.

'Welcome to Coconut Island,' he said.

From the little wooden jetty, Imogen could see the curve of a blindingly white beach, overhung with the coconut palms that cast a jagged shade. A lagoon the colour of a glacier mint and as clear as glass was encircled by a reef, but beyond that there was just the Indian Ocean, stretching out to a horizon smudged with a few billowing clouds. They had been promised seclusion, and seclusion they certainly had.

Set back from the beach and half hidden by a tangle of tropical foliage, from the outside the house was a simple wooden structure with a thatched roof, but inside it was furnished with exquisite style and discreetly fitted with the latest technology from top designers.

The attention to detail made Imogen's eyes pop as Ali showed them round. Outside, there was an infinity pool, a Jacuzzi and a second fabulous bathroom, open to the sky, with a wet area, a waterfall shower and a bath that would hold two easily, all perfectly designed with natural materials to blend into the foliage.

Inside, there was an immaculately equipped kitchen. There were polished wooden floors, long luxurious couches and low tables. There were huge ceiling fans, and a sound system the like of which Imogen had never seen before.

And there was a huge, beautiful bed.

It had to be at least seven feet wide, and made with white sheets of the softest and purest cotton and piled with inviting pillows. A bed made for love.

Imogen, who had been exclaiming with pleasure as Ali showed them round, fell suddenly silent.

She glanced at Tom. His expression was unreadable, but she could imagine all too well what he must be thinking. How could he not be imagining in his turn what it would have been like if Julia had been there with him? If they had been impatient for Ali to leave them alone so that they could fall across that wonderful bed and make love?

It would be heaven. Imogen swallowed, unable to stop herself wondering what it would be like if she and Tom really were on honeymoon, if she was here because he loved her, not because Julia had left him in the lurch.

Too polite to comment on the awkward silence that had developed in the bedroom, Ali continued the tour, showing them the meals that had been left in the fridge, discussing the menu for the next day and pointing out the generator. Then he got into the speedboat and headed back to the resort, leaving Tom and Imogen alone.

They watched the boat speed out through the reef and then veer right in the direction of the islands they had passed on their way, its wake foaming behind it, and then even the sound of its engine vanished.

Imogen listened hard. She could hear the ocean murmuring against the reef, and somewhere a bird called raucously, but otherwise it was utterly quiet.

'Well,' she said awkwardly.

'Well,' agreed Tom in a dry voice.

Biting her lip, she looked out over the lagoon, which was achingly clear and green in the glaring light of midday. A cat's paw of breeze shivered over its surface and rustled the palms overhead, but then it was gone, leaving the scene still and dreamlike in the heat.

'Do you think you can spend three weeks here?' he asked her after a moment.

'Oh, yes, of course! It's absolutely *beautiful*,' she said. 'I feel as if I've stumbled into paradise! I just wish...'

Tom lifted an eyebrow as she hesitated. 'What?'

'I just wish things could be different for you,' she told him impulsively. 'I know how hard it must be for you to have me here instead of Julia.'

'Don't worry about it,' said Tom gruffly. 'I'm more afraid that you'll be bored.'

'Bored?' Imogen stared at him. 'How could I be bored *here*?' she asked, waving a hand at the view.

'You've always struck me as a very sociable person,' he explained to her surprise. She hadn't realised he had observed her at all. 'I see you chatting to people in the office and talking to your friends on the phone.'

Imogen grimaced at that bit. She had hoped Tom hadn't realised how much time she spent on personal phone calls.

'You seem like the kind of girl who likes to have fun,' he went on, uncharacteristically hesitant. 'There won't be much fun with just me for company.'

The truth was, he hadn't been thinking about Imogen. He had been so consumed with the bitterness of humiliation that he had thought only about getting away, and it was only now, very belatedly, that he.was wondering if he had been selfish. Julia had often told him he needed to work on his social skills, but he had never been good at the kind of light-hearted conversation at which Imogen seemed to excel.

She made an unlikely PA, with that slightly chaotic air, but behind the warmth and the friendliness he had noted in her dealings with everyone from the most senior directors to the cleaners, she was unexpectedly practical, and Tom was grateful to her for the way she had dealt with the aftermath of Julia's change of mind. She deserved a better time than he would be able to give her.

Not that there was much he could do about it now. Tom hunched a shoulder. He hated feeling that he had got things wrong. He liked to be in control and know what was going on, and as soon as any emotions were involved, he was neither.

'You make it sound as if I'm a wild party animal,' said Imogen, amused but also secretly flattered. 'To be honest, I spend most evenings watching television with my flatmate and complaining about how nothing exciting ever happens to us. And now I'm here...' She looked around her. 'I couldn't ask for more exciting than this!'

Unless it was someone to share that beautiful bed with, a sneaky voice in her mind had the temerity to point out before Imogen squashed it firmly.

'I promise you I'm more than happy just to look at this view for three weeks,' she told Tom. 'Of course, I'm happy to work too,' she added hastily, remembering their agreement.

'There's no need for you to work today,' said Tom gruffly. 'Since we're here, we may as well make the most of it.'

Imogen beamed at him. 'Sounds good to me.'

'So...what would you like to do? Are you tired?'

'A bit,' she confessed, 'but I want to swim first. I can't wait to get in that water!'

Ali had put their cases together in the bedroom. Tom's was sleek and black, Imogen's squashy and battered, and they sat side by side, looking bizarrely mismatched and yet oddly intimate at the same time.

Imogen fished out her bikini and changed in the en suite bathroom. Adjusting the straps, she regarded her reflection in the mirror dubiously. Had this bikini been *quite* so revealing the year before? It certainly didn't leave much to the imagination!

Why hadn't she stuck more carefully to that diet she had planned in January? If she had known she would be dusting off her bikini in February, she would never have eaten her way through all those packets of chocolate biscuits.

On the other hand, they were all that had got her through some of those long winter afternoons.

It was too late now, anyway. Imogen pulled herself together. Tom already had his laptop open, and when he was working he wouldn't notice if she walked past him stark naked. He certainly wouldn't be eyeing her up and wondering if a one-piece in a bigger size wouldn't have been a better choice, the way another woman would. There was a lot to be said for having a whole beach to yourself.

Still, she wrapped a sarong around her waist before heading out to the living area. Tom might not notice the way she spilled out of her bikini bottoms, but she would, and she didn't want to have to hold her tummy in all the time.

Tom was on one of the couches, leaning forward and frowning intently at the laptop open on the coffee table in front of him, but he looked up as Imogen appeared.

'Don't you want a swim?' she said, feeling self-conscious. He had barely glanced at her before returning his gaze to the screen, but it was enough to make her aware that the sarong was very thin and that, beneath it, she was practically naked.

'Maybe later,' he said. 'I want to check the markets first.'

'OK. Well….I'll be on the beach if you need me.'

When she had gone, Tom let out a long breath and slumped back against the cushions. He had been totally unprepared for the sight of Imogen, barefoot and wearing little more than a skimpy sarong. He recognised the brown hair tumbling to her shoulders, and the wide blue eyes, but had she always had that body? How had he never noticed before what luscious curves she had, or how lush and alluring her skin looked?

And now that he *had* noticed, how was he going to stop?

Tom scowled. He was still bruised from his last encounter with a woman, and he certainly didn't intend to get entangled with another, especially not one who was his PA. It would be totally inappropriate.

He shouldn't even be thinking about how she had looked. He certainly shouldn't be wondering if she would feel as soft and warm as she looked, wondering what it would be like to unwind that sarong and explore that unexpectedly voluptuous body with his mouth and his hands.

Setting his teeth grimly, Tom forced his attention back to the screen. He must be suffering some kind of a delayed reaction to the last few days, he decided. Nothing else could explain the lust that had gripped him when he had looked up to see Imogen just now. It wasn't even as if she was his type. He had never even thought about what she looked like before. His preference had always been for slender, sophisticated women—women who were cool and controlled. Women like Julia.

Julia. The thought of her was like a shock. Had it only been three days since he had been ready to marry her? Tom couldn't believe that he was thinking lustfully about another woman already. He had to stop it, right now, he thought. They had another three weeks to get through—three weeks when he would have to keep his hands firmly to himself.

He could do it. He could do whatever he set his mind to, Tom reminded himself. Hadn't he built an entire career on sheer willpower and determination, on a refusal to let himself be distracted from his goal? He had resisted a lot more tempting distractions than Imogen, and he would resist her too. Quite apart from anything else, he didn't want to distract *her*. They had work to do.

And work was what Tom Maddison did best.

It was hard to concentrate on it right then, though. He was hot and his eyes felt gritty from the plane. A quick dip would refresh him, Tom decided. An image of the lagoon shimmered in his mind, but he dismissed it. Imogen was down there. He didn't want to crowd her.

Odd how vividly he could picture her, he mused, remembering how she had looked, smiling on the boat, her hair tangled around her face and her eyes full of sunshine, how she had looked in that sarong with her shoulders bare.

Remembering that was a mistake.

Restlessly, Tom got to his feet and wandered outside. The infinity pool shimmered invitingly. He would cool off in there and then get back to work.

But the pool seemed empty somehow and when he hung in the water with his arms stretched along the edge he could see the lagoon through the palms and he found himself imagining Imogen down there, on her own.

Really, it was ridiculous to feel that he had to avoid her! They were going to have to get on together for the next three weeks.

It wasn't as if there was a problem, not really. Tom had already rationalised his momentary surge of lust as the simple reaction of a bruised ego. He might be alone on a tropical island with Imogen, but they were both sensible adults. There was absolutely no reason why they shouldn't have the same professional relationship they had always had, and get on with some work.

Work was what mattered.

Hauling himself out of the pool, Tom dried himself off and went into the kitchen. Imogen wouldn't be able to work if she was suffering from dehydration. He would take her a drink.

He found her stretched out on a lounger in the jagged shade of a palm. She had discarded the sarong somewhere along the line and was wearing only a bright pink bikini. Tom's hand wasn't quite steady as he offered her a glass of fresh lime juice.

'Thank you,' she said, sitting up, but her smile as she took the glass from him was definitely tense.

It couldn't be easy for her, stuck here with her boss, thought Tom.

He sat on the edge of the lounger set out beside hers and stared out at the lagoon while he sipped his own drink and willed the image of Imogen in that bikini to stop dancing before his eyes.

He could do this. It was just a matter of getting used to seeing his PA without her clothes on.

There was a strained silence.

'What's the water like?' Tom asked eventually, uncomfortably aware that his voice came out as a rasp, and he cleared his throat.

'Lovely.' Imogen drained her glass and put it down in the sand as she stood up. 'I was about to go back in for another swim,' she said, then hesitated. 'Why don't you come?'

It might be better to do something rather than sit here trying not to look at her, Tom decided. 'All right,' he said, getting to his feet.

They walked over the hot sand together and into the water. It was so clear they could see their feet in extraordinary detail as they waded past the shallows.

'It feels like silk against your skin, doesn't it?' said Imogen, trailing her fingers over the surface.

Tom wished she hadn't mentioned her skin. It was hard enough to keep his eyes off it as it was. As soon as it was deep enough, he dived into the water and swam in a fast crawl out towards the reef.

It felt good to stretch himself physically. It certainly felt less dangerous than standing close to Imogen wearing little more than a few triangles of cloth.

When he stopped at last, he shook the hair out of his eyes and trod water. Here, it had deepened to jade, but he could still see right down to the bottom, some way below. The sun was bouncing off the surface and fracturing the water into silvery patterns, and he had to squint against the glare to find Imogen, who was floating dreamily on her back, legs and arms stretched out like a starfish.

It was very quiet. How long was it since he had stopped like this and just listened to the silence, just felt the sun on his shoulders? His life was so focused, so driven by the need to succeed that he had forgotten how to relax the way Imogen was relaxing. Maybe he had never known how to relax like that, thought Tom, but he had the strangest idea that the tight feeling that had gripped him for as long as he could remember was starting to loosen in the sunlight and the warm silky water.

CHAPTER FOUR

HE SWAM more slowly back to shore. By the time he got there, Imogen was lolling in the shallows. Leaning back on her hands, her head was tipped back as she lifted her face to the sun, but she opened her eyes at the sound of his approach.

'It's incredible, isn't it?' she said naturally enough, but there was still that constraint in her expression and her smile was guarded.

Tom knew how she felt. Imogen was his PA; he was her boss. It wasn't as if they were strangers, but it occurred to him—very belatedly—that they had never had what could properly be called a conversation and now he wasn't sure where to start. They had only ever talked about work, about practicalities, but they could hardly discuss either here, with the light rocking over the water and the hot breeze ruffling the palms.

The situation was more awkward than he had anticipated. The truth was that he had been so desperate to get away from the humiliation of a cancelled wedding that he hadn't really thought what it would be like being alone with Imogen. He had imagined that there would be plenty of room for both of them on the island and, although there obviously was, he could hardly walk past her and ignore her, could he?

After a moment's hesitation, he sat down next to her in the shallows. He would try and avoid her as much as possible, but they were still going to have to establish some kind of relationship for the next three weeks. They couldn't spend their time together in silence. For now he had better try and make a bit of an effort.

Only it was harder than he thought when he was sitting right beside her. He had been careful not to get too close, but he was quite near enough to see how the wet bikini clung to Imogen's breasts.

Near enough to see the droplets of water on her skin and the curve of her mouth.

Near enough to see the sweep of her lashes, the pulse beating in her throat.

Tom cleared his throat and made himself look away. 'The water's very nice,' he agreed.

Imogen dug her toes into the sand and marvelled at his innocuous choice of words. It was more than *nice*. It was magical.

Dazzled by the heat and the light and the colour, she felt as if she had stumbled into another world and she had been sitting very still, half afraid that if she moved it would disappear in a blink and she would find herself back on the Northern Line, battling her way up into the greyness and the rain with the other commuters.

It was all so perfect, the blues and the greens and the pure white beach behind her. The colours were clean and clear and the only sound was the ocean, muted beyond the reef, and the gentle ripple of the lagoon around her ankles.

The only jarring note was Tom. He belonged in the other grey day-to-day world, not in this colourful idyllic one.

Imogen slid a sideways glance at him under her lashes. He was looking out towards the reef, his arms resting casually on his knees, and he seemed at once startlingly familiar and a stranger.

The stern profile, the dark formidable features, the close-cropped hair were the same as ever, but she wasn't used to seeing them etched against a perfect blue sky.

Or on top of a bare chest.

She had known that he was tall and lean, and she had assumed that he would have a decent body, but Imogen hadn't realised quite how good until he had appeared by the lounger wearing only those swimming shorts. It had been impossible not to notice that his legs were long and straight, his chest broad and wonderfully solid-looking, with dark hairs arrowing down to an enviably flat, hard stomach. He had powerful shoulders too, and his skin looked tantalisingly wet and touchable.

Imogen's mouth dried. She was desperately aware of him sitting in the water beside her. Normally she had no problem chatting to anyone, but Tom was hard work at the best of times and now that he was practically naked she couldn't think of a single thing to say.

The next three weeks were going to be awkward if she was going to feel stupidly shy like this the whole time. She wanted to treat Tom exactly the same as always, but how could she when he was sitting there with that body? She wished he would go and put his suit back on. It might not be very practical for the beach, but at least she would feel as if she knew where she was.

The silence lengthened uncomfortably. Imogen was still searching desperately for a neutral topic of conversation when a flash of light beneath the water caught her eye and she leant forward to see another, and then another. 'Look!' she cried, pointing at the tiny fish that darted over the sand and heartily relieved at the distraction. 'Aren't they beautiful?'

'There'll be a lot more out there.' Tom seized gratefully on the conversational gambit. Narrowing his eyes against the glare, he nodded towards the reef. 'I hear the snorkelling is spectacular.'

'I'd love to do that,' she said wistfully.

'You could get out there easily enough. I noticed a boat earlier.'

Imogen looked doubtful. 'I wouldn't know one end of a boat from another. I think I'd be better off swimming! Is snorkelling easy? I've never done it before.'

'I'll teach you if you like,' said Tom, who only moments before had decided that the only way to get through three weeks of Imogen in a bikini was to go their separate ways as much as possible.

'Really?'

So much for keeping his distance! Tom cursed himself for a fool. He couldn't have found a surer way to get close to her in that damned bikini if he'd tried. He was supposed to be getting back to a work relationship, not fooling around in the water.

'We'll have a go tomorrow. After we've done some work,' he added.

'I'd like that,' said Imogen, brightening. Perhaps it would be easier if they did something together. At least then they would have something to talk about.

She leant back on her elbows and looked at him curiously. There was little money in snorkelling, few deals to be negotiated on a coral reef. It seemed an unlikely activity for Tom to take part in. 'Where did you learn to snorkel?'

'In the Caribbean. I had a girlfriend once who went on and on about having a holiday together,' Tom remembered. 'I only went to shut her up, but it wasn't a success. We'd got on fine in London, but I suppose the truth was that we hadn't seen that much of each other. As soon as we got out there, we realised that we had nothing to say to each other. She lay on the beach and I went snorkelling, and once we got back to London I never saw her again!'

Imogen spread her hands, sliding them beneath the silvery sand. 'They say holidays are a real test of a relationship.'

'It certainly was for Helena and I, although according to Helena it was all my fault. She complained I didn't know how to relax, and there's some truth in that. I never know what to do with myself on holiday. I don't think I ever learnt. We never had holidays when we were growing up.'

'What, never?'

'Not the kind of holiday where you go away somewhere different, anyway. I had school holidays, of course, but my mother died when I was small and my father was always working, so I was pretty much left to my own devices.'

'Poor little boy,' said Imogen, but he shrugged off her sympathy.

'I liked it. I started my first business at the age of ten. I used to knock on neighbours' doors and offer to wash cars for a quid, until I realised that I was undercharging!' He smiled wryly at the memory.

'What did you do with your earnings?' she asked, intrigued by the idea of him as a little boy.

'I bought some extra buckets and some more cloths, and gave them to friends in exchange for a percentage of their earnings. By the end of the summer, I had quite a team!'

Imogen laughed. She was feeling better now that they were actually having a conversation. Perhaps this wouldn't be so bad after all. 'It sounds like you were always an entrepreneur!'

'I learnt early on that if I wanted anything, I had to get it for myself,' said Tom. 'Even at ten I could work out the laws of supply and demand. To get what I wanted, I needed money, but to get money all I had to do was work out what everyone else wanted and then make it easy for them to have it.'

'You make it sound so simple,' said Imogen with a touch of bitterness, and he raised his brows.

'It is simple.'

'Working out what people want? Not in my experience!'

He shrugged. 'I never had any trouble knowing what I wanted. It seems to me a lot of people don't *know* what they want. Once you do, you've got a clear objective, and then it's just a matter of working towards it. All you need is a strategy and be prepared to stick with it.'

'That might work in business, but strategies are no use when emotions are involved.'

'No.' Tom thought about Julia and how messy everything had become once he had forgotten just that. 'That's why I stick to business as much as possible. Whenever I venture into emotional territory, it turns into a disaster.'

He hadn't meant to sound bitter, but Imogen shot him a quick glance of concern.

'I'm sorry,' she said. 'I didn't mean to remind you of Julia. I was thinking of myself.'

'Oh?' Tom was glad to turn the conversation away from his inadequacies on the emotional front.

'I always knew what I wanted too, but much good it did me.'

'What *did* you want?'

Imogen sighed and clasped her arms around her knees. 'I wanted my boyfriend to love me again, that was all. I even had a strategy, as you call it. I was going to give him time, and then he'd realise that he missed me.'

'And he didn't?'

'No,' she said. 'He married someone else.'

Tom studied her profile. She had pushed her wet hair behind her ears and she was staring out to the horizon, lost in memories.

'There's no point in wanting something that depends on someone else,' he said after a moment. 'You can only succeed if you want things that you can achieve by yourself.'

Something he should have remembered before he'd asked Julia to marry him.

'But what if what you want is not to be by yourself?' asked Imogen, turning her head to look at him, and Tom found himself trapped by the directness of her gaze.

Had her eyes always been that blue? he wondered, almost startled by the depth of colour. Surely he would have noticed them before if they had?

It must be just the sea and the sky making them look so blue, he decided. A trick of the light.

'Then you probably won't succeed,' he said.

'Success isn't everything,' she pointed out.

'It is to me.'

Imogen didn't answer directly. To Tom's secret relief, she looked away once more to where the ocean surged and sighed beyond the reef.

'I remember in my last year at school, an older girl came to give us a talk,' she said eventually. 'I thought it was going to be really boring. She was a high-flying lawyer, very glamorous, and she seemed to have everything. We were all expecting her to tell us how we had to work hard to succeed, but she said something completely different.

'I've never forgotten,' Imogen remembered. 'She told us that the most important lesson we had to learn was how to fail. She said that we all fail at some time in our lives, and that what counted was not how much money we earned or how much status we had, but how we responded to failure. It was a test of character, she said. Did we let ourselves be beaten, or did we pick ourselves up and start again?'

Tom frowned. He had never let himself consider failure at all. 'And you bought this?'

'Well, it was very uplifting at the time,' said Imogen, almost apologetically. 'Especially for those of us who were more used to failing than succeeding. But I've got plenty of experience of failure now. I have to admit it would be nice to try success some time for a change!'

Tom was still brooding over the idea of failure. 'If you set yourself clear goals, there's no reason not to succeed,' he said.

'That depends on your goals, doesn't it? You can't make someone else love you,' she said a little sadly. 'You can't control how other people will react. If you're going to have any kind of relationship at all, you have to accept that you're not always going to succeed. There's no other option.'

'Unless you give up on relationships altogether.'

'But that's a failure too, isn't it?' said Imogen.

Her words seemed to reverberate over the shimmering lagoon. *Failure…failure…failure…*

Tom stirred uneasily. He wasn't used to failure. He didn't like it. He didn't know what to do with it.

But he had to face it. His relationship with Julia had been a failure. He knew it. Imogen knew it. Everyone knew it.

Humiliation burned in the pit of his stomach and he glared out at the horizon, his shoulders tense and hunched.

'So what did you learn from not getting your boyfriend back?'

Imogen didn't appear to notice the harshness in his voice. 'I learned that I don't want to compromise,' she said. 'I've accepted that Andrew doesn't love me any more. My friends have been telling me that I should get out there again and meet someone else, so I've been trying. I go out on dates, and I really do try to be positive, but I haven't met anyone who could even begin to make me feel the way I felt about Andrew. Every date feels like yet another failure now, so I've decided to stop looking.'

'You're giving up on men?'

'No. I'm giving up thinking that I might settle for something less than perfect.'

There was another long silence, broken only by the rippling of the lagoon and the faint sough of the wind in the coconut palms and, from somewhere in the island, the harsh screech of a bird.

Tom was thinking about what Imogen had said. Julia had tried to settle, he realised. He had only ever been second-best for her. The thought was bitter. Julia had made the right decision in the end, but it had left him feeling a failure.

That was how Imogen said she felt after every disastrous date. Funny, he had never thought of her as having a life of her own before. She had just been a PA and now...

Tom glanced at her. Her eyes were on the horizon, her expression dreamy or perhaps just wistful. She wasn't classically beautiful, like Julia, but there was something appealing about her. Tom couldn't put his finger on it. It might be that lovely lush skin, or the generous curve to her mouth, or perhaps the blueness and brightness of her eyes.

Now...now she was more than just a PA. Tom didn't know exactly what she was, but she was more than that.

Almost as if she could hear him thinking, Imogen turned her head to find him watching her and, as her clear, lovely blue eyes looked into his, Tom found himself struggling to breathe normally.

This was ridiculous, he told himself crossly. It was only Imogen.

'You're getting burnt.' He said the first thing that came into his mind, and touched a finger to her shoulder where her skin was pink. 'Sorry,' he said as she flinched.

Imogen swallowed. 'It's just a bit sore,' she said, not wanting to admit how aware she was of his touch. 'You're right, I'd better go into the shade for a while.'

Clambering inelegantly to her feet, she brushed the sand from her legs and pretended not to notice as Tom straightened beside her. Suddenly, he seemed very close, his chest broad, his shoulders powerfully muscled, his hips lean in the plain swimming shorts he wore, and her mouth dried.

'I might have a snooze,' she said, stepping back as if it would help her suck more oxygen into her lungs. 'It's all catching up with me now.'

'Why don't you go to bed for a couple of hours?'

Imogen managed to shake her head. She would never be able to relax in that bed, imagining what it would be like if things were different, if she could stretch out and wait for Tom to join her underneath that fine sheet, if he were to pull off those shorts and let her run her hands over that smooth, muscled body...

With some difficulty, she wrenched her mind away. 'I like it down here,' she said.

'Up to you.' Tom shrugged, plainly unbothered. 'I'll see you later, in that case.'

Imogen's body was buzzing with a mixture of exhaustion and a prickly awareness, so she didn't really expect to sleep when she lay on the lounger in the deep shade, but tiredness rolled over her like a wave the moment she closed her eyes, and when she opened them again it was to discover that it was nearly two hours later.

Groggily, she got to her feet, still squinting at her watch in case she had made a mistake, but the lengthening shadows told their own story. It looked as if she had had that snooze after all.

Vaguely aware of a lingering embarrassment, without really remembering why, Imogen made her way back to the house. The sun was low on the horizon and the sea lay flat and still while in the undergrowth unseen insects were warming up for a rasping, sawing, shrilling concert to mark the end of the day.

Tom had moved his laptop to the dining table and she could see him studying the screen intently. How many times had she seen him wear exactly that focused expression? Imogen wondered. The line between his brows, the pugnacious set of his jaw, the stern line of his mouth...they were all completely familiar to her after working with him for the last few months.

So why did the sight of him feel like a fist colliding with her stomach, driving the air out of her lungs and leaving her jolted and jarred with the sudden shock of it?

It must be the jet lag catching up on her, Imogen decided, and drew a steadying breath as she put a foot on the veranda steps.

Tom looked up when she appeared in the doorway.

'That was a long snooze.'

'I didn't mean to sleep that long.' Imogen was glad to see he had put on a shirt and shorts. He looked cool and comfortable while she felt hot and drowsy and crumpled after her sleep. At least discomfort helped her shake aside that odd feeling of shocking familiarity.

'I think I'll have a shower,' she said. 'I'm still feeling a bit dopey.'

'You look it.'

His voice was cool, his glance faintly disapproving, and Imogen let out a breath she hadn't realised she'd been holding. It was a relief to realise that he was once more Tom, her irascible boss, a man impatient of weakness or frivolity.

So they had chatted in the shallows for a bit? What else were they supposed to do when they were all alone on a tropical island? Tom might have told her more about himself than she had ever known before, but he had just been making conversation and that wasn't the same as being intimate, no matter what it had felt like.

She certainly wasn't going to start being silly just because she had seen what a good body lurked beneath those suits he always wore. It had just been tiredness making her uncomfortably aware of him as a man rather than a boss, Imogen told herself. She would just have a cool shower and change into something sensible, and they would be back to their normal professional relationship in no time.

The light was fading rapidly as she made her way out to the bathroom. It was open to the sky and the subdued lights made the curving walls and clever tiling look wonderfully romantic. The lack of a door made Imogen a little uncomfortable, but Tom knew where she was, she reasoned. He was hardly likely to come barging in on her and, with no one else on the island, she could hardly ask for more privacy.

She turned her attention to the shower, peering at the controls in the dim light. There were no screens, no panels, just an enormous shower head that stuck out over the tiled floor that sloped slightly to drain. It would be like standing under a waterfall.

Imogen's skin was hot and gritty, and her hair was full of sand. It was going to be wonderful, she told herself as she turned the controls and pulled off her bikini.

With a sigh of relief, she stepped under the cascade of water, only to feel something scuttle horribly underfoot. Something she hadn't seen in the stupid lighting, which was suddenly not romantic at all, but downright dangerous.

Something that had a friend to scrabble over her foot as she jerked it away.

Imogen couldn't help herself. She screamed and leapt out of the water, bolting to the other side of the bathroom without even stopping to grab a towel.

The next moment Tom came skidding round the curving bathroom wall. 'What's the ma—oh!'

He stopped dead at the realisation that Imogen was stark naked.

Imogen's heart was galloping with a mixture of fright and the sheer shock of seeing Tom charge into the room, but for a long, excruciating moment she could only stare back at him from behind the Jacuzzi.

He wondered if she had any idea how she looked, with her hair damp and her skin wet and her eyes wide and dark with fright. Her hand was pressed to her throat where a pulse jumped wildly, and her breasts were rising and falling rapidly as she struggled for breath.

That bikini hadn't left much to the imagination, but Tom was still unprepared for the glorious lushness of her body, and even though his brain was yelling at him to keep his eyes firmly on her face while he backed out, it didn't stand a chance against the pull of instinct which dropped his gaze to skim over those lovely curves.

Imogen saw his eyes drop and, far too late, humiliation jerked her out of her paralysis.

'God, I'm sorry,' Tom managed as she snatched at a towel.

Of course it was far too small, and she had to hold it ridiculously in front of her while she pulled at one that looked big enough to wrap round her, her cheeks burning with embarrassment.

'I heard you scream,' he tried to explain, backing out. 'I thought something was wrong.'

'I trod on something when I got in the shower.' Imogen shuddered at the memory. 'You can't see a thing in this stupid light,' she complained, forgetting how she had gasped at how pretty the room looked at first. 'It was revolting.'

'What was it?' Tom had his voice under better control. At least she was covered by the towel now, not that it made that much difference. The image of her body was still vivid after he had stared like a grubby schoolboy. He shifted his shoulders uncomfortably, mortified by the memory.

'I don't know,' said Imogen. 'I didn't stop to inspect it. It felt disgusting, whatever it was.'

Tom went over to turn the shower off. It gave him a good excuse to look away from Imogen, if nothing else. 'Probably a cockroach,' he said. 'Yes, there he is.' He pointed at the corner, where something dark and shiny lurked, antennae waving malevolently.

Imogen peered nervously round Tom's shoulder. 'Ugh! It's horrible!'

'It probably doesn't think too much of you either after you trod on it.' Tom was finding it hard to concentrate with her so close to him. 'Do you want me to get rid of it for you?'

'Would you?' said Imogen gratefully. She had been wondering how to ask him to do just that without sounding pathetic.

Tom stepped towards the cockroach but it was too quick for him. It dashed for the other wall, and its sudden scuttle made Imogen squeak and jump back. The movement loosened the wretched towel, which promptly started to unwind.

'Oh—!' Imogen only just managed to bite back a curse as she grabbed the towel in the nick of time.

Fortunately Tom didn't notice. He was too busy following

the cockroach around the bathroom, but the faster he stamped, the quicker the insect moved and the more he missed. He muttered furiously under his breath as his shoes rang uselessly on the tiled floor. No cockroach was going to get the better of Tom Maddison!

He looked so ridiculous, stamping around the shower in frustration, and the situation was so bizarre, that Imogen's sense of humour began to get the better of her. It might have been tiredness, or an edge of hysteria, but she could feel laughter bubbling up inside her.

'Gosh,' she said, 'I didn't know you could do flamenco.'

Distracted, Tom stopped in mid-stamp. 'What?'

'A ruthless businessman *and* a hot dancer.' Imogen's expression was innocent as she nodded at his feet. 'You've got to admit, it's quite a combination!'

For a moment Tom could only stare at her. The light was dim but it was enough to see the mischief glimmering in her eyes. A smile was tugging at the corners of her mouth, and all at once he realised how comical he must look, chasing an insect around the shower, watched by his PA, who was utterly naked beneath that skimpy towel.

Did anyone enjoy looking stupid? Tom certainly never had before but, in spite of his exasperation, he felt an answering smile twitch his lips. What an absurd situation to find himself in, but perhaps it was a fitting ending for what should have been his wedding day. It might have started in tragedy, but it was ending in farce.

Without thinking, he lifted his arms, snapped his fingers and stamped his heel dramatically. *'Olé!'* he cried, striking a pose.

It was Imogen's turn to stare, startled by his uncharacteristic lapse into absurdity, and then they both started to laugh at the same time.

They laughed and they laughed, until they were both almost doubled up. It wasn't that funny, but at some level both were aware that their laughter came as much from the release from some unspoken tension as from the humour of the situation.

'Oh dear,' gasped Imogen at last, mopping her eyes with the edge of the towel. 'I think I needed that!'

'And, after all of that, the cockroach has legged it,' Tom realised, looking around the room, as Imogen started to giggle again.

He was feeling a bit odd. He couldn't remember the last time he had laughed like that—laughed *uncontrollably*. Usually, the whole notion of being out of control made him uncomfortable, but now, when he looked at Imogen, it wasn't the scariness of losing control he was thinking about.

It was Imogen's face, still alight with laughter.

It was Imogen's body, beneath the towel that kept slipping dangerously.

He should go before she lost grip of it completely, Tom decided.

'You can have that shower now,' he told her, and then cocked an eyebrow at her hesitation. 'Unless you'd prefer to use the one inside?'

'I would, of course, but then you would think that I'm really pathetic.'

'What, because you're afraid of a little cockroach? Never!'

Imogen made a face at him. 'See, I knew you'd say that! If I went to the other bathroom, I'd never be able to hold up my head again.'

'I won't say another word,' promised Tom, holding up his hands.

'No, no, I'm determined to shower here now. I'm a big,

brave girl now, especially as I know that all it takes to see off a cockroach is a bit of bad dancing!'

He smiled as he turned to leave. 'I'll leave you to it then. Scream if you need me.'

She wouldn't be screaming again, but she needed him, all right. She needed him to go back to being her brusque, irritable boss, thought Imogen, dropping the towel and stretching out her hand to test the temperature of the water. She needed him to stop smiling like that. She needed him to put his suit back on and make her forget that he had that great body.

Imogen had looked forward to the shower, but as she stood under the cascade of warm water she found herself thinking, not about how good it felt to wash the sun and the salt out of her hair but about Tom, and how he had laughed.

Who would have thought that the coolly calculating Tom Maddison would play the fool like that? Imogen smiled as she remembered him striking that flamenco dancer's pose and shouting *olé*! He might have been a different man entirely from the one who barked instructions down the phone or wished her a curt good morning as he strode through her office in London.

This Tom had an unexpectedly wide smile with good teeth, and when he had thrown back his head and laughed, his eyes had creased and the harsh lines of his face had been transformed by amusement. Imogen felt something disturbing start to uncoil inside her at the mere memory, and she shivered uneasily.

The truth was that she was more afraid of that feeling than of the cockroach coming back.

And there was no point going there, she reminded herself sternly. This should have been Tom's wedding day, remember? It should have been Julia standing here, feeling her skin tingle with that heady mixture of sea water and slightly too much sun.

Imogen was fairly sure that Julia wouldn't have screamed at the sight of a cockroach. Or, if she had, she wouldn't have stood there stark naked while those glacial grey eyes swept over her.

But then, of course, Julia would be used to Tom looking at her, Imogen reflected glumly as she dressed. In fact, Julia wouldn't have been showering alone, would she? Tom would have been in there with her, and they would have been too busy making love under that glorious cascade of water to notice a whole parade of cockroaches.

Imogen's cheeks burned at the thought. How awful for Tom to see her instead of Julia at every turn, to have come face to face with his naked PA, whose body could most kindly be described as curvaceous, instead of Julia's slender, perfect beauty. It must have been a horrible shock for him.

Still, she was glad that they had been able to laugh together like that. It felt as if everything had changed now. At least the awkwardness of finding themselves alone together had passed. Of course, there could be few things more embarrassing than your boss catching you stark naked, but there was no point in being shy after that, Imogen decided philosophically. The change in the atmosphere was worth the humiliation.

CHAPTER FIVE

IMOGEN felt quite positive as she dressed, in spite of knowing that her pale aqua sundress was a far cry from the perfect sexy, stylish outfit that Julia would inevitably have had to slip into after her shower. But it would just have to do. OK, so it looked cheap and a little crumpled in these luxurious surroundings, but it might not be a bad thing to have a reminder that she could loll all she wanted in the lagoon but she would always be out of place in these fabulous surroundings.

It wouldn't do to start thinking that the fact that she was here with Tom was anything other than a face-saving measure. He was a successful businessman; she was a temp. He took this kind of designer luxury for granted; her style was cheap, cheery and chain-store. It would be very foolish of her to forget that.

On the other hand, since she was here, she might as well make the best of it. Now they had broken the tension with laughter, perhaps they could at least be friends for the next three weeks. She was never going to replace the svelte, sophisticated Julia, but she could be a friend, even if it was only a temporary one.

Temporary secretary, temporary friend... When would she ever settle to anything permanent? Imogen wondered wistfully.

Not until she was sure that what she had was perfect, she reminded herself firmly.

In the meantime, she was in the middle of the Indian Ocean, on an idyllic island with a man who needed a friend right now. That would be enough, she told herself.

An image of Tom in his swimming shorts flickered distractingly in her brain, but Imogen forced her mind away from thoughts of that lean, tautly muscled body.

Away from the image of his hands.

Of his mouth.

From the memory of how he had looked when he was laughing.

Friends would be enough for now.

Slipping her feet into her favourite sequinned flip-flops, Imogen went out to find Tom.

He was waiting for her on the veranda, his feet up on the railing and a beer in his hand, looking more relaxed than she had ever seen him.

'Better?' he asked as he saw her.

'Much, thank you.'

Tom swung his legs down. 'Would you like a drink?'

He made her a gin and tonic. It was deliciously cold and refreshing, and Imogen sipped it appreciatively as she leant against the railing.

It looked as if she had missed a glorious sunset while she was in the shower. She could see through the coconut palms to where the lagoon gleamed dark and still, and beyond to a vivid streak of crimson along the horizon. Unseen insects were working themselves up into a frenzy of creaking and whirring and sawing and rasping in the tangled foliage, and the air was hot and heavy with the intense scents of the tropical night.

Suddenly something swooped in front of her, and she straightened in surprise. 'Was that a bird?'

'A bat, I think.'

Imogen wrinkled her nose. 'First cockroaches, now bats… Somehow this isn't how I imagined paradise!' she said dryly as she watched the creatures, darting and diving through the hot dark air.

'Don't tell me you're afraid of bats too?'

'Of course not,' she said, shooting him a look. 'I'm not afraid of cockroaches either,' she said, not entirely truthfully. 'I know I screamed, but it was just a shock seeing it there. I wasn't expecting it,' she finished lamely.

Tom looked down at his beer and reflected that he knew how she had felt. He hadn't been expecting to see her without any clothes on either, and that had been just as much of a shock, if in a different way.

'About earlier,' he said abruptly. 'I'm sorry if I embarrassed you, bursting in like that.'

'That's OK. I'm glad you were there. I would never have been able to scare that cockroach away by myself.' Her smile glimmered. 'My flamenco dancing isn't up to much!'

The corner of Tom's mouth lifted at the reminder of what had set them laughing. He was glad Imogen had mentioned it. When she had appeared, looking lush and glowing after her shower, her hair falling damply to her shoulders, he had wondered if the idea that had come to him while she was showering might be asking for trouble, but now the constraint had eased he decided to put it to her after all.

'I've been thinking,' he began.

'Oh?'

He gestured around him. 'This place…it's much more intimate than I was expecting.'

'It's meant for honeymooners,' Imogen pointed out. 'It would be surprising if it *wasn't* intimate.'

'I know,' said Tom with just a touch of his old irritability. 'I wasn't thinking clearly.'

'That's understandable,' she said, instantly feeling guilty. 'None of this can be easy for you.'

'The thing is…' Tom frowned, wondering how best to put it. 'We've got three weeks here,' he began again. 'The chances are that we're going to find ourselves in more embarrassing situations when there's just the two of us.

'I thought with it being a whole island we'd have more space,' he tried to explain himself. It had all seemed so obvious when he was working it out in his mind, but it felt more difficult with Imogen's eyes on his face. He was no good at this kind of stuff. If he wasn't careful, he'd be talking about his feelings.

'As it is, we're going to be effectively living together for the next three weeks,' he ploughed on. 'That's going to be awkward unless we agree to be…I don't know…*normal*.'

'That's just what I was thinking,' said Imogen eagerly.

'I'm just not quite sure what normal is,' confessed Tom.

'Let's be friends. Just temporary ones, of course,' she added quickly in case he thought she was trying to take advantage of Julia's departure.

'Temporary?'

'Well, it would be difficult to go back to working together if we were friends, wouldn't it?'

'Perhaps,' he acknowledged. There was no use pretending it wouldn't be awkward, anyway.

'But, in any case, I'm leaving soon,' Imogen went on, 'so I won't be around much longer.'

'Leaving?' Tom asked, startled. 'Why?'

'I'm going to travel,' she said. 'I've never been outside

Europe before. I've always wanted to go to India, so I'm going to start there and make my way down through South-East Asia to Australia, and I hope that on the way I'll decide what it is I really want to do with my life.'

Now that she had finally given up dreaming of Andrew.

Tom was frowning. 'I didn't know about this.'

'That's why I'm temping,' said Imogen. 'Didn't you know? I'm only filling in until you appoint a properly qualified executive PA.'

He *had* known that, of course. He just hadn't wanted to think about it. He had been too busy steering Collocom away from the rocks to take the time to choose the right person. Besides, Imogen might not be your classically cool and competent secretary, but she had been managing well enough. There had been no reason to think about replacing her.

'When's all this going to happen?' asked Tom, conscious of an uneasy feeling in the pit of his stomach. That wasn't *dismay*, was it?

'As soon as you appoint a permanent PA. I've been saving for nearly a year now, so I'm ready to book my ticket whenever you find the right person. I assumed you were putting it off until after the wedding, but if you interview in April and we have a handover in May, I could be packing my bags in June.'

'June?' No mistaking the dismay now! 'That's only three months away!'

Imogen nodded. 'I know, but if it's awkward when we get back, well, at least it won't be for long.'

Tom looked out into the night and tried to imagine the office without Imogen. Oh, he'd known she would go one day, but he hadn't thought it would be so soon. She was as much part of his life as Julia had been, if not more so. He saw Imogen almost every day, after all. It would be strange without her now.

But it wouldn't be the first time he had had to get used to a new PA, Tom reminded himself, alarmed by the bleak drift of his thoughts. He would be fine.

'That might work out quite well then,' he said, conscious that he sounded as if he were trying to convince himself. 'You're right, it might be difficult to go back to our old boss/PA relationship after being here, but if you're leaving soon, that won't matter.'

'Exactly,' said Imogen, keeping her smile bright.

What had she expected? That Tom would fall to his knees and beg her not to leave him?

No, it would be better this way. There was bound to be speculation at the office when they went back. The sooner she left and got on with her new life, the better, but for now, being friends, even temporary ones, seemed like the best way to get through the next three weeks.

'So are we agreed?' she said. 'As long as we're here, we're not boss and PA any more, but just friends?'

There was only the tiniest moment of hesitation, then Tom nodded. 'Agreed.'

'Great,' said Imogen. 'Now that's settled, let's go and see what's for supper. I'm starving!'

She chatted easily as she set out the delicacies that had been left in the fridge, and Tom found himself almost mesmerised by the readiness with which she was prepared to treat him as a friend. It made him realise how little he had known about her when she was just his PA. He had had no idea that she could be that sharp or that funny, and he watched her as if he had never seen her before as she told him about her friends, about the flat she shared with her friend and the life she led in London, so different from his own.

Suddenly Imogen broke off with a grimace as she

listened to her own words. 'This must all sound so dull to you!' she said.

'Actually, it doesn't,' said Tom, almost to his own surprise. They had found a bottle of perfectly chilled wine in the fridge, and he leant across the table to top up her glass.

Imogen didn't believe him, of course. What had she been thinking of, rabbiting on about wine bars and chaotic supper parties and the snap quizzes she and Amanda held to test their embarrassingly wide knowledge of TV soaps? She cringed at the memory.

'But your life is so much more glamorous!'

She couldn't imagine Tom sprawled in front of the television, for instance. He and Julia would have gone out to smart restaurants or grand parties. They would have been to the opera or polo matches or the kind of clubs she and Amanda only ever read about in magazines.

'Is it?' said Tom. 'My apartment may be bigger than yours, and I may live in a more exclusive part of town, but I don't do much when I'm there. I just work.'

'What about when you were with Julia?'

He shrugged. 'We'd eat out a lot, and yes, there would quite often be some kind of reception, but those events aren't nearly as much fun as they're cracked up to be.'

What *had* he and Julia done together? Tom tried to remember. Julia was into art, but galleries and openings bored him rigid. He had often used work as an excuse not to go with her. Perhaps Patrick had gone instead?

It was all obvious in hindsight, of course, but shouldn't he have wondered how much he and Julia had in common before he'd asked her to marry him? He had thought that a similarly cool and careful approach to life would be enough. How wrong could you be?

He looked across the table at Imogen, whose own approach to life could by no stretch of the imagination be described as cool and careful, certainly not from what she'd been telling him.

'I don't think you'd enjoy my life that much,' he told her. 'It sounds as if you like the one you've got. You've got lots of friends, you seem to have a good time. You've got a job. Why give that up and leave your life behind to travel?'

'Because I need to get away,' said Imogen, her expression uncharacteristically serious.

Resting her arms on the table, she turned the glass pensively between her fingers. 'I spent five years holding on to an impossible dream,' she went on after a moment. 'Five years wanting something I couldn't have. I've finally accepted that it's not going to happen, but I think I need a complete break to do something completely different before I can move on properly.'

'Five years is a long time to want something—or was it some*one*?'

'Someone.' Imogen nodded.

Tom thought about what she had told him on the beach and searched his memory for a name. 'Andrew?'

'Andrew,' she confirmed. 'We were students together,' she told Tom. 'I fell in love with him the moment I laid eyes on him in Freshers' Week and we were inseparable for three years.

'I was so happy all that time,' she remembered, her smile tinged with sadness. 'It never occurred to me that it would end. I just assumed that, once we graduated, we'd get married and spend the rest of our lives together.'

'So what happened?' asked Tom.

'Oh, nothing dramatic. Andrew just…grew out of me.' Imogen managed a smile, but it was a painful one. 'After all, we were very young when we met, just eighteen, and only

JESSICA HART   85

twenty-one when we graduated. People kept asking me what I wanted to do, meaning that I should be thinking about a career, but all I wanted to do was be with Andrew. He was more ambitious. He wanted to be a journalist, and that's what he did. He's doing well, too. He's just been made education correspondent on one of the national papers.'

'And you didn't blend with his décor any more, was that it?'

'No, not really.' It was second nature for Imogen to defend Andrew now. 'Andrew realised that we wanted different things out of life. I was always happy to live in the moment, but he's a planner and thinks about the future in a way I never did. I think he was feeling stifled too, although he didn't put it like that.'

'How *did* he put it?'

'He said he thought we both needed a bit of space. We'd been living together for three years, after all, and neither of us had ever really spent any time on our own. He thought we should have a chance to meet other people before we settled down, and he was right. Twenty-one is much too young to tie yourself down for life—although I didn't think so at the time, of course,' she added with a wry smile.

Tom was trying to imagine Imogen as a student, and realised he could do it quite easily. She would have been exactly as she was now, he thought.

'How did you react?'

'With disbelief at first. Andrew wasn't just my lover, he was my best friend. I couldn't imagine life without him, and it had never occurred to me that he wouldn't feel the same. Then I decided that he was right,' said Imogen. 'It would be best if we had some time apart. So we both went to London, and he got himself a flat and I moved in with Amanda for a while as I was absolutely sure he'd come back. I did a secretarial course, got myself a job and waited for Andrew to miss me.'

'But he didn't?'

'No, he didn't.' Imogen sighed, remembering that time—the slow, sickening realisation that Andrew didn't love her any more. 'I know he's very fond of me, and we've stayed friends, but he didn't need me the way I needed him. I knew in my heart that it was over, but I kept hoping and hoping...'

Her mouth turned down at the memory of her own foolishness. 'And then he met Sara, and it turned out that he needed *her* the way I needed *him*. They got married a couple of years ago, and they're expecting their first baby in the summer.'

Even after all this time it was an effort to keep her voice level.

Tom could see the strain around her eyes and he shifted uncomfortably. He hoped that she wasn't going to cry.

But Imogen was already straightening her shoulders and smiling.

'Do you know the worst thing?' she confided. 'It's that Sara's really *nice*. She makes Andrew happy, and I can see they're perfect for each other. When they got engaged, I used to pray that Andrew would wake up and realise that I was the one he really loved after all, a bit like Julia did with Patrick. I feel awful now to realise I never gave a thought to what that would have been like for Sara.'

Tom shrugged. 'I guess she would have got over it, the way you did. The way I'm going to have to get over it.'

'I hope it doesn't take you as long as it did me,' said Imogen ruefully. 'I've wasted years, convinced that my life was always going to be empty without Andrew. I've tried to meet someone else, but I always end up comparing any man I go out with to him. It took me until last year to really accept that he loves Sara and not me. Even if he stopped loving her for some reason, he still wouldn't love me.

'It's never going to be the way it was before,' she said.

'Andrew moved on a long time ago, and now I need to do that too. I haven't changed since I was a student. It's like I'm stuck in a time warp, where everyone else has moved on and grown up and I've just been drifting, hoping something will change. And, of course, I've realised that the only way something's going to change is if I make it change. If I change myself.'

They had lit the candles on the table, and in the flickering light Tom could see the generous curve of her mouth and the unconsciously upward tilt of her chin. He found himself thinking that it would be a pity if she changed too much.

Imogen sighed a little. 'Anyway, you know what it's like,' she told him. 'I never got as far as planning a wedding, but I understand how it feels when you love someone who decides they don't love you.'

Swirling the dregs of wine in his glass, Tom thought about what she had told him. Imogen always seemed so bright and cheery. He had never guessed that there was a sadness behind her smile.

'I don't feel like that about Julia,' he said abruptly. 'Not the way you felt about Andrew.'

'But you were going to marry her,' said Imogen. 'You must have loved her. You must still love her.'

'Must I?'

Tom's eyes were fixed on the swirling wine, but he was re-membering Julia. 'I desired her, sure, but not with the kind of reckless passion that makes other people lose their heads and, as much as that, I admired her. I still do, I guess. I like her quick wits and cool competence, and I respect everything she's achieved. She worked hard and made a real success of her life. But love her?'

Lifting his eyes to Imogen's face, he shook his head. 'No,' he answered his own question. 'No, I didn't.'

She looked appalled, as if he had kicked away one of the cornerstones of her world, and Tom felt a twinge of remorse, which was ridiculous. 'What?' he said harshly. 'You don't really believe that you have to be in love to get married, do you?'

'But...did Julia know you felt like that?'

'Of course she did. We talked about it when we got engaged, and she said that she felt the same. That's why I was so thrown when she made such a fuss about the wedding.'

Imogen was frowning in bafflement. 'But why get married unless you did love each other? It seems pointless.'

'You don't think it's possible to build a solid marriage based on mutual respect and admiration, and a healthy physical attraction?'

'Maybe, but why would you want to?' she countered. 'I'll only get married if I can find someone who makes me feel the way Andrew did. I want to marry someone I need and who needs me, someone who doesn't think of marriage as a practical arrangement but about being with the one person who fills up all the bits that are missing, who believes that neither of us are complete somehow unless we're together.'

Tom looked uncomprehending, and she tried to explain. 'What's the point of getting married unless you've found the person who makes your heart beat faster, who makes the sun seem brighter, who makes every moment sweeter just by existing? I want to go home at night and be with the one person who can make the rest of the world go away,' she said, 'the one person who, no matter how bad things are, can make it all right just by being there.'

'But that's exactly what I *don't* want,' said Tom, unimpressed. 'I don't want to need anyone else.'

'You don't want to fall in love?'

'No, I don't.' Tom was very definite. 'I've never felt what you felt for Andrew, and I'm glad. You've wasted five years of your life on him, Imogen. Five years! Think of all the things you could have been doing in those five years instead of yearning for the impossible. And knowing what it's like to lose someone you've loved, you're still prepared to risk all that again!'

He shook his head. 'I'd rather have the kind of relationship I had with Julia,' he said. 'True, it ended in humiliation for me, and I can't say I'm happy about it, but my pride is hurt more than my heart. It seems to me that when you fall in love, you lose your senses,' he said. 'You stop thinking clearly. You lose control.'

And that was something Tom Maddison never did.

'Yes, it can make you feel powerless,' Imogen had to admit, remembering how little she had been able to do to make Andrew change his mind. 'You can't make someone love you, that's for sure. But it can also make you feel as if you can do *anything*, and that's always going to be worth the risk.'

'It's not one I'll be taking,' said Tom flatly.

Imogen studied him, mystified. He was a powerful man, much stronger than anyone else she had ever met.

And yet he was afraid of love.

Or was he just afraid of admitting how much he had felt for Julia?

'Well, I'm glad you're OK,' she said at last. 'I thought you must be feeling desperate.'

'I'm fine,' said Tom. 'My ego is massively bruised, but I've got three weeks to recover. I don't think I'll need to take to my bed.'

'Talking of beds…' Imogen hesitated. 'I was thinking I should sleep on one of the couches, and give you the bed.'

'Absolutely not. You're to have the bed.'

'But you're much taller than me,' she protested. 'You'd be

much more comfortable in the bed. There are plenty of places I can sleep.'

'I'm not going to be comfortable, knowing that you're stuck on one of those couches, am I?'

'The same goes for me,' she pointed out.

'In that case, the only answer is for us to share the bed.' Tom raised a brow. 'Are you ready to be *that* good friends?'

No, she wasn't, but it was alarming how ready she was to imagine what it would be like, disturbing how easily she could picture sleeping in the big, beautiful bed with Tom beside her. There would be plenty of room for both of them, but nothing to stop her rolling over in the night and finding herself lying against his lean, hard body.

Nothing to stop her snuggling into his back and sliding an arm over him.

And if she did that, what would Tom do? Would he turn over to face her? Would he pull her closer and explore the curves and contours of her body with those strong, sure hands? Would his lips nuzzle her throat before drifting downwards?

Imogen gulped and jammed the brakes on an imagination that was spinning dangerously out of control.

'I think that really *would* be uncomfortable,' she said with a nervous smile.

'Quite.' Tom's voice was very dry and, when the cool grey eyes looked into hers, Imogen was suddenly convinced that he could see right into her mind.

Clumsily, she pushed back her chair, just in case he really had developed an uncanny ability to read her thoughts.

'Well, I think I'll go to bed.' Was that really her voice? Since when had she taken to squeaking?

'It's been a long day,' Tom agreed, getting to his feet as well.

Imogen stood there, not knowing what to do with her hands

time to start. He didn't want to spend the next three weeks not thinking about her skin, about the curve of her breasts, the silky tumble of her hair, the way her blue eyes reflected the sunshine…

The cushion took another pummelling.

Friends, that was all she had suggested. A friend wouldn't be thinking about that glorious body. A friend wouldn't be fantasising about unzipping that dress, letting it fall in a pool to the floor so that he could explore every inch of that warm, creamy skin.

A friend would remember that she was still more than half in love with her college sweetheart. He would know that she had been hurt and that the last thing she needed was her boss lusting after her body.

No, friends were just…friendly. Friendly was all he could be.

Imogen woke slowly. For a long while she just lay there without thinking, simply savouring the comfort of the bed and the delicious awareness of sunlight striping across her eyelids.

When she opened her eyes at last, the first thing she saw was a huge wooden ceiling fan, turning lazily in the turgid air. At the window, wooden blinds let in bright slivers of light and, as her ears became attuned, she could hear a bird squawking somewhere and the indistinct murmur of the ocean.

In spite of the fan, it was already hot and Imogen stretched luxuriously, filled with a sense of well-being. It wasn't every day you woke up in paradise.

What was she doing in paradise?

Imogen sat bolt upright as she remembered, and she grabbed her watch from the bedside table. It was almost ten o'clock.

Throwing back the sheet, she wrapped a sarong around her and padded into the living area.

It was empty, except for a laptop open on the dining room

table, a cursor winking reprovingly at her, but the smell of coffee drew her to the kitchen tucked away behind a room divider, where she found Tom shaking freshly ground beans into a cafetière.

'Good morning,' she said, suddenly shy.

'Morning,' said Tom.

Imogen clearly thought nothing of hugging her friends goodnight, and he was a little nervous in case she greeted them the same way in the morning, so it was a relief to discover that she limited herself to a smile. He had been braced to resist another hug, but he didn't fancy his chances of keeping his hands to himself, especially not when her blue eyes were clouded with sleep, her hair was tousled and she was wrapped only in a strip of cloth that would unwind at the merest brush of his hands.

Tom concentrated fiercely on the coffee. It was all very well resolving to be friendly, but much harder to remember when she stood there, smiling, looking dishevelled and unaccountably desirable.

Friends shouldn't smile like that, he thought crossly. PAs definitely shouldn't. If Imogen hadn't been both, it was the kind of smile that would make him want to take her straight back to bed.

Luckily she *was* his PA, so Tom turned firmly away to pour boiling water into the cafetière.

CHAPTER SIX

'How did you sleep?'

Extraordinarily, his voice sounded almost normal. It would be hard to guess that his throat was tight and his heart was slamming against his ribs.

'Like a log, thank you,' said Imogen. 'What about you? Was the sofa very uncomfortable?'

'It was fine,' said Tom, who had spent a restless night feeling edgy and hot and confused.

'Good. I was feeling guilty about having that comfortable bed.'

She told herself that was what had kept her awake long after Tom had switched off the last light. He had lain out of sight around the corner, but she had still been desperately aware of him.

It was all very well to talk about being normal, but normal would have been to be lying in this bed together, holding each other, touching each other.

Making love.

But they had decided to be friends instead. Friends was much better than being normal.

Wasn't it?

Of course it was.

In the kitchen, there was an awkward pause. 'Want some coffee?' said Tom after a moment.

'Thanks.'

Fastening her sarong more firmly around her, Imogen perched on a stool at the breakfast bar. 'How long have you been up?'

'A couple of hours. I slept late this morning. I'm usually awake about five.'

'That'll be why you're always at the office before me,' said Imogen, who was a night owl and had to be dragged kicking and screaming out of sleep by a piercing alarm every morning in order to get to work on time.

But as soon as the words were out, she wished that she hadn't mentioned the office. It was too bizarre to be sitting here in her sarong, watching Tom make coffee, and remembering that he was her boss and she was just his PA.

Then again, perhaps she *should* remember that more often. Last night, it had been all too easy to forget.

'You've been working,' she said, nodding at the laptop in the other room.

'I thought I might as well see what was going on.' There was a faintly defensive edge to Tom's voice. 'The world hasn't stopped just because we're here. There are still things to do, and I've got to—'

He stopped. 'Why are you looking at me like that?'

'Are you asking me as a PA or as a friend?'

'As a friend,' said Tom after a moment's hesitation.

'OK, then I think you're mad,' she said bluntly. 'You need a break, Tom. If I were you, I'd take that laptop to the end of the jetty and toss it into the lagoon.'

'What?' He looked absolutely horrified at the thought.

'This is supposed to be a holiday. You shouldn't even be *thinking* about work. Why don't you just relax?'

'And do what exactly?'

'You said you would teach me how to snorkel,' she reminded him.

'Hmm.' He *had* said that, Tom remembered, but he wasn't buying the idea of relaxing for three weeks. Who did she think he was? 'What would you have said if I'd asked you as my PA?'

'Certainly, Mr Maddison, what would you like me to do first?'

His mouth twitched. 'I don't remember you ever being that demure in real life!'

'Of course I was,' said Imogen, pretending to bridle. 'I'm the perfect PA.'

'You think so?'

'I'm reliable, aren't I? And discreet. So discreet, in fact, that you hardly knew I was there half the time. What more do you want from a PA?'

'I knew you were there all right,' Tom said. 'You were always talking to someone.'

But he knew what Imogen meant. He hadn't really been aware of her. It was hard to believe now that he had worked with her for six months and never realised that her eyes were that blue, or her skin that soft. How could he not have noticed her body before? He must have been blind.

All that time Imogen had been there, and he hadn't given her more than a passing thought. The office was never going to be the same again, Tom realised with a sinking heart. Now that he *had* noticed her, he wasn't going to be able to stop. He wouldn't be able to walk past her desk without knowing how soft and generously curved she was beneath whatever prim PA outfit she might be wearing.

Without remembering how dishevelled she looked when she had just got out of bed, with her hair all mussed. Without thinking about the way those dark blue eyes danced when she was teasing him, about the feel of her and the scent of her when she hugged him.

Tom rolled a shoulder uneasily. The office had always been the place he felt most comfortable, but it looked as if that was all going to change. Perhaps it was just as well that Imogen would be leaving soon.

'Is there a problem?' Imogen had been watching his face more closely than he realised.

'Problem? No!' he said quickly.

'So are you going to listen to me as a friend or as a secretary?'

'Both,' said Tom, taking a firm grip of himself. 'I'll teach you how to snorkel and we'll go out to the reef, but it'll be very hot by the time we get there so we won't be able to spend too long. When we get back, I want to do some work and I don't want to hear anything about switching off or relaxing or any of that stuff. Deal?'

'Deal!' Imogen jumped off her stool and grinned at him. 'I'll go and get ready.' Her eyes were bright and blue, and she looked so pretty and so vivid that Tom felt his throat close.

He actually had to clear it before he could speak. 'Have you got anything like an old T-shirt with you?' he asked her, forcing his mind back to practicalities. 'You should wear something over your bikini to stop your shoulders getting burnt.'

'Old T-shirts are about all I *have* got,' said Imogen cheerfully. 'I'd have had much more of a problem if you'd asked me to wear something smart.'

It didn't take long to put on a bikini and a T-shirt and she was back a few minutes later, eager to get going.

Tom had been checking the snorkelling equipment and mentally lashing himself. Somehow things had got off track in the last twenty-four hours. He'd come to Coconut Island to save face, to get away from the pitying looks that were bound to follow him once it became known that Julia had jilted him practically at the altar, and to do some work. It had seemed like a good idea at the time.

He just hadn't counted on Imogen being quite so...distracting. It was time to take control, Tom decided. Yes, she was more attractive than he had realised, and yes, the friends thing made sense while they were here but, when it came down to it, she was still his PA. If he wanted to get any work done here, and once they got home, he had better start remembering that. He needed to get things back onto the friendly but impersonal footing he had originally intended.

So it should have helped that Imogen turned up in a baggy old T-shirt unlike anything Julia would ever have worn. He had always been drawn to women who were well-groomed and dressed with style, so the faded T-shirt ought to have been enough on its own to remind him of all the reasons he shouldn't, couldn't, *didn't* find his PA remotely attractive.

Only it didn't work like that. All the T-shirt did was draw his attention to the swell of her breasts, to the curve of her hips and her bare legs. He watched Imogen slathering them with sun cream and found his mouth drying.

Friendly and impersonal? Yeah, right.

Tom forced his eyes back to the flippers he had been sorting through when Imogen had appeared. No staring, no imagining how it would feel to run his hands up and down those legs. No fantasising about peeling that T-shirt off her...

He could do it, Tom told himself sternly. All it took was a little self-control, and control was what he did best.

'Let's go,' he said gruffly as he handed Imogen a snorkel and mask. 'We'll let you practice in the lagoon first, and then we'll go out to the reef.'

He showed her how to put her face in the water and breathe through the snorkel, and when he was satisfied that she had the hang of it, he tossed the flippers and masks into the little dinghy and started the outboard motor.

The morning air sparkled as they puttered out towards reef. From the boat, the house was quickly swallowed by the foliage until the island seemed no more than a low smudge of dark green between the vast blue arch of the sky and the pale jade of the lagoon. Behind them, the engine spluttered water that glinted like diamonds in the sunlight and left a quiet, rippling wake.

Facing him on the hard seat, Imogen's T-shirt was wet from her lesson and it clung in a most distracting way. Tom had been able to ignore it when he was explaining how to breathe through the snorkel, but now it was an effort to keep his eyes on her face instead.

Her hair hung damply to her shoulders, and her skin was bare and already slightly marked from the mask. She was pretty enough, but not stunning, Tom told himself, reassured that he could be so objective.

Barely had he decided that he could relax after all when Imogen lifted her face to the sun with a sigh of pure pleasure, closed her eyes and smiled, and his hand promptly slipped on the helm, making the boat swing round.

Imogen's eyes snapped open at the sudden movement and Tom's muffled curse. 'What's wrong?'

You are, Tom wanted to shout. *You're wrong. You're supposed to just be my PA. Stop smiling like that. Stop looking like that. Stop making me notice you like that.*

'Nothing,' he said curtly instead and pointed at the reef as if he had been planning to end up at that place anyway. 'We'll anchor over there.'

When the boat was secured, he handed Imogen her flippers and waited until her mask and snorkel were in place before he helped her over the side and into the water. He couldn't do it without touching her, and he was very aware of her arm beneath his hand as he steadied her.

Imogen hung on to the edge of the boat, getting used to the feel of the mask clamped tightly to her face and the snorkel that filled her mouth awkwardly. She watched Tom put on his own flippers and drop neatly into the water beside her, and couldn't help contrasting it with her own lumbering efforts.

Tom surfaced, pulling the snorkel from his mouth and pushing the mask up onto his forehead. 'OK?'

He was very close. Through her mask, Imogen could see him in startling, stomach-clenching detail. His pale eyes were extraordinarily clear in the bright light, contrasting with the darkness of his lashes and the heavy brows. His hair was wet, and droplets of water clung to his face.

She stared at them, half mesmerised by the way they accentuated the texture of his skin, the lines creasing beside his eyes, the roughness of his jaw, and as a drop trickled down towards that firm, cool mouth, Imogen felt as if a hard fist had closed around her lungs and was methodically squeezing out all the air.

Confused by the snorkel, she pulled it out of her mouth so that she could draw a fresh lungful of air and felt immediately better.

'OK,' she confirmed, using her flippers to move away from him in what she hoped was a casual gesture.

He was too close, too overwhelming. It seemed impossible that this was Tom Maddison, that only four days ago they had been in the London office, and he had just been her boss.

He was still just her boss, Imogen reminded herself firmly.

'OK,' she said again.

'Stay close,' said Tom, pulling down his mask. 'And don't touch anything. Just look.'

Imogen nodded, took a breath and replaced the snorkel. She had a momentary panic when she put her face into the water, but then she remembered to breathe as Tom had taught her and the next moment she was floating in the water and looking down at a different world.

Entranced, she drifted along the reef, needing only the occasional gentle movement of the flippers to propel her through the water. It was cooler here, and a lovely deep, dark blue that somehow managed to be clear at the same time so that through the mask she could look right down to the bottom of the lagoon far below. If these were the shallows, how deep was the ocean on the other side of the reef?

Imogen had never seen so many fish before or such vividly coloured creatures. She was a city girl, and in her limited experience British wildlife tended to be brown and grey and black, colours that blended into a drab winter landscape. In comparison, the reef was startlingly bright, with a palette to rival that of the most colourful of fashion designers. The fish swimming beneath her were coloured in blues, greens, yellows, reds and every shade in between, as if a child had been let loose with a box of crayons. They were extraordinarily patterned too, with bold stripes and pretty speckles and strange splodges in a spectacularly gaudy combination of colours.

She had always imagined that coral would be white and bony, but it, too, came in a bizarre range of colours and shapes as it dropped away into the depths. The sun bounced on the surface of the water, filtering down until it caught shoals of tiny fish, invisible until they flashed in the light. Tom touched her arm and pointed down and Imogen's eyes widened at the sight of a huge green fish with a ponderous pout that seemed to be lumbering around the coral outcrops in comparison with the smaller fish that flickered around it.

Imogen was enthralled, but acutely aware at the same time of the sound of her breathing, abnormally loud and eerily laboured through the snorkel, of the feel of the T-shirt wafting around her as she drifted, and of Tom's reassuring presence beside her.

Every now and then a fish would swim up to stare dispassionately into her mask but for the most part they seemed oblivious of the humans hanging in the water above them. There were fish everywhere, swimming along the reef with stately grace, some moving languorously amongst the coral, others darting, drifting, nibbling at tiny plants, flicking busily to and fro. Whole shoals moved as if they were one, accelerating at some unseen signal, and turning together in a shimmer of light.

Absorbed in the magic world beneath her, Imogen was disappointed when Tom touched her arm again and pointed back to the boat but, remembering the deal they had made, she followed him reluctantly.

'That was *fantastic*!' she said as she threw the mask into the boat and clambered awkwardly in after it, too excited by what she had seen to care what she looked like. 'The fish are amazing. I can't *believe* the colours.'

She talked on, squeezing the worst of the wetness from her T-shirt and tipping her head from one side to the other to shake the water out of her ears.

There was a big red mark on her face where the rubber mask had been clamped to her skin, but her eyes were shining and her expression so vivid with delight that Tom felt his throat tighten.

'We can come out again tomorrow if you like, but you've

had enough for today,' he said gruffly. 'You'd get burnt if you stayed out much longer.'

'I think you might be right,' said Imogen reluctantly, twisting her legs round as far as she could. 'I can already feel the backs of my thighs tingling.'

Tom couldn't afford to let himself think about her thighs, or about the way that wet T-shirt clung to her body again. He started the motor with an unnecessarily vigorous jerk of the cord and for the umpteenth time reminded himself what he was doing there.

'We've got work to do, too,' he told Imogen, who was clearly having trouble mustering any enthusiasm at the prospect, although she nodded readily enough.

'Of course,' she said in her best PA voice.

Ali had been in while they were out, and the house was beautifully clean and tidy. The fridge was full of wonderful things to eat, and the bed made with crisp, fresh sheets. Imogen wondered if Ali had noticed that the bed was strangely unrumpled for a honeymoon suite.

'It's like living in a magic castle where jobs get done before you think of them,' she said, helping herself to some fruit. 'I wish I could take Ali home with me.'

'I don't suppose he's checked the stock markets or caught up on all those reports yet,' said Tom caustically. 'There are still some jobs we'll have to do ourselves.'

'Oh, yes.' Reminded of what she was supposed to be doing, Imogen licked pineapple juice off her fingers. 'Is it OK if I have a quick shower first?'

'Good idea,' said Tom, who didn't fancy his chances of concentrating on work if she was sitting there in that wet T-shirt.

It was time to be professional, he decided, opening his laptop a little while later, after he had had a shower of his own.

In spite of the heat, he wished he could put on his suit and tie, instead of shorts and a short-sleeved shirt, which was the best he could do for now. He wished he were back in his office in London, in fact, where he was never distracted and where Imogen only ever wore…well, he didn't know what she wore, but that was the whole point. He never noticed her there at all.

As it was, Imogen had appeared in loose trousers and a sleeveless top. She had done her best to find something appropriate to wear, Tom supposed grudgingly. It wasn't her fault that her hair was still wet, or that her top only seemed to emphasise the shadow of her cleavage. Or that he couldn't stop remembering the sheer delight in her face, the smoothness of her skin when he'd steadied her in the boat.

It wasn't her fault that, for the first time in his life, he didn't know exactly what he wanted, and being unable to focus on a goal left him feeling restless and faintly uneasy.

They did try. They sat across from each other at the table and began by checking their email, but it was hard to care very much about strategic audits or core competencies or competitor analysis when outside the ocean was murmuring against the reef and the sun was slicing through the fringed leaves of the coconuts. Somewhere a bird called raucously and a tiny, almost colourless gecko ran up the wall and froze as if astounded by the sight of two humans staring silently at their computer screens.

Tom couldn't understand it. Until now, work had always been his refuge. He was famous for his ability to focus, in fact, but the words on his computer screen were dancing before his eyes, and his attention kept straying to Imogen across the table. Had she always had that little crease between her brows when she studied the screen? That way of tucking her hair behind her ears?

Sensing his gaze, she glanced up and caught him staring at her. 'Did you want something?' she asked.

Tom scowled to cover his mortification. 'We ought to discuss the new acquisitions strategy.'

'O-kay,' said Imogen cautiously while she racked her brain to remember what he was talking about. Her mind was full of colourful fish and the sunlight on the sea. She couldn't even remember what an acquisition was, let alone how you ever had a strategy for it. London and the office seemed to belong to a different world altogether, a world where Tom Maddison was brusque and brisk and besuited, not lean and long-legged and sleekly muscled.

Not the kind of man who could make her heart turn over just by sitting at the helm of a boat with his hair lifting in the breeze from the ocean and his steely eyes turned to silver in the light.

Tom started talking about some new executive vice president while Imogen searched her inbox desperately for the relevant email, until he stopped abruptly.

'Oh, to hell with it!' he said, throwing up his hands in a gesture of defeat. 'It's too hot to work. Let's go and swim.'

'I've often wondered how people who live in lovely climates ever get any work done,' said Imogen a little while later. They were sitting in the tattered shade of a leaning palm and she curled her toes in the soft sand as she looked out over the lagoon. 'It's bad enough at home when the sun shines. The moment it comes out, I always feel like turning off my computer and spending the afternoon in the park.'

Tom raised a brow. 'Nice to know you've got such dedication to your work.'

'I'm only a temp,' Imogen reminded him, unruffled by his sarcasm. 'Temps aren't supposed to be dedicated. It's different for you. You're responsible for the whole company. If you get it wrong—or decide you'd rather spend the afternoon in the park—then it's not just you that's out of a job. A lot of other people will lose their jobs too.' She made a face. 'I'd hate to have that kind of pressure on me, which is why I'll never have a hugely successful career.'

'Don't you have any ambition?' said Tom, unable to completely conceal his disapproval.

'Sure I do, but it's probably not the kind you would recognise. My ambition is to be happy,' she said simply. Picking up a piece of the dried coconut husk that littered the sand beneath the trees, she twirled it absently between her fingers. 'To see the world, forget about Andrew and find someone who will love me and who wants to build a life with me.'

Imogen glanced at Tom. She could tell that he didn't understand. 'What about you?' she said, pointing the piece of husk at him as if it were a microphone. 'What's your ambition?'

He didn't have to think about it. 'To be the best.'

'Yes, but the best at what?'

Tom shrugged. He would have thought it was obvious. 'At whatever I'm doing,' he said with a hint of impatience. 'If I'm running a company, I'm going to make it the leader in its field, I'm going to win the most lucrative contracts and earn the highest profits. It doesn't matter what the race is for, I'm going to win it.'

'What happens when you *don't* win?'

'I try again until I do,' said Tom. 'The winner is always the one in control, and I never want to be in a position where anyone else can tell me what to do.'

Imogen tossed the husk back into the sand. 'No wonder you don't believe in love,' she said, remembering their conversation the night before.

'I believe in success,' he said. 'And it's not just for me. I take a failing company, I turn it round and I make it the best and, as you pointed out, everyone who works there shares in that success. People are depending on me for their jobs, for their futures. If I fail, they fail too.'

'They'll still have jobs if the company has the second-highest profits,' Imogen pointed out. 'Not winning isn't always the same as failing.'

'It is to me. I'm not prepared to be second-best,' he said uncompromisingly. 'That's why I won't take a day off when the sun shines.'

'And why you're thinking about work when you're sitting in paradise?' She gestured at the view. Coconut palms bent out towards the water, framing the beach and the lagoon between their fringed leaves like an exquisite picture. Beyond the shade the light was hot and harsh, bouncing off the surface of the lagoon and turning the white sand into a glare.

Tom's expression relaxed a little. 'You started it,' he said.

'Did I?'

'You were the one talking about switching off your computer.'

'So I was,' she conceded. She watched a breath of wind shiver across the surface of the lagoon and stir the palms above their head.

'It's hard to imagine that the office exists right now, isn't it?' she went on after a while. 'While we're sitting here in the sun, the girls are in Reception, Neville's in Finance, the other secretaries are sending out for coffee… There are meetings going on and decisions being taken and things are changing without us.' She shook her head. 'It just doesn't seem real.'

'And when we go back, this won't seem real,' warned Tom.

'Well, I for one am going to make the most of it.' Getting up, Imogen dragged her lounger out of the shade. 'I think I'll spend a busy afternoon working on my tan.'

She adjusted the lounger so that she could lie flat and turned onto her stomach before groping around in the sand for the book she had dropped there. Wriggling into a more comfortable position, she smoothed out the page with a sigh of pleasure.

'This is the life! I'm never going to be able to go back to work after three weeks of this.'

Tom watched her with a mixture of disapproval and envy. She had an extraordinary ability to enjoy the moment, he realised. It wasn't something that he had ever been able to do. He was always too busy thinking about what needed to be done at work.

'Careful you don't get burnt.'

'Yes, Mum!' But Imogen pulled the beach bag towards her and rummaged for the sun cream. She supposed she should put some on. Sunstroke was no fun.

Squeezing some lotion into her palm, she slapped it onto her shoulders as best she could.

Tom hesitated, torn between the disquieting temptation of touching her the way he had been thinking about all day and a horrible fear that he might not be able to control himself if he did.

But she couldn't reach her back herself, could she? He could hardly sit here and let her burn.

'Would you like me to put some cream on your back for you?' he offered stiltedly.

It was Imogen's turn to hesitate. The thing was, she would and she wouldn't. The thought of his hands on her skin made her shiver with excitement, but she was petrified in case he guessed quite how much she *would* like it.

But they were being normal here, right? She would burn if she didn't do something about her back, and she wouldn't hesitate to ask any other friend to rub cream in for her.

'That would be great,' she said after a beat.

Reaching behind her, she unclipped the bikini top and lay flat, her arms folded beneath her face and her head pillowed on her hands. She was wearing sunglasses, but turned her head away from him as an extra precaution.

The squirt of the suntan lotion onto his hands seemed unnaturally loud, and Imogen found herself tensing in preparation for his touch. When it came, his hands were so warm and so sure that she sucked in an involuntary breath and couldn't prevent a small shiver snaking down her spine.

'Sorry, is it cold?'

'No, it's fine.' Imogen's voice was muffled in her hands.

Crouching beside her, Tom smoothed cream firmly over her shoulders and up to the nape of her neck, before his hands, slippery with oil, slid down her back, then up, then down again, spreading his fingers this time to make sure her sides were covered.

Imogen made herself lie still but inside she was squirming with such pleasure that she was afraid that she would actually dissolve, leaving a sticky puddle on the lounger. At the same time she was rigid with tension caused by the need not to show it. She mustn't sigh with pleasure, mustn't roll over, mustn't beg him not to stop…

Oh, God, he had started on the backs of her legs now… Imogen squeezed her eyes shut. Thank goodness she had had them waxed before she'd left.

Tom's hands swept down her thighs in firm strokes to the backs of her knees, then on down to her ankles, before gliding all the way back up again. In spite of her best efforts, Imogen quivered.

She was sure that he must be able to hear her entire body thumping and thudding in time with her pounding heart. Part of her was desperate for him to stop before she disgraced herself by spontaneously combusting, but when he did take his hands away abruptly she only stopped herself from groaning with disappointment in the nick of time.

'That should do you.'

If Imogen had been able to hear anything above the boom of her own pulse she might have noticed the undercurrent of strain to his voice but, as it was, all she could do was lie there and hope that he couldn't actually see the heat beating along her veins.

'Thank you.' Her mouth was so dry, it came out as barely more than a croak.

Tom stood up. 'I think I'll get back to work,' he said curtly. 'No, you stay there,' he added as Imogen lifted her head to ask if he wanted her to do anything. 'There's no point in wasting that lotion. I've just got a few things I want to be getting on with.'

'Well, if you're sure...'

'I'm sure,' said Tom. He badly needed to be alone, and the last thing he wanted was Imogen there, wondering why he was so tense or walking so stiffly! 'I'll see you later.'

There *were* things he needed to do but, no matter how hard he stared at the computer screen, Tom didn't seem to be able to focus. His fingers were still throbbing with the feel of her body, so soft and smooth and warm, so dangerously enticing beneath his hands. Even though he had been able to see that she was rigid with discomfort, he had itched to turn her over, to brush the skimpy bikini away and explore every dip and curve of her.

It had taken every ounce of self-control he possessed to take his hands off her and step back.

Tom rubbed a hand over his face in exasperation at himself. Control, that was the key word here.

Control was what he was best at. It was what he *was*. He had never had any trouble controlling impulses before and there was no reason to start now. It was just the heat and the light getting to him, Tom told himself. Or maybe just a reaction to Julia's rejection. That would be understandable enough.

He began to feel a bit better. Yes, all he needed was a little time on his own out of the sun. He would sit here and work, and he wouldn't think about Imogen at all.

He would be fine.

CHAPTER SEVEN

TOM was still at his computer a couple of hours later when Imogen climbed the steps to the veranda. He looked up as she appeared in the doorway and, as their eyes met, the air quivered on the verge of tension before they both looked away.

'Bored?' he asked.

Imogen laughed and shook her head. 'Hardly! I'm thirsty, though, so I came up to get a drink.' She opened the fridge door to find the water. 'How are you getting on? Is everything under control?'

'It is,' said Tom with satisfaction. There was his word again: *control*. It felt right.

He was feeling much more himself. He had read a couple of reports, and fired off some emails. Under normal circumstances, that would have been the work of half an hour, but it wasn't bad, given the amount of time he had spent carefully not thinking about Imogen.

Imogen poured herself a long glass of water and leant against the room divider to drink it.

'I was thinking I might try walking around the island,' she said tentatively.

Left alone, she had found it impossible to concentrate on her book. She was horribly afraid that Tom might have guessed the effect that he was having on her and had been embarrassed. He hadn't been able to wait to get away!

Not that she blamed him. If she had been rubbing lotion onto someone who squirmed like that, she'd have run a mile too.

He had only been putting a bit of cream on her, for heaven's sake! It had been ridiculous to get herself in a state about it, thought Imogen, mortified. They were supposed to be friends, and friends didn't go to pieces the moment the other laid a finger on them. She was determined to find some way to show him that she was back to normal.

'Are you still working, or would you like to come?'

Tom linked his arms above his head and stretched. 'A walk sounds good.' It sounded normal, easy, safe. Controllable. 'I could do with stretching my legs.'

'Great.' Imogen finished her water. 'I'll get my hat.'

It was well into the afternoon by the time they set out, but it was still very hot, in spite of a breeze that ruffled the lagoon and made the palms sigh and rustle overhead as Imogen and Tom headed barefoot along the beach. Imogen had wrapped a sarong around her waist and her face was shaded by a soft straw hat. Beside her, Tom wore shorts and a loose short-sleeved shirt.

They walked in silence at first but, rather to Imogen's surprise, it didn't feel uncomfortable. They splashed around the point where the dense vegetation grew right to the shore and found themselves on the far side of the island. There was little sand to speak of there, but the water was so warm and clear that they were happy to wade ankle deep in the shallows to where the shore curved inwards once more.

Suddenly Tom stopped and shaded his eyes as he looked out to sea. 'Look!'

'What is it?' Imogen's gaze followed his finger until she exclaimed in delight. 'Dolphins!'

In silence they stood and watched a whole pod of dolphins leaping out of the water with breathtaking grace. For Imogen, it was an extraordinary moment. It was as if she had never been fully alive before that moment, and she was aware of everything with a new and fierce intensity.

The sea was the bluest of blues, the heat hammered down, the light beyond the shade of her hat glared. She could feel the sand cool beneath her toes, the shallows rippling warm against her ankles and Tom, still and self-contained beside her, while further out the dolphins played, soaring into the air as if for the sheer joy of it, the water that streamed from their bodies glittering in the fierce sunlight.

Imogen could feel her heart swelling and her throat closed at the rush of emotion. The beauty and exuberance of the scene was so joyous it felt like an unexpected gift.

'Quite something, isn't it?' said Tom.

Unable to speak, she nodded.

After a while the dolphins moved on. Imogen and Tom waited a few minutes in case they came back, but eventually they started walking again.

'I'm sorry Julia's not here with you,' she said quietly at last, 'but I'm glad I came. I'll never forget that, or the reef this morning.'

Tom glanced down but could see little of her expression beneath her hat. 'I'm glad you came too,' he said.

Imogen took a breath. 'How are you feeling?' she asked. 'I mean, really?'

'About Julia? I'm OK,' he said when she nodded. 'And yes, *really*.' He looked away from her, squinting slightly at the bright light bouncing off the water. 'Maybe I should be thinking about her more,' he said slowly. 'I wanted to marry her, after all. I ought to be missing her, but the truth is that I'm not. We never actually lived together, so perhaps it's because I'm not used to her being around.'

He fell silent, thinking about the woman who should have been exploring the island with him. What would it have been like to have been here with Julia? Somehow it was hard to imagine when Imogen was walking beside him, her face shaded by the wide brim of her hat. Her skin was glowing after a day in the sun and he could see the salt drying on her shoulders.

The bottom of her sarong was wet and kept clinging to her calves so that every few yards she had to stop and disentangle herself. As she bent, her tangled brown hair would swing forwards and cover her face until she pushed it impatiently behind her ear.

'I think I miss the idea of Julia more than anything else,' Tom went on at last. 'She was so exactly the kind of woman I'd always imagined marrying: beautiful, very intelligent, glamorous, successful…'

All things she wasn't, Imogen couldn't help thinking.

'Well, you've met her,' he said, unaware of her mental interruption. 'You know how special she was. I was tired of girlfriends constantly demanding attention, insisting that I rang them all the time, forever wanting to cross-examine me about my feelings…'

Tom shuddered at the memory. 'They all seemed to think that I could drop everything at work to dance attendance on them and take them out to dinner or to Paris for the weekend, and if there was a crisis at work, they would sulk.' He lifted a shoulder, irritable at the mere memory. 'I couldn't be bothered with any of that.

'Julia was different,' he remembered after a moment. 'She

wasn't needy or emotional, and she didn't expect me to jump through hoops for her. We understood each other—or, at least, I thought we did,' he amended. 'I had no idea what Patrick meant to her, for instance. When she said that he was just a friend, I never questioned it. I thought she would be the perfect wife.'

He paused, remembering. 'I suppose the truth is that it wasn't her I really wanted, but someone to go home to. Someone who would make me comfortable, who would be able to cope with any corporate entertaining and who wouldn't make a fuss about the time I spent at work.'

'It sounds to me as if you wanted a housekeeper, not a wife,' said Imogen with a certain tartness. 'Why didn't you just hire someone?'

'Because I don't sleep with my employees.' Tom's voice was level, and Imogen flushed beneath her hat.

Of course he would expect to sleep with his wife, but she didn't really need to have that fact rammed down her throat. She didn't need to imagine being that wife, making love with him every night, waking up with him every morning. Especially when it was never going to happen.

'As one of your employees, that's good to know,' she said as crisply as she could.

Tom slanted her a quick look. 'It's not just about sex,' he said. 'I wanted an equal, someone I could talk to, someone to support me—what was so wrong with that?'

'That depends on what you were going to offer her in return.'

'A lot of money,' he said. 'Security. Comfort. Trust. Respect. Honesty. Fidelity. When I make a promise, I keep it. I wouldn't have taken wedding vows unless I was going to stick to them.'

It wasn't a bad deal, Imogen supposed. She knew people who had settled for less.

He had offered Julia everything except love. Imogen wasn't surprised that Julia had thought that she would marry him, but it wasn't a surprise either that she hadn't been able to go through with it.

Tom might not think love mattered, but it did.

'You don't approve?' He was watching her more closely than she realised.

'It's not up to me to approve or disapprove,' said Imogen carefully. 'It just wouldn't be enough for me.'

'What more do you want? Oh—love, I suppose?'

'Yes, love,' she said evenly, ignoring the dismissive note in his voice. 'What good is respect or security or all that stuff if you're not with someone who makes you feel…oh, I don't know…'

How could she explain to someone like Tom? '…like one of those dolphins we saw,' she tried. 'They looked so…so *joyous* leaping out of the water, didn't they? As if they were exactly where they wanted to be, doing exactly what they wanted to do. That's how it feels when you're in love,' she told him. 'I'm not getting married until I feel that way again.'

Tom shook his head, unconvinced. 'You're not being realistic, Imogen. You want everything to be perfect, but nothing ever is. Look at Coconut Island,' he said, gesturing around him. 'They said it was paradise, and it is—but there are still cockroaches and bats and who knows what else lurking in the undergrowth.'

Imogen cast a nervous glance at the vegetation smothering the shore. She hadn't thought about what else might be sharing the island with them and wished that Tom hadn't put the idea into her head. What if there were snakes? Mentally resolving to stick to the beach at all times, she edged further out into the water.

Tom was still talking about the need to adjust her ideas. 'You're holding on to a fantasy,' he told her.

'So I've been told,' said Imogen with a slight edge. 'Amanda thinks I ought to compromise, and go out with men who aren't absolutely perfect, but I don't want to do that. I've been in love. OK, it didn't work out, but I'm not prepared to settle for anything less.'

'You're just setting yourself up for disappointment,' he warned, and she put up her chin.

'Well, we'll have to agree to disagree, won't we? It's just as well we're not thinking of getting married, isn't it?'

There was a tiny pause. In spite of himself, Tom's mind flickered to Imogen's warm, smooth body, to the feel of her hug and the laughter in her eyes. It might be nice to go home to that every night.

But that would mean feeling unsettled the whole time. Imogen would want him to love her and make her feel like a bloody dolphin! Tom recoiled from the very thought. His whole life would slip out of control in no time. No, he couldn't cope with that at all.

'Yes,' he agreed. 'Just as well.'

That first day set the pattern for the week. Walking round the island at the end of the afternoon became part of their routine. Imogen never got tired of the reef and was eager to get out there every morning. For the first couple of days, she sat down at her computer when they got back, but in the end Tom told her gruffly that there was little point in her being there and that she could do as she pleased.

Imogen didn't put up much of a protest, it had to be said. It was impossible to concentrate, anyway, and she hoped that eventually Tom would get the idea of not working as well and learn to relax instead.

Not that there was much sign of that yet. Imogen had no idea what he was doing, but he seemed to spend hours at his laptop while she was on the beach. It was a shame that he was such a workaholic, she thought. He wasn't having much of a holiday and, when they did spend time together, they were getting on surprisingly well. Sometimes he would bring her a drink, or join her for a swim, but he never stayed for long and always made an excuse to get back to his computer.

Tom was not, in fact, doing nearly as much work as Imogen thought he was. Oh, he spent a lot of time sitting and looking at the screen but he was finding it increasingly hard to concentrate.

Imogen was a constant distraction, and his mind had a disturbing tendency to drift towards her at inappropriate times and in frankly inappropriate ways. It made Tom very uneasy. He had never had this problem focusing before.

The truth was that he was deeply tempted to succumb to this unexpected attraction, but how could it possibly work? When it came down it, Imogen was still his PA and it was hardly any time since he was supposed to be marrying Julia. She wasn't going to believe him if he told her that he was fast becoming obsessed with her, was she?

Of course, it was just a physical obsession, Tom reassured himself, and obviously well under his control. Which was just as well, given that Imogen was clinging to her ridiculous fantasy about love.

No, it would never work. Besides, none of this would seem real when he got home, Tom would remind himself whenever he wavered from his decision. It was all too easy to get carried away by the seductive glitter of sunlight on the lagoon and the hot, starry nights. Back in his cool, well-ordered London life he would be very glad that he hadn't made a move.

In the meantime, he was doing his best to maintain some distance. It was a little easier once he had told Imogen that he didn't expect her to work after all. Tom had been afraid that if she carried on sitting across the table from him she would realise just how little work he was actually doing.

Otherwise, things were OK if they were doing something—snorkelling or swimming or walking or eating—but he avoided the beach as much as possible. When Imogen was just *there*, looking touchable, his hands would start to twitch alarmingly and he had to take himself off in case they reached for her of their own accord.

The evenings were tricky too, but at least then it was dark. Together, they would sit and watch, mesmerised, while the sky softened and glowed and the sun sank towards the horizon and disappeared at last in an extravaganza of fiery colour. The sudden darkness brought a raucous chorus of insects and the bats, swooping and diving through the hot air.

Tom was always achingly aware of Imogen beside him then. Every evening she showered and changed into a dress, and he could smell the soap and sunshine on her skin, and in the freshly washed hair that tumbled loose to her shoulders.

But he could handle it. It was under control.

'I don't like the look of that.' Imogen stopped in the shallows and pointed at the horizon, which was boiling with dark, dense, billowy clouds.

It was very hot and even the water around her ankles felt warmer than usual. The circuit of the island involved more wading than walking, but it was already familiar. Imogen did a quick calculation. This was the fifth time they had done it, but the first time she had noticed clouds like that. They were a long way away, it was true, but there was something menacing about them, and she watched them uneasily.

'I hope there's not going to be a storm.'

Tom eyed the horizon. 'It's looking pretty black,' he agreed. 'We might well get some rain.'

'I don't mind rain. It's thunder and lightning that make me nervous.' Imogen hugged her arms together. 'I know it's silly, but I hate storms.

'When I was little, I went on a camping trip with my friend and her family,' she said. 'We were staying on a campsite by a river, and there was a terrific storm in the middle of the night. Thunder, lightning, torrential rain, wind…the full works. It was chaos,' she remembered with a shudder. 'There were tents blowing away, and people screaming and the river flooded…

'I was only seven and I was terrified, although it turned out in the end that no one had been badly hurt or anything. But the tents were ruined and everything was such a mess that we went back early. When we got home, my mother had to tell me that my granny had died suddenly while I'd been away.'

The memory still made Imogen sad. 'She'd been living with us and I absolutely adored her. I was devastated, and I suppose it got all muddled up in my mind. I thought that the storm had somehow killed Granny, and the next time there was thunder and lightning I got absolutely hysterical.'

Tom's expression was hard to read and she trailed off, feeling foolish. 'I told you it was silly,' she apologised.

'It's difficult to get things that happen to us as kids into proper perspective,' he said. 'Even when we're grown up and understand what really happened, we still feel it the way we did then. My mother died when I was five,' he said abruptly. 'I don't remember much about her––it's more of an impression than a specific memory—but I remember exactly the tweedy jacket my father was wearing when he came back from hospital to tell me. It felt rough when he hugged me, and I can still see those leather buttons. Even now I'll sometimes catch a glimpse of someone wearing a jacket like that and I'll feel a mixture of confusion and distress, just like I did then.'

He had kept his account deliberately dispassionate, but Imogen felt tears sting her eyes at the thought of the small boy learning that his world had fallen apart.

'How awful for you.'

'I was all right.' She was unsurprised when Tom brushed her sympathy aside and carried on splashing through the shallows.

'I don't think I really understood what my father meant,' he said. 'They hadn't told me that she was ill, and I was just aware that nothing was happening as it should any more. I remember not understanding why the house was a mess or why we didn't have meals at the proper times any more.

'Of course, I can see now that my father was struggling to cope, and doing the best that he could. Tidying the house wouldn't have been top of his order of priorities, but it bothered me at the time. That level of disorder still makes me uncomfortable,' he added in a burst of confidence.

No wonder being in control was so important to him, thought Imogen, wading through the warm water beside him. His mother's death would have disrupted everything that he took for granted. As a small boy, he must have felt utterly powerless. She could see how building an orderly world that he could control would be a way of coping with the loss of the most important figure in his life.

His distrust of emotions made more sense now. Tom might think that he was being realistic, but inside he was still the boy who had lost the woman he loved the most, and was afraid of feeling that bereft again. It was easy to see how a small child, unable to understand death, would think that he had been abandoned by his mother, would feel at some level that she wouldn't have left him if he'd been good enough. That would certainly explain his drive to succeed, to prove again and again that he *was* good enough.

And now Julia had abandoned him too. Imogen's heart cracked for him, and she slid a glance under her lashes. She knew better than to say anything, but she felt desperately sorry for him. It wasn't surprising that he was so wary of love. Falling in love would mean letting go of everything that had made him feel safe since he was a child.

It was a shame, Imogen thought. If only Tom would take the risk, he could make some woman very happy. Behind that brusque exterior was a man who was strong and steady and fiercely intelligent, with an unexpectedly dry sense of humour. The more time she spent with him, the more she found herself liking him.

And the more attractive she found him.

Night after night, she would lie alone in the big bed and think about Tom on the sofa, just round the corner. In the darkness she would remember how he looked when he came out of the water, brushing his wet hair back from his forehead. His legs were long and lean, his chest broad and his shoulders powerful. Imogen's mouth would dry at the memory.

It was getting harder and harder to remember that she was supposed to be treating him like any other friend. She was reluctant to offer to rub sun cream into his back too often, not because she didn't want to touch him, but because she wanted it too much. Tom often hesitated before accepting, and Imogen was convinced that he knew how much she loved the sensation of feeling the leashed power of his body beneath her hands, in spite of her best attempts to appear brisk and unconcerned. His skin was warm and sleek and matt and, when she felt his muscles flex at her touch, her stomach tightened and heat roiled through her.

It was all she could do to stop her hands sliding all over him. She longed to explore all that solidity and strength, to touch her lips to the back of his neck and kiss her way down his spine and then turn him over and start all over again. Sometimes Imogen felt quite giddy with it, and snapping the lid back on the bottle and stepping back took such a heroic effort that she had to sit down and close her eyes.

And remind herself of all the reasons why she had to keep her hands firmly to herself.

It would be a huge mistake to forget how incompatible they were. She might understand now why Tom was so resistant to the idea of love, but that didn't change the facts. She would be mad to even think about falling for a man who was incapable of loving her back. All he could ever offer was a physical relationship, and that wouldn't be enough for her.

Would it?

'It's hot tonight.'

Dropping onto the wicker seat next to Tom's, Imogen lifted the hair from her neck in a vain attempt to cool it and he got a whiff of shampoo. He couldn't recognise the scent—limes, perhaps, and something else—but it was clean and fresh and innocently alluring, rather, he realised with something approaching dismay, like Imogen herself.

She was wearing loose silky trousers tonight, but with a strappy top that left her arms and shoulders bare. Tom was sure that she hadn't set out to look seductive, but all she had to do was sit there in her very ordinary clothes and he was wondering what it would be like to run his hands down those smooth arms, wondering how warm her skin would feel, how easily those tiny strips would slide from her shoulders…

Swallowing, he got up to make her a drink. 'I think we may be getting that rain soon,' he said. When in doubt, stick to the weather.

'Really?' Imogen looked out at the lagoon with a frown. In the last flush of the sunset, it gleamed like burnished copper, its surface glassy and still.

'It's very close,' he pointed out, 'and those clouds were behind us, remember? Just because we can't see them doesn't mean they're not there.'

Imogen pulled a face. 'Creepy thought.' Not being able to see it only made the gathering storm seem more menacing.

Uneasily, she pulled her legs up so that she could hug her knees. 'I think you must be right, though. It feels eerie tonight. It's as if the whole island is holding its breath.'

The air was suffocatingly hot and heavy. It seemed to wrap itself around them as Tom handed Imogen her drink and sat back down beside her.

'Listen!' he said, holding up a finger.

Imogen cocked her head on one side. 'I can't hear anything.'

'Exactly. Usually you can't hear yourself think for the insects but there's not a peep out of them tonight. It's all quiet.'

'So it is.' In spite of the heat, she shivered. 'No bats either. It's uncanny.'

The last stripe of scarlet along the horizon slipped away and the darkness swooped after it, swallowing up the last gleam of light in the sky. It felt more intense than usual, and Imogen was sure that she could feel the blackness boiling angrily up behind them.

The silence was making her stomach churn, and she bit her

lip and hugged her knees more tightly, unsure whether she
longed for something to happen to break the suspense, or
dreaded it.

A lamp inside threw a dim yellow glow through the
window onto the veranda. It was enough for Tom to see a
pulse hammering in Imogen's throat. Her whole body was
rigid with tension, and he remembered what she had told him
earlier about her fear of storms.

'Come here,' he said, and held out his hand.

Imogen didn't even hesitate. She took it gratefully, and the
fear that had been jittering just below her skin steadied the
moment his fingers closed firmly around hers. His clasp was
warm and strong as he drew her down onto the seat close
beside him. He didn't tell her not to be frightened, but just put
his arm around her and held her close against the hard security
of his body.

Her heart was booming and thudding, but now she didn't
know whether it was from fear or from a desperate, churning
awareness of Tom's nearness. He was so solid, so steady, so
gloriously reassuring, that she wanted to burrow into him, but
she made herself sit still, comforted by the strength of his arm.

As every evening, he was wearing cool chinos and a loose
shirt. Tonight, for the first time, she was close enough to feel
that it was made of the finest cotton, close enough to breathe
in its indefinably expensive smell, mingled with the clean,
wonderfully male scent of his skin.

Imogen was so distracted by the feel of him that she almost
forgot the threatening storm until the blackness was fractured
by a great fork of lightning, followed a few seconds later by
an ear-splitting crack that sent her heart lurching into her throat.

Tom felt her jump and tightened his arm around her. 'Here

we go,' he said cheerfully. 'Looks like it's going to be a big one, but you're safe with me.'

And, incredibly, safe was exactly how Imogen felt, even though the sky was lit up again and again in a spectacular display, and the sound of the thunder ripped through the silence and reverberated all around them. It went on for long minutes before stopping as abruptly as it had begun.

'Wow,' she said unsteadily into a silence that still echoed with the crack of thunder. Normally the first hint of lightning had her literally cowering under the blankets, and she had never seen anything like that display of ferocious power. She moistened her lips, very glad of Tom's massive, reassuring presence. 'Do you think that's it?'

But that was only the beginning. Before Tom had a chance to reply, the wind was upon them. Like a wild animal, it snarled through the palms, shaking them in savage fury until they bent like saplings. It thrashed its way into the under-growth, whipping the foliage from side to side, and hurled itself at the house.

And then the rain hit them.

Imogen had never seen rain like it. It fell like a wall of water, thundering down onto the veranda roof and hammer-ing into the sand. The noise was deafening, brutal, and she huddled closer into Tom's side.

'All right?' He had to shout over the sound of the rain, but she could still hardly hear him.

She had been watching the rain with a mixture of awe and terror, but at his question she pulled away slightly so that she could look up at him. The silvery eyes gleamed back down at her and she realized, to her astonishment, that the corners of his mouth were turned up. He was actually smiling!

'You're *enjoying* this!'

Tom's smile broadened at the accusing note in her voice. 'I like storms,' he admitted. 'Don't you think this is exciting?'

Now he came to mention it, that *was* excitement quivering along her veins, but it wasn't due to the storm. It was being pressed close into his body, knowing that if she turned her head just a little bit more his throat was only inches away. It would take so little to lean into him and touch her lips to his skin and, once she'd done that, she could blizzard tiny kisses along his jaw to his mouth.

And, if she got that far and he was still smiling, she could find out if his lips were as cool and firm as they looked. She could kiss him the way she had been trying so hard not to think about kissing him all week. She could squirm onto his lap and wind her arms around his neck and perhaps Tom would kiss her back. Perhaps his hands would slide over her, perhaps he would peel off her clothes, perhaps he would take her inside to that big bed and make love to her…

Imogen gulped. Tom was talking about the storm, remember? '*Exciting* isn't the word I'd use,' she managed.

Tom laughed and pulled her closer. He hadn't meant to, but she fitted so perfectly into him, and she was so soft and so warm and so gorgeous that his arm seemed to tighten of its own accord. The storm was awesome, without a doubt, but the millions of volts crackling across the sky were muted compared to the feeling that jolted through him whenever Imogen shifted slightly and the thin material of her dress beneath his hand slithered over her skin.

Even as he looked down into her face, Tom knew that it was a mistake. The muted glow of the lamp inside was just enough for their eyes to meet, and once they'd snared they were both caught. Tom's smile faded slowly as her gaze held his. He knew just how blue her eyes were, but in this light they were dark and deep and he was drowning in them.

The sound and fury of the storm was forgotten as something undeniable crackled into life between them. Imogen couldn't have looked away if she had tried. It was as if some irresistible force were drawing them together, and her blood drummed with anticipation.

At last—at *last*—he was going to kiss her, and she was going to kiss him back, just as she'd dreamed about. She wasn't going to think about anything except how good it was going to feel. Parting her lips, she lifted her face as Tom lowered his head…

CHAPTER EIGHT

A SUDDEN jagged flash of lightning severed the dark and thunder crashed so terrifyingly close to the house that they both flinched apart in the blinding light. The next moment it was gone and they were plunged into utter darkness.

Imogen stiffened, the old fear clutching at her throat.

'The generator's gone,' Tom yelled in her ear. 'Don't worry. There's a flashlight inside.'

He took his arm from round her and she grabbed him in panic, frantic at the thought of waiting alone in the dark with the storm screaming around her. 'Don't leave me!'

'I'm not going to leave you.' He took firm hold of her hand. 'Come with me. It'll be fine once we get some light.'

Without even a glimmer of starlight, the depth of the darkness was disorientating. Hand in hand, they groped their way to the door and then inside. Tom remembered Ali showing them the flashlight and how to light the gas lamps—for just such an eventuality, he supposed—but it still took some time to find it and, when his hand did finally close on it, he exclaimed with relief.

'At last!'

He clicked it on and they both blinked at the brightness of

the beam. To Imogen's relief, the blackness that had been pressing so heavily around them shrank back instantly.

'That's better,' said Tom, and it was, until he looked down to see that he was still holding Imogen's hand. 'Are you OK?' he asked carefully.

She followed his gaze to their linked fingers and a flush crept up her cheeks. 'Yes, I'm fine,' she said, awkwardly disentangling her hand.

Funny, thought Tom. That didn't feel better any more.

He had been so close to kissing her. If that lightning hadn't taken out the electricity just then, he wouldn't have been able to stop himself. And where would that have ended?

Tom knew where. In that bed, and in the very situation he had just managed to convince himself that he should avoid.

Imogen was clearly thinking better of things as well. He had noticed how quickly she had withdrawn her hand from his, and now she was hugging her arms about her nervously. She might still be spooked by the storm, but he thought it was more likely that she was unnerved by the fact that her boss had almost kissed her.

Best to pretend that nothing had happened, he decided.

'Well,' he said, a little too heartily, 'let's light the gas lamps and then we may as well have something to eat. There are plenty of salads in the fridge.'

Imogen never forgot that meal in the hissing light of a gas lamp while the rain crashed onto the roof and her fingers twitched and tingled where they had been curled around Tom's. She couldn't keep her eyes off his lean, solid body, massive and reassuring in the wildness of the dark night.

She tried not to stare, but her eyes kept skittering back to him, only to skitter away again the moment they collided with his pale grey gaze. Not that it mattered where she looked;

all she could see were the hard angles of his face, his hands, his mouth. His *mouth*... Had he always had that mouth?

It was just the shadows cast by the lamp, Imogen tried to tell herself. Just the power of the downpour, the energy of the lightning, that was making her feverish. Just the storm that was raging outside and deep inside her, fizzing like lightning in her blood and making her heart thunder so loudly that if it hadn't been for the rain, Tom must surely have heard it.

It was almost a shock when the rain stopped as abruptly as it had begun. One moment it was pounding down, the next there was an uncanny silence, broken only by the steady drip, drip from the huge tropical leaves outside, before the insects erupted into frenzy and the whole island steamed in the aftermath.

Imogen knew just how it felt. Leaping up, she made a big show of clearing away the plates and putting the food away. Tom hadn't said anything but it was obvious that he had changed his mind about kissing her.

It had been too easy to get carried away by the darkness and the drama of the storm, she reminded herself. And put herself in Tom's position. He was only a man, after all. She had been young, female and alone with him in the dark. Who could have blamed him for being tempted to forget Julia's rejection with someone who was clinging to him like a limpet?

Or for thinking better of it when the lights came on again?

It was just as well nothing had happened, Imogen decided. It would have made it very awkward. Tom was still her boss, and they were going to have to go back to working together in a couple of weeks.

And even if he *had* kissed her, it wouldn't have meant anything. She didn't want to be just a poor substitute for Julia, did she?

Did she?

No, Imogen told herself firmly. Absolutely not. She had narrowly escaped making the most enormous fool of herself, and it wasn't going to happen again. From now on, there would be no holding hands, no pressing herself against him, no fantasising about kissing him. They had agreed to be friends and a friend was all she would be.

Imogen woke the next morning to a bright blue sky. The air was rinsed and sparkling and when they set off for the reef as usual, the water was so still and so clear that it was hard to believe in the ferocity of the storm the night before. If it hadn't been for the intensity of the island scents, heady and lush after the rain, Imogen might have thought it had all been a dream.

She was hoping that excruciating awareness of Tom would turn out to have been a dream too, but if anything it was worse in the diamond-bright light, when every line around his eyes, every crease in his cheek, seemed extraordinarily clear, and when the severe planes and angles of his face were etched against the blue sky.

Remembering her vow, though, Imogen chattered brightly all the way to the reef, and gave what she thought was an excellent impression of a girl too inane to harbour lustful thoughts about her boss.

It was a relief to put on the mask and snorkel, to hide her face in the water and lose herself in the absorbing world beneath the surface. The silence was soothing. There was just the coolness of the water and the sound of her breathing and the fish drifting below in a spectacle of colour, and by the time Tom indicated that they should go back, she was feeling much more herself. She was able to be really normal as the little boat skimmed over the water, and her spirits lifted.

See, she could do this, she congratulated herself as she settled onto the lounger in the sun a little later and opened her book. Last night had been an aberration. She would blame it all on the storm. All she had to do was carry on treating Tom as a friend and enjoy the holiday. She would have to worry about how they got back to a working relationship when they got home.

One thing was sure, she couldn't see them being friends in London. Their lives were just too different. Tom wouldn't be happy slobbing out on the sofa while she and Amanda gossiped, dissected the latest celebrity mags and tested each other on developments in the latest soaps. He wouldn't offer to ring for a takeaway when it turned out there was nothing in the fridge, or want to lie in bed until lunchtime on a Sunday.

And he would never be able to cope with their messy flat, Imogen realised, remembering his need for order and control. He needed someone like Julia—gorgeous, glamorous Julia, who probably drifted around art galleries looking intelligent on Sundays and no doubt lived in an immaculately tidy apartment.

No, they might be friends on Coconut Island, but there was no point in thinking that it could be the same in London.

When Tom appeared with a glass of fresh lime juice a little later, she put her book down with a cheerful smile.

'You make a great barman,' she told him. 'I'll owe you lots of coffees at your desk when we get back to the office.'

No harm in reminding him that she hadn't forgotten reality, no matter how much it must have seemed it the night before when she had clung to him and her eyes had been crawling all over him.

'Actually, it's Ali you should be making the coffee for,' said Tom, sitting sideways on the lounger next to hers. 'He made these. He was just finishing tidying up after the storm when I was checking my email.' He swirled lime juice around his glass with a faint frown. 'Does tonight mean anything to you?'

'No. Should it?'

'He was trying to tell me about something that had been arranged for tonight, but I couldn't get what he was talking about.'

Imogen pulled a face. 'No idea. Perhaps there's a party or something at the resort? He could have been asking if we wanted to go.'

'God, I hope not,' said Tom in dismay. 'I said yes, OK, just because it seemed easier than trying to understand. But maybe you'd like to go and meet other people?' he added belatedly.

Normally she would have loved the idea of a party, but there was nothing Imogen wanted to do less right then. There were only two weeks left, she had remembered earlier, and she didn't want to share Tom for even a minute of it with anyone else. But she couldn't tell him that in case he thought she was needy and reading too much into what had—or hadn't—happened last night.

'It might be fun,' she said as casually as she could. 'Let's see what happens tonight.'

'Are you dressed?' Imogen heard Tom call from the veranda that evening as she put on her lipstick. 'Ali's here with the boat.'

Just in case it turned out that they were going to a party, Imogen had put on her only smart dress. It was a pale creamy yellow and made of a gorgeous silky material that slithered coolly over her skin and was perfect for putting on after a day in the sun. She had tried to be sensible and sit in the shade as much as possible, but even so the sun had turned her skin to a warm gold and her hair was streaked with blonde. The dress set her new sun-drenched colouring to perfection.

'I wonder what's going on,' she said to Tom, fixing in her earrings as she joined him on the veranda.

'Let's go and see.'

Barefoot like Imogen, Tom led the way down to the jetty. He was browner too, and his silver eyes made an even more startling contrast than usual with his tanned skin. Following him along the jetty, Imogen found her eyes resting hungrily on his back, and she squirmed at the guilty desire that swirled deep inside her like liquid gold.

Stop it, she told herself sternly. Don't look at him. Don't even *think* about it.

Ali was waiting for them in a dinghy at the end of the jetty. All smiles, he gestured out to a beautiful wooden boat waiting beyond a reef.

'For you,' he said.

'It doesn't look like a party anyway,' said Tom in relief.

Imogen was watching the boat. 'Isn't it lovely? It's called a *dhoni*, I think. I remember reading about them when I was booking the island. Apparently they're fabulous for a sunset cruise. I wonder if that's what this is?'

'You didn't book it?'

'No, but it's possible Julia did,' she said slowly. 'She asked me for all the details of the resort at one point. Maybe she was planning a surprise for you?'

'Well, we may as well find out.' Tom pointed at himself and Imogen, and then at the boat with a questioning look at Ali, who nodded vigorously.

'Yes. Come, come.' He waved them towards him.

'He seems to be expecting us,' said Tom. 'What do you want to do? I can tell him there's been a mistake, or we can go along and see what happens.'

'Let's go,' she said. 'It'll be fun.'

The *dhoni* rocked gently as they climbed on board. Tom and Imogen were shown to the prow, which had been laid with luxurious cushions, and they settled down, feeling self-conscious as the crew pulled up the anchor and hoisted the square sail.

Once the sails were up and filled, the engine was cut and there was just the slap and rustle of the waves against the wooden hull. The sea breeze lifted their hair and filled their nostrils with an ocean tang, while the water deepened to a dark, beautiful blue and the setting sun turned the light to gold.

'I don't know whose idea this was, but it was a great one,' said Imogen, thrilled by the lift and fall of the boat.

Tom watched her smiling with pleasure, and his throat ached. She was all warmth and light in the sunset. Her skin was honey-coloured, her hair bleached with sunshine, and the pale yellow dress clung enticingly to her curves and fell in soft folds around her bare legs.

The urge to reach for her, to slide his palm up over her smooth knee, beneath her skirt to explore her thigh, was so strong that he got abruptly to his feet to lean on the side of the boat.

'Dolphins,' he said, pointing, relieved at the distraction.

'Where?' Imogen jumped to her feet to join him. 'Oh, yes! Oh, aren't they *wonderful*?'

Face alight, she leant beside him, her arm only inches from his. She wasn't looking at him. She was watching the dolphins with delight as they played in the frothy wake from the prow, leaping and rolling with effortless grace through the water. A warm breeze blew her hair around her face and she held it back as best she could with one hand.

'This is all perfect.' She sighed, turning to him with a smile.

'Yes,' he said, but he was looking at her rather than the dolphins. 'It is.'

That was when Imogen made the mistake of looking into his eyes, and her smile faltered. It was just like the night before, when at least there had been the excuse of darkness for gazing back at him. Now she had dolphins to watch, the boat to discover, the thrill of the deep, dark ocean and the beauty of the sunset to distract her, and yet she still couldn't wrench her eyes from Tom's silvery-grey ones. They held an expression she had never seen before, one that she couldn't identify but which made her heart kick into a new, slower, re-verberating rhythm that sent the blood humming along her veins and lit a tremble of heat deep inside her.

Held together by an invisible skein, neither of them noticed that the sails were being lowered. They were oblivious to the boat turning or Ali readying the dinghy once more, and only a shout from the captain to a member of the crew jerked them back to awareness of where they were.

They both looked quickly away.

Tom cleared his throat. 'What's happening now?'

'I'm not sure. We're stopping for some reason. It's just a sandbar, but there's someone there…' Imogen peered over the beautifully carved wooden rail, not sure whether she was relieved or sorry at the distraction.

So much for all her stern resolutions this morning about putting last night behind her. All it took was one look in Tom's eyes and she was lost. Her pulse was thumping and she felt ridiculously shaky.

'It looks as if we're going ashore,' she said, forcing a smile, but avoiding his gaze. 'I've always wanted to go on a magical mystery tour, haven't you?'

'No,' said Tom, who was way out of his comfort zone. 'I like to know where I'm going.'

But he went readily enough when they were gestured to the

dinghy, and then ferried across the translucent shallows to the sandbar. Once there, it seemed obvious that they should get out, so Tom helped Imogen jump onto the sand and looked enquiringly at Ali.

'For you,' he said, pointing them towards a frail elderly man dressed in immaculate white who seemed to be waiting for them.

'What's going on?' Tom muttered out of the corner of his mouth as they headed obediently towards the old man.

'I've got no idea,' confessed Imogen, baffled, but when they got a bit closer she saw that a circle had been drawn in the sand and she stopped and tugged at Tom's sleeve.

'What is it?'

'I'm getting a bad feeling about this,' she whispered.

Tom glanced at the elderly man and then back at Imogen. He was just an old man, surely? What was so threatening about that?

'I think it might be set up for a wedding ceremony,' she told him.

'What?'

Tom's voice rose and she shushed him quickly. 'I read about it when I was finding out about honeymoons here for you. You can't actually get married here because it's a Muslim country, but you can have a special ceremony to bless your marriage or renew your vows.'

'And you booked one?' he asked, aghast.

'Of course not,' hissed Imogen, 'but what if Julia did? She might have thought it would be romantic. There's so much organisation that goes into a wedding, it sometimes seems hard for the bride and groom to really enjoy it and think about what they're promising in the ceremony. This way you'd have had time to relax after the wedding and say your vows again when you could really concentrate on each other.

'I think it's a nice idea,' she finished defiantly, reading the scepticism in Tom's expression without difficulty.

Now Tom thought about it, Julia *had* dropped some cryptic comments about their vows but he hadn't been listening properly. If he had, he would have told her that he couldn't imagine anything worse.

But it was too late for that now. 'If all this was booked in advance, why didn't they tell us anything about it when we arrived?'

'Perhaps they did,' said Imogen, remembering how distracted they had both been at the resort. 'Neither of us were really paying much attention to what the manager was saying.'

'I suppose not. God, what a mess!'

Tom cast a glance at the old man, who smiled encouragingly and beckoned them closer.

'What are we going to do?' asked Imogen in an urgent undertone.

'We'd better bluff it out,' Tom decided. 'It's too difficult to try and explain now. You're sure it's not a legal ceremony?'

'It's just symbolic.'

'There you are,' he said, taking her arm. 'It won't mean anything. Better five minutes of mumbo-jumbo than half an hour of awkward explanations.'

'I don't know…' Imogen hung back, not at all convinced, but Tom was urging her forwards and suddenly she was looking into the old man's face. It was very calm, and his eyes were wise.

'Your name?' he asked her, gesturing her into the circle.

'Imogen.'

'And Tom,' Tom supplied quickly before he was asked and stepped into the circle facing Imogen.

The celebrant nodded. 'You have come to celebrate your love for each other?'

'Er…yes.'

If he was surprised at their hesitation, he didn't show it. 'There are just the two of you. That is good,' he said. 'This is about you and no one else. This is your circle. Stand inside it, share it. It binds you together. It represents oneness—your oneness with each other and with the earth. It represents your love.'

Imogen bit her lip. It felt all wrong to be deceiving him, but it was too late to go back now. It didn't mean anything, she tried to remind herself, but as the old man's gentle words of blessing fell, an invisible net seemed to drop over the circle where she and Tom stood in the sand, drawing the two of them tighter and tighter together and cutting off the rest of the world.

The sun was setting fire to the sea that stretched all around the sandbar. It was an extraordinary, dream-like feeling to stand there in that blazing golden light, to be astonishingly aware of the soft white sand beneath her feet, and of Tom's hands holding hers in a warm, strong clasp.

Imogen didn't want to look at Tom, but she couldn't tear her eyes from his and she found herself hanging on to his hands as if he was all that could keep her anchored in reality.

The ceremony was very simple, and very moving. Held by the silver of Tom's eyes, Imogen heard the old man talking about love, about commitment, about finding completeness together, and every word seemed right.

'Imogen,' he finished at last, 'is this man, Tom, the man you love?'

She swallowed. 'Yes,' she said huskily, and her heart rang with the knowledge that it was true.

'Tom, is this woman, Imogen, the woman you love?'

Tom's voice was steadier than hers. 'Yes.'

'Imogen, take Tom's heart, hold it safe. And, Tom, take the heart Imogen gives you and cherish it. Love each other, be true to each other, find peace in each other. Find joy in each other always.'

Ridiculously, Imogen felt her eyes sting with tears. 'I will.'

'I will,' said Tom after the barest of pauses.

'Promise this with a kiss.'

Imogen's eyes locked with Tom's. She saw something flare in the silver depths, and her breath caught.

He was going to kiss her. Of course he was going to kiss her. He had no choice but to kiss her.

At last—at last!—he was going to kiss her.

The corners of Tom's mouth turned up very slightly as he let go of Imogen's hands to cup her face between his palms.

'I promise,' he said softly, so softly that she wondered if she was even supposed to hear it, and then his mouth touched hers.

His lips weren't cool at all. They were warm and firm and sure and so wickedly exciting that Imogen gave a tiny gasp, taken unawares by the intensity of the response that rocketed through her.

Tom's hands drifted down to slide beneath her hair so that he could cup her head and deepen his kiss, and Imogen's world dissolved into giddy delight as she let herself kiss him back the way she had so longed to do. Leaning into him, she slipped her arms around his waist and held tight to the sweetness of the moment.

It might turn out to be a mistake, she knew, but right then it felt utterly right and she murmured an inarticulate protest when Tom reluctantly broke the kiss and lifted his head.

Both of them had forgotten the old man, who was still standing there, watching them with a faint smile. Still reeling from the kiss they had shared, they barely noticed as he deftly looped their wrists together with a knotted twine made from shredded leaves.

He made a beautiful gesture with his hands. 'It is done,' he said simply and stepped back. 'You are bound together, and now you are one.'

'What have we done?'

All smiles, Ali had escorted them back to the *dhoni*, where Imogen had been greeted with a garland made of frangipani flowers. The heady fragrance was making her feel slightly sick as she and Tom were left alone in the prow at last. Or perhaps it was the way her senses were still spinning from the realisation of how much she loved him?

How much, and how hopelessly.

Now, as the sails unfurled and the boat dipped gently into the swell, Imogen held onto the rail, afraid that her trembling legs wouldn't hold her up any longer.

'We haven't done anything,' said Tom, unfastening the twine around their wrists. He hesitated, just for a moment, and then dropped it into the sea. 'It was a ritual,' he said. 'It didn't mean anything.'

Imogen watched the loop disappear and wanted to cry. It hadn't felt meaningless. 'We made promises,' she said with difficulty.

Tom looked away. She was right. And wasn't he the one who prided himself on always keeping his promises?

It had been the strangest of experiences, standing in that circle with Imogen. He had been feeling exasperated at the whole muddle, Tom remembered, but the moment he'd taken her hands and looked into those blue, blue eyes an inexplicable sense of relief had swept over him, as if, without knowing quite how it had happened, he'd found himself at exactly the right place at exactly the right time, doing just what he'd needed to do.

And then he had kissed her, and her sweetness had made him reel. The taste of her, the feel of her, the softness of her lips and the silkiness of her hair around his hands was still thrumming through him, beating insistently along his veins and making him feel…what? Edgy? Apprehensive? *Excited?*

Surely not.

'It wasn't real,' he said, wishing he didn't sound so much as if he were trying to convince himself. 'We're not really married.'

They couldn't be married. Neither of them wanted to be married. It was ridiculous to think anything had happened on that sandbar.

'No, of course not.' Imogen mustered a smile. 'I can hardly believe it actually happened, to tell you the truth. It was like a dream.'

'This whole week has been like a dream,' said Tom, coming to join her at the rail. 'It's as if we're in a kind of bubble with no connection to life at home.'

She nodded. 'Yes, that's exactly what it feels like.' She managed another smile, a better one this time. 'It's going to be a shock to wake up when we go home!'

'We don't have to wake up just yet.' Succumbing to temptation, Tom took Imogen's hands and turned her gently to face him. 'We could keep the dream going a little bit longer.'

His fingers were warm and persuasive around hers, and Imogen felt dizzy at his nearness again. 'The dream?' she croaked.

'That we're here because we want to be together,' he said. 'We both know it's not true, and that it couldn't last even if it were. As soon as we get back to London, everything will be different. The dream will be over. We won't be able to get it back, and we won't want to.'

Was he making any sense? Tom wondered. He wasn't sure if

he understood himself what he was trying to say to Imogen, and part of him was already wondering if he was making the most terrible mistake. But another, stronger part was urging him on.

'We're not the same people here that we are in London,' he said. 'We want different things at home but here…maybe here we want the same. I know what I want. I want to kiss you again. I want to touch you again. I don't want to spend another night on that damned couch thinking about you alone in the bed and wishing that I could be with you.'

Imogen was looking pole-axed, the blue eyes wide with astonishment. She opened her mouth to speak, but Tom was afraid to hear what she was going to say and he rushed on before she could start.

'I know you're still hung up on Andrew. I know you're hanging out for something perfect that I can't give you, but I was just thinking that while we're here, maybe it *could* be perfect. We both know this isn't real, but we've still got two weeks. Why not make the most of it?'

'You mean as if this really was a honeymoon?' Imogen found her voice at last. 'As if we meant those vows we've just taken?'

'Yes,' said Tom. 'We're not talking about forever,' he added quickly. 'As soon as we get back to London, we can forget about this time. We can pretend it never happened. But for now…now there's just the two of us, and we can…we can love each other, just like we've just promised.' He paused, looking down into her face, trying not to show how desperate he was for her to agree. 'What do you think?'

Imogen's fingers twined around Tom's. *It couldn't last*, he had said. *We're not talking about forever.* She was going to hurt when it was over, when she had to go back to being his PA and greeting him coolly every morning.

But she was going to hurt anyway, Imogen realised. That was what happened when you fell in love with a man like Tom.

It wasn't supposed to be like this. She had wanted the perfect relationship. She wasn't supposed to fall in love with a man who didn't do love, who would give her two weeks and no longer.

But she had done it anyway, and wasn't two weeks better than nothing? At least when they said goodbye, as they would in two weeks' time, she would have some memories to treasure. That would be all she would have, Imogen knew. There was no point in hoping that the dream would last.

Find joy in each other, the celebrant had told them. She could choose that, or she could choose to be sensible.

Imogen chose joy. It would be temporary, like everything else she did, but it would still be joy.

And how else was she to resist him for the next two weeks?

Smiling, she tugged her hands from Tom's to rest them flat against his chest and looked up at him. 'I think it's a very good idea,' she said.

Tom stared at her for a moment, as if hardly daring to believe what she had said, and then his eyes blazed and an answering smile illuminated his face. Sweeping her into his arms, he kissed her fiercely, hungrily, and Imogen melted into him, warm and willing, her fingers clutching at his shirt to stop herself from dissolving with sheer pleasure as the heat washed through her.

Giddy with the glorious relief of being able to kiss each other, touch each other, the way they had wanted to all week, they sank down onto the cushions under the darkening sky, crushing the frangipani garland between them. The fragrance of the creamy yellow flowers enveloped them, while the boat rose and fell, and there was only the shush of water against the hull, the creak of wood and the occasional flap of the sail.

The crew talked quietly at the back, giving Tom and Imogen complete privacy, but they were aware only of each other in any case. Tom's body was hard and heavy as he pressed her into the soft cushions, his hands sliding possessively under the yellow dress.

Imogen wrapped her arms around him and forgot everything else. She was sinking under a tide of heat. Every now and then she would surface, gasping, almost frightened by the need to touch him everywhere, feel him everywhere, and a tiny part of her would wonder if she was making a terrible mistake. But how could it be a mistake when his lips felt this good, when his mouth was this exciting, when his hands were moving over her, tracing wicked patterns of desire, and she was unravelling with the need for more, more, more…?

The stars were out above Coconut Island when they made their way back along the little jetty. Afterwards, Imogen could never remember exactly how they had got there. Ali must have taken them in the dinghy, she supposed, but all she remembered was the feel of the smooth bleached wood beneath her bare feet and the gentle slap of water against the posts. She was preternaturally aware of everything: of the silky dress whispering against her legs, of Tom's warm grip on her hand, of her mouth still tingling, her body still thumping with desire.

It all looked so familiar, she thought as they climbed the veranda steps. It all looked exactly the same when it should be different. Everything had changed since they had walked down these same steps to see Ali waiting for them at the end of the jetty.

Then they had been boss and PA; now they were husband and wife.

CHAPTER NINE

EXCEPT that they weren't, not really. Imogen's steps faltered at the sudden moment of clarity.

Tom was behind her, nuzzling her neck as he guided her through the door and pushed her back against it so that he could kiss her again, his hands hard and urgent. 'What is it?'

'You…you don't think we'll regret this?' she asked unsteadily, trying to hang on to the last shreds of rationality but it was hard when the feel of his lips on her bare shoulder was enough to make her inhale sharply.

'We're going to have to go back to working together,' she reminded him with difficulty as he started kissing his way down her throat. 'How are we going to do that if we…?'

'How are we going to spend the next two weeks if we don't…?' countered Tom, smiling wickedly against her skin. His fingers had found the zip of her dress and were easing it down. 'Let's just forget work for now.'

Imogen shivered at the sureness of his touch. She had a hazy idea that it wasn't going to be as easy as he made out, but she couldn't think, not with his hands sliding over her, not with his mouth devastating the last of her defences, not with the heat pooling deep inside her. It spilt feverishly along her veins until she stopped trying to think at all and gave herself up to the deep, dark spool of desire, to the feel of his mouth and his hands and his lean, hard body.

The bed was wonderfully wide. It was like being cast away, with the deep thrill of knowing that they were completely alone. There was no one to see them, no one to hear them. There was just the two of them, entwined, where nothing mattered but touching and tasting and feeling.

'Let's just think about being here,' whispered Tom in her ear. 'Let's just think about now.'

And so Imogen closed her mind to the future and did just that.

The days that followed stayed forever golden in Imogen's memory. At one level, things went on much as they had done before. In the mornings they explored the reef, while afternoons were spent on the beach, swimming, reading or just lying in the shade and talking.

Often Imogen was content just to sit and gaze at the sea, marvelling at the intensity of the light, of the blueness and the greenness and the pristine whiteness of the beach. She would inhale slowly, savouring the wonderfully clean, invigorating smell of sea and sunlight, feeling the heat in her nose, watching the way the breeze made the palms sway and sent their tattered shadows dancing over skin and sand.

She had never seen things so clearly before, had never been intoxicated by smell and touch and taste the way she was now. It was as if all her senses were supercharged with Tom at her side.

The laptop lay unopened now, as Tom succumbed to the dream-like atmosphere of the island. He liked to get up early in the morning, when Imogen was still asleep, and walk down to the jetty, when the light was pearly and the lagoon was quiet and still.

Imogen preferred the early evening. She loved washing off the tingling, salty feeling of too much sea and too much sun, and changing into something loose and comfortable. Tom would have made a cool drink by then, and they sat on the veranda together, watching the sun set. A hush fell over the island then, and in silence they watched the sky flush pink, deepening with astonishing speed to a blaze of orange and scarlet, while the sea shimmered and they both remembered standing on the sandbar, promising to love each other for ever in the same glowing light.

Once it had faded, the tropical night dropped with a speed Imogen could never get used to. It was the signal for the cicadas to start whirring and they would sit on, waiting for the bats to come swooping past the veranda and spotting the little geckos that darted up the walls.

Imogen wished they could stay on Coconut Island for ever. She loved the colours, the smell of the dried coconut husks on the beach, the hot wind that soughed through the trees and ruffled the surface of the lagoon.

Most of all, she loved being with Tom. She loved the long sweet nights, the mornings when he returned from his walk to wake her with drifting hands, the afternoons in the shade. She loved every moment when he touched her, every second that she could reach out for him and find him there.

But beneath the pleasure she took in every moment lurked the knowledge that it couldn't last. Imogen tried desperately to forget that this time would pass but, just when she least needed a reminder, some stern, sensible part of her brain would put up its hand and point out that the days were passing and that before too long she would have to go back to the greyness of London in March. Back to the squash of commuters on the Tube, coats steaming with rain, back to dripping umbrellas and Monday mornings. Back to being Tom's PA.

There would be no more nights together, no more lazy afternoons.

No more loving.

Imogen would push the thought away, but the days passed in relentless succession and suddenly it was their last evening on Coconut Island.

Leaning on the veranda railing next to Tom, she watched the sun setting in a blaze of crimson behind the reef.

I'm not ready, she wanted to cry. *I can't face this yet.*

But she would have to find a way to face it, and to reassure Tom that she hadn't forgotten what they had agreed.

She turned her glass between her fingers. 'Funny to think this is the last time we'll do this,' she said.

It was the last time they would watch the sun set together. The last time they would sit in the dark and watch the bats swoop and dive. The last time they would listen to the insects ratcheting up their whirring, creaking, rasping chorus.

The last time they would make love in that big bed.

She had known this time would come, Imogen reminded herself, squaring her shoulders. It wasn't as if it was a surprise. She had known all along that it would come to this.

'This time tomorrow we'll be back in London.'

'Yes,' said Tom heavily.

He ought to be glad. He would be going back to the office, back to where everything was straightforward and he knew where he was. He would be in control of his life again, not like here.

It was different here. The sun and the sea and the quietness had worn down his defences, and he had forgotten the lessons he had learnt so carefully—to guard his feelings, to keep control. He had let himself relax and lose himself in Imogen.

It had felt so right at the time but now Tom was beginning to wonder if he had made a terrible mistake.

At the time, it had seemed a sensible idea. Why spend another two weeks feeling frustrated when they could come to an agreement as two consenting adults? It was all going to be so easy. They had a definite time limit. There would be no awkward discussions about when or how to say goodbye. The two weeks would end, and it would be over. Simple as that.

But he hadn't counted on how quickly he would get used to Imogen, to her laughter and her warmth and the wild, unexpected passion that had ensnared them both.

He hadn't counted on the way his body would crave hers like this. He had always been so controlled, and yet now he had this constant urge to touch her, to slide his hands over her and taste the sun and the salt on her skin, to feel her smile against his throat.

He wouldn't be able to do that any more.

Tom tried to tell himself that it would be fine, that he would have work to distract him, but whenever he tried to imagine sleeping without Imogen's softness curved into him, or waking early in the morning and not being able to turn to her, he felt something twist uncomfortably deep inside him and a bleakness crept into his chest.

'Perhaps it will all feel different when we get home,' he said, hoping that it was true.

'I'm sure it will,' said Imogen brightly. 'It's been lovely, but we both know it's not real. Real will be going into work on Monday morning, and dealing with everything that's happened while we've been away. We'll be too busy to remember anything but the fact that I'm your PA and you're my boss.'

She seemed very confident, thought Tom, but why wouldn't she be? They had made a deal that this would be a time out of time. He could hardly blame her if that was how she was treating it. It had been his idea, after all.

The sunset was as spectacular as ever, but Tom didn't even see it. He was confused and uneasy at the way everything was slipping out of control. How had it happened? When had he started to *feel* like this?

It had been easy when he was with Julia. He had known exactly where he was and what he wanted. But with Imogen… The truth was that Tom had never felt the way he did now. Intellectually, he could see that she was the last kind of woman he should fall in love with, but somewhere along the line she had become essential to him in a way he couldn't define. All he knew was that after living with her, laughing with her, loving with her, the thought of life without her made him feel inutterably bleak.

If this was love, Tom didn't like it.

This wasn't the joyous feeling Imogen had described. It was the gut-wrenching sensation of standing on the edge of an abyss.

And what if it *wasn't* love? Tom didn't trust this new feeling. It was too uncomfortable, too unfamiliar. He certainly didn't trust it enough to say anything to Imogen. Less than a month ago, he had been sure that he wanted to marry Julia. Why would Imogen believe that he had changed his mind so completely? Tom wasn't even sure that he believed it himself.

Hadn't they been clear right from the start that this was just a temporary thing? They were making the most of things, no more than that. What they had found together wasn't important. It wasn't something that could last.

No, he couldn't say anything, he had decided. If he blurted out that he was in love with her, he would embarrass her, and if it turned out that he didn't once they got home, he would hurt her, and Tom couldn't bear the thought of that.

And, of course, if he did say something, Imogen might say no. She might reject him, and Tom wasn't sure that he could handle that either. Not again.

The truth, he acknowledged to himself, was that he didn't dare say anything. He couldn't risk everything he was on feelings that he wasn't sure about. And so he had been imperceptibly distancing himself over the last two or three days. Better to wait until they were home, he convinced himself, and he could tell whether these strange new feelings were real or just part of this fantasy place.

Imogen had picked up on his subtle withdrawal and had drawn her own conclusions. Tom was already thinking about going home, about working together again, she decided. Was he trying to find the words to remind her that what they had was only ever intended to be temporary? She would have to make things easy for him. He would be dreading a conversation where feelings might be mentioned.

She wasn't looking forward to it herself, but it had to be done. They couldn't just leave and not acknowledge what the last three weeks had been like, but she would have to make it clear that she understood completely that tomorrow it would be over.

Tom still had the fallout from his engagement to Julia to face on his return. He would be preoccupied with that and with work. If she told him how desperately she had fallen in love with him it would just make him acutely uncomfortable. He didn't need that to deal with as well.

No, the best thing she could do for him was to get back to normal as soon as possible; the best thing she could do for herself was to stop fooling herself there could ever be any future in it and make a new life for herself.

The best thing for both of them would be to pretend that these last three weeks had never happened.

Imogen set her glass on the railing, put on a big smile and turned to face Tom properly.

'It's been so wonderful,' she told him. 'I'll never forget this time we've spent together, Tom. It's going to be hard getting used to travelling in less than the lap of luxury, but whenever I get to a beach or see a palm tree, I'll think of you.'

Whenever she closed her eyes or felt the sun on her face or lay in the dark, she would think of him.

She would think of him with every breath, miss him with every beat of her heart.

Tom eyed her broodingly over the top of his glass. 'You still want to go travelling then?'

'Of course.' Imogen kept her smile bright. 'Even more so now, in fact. Being here has given me a real taste for travel.'

She turned back to look out at the lagoon. There was a crimson line along the horizon where the sun had finally disappeared, and the darkness was closing in. The bats would be out any minute now.

'I may not find anywhere as perfect as this, but there will be other beautiful places,' she said.

Places without Tom.

A silence fell. The shrilling of the insects was very loud as it stretched and stretched, until neither could stand it any longer. Inevitably, they both spoke at the same time.

'Imogen—'

'Do you—'

Both stopped awkwardly.

'You first,' said Imogen.

'I just wanted to say…well, it's going to be hard to talk about this when we get back,' said Tom 'It's probably better if we don't, if we just pretend this time never happened, but I want you to know that I'm grateful for everything you've done.'

'You don't need to thank me,' said Imogen. 'I've had a wonderful time.'

'Really?'

'Really,' she said and, as their gazes locked and held, Tom reached out and drew her towards him.

'I'll miss you,' he confessed.

'I'll miss you too,' she whispered, her arms sliding round his neck. 'It's hard to believe that this time tomorrow this will all be over.'

Tom bent his head to find her mouth. 'It's not over yet.'

Imogen swallowed hard as the plane descended through the grey clouds above Heathrow. This was it. The end of blue skies, the end of bright light, the end of the dream.

They had had one last bittersweet night of loving, but that morning they had dressed in silence. Tom had put on his suit again for the journey back. Imogen was wearing the jeans and top that she had travelled out in. After all this time in little more than a sarong, the clothes felt heavy and constricting and her sandals were awkward to walk in.

When Ali had appeared with the dinghy to take them back to the resort, Tom had helped her into the boat for the first stage of that long, inexorable journey. It would be the last time he touched her.

Imogen felt like a snail being torn from its shell, wrenched away from the island, away from the warm blue ocean, dragged across the skies when, with every fibre of her being, she longed to be back under the coconut palms, sitting next to Tom and watching the breeze ruffle the still surface of the lagoon.

Tom was sitting beside her on the plane, but there the similarity ended. They had spoken little on the long flight. His face was set in grim lines, just as it had been on the journey out, and, sensing his withdrawal, Imogen lifted her chin and withdrew in her turn.

He needn't be afraid that she was going to cling, she told herself. She had no intention of embarrassing him by telling him how much she loved him. That hadn't been part of the deal at all. Tom Maddison wasn't the only one who kept his promises.

Down, down into the cloud cover sank the plane and Imogen's heart sank with it. Staring out of the window, she felt a pang as the last of the bright blue sky linking them to the Indian Ocean disappeared and the light dulled and it was just London in March, grey and overcast.

Then it was all happening too fast. They were first off the plane, their baggage appeared quickly and they were heading through Customs before Imogen had a chance to think about how she was going to say goodbye to Tom, before she could find a way to pretend that her heart wasn't breaking.

She tried to stall, wishing frantically that time would somehow slow down, but Tom was already striding onwards, eager, it seemed, to get back to real life. He paused at the exit, his hard gaze sweeping over the crowd in the Arrivals Hall until he identified his driver.

'There's Larry.' He headed towards him. 'He should have the car waiting just outside. Where would you like to go?'

'Actually,' said Imogen, hanging back, 'I think I'll get the Tube.'

Tom frowned. 'It'll be much quicker in a car at this time of day.'

'It's not that.' She forced a smile. 'I think I need to start getting back to normal,' she tried to explain. 'I've had three weeks of lovely luxury, but that's not my life. The next time I'm at an airport, I'll have a backpack and the cheapest ticket I can get.'

Her bag was slipping from her shoulder and she hoisted it back, keeping her smile firmly in place. 'I may as well get used to it now.'

Panic gripped Tom by the throat. He had spent the flight planning how to say goodbye. He couldn't do it on the plane, with flight attendants hovering the whole time. There were too many other people at the baggage carousel. The back of the car would be their only chance for any privacy, he had decided, but now Imogen wanted to say goodbye there and then in the middle of the busy terminal and the careful words he had prepared were promptly wiped from his memory.

'Whatever you like,' he said stiffly instead.

That reference to travelling had obviously been designed to remind him that she had plans that didn't include him. Perhaps it was just as well they would say goodbye here. God only knew what would have come tumbling out if they had been alone in the back of the car with him trying to keep his hands off her.

'So...' Imogen lifted her arms a little helplessly and dropped them back to her sides '...I guess this is it.'

'Yes,' said Tom. There was a sharp ache in the back of his throat. 'I guess it is.'

'See you on Monday, then?'

He nodded. 'Have a good weekend.'

'You too. Well...bye, boss.' From somewhere Imogen produced a brilliant smile, then she turned and walked away towards the signs for the Underground.

'Goodbye, Imogen.'

Tom stood in the busy concourse with the crowds surging around him and watched her go, and felt bleaker than he ever had in his life. He wanted to run after her, to stop her going through the ticket barrier, to drag her onto the next plane to the Maldives.

But he couldn't do that. Imogen had her own life, her own plans, and she had made it very clear that they didn't include him. She was off to see the world. That was what she wanted, what she needed to do. She was young, beautiful, outgoing. Why would she stay with a man like him—older, driven, a self-confessed workaholic?

He was no fun, Tom knew. He had always been too busy striving for success to be distracted by fun. Imogen deserved someone who would cherish her gaiety and ability to live in the moment. She deserved better than him.

He was better off on his own, anyway, Tom decided, making a determined effort to shake off the sickeningly empty feeling. He couldn't manage this relationship business. He had tried commitment with Julia, and look what had happened! Failure and humiliation.

He wasn't risking rejection again. He might miss Imogen a bit when she went, but he would get just as used to the new PA eventually, and she wouldn't distract him the way Imogen did now. It wasn't as if he and Imogen could ever have had anything in common, Tom reminded himself. They were too different. It could never have lasted.

No, Tom thought as he turned to find his driver, it was all for the best.

Imogen tugged at her jacket as she watched the lift doors close. Her suit felt heavy and uncomfortable, and her feet were cramped in the unfamiliar shoes.

It had been a long weekend. She had smiled and smiled when she'd got into the flat, but Amanda hadn't been fooled for a minute.

'I *knew* this would happen! You're in love with him, aren't you?'

Imogen opened her mouth to deny it and then admitted defeat. 'Yes,' she admitted, 'I am.' But her voice cracked and, in spite of herself, her brave smile wavered and collapsed miserably. 'But it's hopeless, I know that. He doesn't want me now.'

It didn't take long for Amanda to get the whole story out of her. 'I don't think you should give up so easily, Imo,' she said when Imogen had finished and was scrubbing her wet cheeks with a tissue. 'It sounds to me as if this Tom wanted you just as much as you wanted him.'

'That was on the island. He made it very clear that it was just a temporary thing.'

Amanda sniffed. 'Hmm, well, in my experience, it's not what men *say* that matters, it's what they *do*, and he wouldn't have been sleeping with you unless that's what he wanted. It's all very well to decide that you're going to forget it ever happened, but it'll be a very different matter when you're working together. If you're going to be remembering what it was like, chances are that he's going to be doing the same.'

Was it possible? Imogen wondered. Could Tom be missing her too? Or had he already filed her mentally under 'finished business'? He had emotions, she knew, but he kept them locked tightly away, the way he had learnt to do ever since he was a small boy, learning that his mother wasn't coming back. It would be too much to expect him to suddenly get in touch with his feelings, or to assume that those feelings might be about her. It wasn't that long since he had been hurt by Julia, after all.

But...

But perhaps Amanda was right and she shouldn't give up all hope, Imogen began to think tentatively. Surely Tom couldn't have kissed her like that, made love to her like that, if he didn't feel *anything* for her? He had never actually said what he felt, but the physical connection between them had been real enough.

She missed him dreadfully. She missed his lovely, solid male body next to hers. She missed the sound of his voice, reverberating over her skin. She missed the smile in his eyes when he drew her to him.

If she could have that again, might that not be enough? Imogen wondered as she lay achingly alone in her bed. If she could hold him again, feel him again, this awful ache might not be so bad. Tom might not be ready to fall in love, but perhaps he would consider continuing the arrangement they had had on the island…

The idea slid into Imogen's mind and stayed there, impossible to dislodge. But why *wouldn't* it work? she reasoned. She wouldn't ask for commitment. She wouldn't expect him to tell her he loved her. All she wanted was to be with him.

She couldn't blurt it out, of course. Tom would be horrified if she went all emotional on him. She would have to see what he was like on Monday, but if he had missed her a fraction of the way she had missed him, perhaps there was a chance…

It was enough to set Imogen's blood fizzing at the thought of seeing him again as the lift slid upwards. She was sharing it with two others and, although she only recognized them enough to smile, she was burningly aware of their interested glances. They obviously knew exactly who she was.

She had already had a taste of the speculation rife in the office about what she and Tom had got up to while they had been away. The girls on the reception desk had welcomed her back, exclaimed over her tan and clearly not believed a word of her insistence that it had been no more than a business trip.

There would be more of that to come, Imogen knew.

Perhaps she should wait until the intense interest had died down before she said anything to Tom about resuming the relationship they had had on the island. She certainly wouldn't embarrass him by acting all doe-eyed around him.

In fact, she should make it clear that she was sticking to their agreement to pretend that nothing had happened until she had some sense of what Tom himself wanted.

Still, her heart hitched in anticipation as she nodded goodbye to the others, stepped out of the lift and hurried along the opulent corridor to her office. The trouble was that she had been thinking too much. Better to just go in and be herself, instead of preparing what she would say. She hadn't had to prepare on Coconut Island, so why start now?

But, after all that, Tom wasn't in his office. Bitterly disappointed, Imogen sat at her desk and spun slowly in the chair.

It felt odd to be back. The island still seemed real, and all this a not wholly comfortable dream. She looked at her watch. This time the week before they had been snorkelling. She had a sudden vivid picture of Tom surfacing beside her, pulling off his mask, flicking the water out of his hair and smiling at her. The sunlight bouncing off the water had thrown a rocking pattern over his skin, and his eyelashes had been dark and spiky and a startling contrast to the silver-grey eyes.

The memory pierced Imogen like a skewer and she swung her chair back to face her desk and switched on her computer. Distraction, that was what she needed.

Her inbox was dauntingly full. It was a long time since she had last checked her email on Coconut Island, since Tom had pushed his laptop aside and suggested a swim instead. Imogen could still feel the delicious coolness of the lagoon as she sank into the wa—

But she wasn't supposed to be wallowing in those memories. She caught herself up guiltily and scowled at the computer screen as she forced herself to concentrate. Working doggedly through the messages, she did so well that she didn't even notice that Tom had arrived and was watching her from the doorway.

It had been the longest weekend of Tom's life. He had spent it in his sterile apartment, trying to work out what was so different now and, when he did, it came as a shock.

He was lonely.

Tom was furious with himself. He had *never* been lonely. On the contrary, he'd always felt most comfortable on his own, but now...now he was used to Imogen being there. He missed her sweetness and her warmth, and without it he felt cold and somehow empty.

He told himself that he just needed a couple of days to adjust. He thought that he *had*, but the sight of Imogen at her desk left him feeling literally gutted, as if a great fist had reached inside him and wrenched out his entrails.

Engrossed in her emails, she looked composed and unfamiliar, as if she had never laughed in the sunshine, never rolled on top of him and let her hair tickle his bare chest, never teased him with soft kisses.

Never stood on that sandbar and promised to love him for ever.

The suit, the hair pulled back from her face, the air of efficiency all spelt a clear message. She was sticking to the agreement they had made. She was pretending that the past three weeks had never happened and that she was just his PA once more.

He should be grateful, Tom knew. Imogen was making things easy for him. This was his chance to step back and decide how he really felt, but all he could think was that she was making it impossible for him to stride over to the desk, yank her up and into his arms and kiss her the way he really wanted.

That would be madness, of course. It would be a ridiculous, rash, *risky* way to carry on. It would mean he had lost control altogether, and control was all he had to hang on to at the moment.

So in the end all he did was wish her a good morning from the safe distance of the doorway.

Imogen's head jerked up and Tom was momentarily comforted by the blaze of expression in her blue eyes, but it was so quickly veiled that he wondered if he had imagined it just because he wanted to see it so much.

'Good morning,' she replied with some constraint. 'Did you have a good weekend?'

Her cool politeness sent ice creeping over Tom's heart. It was just as well he hadn't grabbed her and kissed her.

'Yes, thank you,' he replied, equally polite, equally cool. There was no point now in confessing to Imogen that he had spent his entire time missing her. 'And you?'

'Fine, thanks,' lied Imogen.

There was an awkward pause.

'You're in early,' said Tom eventually.

'I wanted to get on with things,' she said. 'There's lots to do.'

CHAPTER TEN

THE memory of the island was thundering around the room but Imogen wasn't going to be the first to mention it. What could she say, anyway? *Oh, remember how we lay on the beach and looked at the stars? Remember how it felt to hold hands and feel as if the earth was turning beneath us? Remember how we made love right there and then had to shower off all the sand before we went to bed?*

So she smiled coolly without quite meeting his eyes and handed him a folder. 'These are the most urgent messages.'

Daunted by her composure, Tom took the folder but didn't open it. 'Have you still got the key to Julia's flat?' he asked abruptly.

'I should have.' Imogen rummaged in her drawer. She had used the key when she had returned the wedding presents before they'd left for Coconut Island. 'Yes, here it is,' she said, producing the key and forcing her mind away from the island. Stupid how it took so little for the memories to come swirling back. 'Do you need it back?'

'I was wondering if you could do a job for me,' said Tom, and she assembled a smile from somewhere.

'That's what I'm here for.'

'I spoke to Julia at the weekend,' he told her. 'It turns out that Patrick is going to work in some out-of-the-way place in South America, and Julia's going with him. I can't see her lasting out there,' he admitted, 'but she seems determined to start a new life.

'She hasn't got time to come back to London and sort out the apartment before she goes,' he went on, 'and the agents need it to be cleared so that they can let it again. She just took a small bag with her when she went off with Patrick and, although she hadn't moved everything over here, there will still be some clothes and other stuff left. She says she doesn't want any of it,' Tom finished, 'so she asked if I would get rid of anything that's there. It can all go to charity or the dump.'

Imogen ached at the distant note in Tom's voice. Talking to Julia must have been difficult for him, she knew. He had told her that he didn't love Julia, and Imogen believed him, but she knew how much the other woman's rejection had hurt his pride. Imogen had found it hard settling back into normal life, but how much harder must it be for Tom, who had had to return to an empty flat and the reminder that the perfect life he had planned with Julia had fallen apart?

'Would you like me to deal with that for you?' she said, anticipating his request.

'Thank you,' said Tom.

His formality broke Imogen's heart but she kept her smile in place. 'I'll get on with it as soon as I can.'

In fact, it wasn't until after work that Thursday that Imogen had time to get to the exclusive apartment Julia had rented in Chelsea.

It had been a very long four days, and Imogen was exhausted with the effort of keeping a smile on her face and parrying the not-so-subtle questions of her colleagues, who were desperate to know more about the time she had spent with Tom. Which was hard when she was just as desperate *not* to think about it.

She and Tom had both been careful to avoid any reference to Coconut Island. Inevitably, the atmosphere in the office was strained, but Imogen didn't think they had been doing too badly until one of their senior shareholders had come to see Tom earlier that afternoon. When the meeting was over, Tom had walked him out to Imogen's office and helped him on with his coat while he'd continued to complain about protection orders.

'The world's run mad.' He snorted. 'Next thing we know, flies and slugs will have protection orders! Last year we had bats roosting in the roof and we weren't allowed to get rid of them! Absolutely ridiculous,' he grumbled. 'Bats, I ask you! Horrible little things. Have you ever seen them?'

Over his shoulder, Tom's eyes met Imogen's. 'Yes, I have' was all he said, but it was as if they were both transported back to the veranda on Coconut Island, to the hot tropical dusk and the bats darting and diving in the air. Imogen could practically feel the chair beneath her thighs, almost smell the frangipani drifting through the darkness, and hear the insects whirring and chirruping.

She knew Tom was remembering too. She could see it in the silver-grey eyes as their gazes locked and there was just the two of them, held in thrall by the memory of those long, sweet evenings.

'Well, I'd better get on,' the shareholder was saying, digging in his pockets for his gloves. 'Good to see you again, Tom. Oh, and by the way, I meant to say that I was very sorry to hear about that business in February,' he added gruffly.

'Business?' Tom sounded distracted.

'Your wedding...most unfortunate.' He was obviously embarrassed at having to be specific.

'Oh, that…yes…thank you.'

Imogen was thinking about that exchange as she put the key in the lock and let herself into Julia's apartment.

Tom hadn't said anything when he'd come back from escorting the shareholder to the lift but something had changed with that meeting of their eyes, Imogen was convinced, and she hugged the possibility to her. Perhaps she didn't need to despair, after all.

Wandering from room to room in Julia's gorgeous flat, Imogen let herself dream. Maybe she would go into the office tomorrow and be talking about work when Tom would throw the file they were discussing onto the desk and say he couldn't bear it without her any more. He would sweep her into his arms and tell her she was the one he really wanted. He'd beg her to marry him and stay with him for ever.

Even if he didn't tell her that he loved her, it would be enough, Imogen decided. A man like Tom couldn't suddenly pull all his emotions out of a hat, but there *had* been a chemistry between them, and today it had seemed as if it was still there. They could build on that. She could teach him how to love. She didn't care as long as they could be together.

They could live somewhere like this. Imogen loved this apartment. It had lots of space and light, with a wonderful view of the Thames. She couldn't help comparing it with the flat she shared with Amanda. There was nothing wrong with that, but it was very small and a bit shabby. They had fun there, of course, but this was the kind of place you lived in when you were grown up, when you had made a success of your career and were going to marry a man like Tom.

Dreamily, Imogen opened the wardrobe in the bedroom. Julia hadn't spent much time in London, but it was still full of beautiful clothes. Imogen whistled soundlessly as she checked the labels. Amanda would be wild with envy. This lot ought to raise a lot of money for some lucky charity shop.

Fantasising all the while about living there with Tom, Imogen folded the outfits carefully and put them on the bed, ready to be packed into boxes for collection. She would have to deal with Julia's wedding dress separately. It was hanging in a gorgeous cover behind the door and was much too big to fit in any of the boxes.

Imogen couldn't resist having a look at it. Drawing down the zip, she let out an involuntary sigh of longing. It was exquisite. Very gently she touched the shimmering ivory fabric, marvelling at the detail in the delicately beaded design. Julia had sent her a sketch of the design, but she hadn't realised how beautiful it would be when it was made up. This was the wedding dress every girl dreamed of, a dress that would make you look like a princess—gorgeous and utterly romantic.

Lifting it down, she drew off the cover and held the dress up against her, imagining wearing it at her own wedding.

She was walking down the aisle on her father's arm in the village church. He was bursting with pride, her mother was sniffing into a handkerchief, her brothers were rolling their eyes but happy for her anyway. Amanda was there too, ready to step up and take her bouquet when the moment came.

Imogen could practically feel the stone floor beneath her feet and smell that mixture of musty kneeling cushions, old hymn books and wooden pews worn smooth by generations.

In her mind, she looked towards the altar and there was Tom, looking devastating in an austere morning suit. For a moment, she wondered if it could possibly be true, but then the stern features softened as he turned to watch her coming up the aisle, and he smiled at her, the silvery-grey eyes alight with love…

Reluctantly, Imogen wrenched herself from the dream and

stroked the beautiful dress longingly. What would it be like to wear a dress like this?

Find out.

The thought slid insidiously into her head and lodged there. Why *not* try it on, after all? It wasn't her dress...but Julia didn't want it. What harm could it do, just to see what she would look like as a bride?

Imogen dithered, then made up her mind. Quickly, she pulled off her clothes and examined the dress in her bra and knickers. Unzipping it carefully, she stepped into the skirt and pulled up the bodice in front of the mirror. The heavy silk felt gorgeous against her skin.

Smiling at her reflection, Imogen reached for the side zip—and the dream promptly shattered under the crashing fist of reality.

There was no way this zip was ever going to do up with her inside it.

Imogen watched her smile wiped out by a wash of humiliation, and a blotchy tide of embarrassed colour surged up her throat. There might as well have been a crowd of spectators, pointing and jeering.

What had she been *thinking*? She knew how slender and elegant Julia was. She had to be a good three sizes bigger than Tom's erstwhile fiancée. Of *course* she wasn't going to fit into Julia's dress.

Of course she wasn't going to fit into Julia's life.

Because that was what she really wanted, Imogen realised dully. She wanted to be slim and sophisticated and beautiful and clever and the kind of woman Tom really wanted to share his life. But she wasn't any of those things. She had to face reality, and the reality was that Tom Maddison was out of her league. He was never going to love her. If he couldn't love

Julia, he couldn't love anyone, and she would be fooling herself if she let herself believe otherwise.

And Imogen needed to be loved. That had been the dream, she understood now. It wasn't the wedding, or the dress. It was that moment of looking at Tom and believing that he loved her.

Well, it wasn't going to happen, and she had to accept that. No matter what she told herself about chemistry, it wouldn't be enough.

A fantasy, Tom had called it. Well, maybe it was, but Imogen knew that nothing else would do. *I'm not prepared to settle for anything less than love*, she had told him, and she was right. She had thought that she could compromise, but she couldn't.

Miserably, she stepped out of the dress and put it back on its hanger, before carrying it over to lay it on the pile destined for the charity shop. Someone was going to get a fabulous bargain.

But it wasn't going to be her.

'That's it for now.' Imogen closed her notebook and got to her feet. 'Except…' she fished in a folder for a piece of paper and passed it across the desk to Tom '…I thought you would like to see the job description I've prepared.'

'Job description?'

'For your new PA.'

Tom felt as if she had reached across the desk and slapped him.

'You're leaving?'

'I told you that I was planning to travel.'

'I thought you said June?' The words felt unwieldy in his mouth and he had to force himself to take the sheet of paper.

'I've advanced my plans a bit,' said Imogen. 'I've got a great deal on a flight to Australia leaving in a month.'

A *month*? Tom felt sick. She obviously couldn't wait to get away.

He stared at the job description, but the words danced in front of his eyes. He should have expected this, he knew. It wasn't as if she hadn't told him very clearly that she wanted to travel. Now he felt a fool for letting himself hope that she would want to stay after all.

It had been stupid of him to even think about trying to find a way back to how things had been on the island.

He had wanted to be careful, knowing that it would be a mistake to rush into anything. Even if Julia's desire to rush into marriage hadn't taught him a lesson, Tom needed to be sure about what he felt. Imogen wasn't like any other girl-friend he had ever had. She didn't fit into his life the way Julia had. She was disturbing, distracting. She had thrown him into turmoil and made him question everything he'd ever thought he wanted. Tom didn't like the way it left him feeling churned up and out of control.

There had been part of him hoping that this feeling would pass. He didn't want to hurt Imogen by telling her that he wanted her, and then realising that he didn't. Tom knew what it was like to be messed around, and he wasn't going to do to Imogen what Julia had done to him.

It was just as well he hadn't said anything, Tom decided. Imogen had obviously been making her own plans, and it would have been awkward for her to find a kind way to let him down. At least this way he would be spared the humiliation of having his feelings thrown back in his face.

This way, he hadn't risked exposing himself only to be left again.

It was probably all for the best, in fact.

'That looks fine,' he said and handed the job description

back to Imogen, not having read a word of it. 'Pass it on to HR and tell them it's urgent. I want someone in place before you go.'

Imogen took a final look around her office. No, not hers. It had only ever been temporary, like everything else in her life. She had a temporary job, a temporary relationship on the island, and now she was going off on a temporary trip. When she came back, Imogen vowed, she was going to settle and make something permanent.

But the only permanence she wanted was Tom. The last month had been horrible. Oh, she had put a good face on it. She had smiled and pretended that she was looking forward to her trip. She had told herself that once she got to Australia everything would feel different, but that was what she had told herself after Coconut Island, wasn't it?

Imogen didn't believe it now. She knew that wanting Tom didn't get easier, that loving him didn't get any less. Her memories of the island were no less vivid now than they had been the day after they came back. She couldn't bear the thought of leaving him, but she couldn't bear to stay. Much better to face reality. It would be all too easy to waste her life hoping for the impossible.

What was the point of hankering after a man who didn't know how to love? She might love Tom, but he could never make her happy. She needed to love someone who would love her back, who needed her the way she needed him, and that someone wasn't Tom.

For the past month he had been distant and their conversation largely limited to work, although every now and then he had asked after her plans, as if to underline the fact that he was perfectly happy with her going. He had appointed a new

PA, a coolly efficient woman called Judy with impressive qualifications and tons of high-level experience, who would suit Tom perfectly. He wouldn't miss *her* at all.

Facing reality hurt.

'Come on, Imogen, we're all waiting for you.' Sue from HR was beckoning from the door. 'You can't be late for your own farewell party.'

'I've never had a party when leaving a temp job before,' said Imogen as they made their way down to one of the conference rooms. She was baffled by the fuss everyone was making. 'I've only been here a few months.'

'It feels like longer,' said Sue. 'We're all going to miss you. Wait until you see the turnout!'

Imogen's throat tightened when she saw how many people had come to say goodbye and wish her well. She smiled shakily. 'Stop being so nice! You're going to make me wish I wasn't leaving.'

'Oh, yes, of course you'd rather stay here with us than go to Australia!'

There was much good-natured envy of her travels. Imogen plastered on a big smile and agreed that she was incredibly lucky, but all the time she was aware that Tom wasn't there. He had had to go to a meeting, but he had said that he would be back in time for her farewell party.

Imogen dreaded saying goodbye to him, but perhaps it would be better to do it in front of everyone else. An audience might stop her making a complete fool of herself.

'Where's the boss?' grumbled Neville from Finance. 'We can't start the party until he's done the speech.'

'We can't start the party until he's gone,' said someone else. 'He's not exactly a bundle of fun, is he?'

Imogen wanted to tell them they didn't know what he was

really like, but there had been more than enough interest in her relationship with Tom. She was fairly sure that a lot of those there were hoping that there would be some juicy titbit of gossip in his speech.

'Here he is now,' she heard someone say, and she turned to see Tom filling the doorway, looking stern and massive and gorgeous. Imogen's heart ripped at the sight of him. How did he do that? All he had to do was stand there and look like that, and her breath caught and longing snarled in her like barbed wire.

Across the room his eyes met hers for a long, jarring moment, then he was looking away, inclining his head to hear something the Director of HR was saying. He nodded, and then stepped up onto a dais at the front of the room.

Imogen was being nudged forward too. She knew what to expect. She had been to enough excruciating farewell bashes. There would be an awkward speech, the presentation of a jokey present and a gift token of some kind, and then it would be her turn to make a speech. Well, there was nothing to be done but hope that it was over as soon as possible.

But what if Tom left as soon as the speeches were over? She wouldn't have a chance to say goodbye to him properly, Imogen realised in a sudden panic. She didn't want to say it in front of everyone after all. She wanted to tell him what he had meant to her, but how could she do that with them all watching? *I love you* wasn't the kind of thing you could say with an audience.

Someone was chinking a glass, and the room fell silent while Imogen was still feverishly trying to work out how she could tell Tom what she felt. All at once it was imperative that she did. How could she have even thought she could go away without saying anything?

She barely heard the Director of HR introducing Tom, but

she saw Tom take a step forward and clear his throat. He looked very grim, as if he would rather be almost anywhere else, and Imogen didn't blame him.

Tom looked at the sea of faces turned expectantly towards him. They were all waiting for him to deliver the usual tribute: always ready with a smile…will be much missed…wishing her all the best on her travels, blah, blah, blah. Tom had it all ready but, as he opened his mouth, he realised that he couldn't do it. He couldn't trot out some bland speech to Imogen. He couldn't pretend that she was just like everyone else when his heart was seething with the truth.

'You're all here because, even though Imogen hasn't been here very long, she's become part of the company,' he began slowly. 'She's been a good colleague to you and I'm sure you're going to miss her, but you're not going to miss her the way I will. When Imogen walks out of the door tonight, it's going to be like a light in my life that's been switched off.'

There was a sudden riveted silence in the room as everyone did a double take and checked with their neighbour that they hadn't misheard.

'The thing is, I've got used to her smile, to the way she sucks in her breath when she's annoyed.' Tom could hardly believe what he was saying, but the words just kept coming. 'I'll miss how she laughs on the phone, the perfume that she always wears. I'll miss the way my heart stops whenever she walks into the room, and how the day seems brighter and better when she's there.'

The room had fallen utterly silent by now, but Tom had forgotten everyone else. His attention was fixed on Imogen, who had been pushed to the front and was staring at him, blue eyes enormous. Now that he had started, it was easy, he realised.

All he had to do was tell her everything that had been churning inside him since they'd returned from Coconut Island.

'I'm sorry if I'm embarrassing you,' he told her. 'If it's any comfort, I know I'm making the most colossal fool of myself too, but I just can't let you go without telling you how I feel. I've tried not to need you. I told myself that I would soon get used to it once you'd gone, but it's too late for me now. If you're not there, I can't get comfortable, nothing seems quite right, and when I look at what my life will be without you, I don't see success, I just see a flat, empty tundra I have to get across somehow.'

Imogen was still staring incredulously. Tom didn't blame her. He had never taken such a risk before, had never felt as if he were at the mercy of forces beyond his control the way he did now. He was terrified.

'I love you,' he told her, without taking his eyes from hers. 'There, I've said it! I didn't want to fall in love with you—I didn't think I *could*—and I've been trying to persuade myself that what we had on Coconut Island was just a temporary thing. I told myself this feeling would go away, but, Imogen, I don't think it's going to,' said Tom quietly. 'I think I'm going to spend the rest of my life missing you and the way you make me feel.

'I wasn't going to say anything,' he went on after a moment. 'I thought it would be awkward and embarrassing for both of us—as indeed it has been!' he added with a rueful smile. 'But you told me once that sometimes we have to be prepared to fail, and I guess that's what I'm doing now, but I don't want you to go without telling you what you've done for me. You've changed my life. I didn't understand when you told me that you were looking for someone who would complete you, but I do now. You've made me realise that I don't have your warmth and your laughter and that without them, without *you*, I'll never be quite right.'

He hesitated, wondering if he was making sense. 'I thought I was comfortable before. I thought I knew exactly what I wanted and what I needed to do, but the truth is that knowing you is the only thing that makes my life feel worthwhile.'

To his horror, Tom saw tears shining in Imogen's eyes. 'You don't need to worry,' he hurried on. 'I'm not expecting you to say anything. I know you've got plans, and I hope you'll have a wonderful time. You deserve to be happy. I just wanted…just wanted to thank you,' he said, losing the thread at last. 'For everything you've been, and everything you've done. I'll never forget you.'

There was another deafening silence. Nobody moved. They were clearly all waiting to see if he was planning on humiliating himself some more.

Imogen opened her mouth and then closed it again, unable to speak.

'Anyway,' said Tom too heartily, 'I believe we have a present for you.' He picked it up from the table and stood holding it, not sure what to do with it next.

He felt as if he had jumped off the edge of a cliff and was still bracing himself for a crash landing. It was a little late to realise that he had absolutely no idea of how he was going to get himself out of here.

But Imogen was moving at last. She stepped onto the dais while the entire room held its breath.

'I don't want a present,' she said very clearly, finding her voice at last. 'You've just given me everything I could ever want or ever need.'

Half the women in the room sighed.

Was that a smile tugging at the corners of her mouth? Hope

began to beat wildly against Tom's ribs as he looked into Imogen's blue, blue eyes.

The Director of HR cleared his throat. 'I think perhaps Mr Maddison would like to say goodbye to Imogen alone,' he said firmly. 'The rest of us can continue the party in the pub.'

Reluctantly, people began to leave, looking over their shoulders at the scene at the front of the room, where Tom and Imogen stood facing each other, apparently oblivious to the room emptying.

Even when the door had closed behind the last of them and cut off the buzz of speculation outside, neither of them moved immediately.

'Sorry,' said Tom. 'Was that very embarrassing?'

'Very,' said Imogen unsteadily. 'And very beautiful.'

Stepping closer, she took the present from his nerveless hands and put it carefully on the table.

'Did you mean to say all that tonight?' she asked him.

He shook his head. 'I had another speech entirely prepared but, when it came to it, I realised I just couldn't do it. I couldn't say goodbye to you like that. I can't say goodbye to you at all.'

'Then don't.' Imogen closed the distance between them at last. Putting her arms round his neck, she pressed her face into his throat. 'Don't say goodbye, Tom. I can't bear it if you do.'

Instinctively, Tom's arms closed around her and he drew her hard against him, breathing in the scent of her, savouring the warmth and softness of her, his head reeling with the relief of holding her again.

'Imogen…does that mean you'll stay?'

'I will if you want me.'

'Want you?' Tom laughed raggedly. 'Imogen, you have no idea how much I do! I'm so in love with you, I don't know what to do with myself. You've turned my life upside down, and now you're the only one who can put it all right again.'

'But I'm so ordinary,' Imogen protested, pulling back slightly to look up into his face.

'You're not ordinary,' he said. 'You're beautiful and warm and loving and true. Are you thinking about Julia?'

'Of course. You've got to admit we're very different, and she was so much more suitable for you.'

'Suitable, maybe,' said Tom, 'but she wasn't you, and she didn't make me feel alive the way you do. She didn't make me the kind of man who takes crazy risks like the one tonight, and when I was with her I didn't feel as if I was in the only place I wanted to be, the way I feel when I'm with you.'

He pulled her back against him, sliding his hands under her hair to hold her head still. 'If it comes to that, do you think I don't know that *I'm* not suitable for *you*? I just wish I could be the man you really want.'

'But you are.' Imogen put her fingers over his mouth. 'Tom, you are,' she told him.

'You said you weren't prepared to settle for anyone less than perfect,' he reminded her. 'I'm not perfect.'

'No, you're not. You're really quite difficult at times,' she said, softening her words with a smile, 'but I love you anyway. And I'm not perfect either, but when we were together…the way you make me feel…*that's* perfect.'

A smile started in the silver-grey eyes and spread slowly over his face. 'Do I make you feel like a dolphin?' he asked, half joking, half hopeful.

Imogen remembered the dolphins soaring out of the sparkling sea into the sunlight and smiled back at him. 'That's *exactly* how I feel when I'm with you!'

Tom kissed her then, a long, deep, hungry kiss that left her breathless and blissful, and when he broke for air she wound her arms around him and kissed him back, while joy spilt through her in a glorious, giddy rush.

Imogen never knew how long they kissed there, or at what point they moved, but when she came up for air, Tom was leaning back against the desk and she was wedged between his legs. Heaving a sigh of happiness, she rested her head on his shoulder and felt his hands smoothing possessively up and down her spine.

'Why were you going to leave if you loved me?' he asked.

'Because I was afraid that if I stayed I would end up compromising. You'd been so certain that you would never fall in love, and I could see myself spending years just hoping and hoping that the impossible would happen.'

'The way you did with Andrew?'

She nodded against his shoulder. 'I told myself I had to face reality, and I didn't think I could do that, seeing you every day. I thought it would be easier to go to Australia, where there were no memories, and then you stood up there in front of all those people and told me that you loved me and I thought my heart was going to burst. I still can't believe this isn't a dream,' she confessed.

'If it is, we're both in it,' said Tom, kissing her softly. 'Now we've both got to face the reality of loving each other.'

Imogen nestled closer. 'That's one reality I don't mind facing!'

'Then we'll face it together.' He rested his check against her hair. 'Do you remember that ceremony on the sandbar?'

As if she could forget! 'That's when I first knew I loved you,' Imogen said, loving the feeling of being held tight against his hard, solid body. Of feeling safe. Of feeling cherished. 'I meant every word I said that day and I'm like you, I keep my promises.'

'I'm glad to hear it,' said Tom. 'So shall we make it legal and get married properly?'

Imogen's eyes were shining as she tipped back her head and smiled up at him. 'Yes, let's do that,' she said, and the warmth in his expression as he smiled back made her heart turn over.

'And where would you like to go on honeymoon?' he asked.

Imogen laughed, remembering how he had asked her that once before on a wet January day. 'We've already had a honeymoon!'

'We'll have another,' said the workaholic. 'I'll arrange it all. It just so happens that I know the perfect place...'

The old man was waiting for them on the sandbar, just like before. The sky was flushed with a gold that was just beginning to burn red. Tom took Imogen's hand and they walked across the sand towards him.

They had been married the week before in the little church in the village where Imogen had grown up. That had been a traditional wedding, and a very happy day, surrounded by family and friends, but the ceremony on the sandbar was just for the two of them.

It was six months since they had last been on Coconut Island, but the lagoon was as beautiful as ever. They spent their days just as they had done before, and in the evenings they sat on the veranda and watched the bats come out after sunset. It was all just the same—except this time Tom was her husband, not her boss, and Imogen hadn't known it was possible to be this happy.

Imogen had loved her wedding, but deep down it felt as if it wasn't until they had been through this ceremony again that she and Tom would really be married. She was wearing the wedding dress that had looked elegant and summery in the village church, but which she had chosen with the sandbar in mind. This time she was barefoot, and the chiffon layers stirred around her in the light ocean breeze as she laced her fingers with Tom's and stepped into the circle with him.

This time there was no hesitation, no awkwardness.

This time it was real.

If the old man thought it was odd that they were apparently renewing their vows so soon, he gave no sign of it. He went through the ceremony with quiet dignity and this time every word resonated along Imogen's veins.

'Love each other, be true to each other, find peace in each other,' he finished at last. 'Find joy in each other always.'

Tom and Imogen smiled as they drew together for a kiss. 'We will,' they said.

THE *Balfour* LEGACY

EIGHT SISTERS, EIGHT SCANDALS

VOLUME 1 – JUNE 2010
Mia's Scandal
by Michelle Reid

VOLUME 2 – JULY 2010
Kat's Pride
by Sharon Kendrick

VOLUME 3 – AUGUST 2010
Emily's Innocence
by India Grey

VOLUME 4 – SEPTEMBER 2010
Sophie's Seduction
by Kim Lawrence

8 VOLUMES IN ALL TO COLLECT!

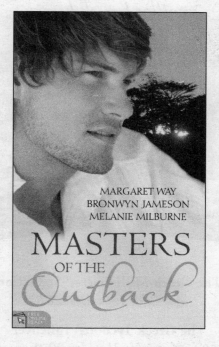

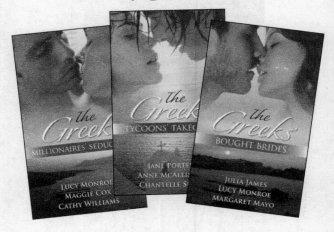

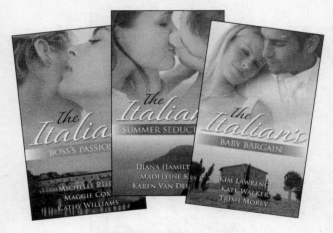

Three gorgeous and sexy Mediterranean men

RAYE MORGAN
CAROL GRACE
DONNA ALWARD

MEDITERRANEAN
Men & Marriage

– but are they marriage material?

The Italian's Forgotten Baby
by Raye Morgan

The Sicilian's Bride by Carol Grace

Hired: The Italian's Bride by Donna Alward

Available 2nd July 2010

www.millsandboon.co.uk

M&B

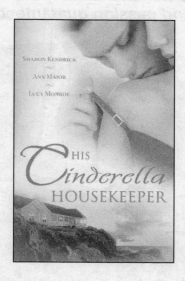